## Praise for *The Beautifi...*

"Oh, the dark secrets that can be hidden in the openness of the Iowa landscape. Nicole Baart has given us such fully drawn characters and compelling relationships that only the hardest of hearts wouldn't be won over by *The Beautiful Daughters*."

—WILLIAM KENT KRUEGER, *NEW YORK TIMES* BESTSELLING
AUTHOR OF *ORDINARY GRACE* AND *MANITOU CANYON*

"Compelling and exquisite. . . . Baart has crafted an unforgettable novel filled with characters and places so rich, they spill from the pages in beautiful, slow motion passages that you'll savor again and again . . . one of those special novels that will stay with you long after you've turned the last page."

—ROBERTA GATELY, AUTHOR OF
*LIPSTICK IN AFGHANISTAN* AND *THE BRACELET*

## Praise for *Sleeping in Eden*

"Baart expertly unravels the backstory of her intriguing characters, capturing the nuances of both life-tested relationships and the intense passion of first love. Ripe with complex emotion and vivid prose, this story sticks around long after the last page is turned."

—*PUBLISHERS WEEKLY*

"Baart's eloquent prose draws the reader into the tragic tale. At times a love story, other times a mystery, this is overall a very purposeful piece of fiction."

—*RT BOOK REVIEWS*

"A taut story of unspoken secrets and the raw, complex passions of innocence lost."

—MIDWEST CONNECTIONS PICK, MAY 2013

"Intense and absorbing from the very first page. Written in lovely prose, two seemingly different storylines collide in a shocking conclusion."

—HEATHER GUDENKAUF, *NEW YORK TIMES* BESTSELLING AUTHOR
OF *THE WEIGHT OF SILENCE* AND *MISSING PIECES*

"Bittersweet and moving . . . will haunt you from page one. Nicole Baart writes with such passion and heart."

—SARAH JIO, *NEW YORK TIMES* BESTSELLING AUTHOR
OF *BLACKBERRY WINTER* AND *THE VIOLETS OF MARCH*

"Emotionally gripping and perfectly paced, *Sleeping in Eden*'s taut story line and profound characterizations will keep you turning the page until the richly satisfying end."

—AMY HATVANY, AUTHOR OF *OUTSIDE THE LINES*
AND *IT HAPPENS ALL THE TIME*

"Vivid storytelling with a temporal sweep. In Baart's cleverly woven mystery, the characters' intertwined fates prove that passions transcend time—and secrets will always be unearthed."

—JENNA BLUM, *NEW YORK TIMES* AND
INTERNATIONALLY BESTSELLING AUTHOR

## Praise for *Far from Here*

"Nicole Baart is a writer of immense strength. Her lush, beautiful prose, her finely drawn characters, and especially her quirky women, all made *Far from Here* a book I couldn't put down."

—SANDRA DALLAS, *NEW YORK TIMES* BESTSELLING AUTHOR
OF *PRAYERS FOR SALE* AND *THE LAST MIDWIFE*

"A rare journey to a place that left me healed and renewed. . . . A tribute to love in all its forms—between a man and a wife, between sisters, and among mothers and daughters—my heart ached while I read *Far from Here*, but it ached more when I was done and there were no more pages to turn."

—NICOLLE WALLACE, NEW YORK TIMES BESTSELLING<br>AUTHOR OF EIGHTEEN ACRES

"Nicole Baart's tale of the certainties of absolute fear and the uncertainty of love whirls the reader up and never lets go."

—JACQUELYN MITCHARD, NEW YORK TIMES BESTSELLING AUTHOR<br>OF THE DEEP END OF THE OCEAN AND TWO IF BY SEA

"Gorgeously composed . . . a candid and uncompromising meditation on the marriage of a young pilot and his flight-fearing wife, their personal failings, and finding the grace to move beyond unthinkable tragedy. . . . Pulsing with passion and saturated with lush language . . . will leave an indelible mark."

—PUBLISHERS WEEKLY (STARRED REVIEW)

"Nicole Baart is a huge talent who has both a big voice and something meaningful to say with it. *Far from Here* is a gorgeous book about resilient people living in a broken world, finding ways to restore hope and even beauty in the pieces."

—JOSHILYN JACKSON, AUTHOR OF GODS IN ALABAMA<br>AND THE OPPOSITE OF EVERYONE

ALSO BY NICOLE BAART

*The Beautiful Daughters*

*Sleeping in Eden*

*Far from Here*

*The Snow Angel*

*Beneath the Night Tree*

*The Moment Between*

*Summer Snow*

*After the Leaves Fall*

# Little
# Broken
# Things

*A Novel*

# NICOLE BAART

**ATRIA** PAPERBACK

New York • London • Toronto • Sydney • New Delhi

**ATRIA**
PAPERBACK

An Imprint of Simon & Schuster
1230 Avenue of the Americas
New York, NY 10020

This book is a work of fiction. Any references to historical events, real
people, or real places are used fictitiously. Other names, characters, places,
and events are products of the author's imagination, and any resemblance to
actual events or places or persons, living or dead, is entirely coincidental.

Copyright © 2017 by Nicole Baart

All rights reserved, including the right to reproduce this book or
portions thereof in any form whatsoever. For information, address
Atria Books Subsidiary Rights Department, 1230 Avenue of the Americas,
New York, NY 10020.

First Atria Paperback edition November 2017

**ATRIA** PAPERBACK and colophon are trademarks of Simon & Schuster, Inc.

For information about special discounts for bulk purchases, please
contact Simon & Schuster Special Sales at 1-866-506-1949 or
business@simonandschuster.com.

The Simon & Schuster Speakers Bureau can bring authors to your
live event. For more information or to book an event, contact the
Simon & Schuster Speakers Bureau at 1-866-248-3049 or visit our
website at www.simonspeakers.com.

Interior design by Dana Sloan

Manufactured in the United States of America

10   9   8   7   6

Library of Congress Cataloging-in-Publication Data is available.

ISBN 978-1-5011-3360-2
ISBN 978-1-5011-3361-9 (ebook)

*For Eve*

Broken things are loveliest

*—Sara Teasdale*

# Little Broken Things

THE LITTLE GIRL'S HAIR is fine as cornsilk. It pours through the scissors like water and spills to the floor, a waterfall of white.

"Beautiful," I breathe, squeezing her narrow shoulders with hands that tremble. My voice wavers, too, and I swallow hard. *Not now.* "You look like Tinker Bell."

"I don't want to look like Tinker Bell." One small hand reaches up and up, searching for the fountain of curls that cascaded down her back only moments before. Now ringlets frame her ears, perfect curlicues that tickle the nape of her neck and flirt with the greening Hello Kitty earrings she's been wearing day and night for at least a month.

The earrings will have to go. And the telltale glimmer of her almost silvery-blond hair.

"Look what I have," I say, trying to distract her. Circling her tiny waist with my hands, I spin her on the kitchen stool so that we're nearly nose-to-nose. I press a quick, awkward kiss to her damp forehead, sweaty from the game of hide-and-seek I used to set the stage for all that is to come. Children are not my specialty, but somewhere along the way I learned that they're just like adults in one regard: they purr when petted just so. It feels wrong to use kindness as a tool, but I'm doing what I have to. "It's a surprise."

"What?" A thin eyebrow quirks knowingly, skeptically. The girl is only six, but she's an old soul. A single word can flip the tables. Make me feel as if we've switched places and I'm the child, the kindergartener before me a grown woman. So much wiser than I was at six and sixteen and twenty-six.

"You have to pick." The boxes are on the counter and I grab

1

them quickly, one for each hand, and hold them behind my back. "Chocolate mousse or ginger twist?"

The girl's nose crinkles, confused. "We already had ice cream," she says. "Cookie dough."

Of course she's bewildered. There isn't often ice cream in the freezer. Or bread in the pantry, or milk in the fridge for that matter. And now: Chocolate? Ginger? After ice cream and hide-and-seek and undivided attention? It's as magical and mystifying as the haircut, the flaxen curls that tumbled in lacy patterns across the dirty linoleum floor. We've slipped into a fairy tale, but she has yet to realize that we're stumbling down a thorny path, lost in a dark and wicked wood.

"Chocolate mousse?" I press, because fear is creeping in. I'm going numb and will soon be paralyzed, incapable of doing what I have to do. The list of my weaknesses is long and varied, but none so great as my tendency for inertia. At the moments I most need to *go*, I find myself crippled and terrified. Trapped. That isn't an option now.

"Ginger twist," the girl says. To be contrary.

"Good choice," I force myself to say. "I always wanted to be a redhead."

Another nose wrinkle, but I can't explain. She wouldn't understand anyway. I just yank the tab on the box and fish around for the clear plastic gloves that wait inside. There is also a disposable cape and I sweep it around her with what I hope is a flourish. I'm starting to quiver, my entire body seizing as if I'm on the verge of hypothermia. Never mind it's August and there is a thin bead of sweat slipping down my spine. "You'll look just like Annie."

"I thought I looked like Tinker Bell." There is a hitch in her voice now, a dark shadow on the horizon that forecasts tears.

*No.* If she cries it's over. I won't be able to follow through. "We're going to play a game." I sound insistent, maybe even desperate.

"I don't want to play a game."

"It'll be fun, I promise." I squeeze the dye into the little black bowl and add the developer. The odor of ammonia rises in the kitchen, the tang of chemicals and cat urine reminiscent of things I've worked hard to forget. It's a trigger I wasn't expecting, so overwhelming I have to grip the edge of the counter, squeeze my eyes shut against the mushroom cloud of emotions that turns my heart toxic. "You love games."

"I said, I don't want to play a game." The girl slides off the stool with a grunt, but I whip around and catch her under the arms before she can get too far.

"Sit still, damn it!" Shouting at her won't help matters at all, but I've never been very good at keeping my temper. I thrust her back onto the stool. Feel guilty that I don't feel guilty about it. "I told you to sit still."

"No, you didn't." But it's nothing more than a whisper.

Vaseline would stop her delicate hairline from flushing with the hint of an angry rash, but there isn't time for that. Or for waiting the full twenty minutes for the color to develop. And when I push her small head down beneath the stream of cold water gushing from the rusty faucet in the kitchen sink, I only allow myself a teaspoon of remorse. We don't have a choice. I can't let myself forget that. Not even for a second.

"There you go," I say, after it's all over. I towel her cherry-colored curls with more force than necessary, ignoring the dye that bleeds onto the white towel and ruins it. "I don't even recognize you."

Of course, I do. There is nothing that can be done for her eyes, stone-colored and distinctive simply because they are every color and no color at all. They're eyes that require a second glance: creamy smooth as a latte when she's calm, dark as a thunderstorm when she's upset. Grayish now, and sad, but as I watch, her eyes seem to change. It's the hair color. It has to be. Her gaze is suddenly unfamiliar beneath the fringe of red. A bright, suspicious green that is so shocking it turns the kitchen cold.

"I love you," I say abruptly, surprising myself. It's not something I say. Not often. And certainly not with the depth of emotion behind it that I feel in this moment.

I reach out tentatively and take a single coil of her bright hair between my thumb and forefinger. It's the only way I dare to touch her. I long to pull her into my arms and never let go, to press her against me and *run*. "You're my brave girl," I tell her.

It's the closest I come to saying goodbye.

# Day 1

---

## Wednesday

*Wednesday*

*4:48 p.m.*

**NORA**

*I have something for you.*

> **QUINN**
>
> *Sounds mysterious.*
>
> *Give me a clue.*
>
> *Seriously, Nora. Don't be a tease.*
>
> *Nora?*

# QUINN

KEY LAKE WASN'T DEEP. It wasn't particularly lovely either, but the tree-lined shores fit together like a jigsaw puzzle, and there was something dusky and mysterious about the slant of light when the sun began to set across the water. The lake had a beauty all its own, and Quinn tried to remind herself of that as she sat on the edge of the dock, her toes ringed by specks of bright green algae. If she leaned over far enough she could see not just the bubbles from Walker's submerged snorkel but the shape of him, too. Murky and indistinct beneath the slightly brackish water. But there he was. Diving. Hers.

When he broke the surface, Quinn stretched out her foot, toes curled like a ballerina en pointe, and he placed a piece of smooth glass on top of it with a smile. "It's not a slipper," he said after taking the mouthpiece of the snorkel out from between his teeth. "But we could call you Cinderella all the same."

"Does that make you Prince Charming?"

"Not even close." Walker palmed the piece of glass and moved through the lake as silent and smooth as the little waves that lapped at the posts of the old dock. Then he pulled himself up and out, spilling water from the fine lines of his body, naked but for the boxers. He settled himself on the dock beside her, cool and dripping.

"I wish you'd put on a proper swimming suit," Quinn protested, but something deep in her stomach knotted at the sight of him. Her husband wasn't handsome so much as he was striking. It was impossible to meet Walker Cruz and not stare. It was the breadth of his strong hands, the ropy muscles of his dark forearms. The five o'clock shadow that he let curl into an honest-to-goodness beard when he was too preoccupied with a project to shave. Most appealing and confusing to Quinn was the intelligent, peculiar flash of his copper-flecked eyes. Sometimes, when he looked at her, Quinn felt like he was a stranger. Even though she slept beside him every night.

"Your boxers are practically see-through," she told him. "My mom has a telescope, you know."

Walker shook his head and scattered droplets of water over Quinn. "Mrs. Sanford can look to her heart's content." He laughed, dismissing the house across the lake with a flick of his fingers.

Quinn didn't have to look to know that the windows of her childhood home winked black as the sun slipped behind its brick walls. Maybe her mom was watching. Maybe not. She tried not to care either way, but it was hard not to. Indifference was for people who had no reason to care. Unfortunately, Quinn had many reasons. For starters, the fact that she and Walker were living in her mother's rental. Or that they were both—temporarily, she hoped—unemployed. And, of course, there was Walker himself. It didn't matter that Quinn loved him; her mother thought he was unsatisfactory—and she made little attempt to hide her disdain.

"Hey." Walker put a damp finger under her chin and tugged her face toward his own. His kiss was wet and warm. He tasted of lake water and the Chardonnay they had with grilled chicken for supper: buttery and crisp. "It's temporary," he reminded her.

"Define *temporary*," Quinn murmured against his lips, but he was already pulling away.

"You didn't like Los Angeles."

Quinn made a noise in the back of her throat. "It's better than here."

But Walker would not be so easily disregarded. "We'll be gone before winter."

"It's August," Quinn said as if that was proof. That winter was coming. That they had already lingered here too long. Paying her mother half of what a summer vacation rental normally brought in and validating Elizabeth Sanford's many warnings about the financial instability of marrying a struggling artist.

"My piece will sell," Walker said, and the glint in his eye was almost enough to make Quinn believe. Almost.

"Can I see it?"

He shook his head but held up the polished, cloudy glass between his thumb and forefinger. "A hint," he said, and the smile that played on his lips was enough to make Quinn grin back in spite of herself.

"You're crazy," she said.

"Crazy genius? Or just *crazy* crazy?" Walker pushed himself up and offered his hands to Quinn, the glass still clutched between his last two fingers and his palm. She could feel the cool smoothness of it pressed between their skin when he lifted her.

"Just crazy, I think."

Quinn could have argued, but she wasn't in the mood. Walker's feet made a set of perfect footprints on the worn boards of the dock, and she followed them carefully, her own small feet swallowed up by the dark silhouette of his. Their life wasn't crazy. Not exactly. It just wasn't what Quinn had always hoped it would be.

At the edge of the dock, Walker stopped and slid his feet into the ratty flip-flops he had kicked off earlier. Between the dock and the house was a stretch of shorn grass that refused to grow properly because of the sandy soil beneath. It was rough and sprinkled with thistles, but it was perfect for bocce ball and lying on a towel in the sun, the two pastimes that had dominated their summer routine—if the lazy, haphazard way they filled their days could be called a routine.

They were waiting. Waiting for something better. Waiting for inspiration to strike. But lately Walker had been too busy in the boathouse he had transformed into an art studio to play or lounge with her. To wait. Quinn was happy for him, truly she was, but she didn't like being locked out of any area of his life. Walker's art was the worst. She felt small in the bald-faced hunger of his need for texture and color and light. The way he shivered at the sight of prairie grass bent by a storm or a branch that had fallen askew, crooked and disturbing as a broken limb.

Quinn wasn't nearly so deep. She felt lost in her husband sometimes. Like she was drowning.

"You coming in?" she asked, trailing a finger down his damp arm. "You'll need to change."

It was an excuse. She craved him like water, the almond slant of his eyes, the way his skin was as dark and fine as sun-warmed soil. He had a slight accent from summers spent in Mexico City with his father's family, and a lilting softness that rounded his consonants courtesy of his Ghanian immigrant mother. Quinn loved it all.

Her husband was so *extraordinary*. Set apart. Quinn ached for him, for something more than a mere wedding band to bind them together. She was his, heart and soul and body and mind and anything else she had to give. Quinn just didn't know if he was hers in the same way.

"I have clothes in the boathouse," Walker said. He was already distracted, his gaze on the high windows of the old, box-shaped building that housed his fever dream. It had been many long months since Quinn had seen him this way, but now he was a man consumed. There was little room for anything else. Even her. She let her hand fall to her side.

"Okay," Quinn said. "Don't be too late."

He took several steps away from her, dismissed, his mind obviously on whatever awaited him in his makeshift art studio. But as Quinn watched, he caught himself and paused, gave his wife a final second of his attention. "You all right?"

"I'm fine," she assured him. "Go." She hadn't told him about her sister's text. And she wasn't about to when he was already concentrating on something else.

*I have something for you.*

What was Quinn supposed to do with that? A single cryptic message was typical Nora, and Walker would tell her as much. He wouldn't give it another thought, and his nonchalance would only make Quinn feel silly for wondering. For worrying. But she couldn't help it. *I have something for you* implied a transaction of sorts. She hadn't seen Nora in over a year and she longed for her older sister with an almost childish desperation. They had never been close, not really, but absence and an air of mystery had rendered Nora the stuff of dreams. Her random texts and even less frequent phone calls felt almost illicit, dangerous, though as far as Quinn knew the worst thing her sister had ever done was walk away from a full-ride scholarship to Northwestern and shrug off Sanford family expectations.

Quinn envied her sometimes.

Walker didn't seem to notice that anything was wrong, and he winked at Quinn as he walked away, his flip-flops slapping his heels in rhythm as he carried his find to the boathouse.

It wasn't much, that tiny piece of glass. Walker's installations were usually magnificent in size and stature, and Quinn had a hard time reconciling the artifacts he was digging up from the lake with the immense sculptures her husband was known for.

He had been almost spiritless since they moved from Los Angeles to Key Lake, Minnesota, at the beginning of the summer. At least, artistically speaking. Quinn had loved the undivided attention she'd received for the nearly two months of Walker's creative dry spell, the way that he trained the intensity of his concentration on her. She was his outlet for the long, hot weeks of June and July, her body and the plane of her hips, the way that her back lowered to her narrow waist, the object of his obsession. Walker had always been a singular man, devoted and laser-focused since the moment she met him in an introductory art class in college. He had been the professor's work study, but Walker ended up teaching most of the class. And Quinn had admired his obvious devotion from the start. She'd wished maybe she had more of whatever Walker possessed hidden somewhere in her own soul.

Quinn wasn't nearly so exceptional. But she was determined. And as far as she was concerned, this humiliating homecoming, these months of living under the watchful, disapproving eye of her mother, were nothing more than a detour.

She shielded her eyes against the sunset and stared across the lake, daring Liz Sanford to stare back. All at once she was grateful for Walker's boxers, for the unruly flip of his dark hair, for the way her life was on display. Even an enigmatic text message from her sister couldn't get Quinn down. She knew what she wanted. And this time she wasn't going to let anything stop her.

# NORA

NORA GLANCED IN the rearview mirror and saw that the girl had buried herself in the dusty car blanket. It was wrapped completely around her, a plaid cocoon from which only the toe of one purple sneaker peeked out. She wasn't even sitting up anymore. Instead, her seat belt was pulled taut over the soft mound of the blanket and her tightly curled body, the fabric twisted so that Nora wondered if the restraint was doing any good at all. Maybe this wasn't safe. Maybe transporting a child required a special endorsement on her driver's license. Nora remembered the complicated five-point harness of the little girl's toddler days and wished she would have remembered to grab the booster seat.

The last few hours had been a fog. A grueling blur of tears and exhaustion. Of trying to comfort and failing miserably. Nora couldn't help it—she was tense, scared, and the child had wilted beneath the strain of the stifling atmosphere in Nora's apartment. She sat with her back tight in a corner and cried as though the world would end. Hot dogs didn't help, though Nora drowned them in ketchup just the way the girl liked. Neither did cartoons, but the only kid-friendly TV shows were reruns of *SpongeBob SquarePants*. The child had seemed more afraid than entertained.

Nora had been there when the girl was born, a truly terrifying affair that disabused her of the notion of ever having children of her own. When it was all over and the doctor had cheerfully announced, "It's a girl," Nora had taken the nameless infant into her own arms. She felt all elbows and thumbs, awkward and angled, as she cradled the tiny bundle, a hesitant participant in what should have been a natural rite of new life. The baby wasn't quite what she expected either. The skin on her newborn cheeks was white and peeling, her fingers so diminutive that Nora hardly dared to touch them for fear they would splinter. But the infant was wide-eyed and quiet, her lips parted as if she were about to say something.

"She's amazing," Nora said. And she was. But she was also strange and unnerving and miraculous. "What are you going to call her?"

"Her name is Everlee."

"It's pretty," Nora forced herself to say. But she hated it. And in the years after, she used every excuse she could not to call the girl by her ill-chosen name. Sweetie or honey or bug. Anything but Everlee. She had a hard time even *thinking* the name.

"Honey?" Nora called, shifting her eyes to the rearview mirror again. The child was still balled up under the blanket. Maybe she was sleeping. She certainly needed it. "Sweetheart, can you hear me under there?"

No answer. But then, she wasn't much for talking and never had been.

"We're going to play a little game, okay? A pretend game." Did this sound like fun? Nora hoped so. She wanted to make it as painless as possible. "It'll be great. Like playing dress up, only we're going to put on a different name. Just for a little while. You get to pick what you want to be called. Won't that be fun?"

Silence. Nora could see the blanket shift a bit in the rearview mirror, but it seemed she was only pulling the swaddle tighter.

"What's your favorite name? Should we call you Courtney? Or Piper? What about Olivia like in those books I bought you?"

Not even a flicker this time.

Nora sighed and adjusted her sunglasses as the sun dipped closer to the horizon. The sky was all vivid pastels, long sweeps of clouds like brushstrokes as she drove into the light. It was too cheery for her errand. So picture-perfect it was almost artificial. It reminded her of the place she was going, and not in a good way.

*I have something for you*, she wrote, and then couldn't think of anything else to say.

What *could* she say? *Get the guest room ready, I'm strapping you with a reticent six-year-old for I don't know how long. Oh, and I don't intend to tell you a thing about her.*

Nora knew how that would go over.

Details. Quinn would want details and an annotated outline and the entire freaking story beginning with the very moment that the girl was conceived. And Nora couldn't tell her anything.

Perfect little Quinn. Lovely, good, careful Quinn, who played the part of the wide-eyed baby sister so beautifully. Her degree was in secondary education, high school English to be exact, but Nora understood that she was better suited for preschool even if Quinn wouldn't admit it herself. Quinn was an optimist, a happy girl who had once been both the head cheerleader for the Key Lake Titans and the vice president of the student body. She was supposed to marry the captain of the football team and have lots of adorable babies to populate Key Lake. But Quinn had uncharacteristically gone against everyone's expectations and decided to do something different altogether.

Quinn was trying to be someone she was not. Marrying that unbearably sexy, but totally weird, artist. Moving to Los Angeles. Pretending she could handle a roomful of teenagers when Nora fundamentally understood that high school students would eat her sister alive.

The last time Nora saw Quinn, her hands and wrists were hennaed, elaborate flowers and intricate designs crisscrossing her fair skin like a map. Walker was experimenting with graffiti and tattoos, and his wife had become his favorite canvas. That had been almost two years ago, a rare family Christmas at the Sanfords', and Nora had felt downright sorry for her sister. Quinn seemed bewildered by her own life. She stared at her husband with a naked longing, a look that made Nora feel as if she had witnessed something shamefully private. But then Quinn's eyebrow would quirk and it was as if Walker was a complete stranger to her. Lips slightly parted and head tipped just off-center, she gazed at her own husband as if seeing him for the very first time. It was unsettling. The henna began to smudge partway through the day and Quinn drank just a bit too much champagne during the gift opening and began to seem blurry and indistinct herself. She was melting away, fading like the orange dye that stained her hands.

But Quinn was great with kids. At least, she had been. A dozen years ago.

"What about Annie?" Nora asked, directing the question to the back seat. "I love the name Annie. To match your hair."

A shuffle. The slightest scuff of blanket on car upholstery.

Did she say something?

"What?" Nora tilted her head so that her ear was angled toward the back seat while her eyes remained on the road. The last thing she needed to do was end up in a ditch with a child bundled like a caterpillar in the back. The girl would look like the victim of a poorly planned abduction. "Did you say something, love?"

"I want to go home."

"I want that, too," Nora said, because she didn't know how else to respond. And it was true. But it wasn't possible. Not anymore. Not for either of them ever again.

Nora stifled a shiver and told herself that the goose bumps sprinkled across her arms were because the air-conditioning was on too high. She reached for the vent, angled it down and away, and then grabbed her phone from its resting place in her cup holder. The girl would probably be scarred for life, would grow up to text and drive and kill herself in a fiery crash, but Nora set a bad example anyway. One eye on the road and the other on her screen, she pecked another text to Quinn: *I'm coming.*

*Wednesday*

*9:10 p.m.*

> **QUINN**
> What's that supposed to mean?

**NORA**
Meet me.

> **QUINN**
> Now? Where?

**NORA**
Boat ramp.

> **QUINN**
> Redrock Bay?

**NORA**
10.

# LIZ

THE COMMERCIALS LIED. None of those artificial glass cleaners could come close to the power of vinegar and newspaper. A little warm water in a bucket, a tangy splash of vinegar that probably should have put her in mind of pickles but instead made Liz think: *clean*. She had a special cloth that she reserved for this purpose alone; hand-washed weekly so that it would never become sullied by detergents or coated in buildup from the Island Fresh Gain fabric softener that she liked to use on her sheets. All Liz had to do was dip the cloth in the vinegar water, scrub the window one pane at a time, and then dry the streaks with a handful of crumpled newspaper. Usually the *Key Lake Gazette*, which wasn't good for anything else anyway.

Liz Sanford's windows sparkled.

So did the lens of her telescope.

It wasn't hers, not really. It had been Jack Sr.'s before the day less than two years ago when he claimed he had a twinge of heartburn and died in his leather La-Z-Boy while Liz washed the supper dishes. By hand, of course. Only people who didn't care about the state of their china would dare to use a dishwasher.

She felt guilty sometimes. Guilty for sending Jack to his office with a Tums in hand and then humming to herself as she lathered the two Crown Ducal Bristol-Blue dinner plates they had used for what would be Jack's last meal. Guilty because Liz didn't check on him until almost twenty minutes later, when the silver was nestled in

19

the drawer and the Waterford crystal wineglasses had been placed in their designated spots in the reclaimed-barn-wood hutch. By that time he was already cool to the touch.

The grief counselor (her physician had insisted she see him—Liz had only gone twice) assured her that it wasn't her fault. Nor could she blame the rib eye they had enjoyed that night. The diced potatoes she had crisped in butter and bacon fat. The warm white bread that her husband had torn off in hunks and dredged through the drippings the steak left behind.

Jack Sr. was the picture of health before he suddenly wasn't. He had never been corpulent or breathless or sweaty, all things that would have repulsed Liz. In fact, he'd been tall, quite trim. He even had a full head of tawny hair when he died—though his tidy goatee was more silver than gold. Jack's death taught Liz that sometimes the surface is not an accurate indicator of what lies beneath. Sometimes these things *just happen*. There's no way to know. No way to predict.

No one to blame.

Liz didn't go back to the grief counselor because she decided that she *didn't* blame herself. Guilt was a sneaky emotion, a scavenger that fed on scraps meant for the burn pile, and she managed it quickly when it reared its ugly head. Liz had been a good wife. Of that there was no doubt. Jack was her king and his home was a castle, neat and spotless, the decor so subtle, so tasteful that Liz sometimes stopped with her fingertips on the slate slab counter because she was overcome by the synergy of her own design. Good lines, soothing colors, leather and wood and earth and stone. But Liz also knew the power of fire, and her fabrics were a spark of inspiration in the most unusual of places. Carnelian and tangerine, indigo and pink stirred so soft it looked like the raspberry sorbet she had loved as a girl.

Liz wasn't an artist—she would never stoop so low as to call herself *that*—but she was artful. In her kitchen, in her garden, in her bedroom. When Quinn eloped and Liz could hardly breathe for the disappointment, she mustered up one piece of advice and handed it to her daughter like an ill-suited gift.

"Never say no," Liz whispered, hugging her daughter stiffly, pretending that all was well and would be well when she knew that it would not.

"What?" Quinn tried to pull away but Liz held tight, bony arms pressing the lush curves of her youngest close.

"If he ... *wants you*, don't ever turn him down." It was advice her own mother had given her, and Liz followed it with religious fervor. If her daughter was disgusted by the sudden intimacy of her counsel, Liz didn't care. She knew how to keep a husband happy—in a dozen different but equally important ways. And though she doubted the unfortunate union between her baby and *that artist* would last long, she couldn't entirely abandon her offspring.

It was this singular dedication to the fruit of her womb that absolved Liz of any guilt she felt when she bowed her head over the telescope and peeked in on Quinn and Walker from her vantage point across the lake. From what Liz could tell, Quinn had taken her advice to heart—even if she had blushed crimson and hurried away when Liz had given it. Not that Liz needed or even wanted to know details. She was no voyeur and quickly took up her dust rag, her vacuum, her apron at the slightest indication that things were turning romantic across the lake.

If only she could peek in on Jack Jr. and Nora as easily as she looked after Quinn. Liz had never exactly been the mother-hen type, but she did love her kids. And she liked to offer her advice when necessary.

Besides, it wasn't all mere observation. Liz had learned something from her surveillance and it justified what others might consider untoward. It seemed, after just a few months of haphazard examination, that her daughter and son-in-law had two settings: together and apart. Together was cover-ups abandoned on the deck, doors half-closed, hair disheveled. Apart was Walker in the boat-house and Quinn, alone.

They would never last.

What would Jack say if he could peer through the telescope? What would he think of Liz's impetuous decision to offer the un-likely couple the swankiest lake rental they owned? Most impor-tant, what would Jack *do*? But though she fretted over this question at night, propped in the very middle of her now practically obscene king-sized four-poster bed, night creams and wrinkle emollients making her skin as slick and shiny as an oil spill, Liz was baffled.

She had spent three-quarters of her life with him, but she had absolutely no idea what Jack Sr. would do.

Besides, of course, keeping tabs on his daughter through the antique telescope that was ostensibly purchased for bird-watching.

In some ways, Liz thought of the telescope as her husband's leg-acy. It was more meaningful than the rental properties that were scattered around the lake or even the contents of Jack's safety de-posit box. Liz had always known the box existed, but never officially saw it until the week after the funeral when she entered the Key Lake Union Bank as the newly widowed Mrs. Sanford, key to the mysterious repository in hand. There wasn't much inside. A copy of their will, Jack's father's class ring set with an emerald that Liz was sure was authentic. But at the very bottom, Liz was shocked to find a letter that she had written nearly forty years before. It was a love letter of sorts, though Liz wasn't sure it could be called that since it lacked the usual frippery of such correspondence. She did not dot her *i*s with hearts or tell Jack that she loved him. It was really quite matter-of-fact, a note passed in their senior world history class that informed him of a party that weekend and her wish that he would attend. With her.

It was the beginning. Liz had forgotten that she had been the one to start it all.

How bold.

Liz liked herself a little more, remembering.

And she liked the way she felt when she put her eye to the telescope for the very first time, less than a week after Jack had passed. Liz hadn't bothered with it before, but now that her husband was gone it felt like something that she should do. After all, Jack had once spotted a house fire through that telescope. He'd called 9-1-1 before anyone else even realized what was happening. Another time he spied a stranded boat that had dropped a propeller, and then rescued the family himself. Their telescope was a service to the lake. *Their* telescope. But now it was hers.

Liz took to it quickly. In fact, she rarely walked through the living room without pausing for a gander, a tiny hit that strengthened her ties to the small lakeside community. She was just a part of the tapestry—much like a paisley flourish on the expensive fabric she designed—doing what she could to ensure the peace and stability of the place that she called home.

And Liz was performing this important task late one evening as she headed to bed, wrapped in a silk robe embroidered with trailing orchids and sipping an herbal tea that her nutritionist swore would erase crow's-feet while she slept. It was just a teensy peek, a moment of curiosity that should have yielded nothing more than the faint glow of bedside lamps between the drawn shades of nearly every home around Key Lake.

But instead of being greeted by the orange flicker of the occasional bonfire on the rocky shoreline, Liz found her gaze yanked to the A-frame where Quinn and Walker lived. All the lights in the boathouse were on (not unusual) but the cabin was black (very unusual). Even more alarming was the flicker of headlights through the trees as a car pulled down the long gravel driveway away from the house. It was that ridiculous purple Kia Quinn and Walker owned.

*Apart.*

Liz glanced at the clock above the mantel. Almost 10:00 p.m. She didn't know whether to be happy or concerned that Quinn was leaving her husband at such an odd hour, but she did know that something had taken root in her chest. It was a fledgling thing, a hope or a wish or a fear so thin and gauzy it didn't yet have an object or even a name. Liz straightened up quickly and smoothed her silky robe. Smiled.

Something was about to change.

# QUINN

QUINN LEFT WITHOUT telling Walker where she was going.

Nora could do that to her. They weren't close, hadn't been for years. Or ever, for that matter. And yet, one word from her sister and Quinn was all too happy to *go*.

It made her irritable, and it wasn't like Quinn to be moody. Even when Nora was going through her teenage activist stage and the Sanford house felt more like a war zone than a home, Quinn tried to keep everyone chummy and smiling with fresh-baked banana bread and a steady stream of heartwarming clichés.

"You shouldn't provoke them like that," Quinn once chided Nora. Her sister had come downstairs for school wearing a T-shirt with curlicued letters that read "Ask me about my radical feminist agenda." Of course, it made Jack Sr. see spots. Their older brother, Jack Jr.—JJ—wasn't buying it either, and a shouting match ensued that only ended when their father insisted Nora remove her T-shirt and she obliged. In the middle of the kitchen. Just a few inches of the pale skin of her slender midriff made Jack quickly retract his demand, and he and his son all but fled the room.

Nora scowled at their retreating backs.

"He loves you, you know," Quinn said around a mouthful of Cheerios.

"Shut up, Quinn." Nora straightened her shirt with a tug.

"What did I do?"

"If you're not part of the solution, you're part of the problem."

Quinn didn't even know what the problem was, much less how to be part of the solution. And whenever she tried to share anything troublesome in her life, Nora assured Quinn whatever she was facing was a first-world problem and she should get over herself.

"First-world problems," Quinn muttered as she flicked on the blinker and pulled down the long drive that led to Redrock Bay.

It was just before ten, but the surface of Key Lake was deep purple in the fading twilight. The single-lane gravel road forced Quinn to slow down as it curved through the trees, away from the water, but not before she sent a spray of dust and rocks pinging into the shallows.

She wished she had a friend. Someone to call as she hurtled through the night toward Nora and her cryptic decree: *I have something for you.* But the thought was so pathetic that Quinn was embarrassed for herself. As if she was so unlovable. So awkward and eccentric she was incapable of forming meaningful relationships. It wasn't that and she knew it. Quinn was good with people, quick to make friends, and perennially popular. But Key Lake was an anomaly.

There were girls left over from high school, a handful of old friends who had married their childhood sweethearts and moved into cute little houses in the center of town just like their parents always hoped they would. Quinn had been like them once—idealistic and more than a touch naive—but these women were so different from the teenagers they had been that she hardly recognized them. Or maybe Quinn was the one who had changed.

The first weekend that Quinn and Walker were back in Key Lake, the old guard invited them to a barbecue at Redrock Bay. The man-made beach was in the heart of Key Lake State Park, a bit of an inconvenience if you didn't have an annual pass and had to pay the six-dollar daily fee, but worth it for the fine sand and the view of the serpentine lake as it meandered around the peninsula. It was a place rife with fond memories, and Quinn found herself warming slightly to the idea of living in her hometown after swearing she'd never again be counted on the Key Lake census. But there they were, meeting friends on a hot summer night for a party on the beach. Boxes still littered the floor of their temporary home, they hadn't even made a proper grocery run yet, but maybe lake life wouldn't be as bad as she thought. Perhaps she and Walker could actually be happy here.

They bought an annual pass at the ranger station and affixed the sticker to the windshield of their rusty hatchback with an air of optimism. Walker had spent the better part of the afternoon looking for the case of wine they had shipped from LA, and when he finally found it in the closet under the stairs, he chose Quinn's favorite: a bottle of Méthode Champenoise because it was sparkling and light, festive. He pulled it out of the back seat with a flourish as Quinn grabbed the fabric grocery bag that contained her homemade tapenade and a crusty baguette of Walker's own creation. When he wasn't working on a project, he put his hand to bread. Focaccia and boule and a brioche that was so buttery it tasted more like cake than bread. Quinn was suddenly, overwhelmingly proud. She couldn't wait to introduce her wonder of a husband to the people who had once been the center of her universe.

They emerged from the trail that led from the parking lot to the beach, breathless and expectant, cheeks blushed with lust for each other. Walker and Quinn had married for longing, and as they cleared the trees Quinn was sure the passion of their relationship was written all over her face. She put a hand to her cheek and tried to steady herself as she waited for the inevitable shouts and clumsy embraces, the cheerful reunions made awkward by their stale familiarity.

No one noticed them.

Quinn glanced around the beach, cataloging people in her mind and noting differences as clinically as a psychologist. Kelly's hair was short, shorn at her jawline in a cut that was stylish, but a poor choice for her round face. There was a baby on her hip, chubby and grasping, and he squealed as he reached for the blunt ends of her hair and missed. Kelly was deep in conversation with Ryan. Sarah's husband? It was hard to remember. Sarah had ping-ponged between Ryan and Mark for years. Quinn could hardly believe they were all still friends.

There were twenty-some adults spread out across the beach, clustered in twos and threes like Kelly and Ryan or standing ankle-deep in water as they dipped the fat toes of their matching babies in the cool lake. Quinn's friends were changed, all of them, older and softer, a few of the men sporting a little salt and pepper at their temples and the women wearing practical tankinis instead of the sexy two-pieces they favored back when Quinn had known them so well. She fingered the long string of her own black bikini where it looped out from beneath the collar of her T-shirt and felt almost indecent.

Part of her was jealous at the patent motherhood around her, of the life she was supposed to have. It had been within her grasp, all of it. The little house, the small-town simplicity, a spot firmly in the center of this tight-knit circle. Quinn had once been the queen bee, her kingdom complete with faithful subjects and a man (boy?) who she believed was the love of her life. But sometimes things are far more layered than they seem. More complicated, impenetrable. Quinn had hated this world and the sticky, menacing gospel of exclusivity and self-preservation it preached.

She still did. Even as she deflated a little, Quinn was filled with a sort of ferocious pride in the lavish curves of her own unblemished body. She felt like an ingénue in a crowd of worldly women. A child herself at twenty-five, but markedly different, younger somehow, than the women who were her peers. Just stepping foot on the beach had suddenly and irrevocably thrust her beyond the border of some inner sanctum. Quinn was not a woman who *knew*. Who had crossed the divide and bore the scars to prove it. She both loved and loathed herself for it.

The one thing that Quinn was not conflicted about was the overwhelming urge to flee. They didn't belong here.

"Let's go," Quinn whispered to Walker. His hand was in the back pocket of her jean shorts and she was gripped by a need to be alone with him. To prove that though her body failed at what it was supposed to so naturally do, it never faltered when Walker trailed his mouth across her skin.

"Too late," he whispered back.

Kelly had spotted them and there was a tepid facsimile of the warm welcome that Quinn had hoped for. One-armed hugs around toddlers, halfhearted hellos as infants screamed for attention. A picnic table was laid out with potato chips and pasta salad, and Theo was roasting hot dogs over a fire, six at a time on a two-pronged stick lined up in a perfect, nauseating row. No one touched Quinn's tapenade, and when Walker offered wine the men looked affronted while the women assured him that they were *breastfeeding*. As if he should have known just by looking at them that they were ripe and life-giving and incapable of imbibing even a sip.

Quinn shuddered, remembering. She and Walker had left long before it was polite to do so, claiming exhaustion though they were anything but. They made it halfway back to the car before they fell against each other. Lips. Hands. Clothes damp and clinging. Fingers frantic on hot skin and the taste of salt mingled with expensive French wine. They had finished off most of the bottle by themselves and it made them weak. They surrendered to the ache that brought them together in the first place, that sustained them in those harsh, artificial years in LA, and that would carry them through the brilliant glare of a Minnesota summer. It was enough, Quinn told herself. She didn't need diapers and the toothless grin of a little person who looked like Walker but had her periwinkle eyes.

But she did.

*They* did.

Quinn sighed as she pulled into the empty parking lot by the boat docks and turned off her car. When the engine went silent she could suddenly hear the hum of the waxing night through her open window, the forest coming alive as the first stars began to prick the sky above her. Frogs, and cicadas in the trees, water lapping hungrily at the shore. Maybe she should have been afraid. In LA, Walker had worked hard to convince her that a measure of fear was healthy, essential. He showed her how to splay her keys in between her fingers and made her promise to always be aware of her surroundings. Of people who might lurk in the shadows.

There was nothing ominous about Key Lake. Quinn left the key in the ignition and the car unlocked when she got out of it.

It was just like Nora to be late. Quinn walked to the nearest boat dock and wandered all the way to the end, forcing herself to leave her phone in the back pocket of her shorts instead of checking it yet again. It was set to ring and vibrate—she wouldn't miss a call or a text. But that didn't stop her from worrying, from nursing a familiar ache that started a slow, dull throb at the thought of her sister. No, it was more than that. Nora's abandonment was a swath of scorched earth, black across the landscape of Quinn's past. A tendril of smoke whispered from the ashes.

*What now, Nora?*

Quinn swallowed the hope that floated up and up in her chest. Tried to prepare herself for the worst.

# NORA

IT WAS ALMOST ten thirty when Nora finally wound her way down the road to Redrock Bay. A sign near the ranger station at the entrance to the park admonished her to pay for admittance utilizing a wooden drop box and the honor system, but she drove right past it. She didn't plan on staying long.

The small parking lot near the marina was empty save for a purple hatchback with California plates. Quinn was standing beside it, her legs and arms bare and golden in the glow of the headlights as Nora swung the car around. She hadn't expected to feel much of anything, but the enormity of seeing her sister after so long hit Nora square in the chest. She struggled to breathe.

Quinn looked warm and wholesome, her skin tanned and her dirty blond hair pulled back in a high ponytail that put Nora in mind of her sister's cheerleading days. At twenty-five, she still shimmered like a teen, her limbs smooth as pulled taffy, her expression so earnest, even at a distance, it was easy to tell that she still longed for approval. *Love me*, everything about her seemed to whisper. And it was impossible not to love Quinn. But sometimes, it was hard to like her.

Nora squeezed the steering wheel until her knuckles glowed white in the dashboard lights. A part of her wanted to put the car in reverse and speed away, leaving Quinn in a cloud of dust. But it was too late for that.

"I'll be back in just a minute," Nora finally said, clicking off her seat belt and swiveling around to consider the blanketed girl. The

31

child had tugged the fabric below the line of her sea-glass eyes and was regarding Nora with an indecipherable gaze. "What do you think?" Nora attempted a smile but it felt fake and fragile on her lips. "Amy? Should we call you Amy?"

Nothing.

Nora sighed and stepped out of the car, leaving the door ajar so that the girl didn't feel completely abandoned. What to do? Wave? Smile? The gravity of the situation made Nora's feet feel weighted. She was halfway to Quinn and had no idea what to say to her sister.

But Quinn didn't hesitate.

"Nora!" Quinn flung herself across the remaining distance between them and crushed her sister in a hug. "I didn't think you were going to come!" Then she backed away and held Nora at arm's length, a frown cutting a perfect line between her eyebrows. The wrinkle reminded Nora of their mother. But she would never say so to Quinn.

"Hey, Q."

"I should hit you."

"Maybe," Nora agreed. She didn't bother to apologize.

So Quinn wound up and smacked her in the arm, hard enough to sting but not hard enough to leave a bruise. It was a sisterly science, an exact measurement of force and velocity divided by the profound desire not to get on the wrong side of Jack Sr. He wasn't a fan of fistfights between girls, even if JJ—the perfect child—had been the one to institute the mild sibling abuse that marked their home.

"I deserved that," Nora said as her baby sister worried her lip.

"You cut your hair."

Fingering the nape of her neck, Nora toyed with the feathered ends of her blond fringe, the frayed, wavy edge that made her look like a rock star. All she needed were tattoos and an abundance of earrings, but Nora had an unusual affinity for the purity of her own body. She had no desire to be branded or pierced, save a tiny tattoo on her shoulder in the shape of an arrow—her best friend, Tiffany, had a matching one—and when she dabbled in drugs it was only because she was an angsty teenager and that's what angsty teenagers did. She didn't like the way they made her feel. Nora figured she wasn't the addictive type.

"I needed a change," she offered, knowing that the haircut must be a shock to Quinn. The last time they'd seen each other, Nora's flaxen waves had nearly touched her waist. Now, a long sweep of bangs complemented her cheekbones, and short layers exposed her neck and jaw. The overall effect was an aura of self-possession, of power. She used it to her advantage.

"It looks great." But Quinn's eyes were narrowed, hurt. They were strangers, and the strain of their awkward conversation was apparent. Nora wished she could rewind the clock, right past wrongs. But she couldn't worry about Quinn's feelings right now.

"Thanks."

"It's good to see you. I mean . . ." Quinn didn't finish, and didn't have to. Nora could see it all written across her face. *I'm lonely. I wish things were different. I'm so angry at you. I miss you.*

"It's good to see you, too," Nora said, because what else could she say? She didn't want to see her sister now, under these circumstances, but what choice did she have? Quinn wasn't the only Sanford sister whose life hadn't turned out the way everyone had planned.

"Let's get out of here," Quinn suggested with an air of finality. "Let me buy you a drink. Malcolm's serves Guinness now. Crown and Coke?" Quinn was already walking back to her car, clearly expecting Nora to follow so they could slide into one of the tattered booths at Malcolm's on the Water and pretend things were different.

"Quinn, stop." Nora hadn't followed a single step, and when Quinn turned around the distance between them seemed unexpectedly large. "I don't have time for a drink."

"But you came all this way."

"I can't—"

"It's late." Quinn shrugged one shoulder and offered up her most charming smile, dimple on the right. But there was something sharp in the line of her mouth. Unforgiving. "Spend the night. Walker is working on a project and the house is so big. You can have the suite off the kitchen. I'll make you crepes in the morning, whipped cream and all." Was she being sarcastic? Nora couldn't tell.

Nora didn't mean to be harsh, but she shook her head and fixed her sister with a warning look. She had used this particular glare a thousand times throughout their childhood, and Quinn recoiled just like she had when she was eight and still in lopsided pigtails.

"What?"

"I need you to do something for me. To keep something safe," Nora said.

Quinn put her hands on her hips. "Okay. There's a safe in the master bedroom of the cabin. Walker knows the code."

"That's not what I mean."

"Then . . . ?"

"You have to promise me something first."

Quinn raised an eyebrow. "You're not involved in anything illegal, are you?"

"No," Nora said quickly, but the truth was, she had no idea if what she was doing was illegal. "No, it's not illegal. I just need to know that you're going to take this seriously. That you're going to do what I'm asking you to do."

"Fine," Quinn said.

"No, not fine. That's not good enough."

"Damn it, Nora. What do you want from me?" Quinn threw up her hands. "I don't even know what I'm promising!"

"That you'll be careful and wise. That you won't tell anyone . . . what I've given you. That you'll trust me to take care of things and not take matters into your own hands."

"You're scaring me." Quinn crossed her arms over her chest, and the protective movement reminded Nora of when Quinn was little and would hide from JJ with her arms folded over her head as if the act of covering herself alone made her invisible.

"There's nothing to be scared of." But Nora wasn't so sure of that. "It's just a bit of a crazy situation and I really need someone I can trust. I trust you, Q. I believe that you'll do the right thing."

Quinn bit her lip as she considered this, but Nora could tell that she had gotten through. Her younger sister loved people. Loved them unabashedly and to a fault. It made her an easy target, though Quinn was far from gullible. She didn't comply because she didn't understand the implications, she just sincerely wanted to be helpful. To make everyone happy. To promote peace. There weren't many people in the world as caring and guileless as Quinn Sanford. No, *Cruz*. Nora wondered if she'd ever get used to that. And she wondered if she could ever forgive herself for using Quinn in this way. For putting her in danger? But no, there would be no danger. They had worked out every detail.

"What do you want from me?" Quinn asked.

But Nora had already turned to the car. She didn't see Quinn's expression change from skeptical to hopeful, and if she had, she wouldn't have known what to make of such unvarnished wistfulness anyway. Instead of worrying about her sister, Nora pulled open the passenger side back door and bent low.

"We're here," she said, smoothing corkscrew curls away from the tender curve of her cheek. The child was uncovered to her shoulders, but in the faint glow of the dashboard lights Nora could see that not much had changed. She was staring straight ahead, her emotions buttoned tight as a corset and her little jaw fixed.

"Hey," Nora whispered, her resolve weakened by the child's combination of strength and vulnerability. "You're going to like Quinn. She's my sister. She's really, really nice, and she makes the best chocolate chip cookies I've ever had. You like chocolate chip cookies, don't you?"

The girl blinked slowly, but otherwise didn't move or acknowledge that Nora had spoken at all.

"And she loves to read books. With voices." Nora had no idea if there were children's books in the cabin, but surely Quinn would rise to the occasion. Would make trips to the library and the quaint gift shop on Main to buy a plush lovey that Everlee could snuggle while they curled up and read together. *No*. No trips anywhere.

And not *Everlee*. She couldn't call her that anymore. At least, not out loud.

"Have you thought about a name?" Nora asked. "We're going to take a little break from Everlee for a couple of days. Remember?" She eased herself onto the bench seat beside the girl's bowed head. A part of her wanted to scoop up the blanketed bundle and brush her lips against the place where the child's hairline formed the bow of a perfect heart. She wanted to call her *buttercup* and tickle the spot beneath her slight rib cage that always elicited a giggle.

Instead, Nora sighed and patted her shoulder. "Come on, sweetie. It's time to go, okay?" And because she still didn't answer, didn't protest at all, Nora slid her hands underneath the balled-up six-year-old and awkwardly cradled her. She should have been heavier than she was, at least Nora thought so, and she made a mental note to suggest that Quinn feed her more. Peanut butter and eggs and chunky guacamole with chips. Things to put some meat on her tiny bird bones.

It was difficult to ease out of the car with the child in her arms, but Nora managed. As she stood, she intentionally avoided looking at Quinn. She focused instead on securing the weight in her embrace, on the short list of things that she had to convey. *Don't overdo it on the dairy. Make sure there is a stockpile of ketchup. And whatever you do, keep her hidden.*

"Nora?" Quinn's voice was a high squeak. She hurried over to where her sister stood, still trying to shift and shoulder the bulk against her chest. Quinn extended a hand to fold back the blanket and regard the girl circled in Nora's embrace. "Who is this?"

"A friend." Nora rushed on before Quinn could ask more questions. "I need you to keep her for a while. It's a long story and I'll tell you later, but for now I need you to trust me. I need you to please just do what I ask."

A note of desperation rang in her voice even though she had tried to sound casual. There was nothing casual about this. No way to downplay the fact that there was a child cradled between them.

"Nora." Quinn's wide eyes spoke volumes. "I don't know if I can do that."

"You have to." Nora gave up trying to comfortably hold the girl and set her down on the gravel road. She unwrapped the blanket, folded it over once, and then settled it over the child's narrow shoulders. Nora half expected her to start crying again, or at least complain, but she just stood there, mute, and stared at the ground by her feet. "Promise me you'll keep her safe."

"Nora—"

"Don't let anyone know that she's staying with you, okay? Not Mom and not—" Her voice snagged in her throat. She swallowed hard. "Not JJ, okay?"

"Yeah, 'cause I tell JJ everything." Quinn rolled her eyes. "We're BFFs. Come on, can we please talk about this? Alone?"

Nora put her hand over the girl's mussed curls. "No. We can't. I need you to take care of her for a couple of days while I sort something out. She's the sweetest thing, Q. It'll be a piece of cake. And when this is all over I'll find a way to make it up to you."

Quinn was shaking her head. "I don't want you to make anything up to me, but you can't do this. You can't just leave her here, Nora. She doesn't even know me. I don't know her. What's her name?" Seemingly thinking better of her question, Quinn sank to her knees and gave the child before her a warm, if hesitant, smile. "What's your name, honey?"

Nora saw her chance. She ruffled the girl's hair with what she hoped was a tangible affection and then hurried over to the car. It was running, her door open, and she was inside before Quinn could realize what was happening. Rolling down the passenger window, Nora called through it as she backed down the long drive. "Don't tell anyone where she came from, okay? Just stay home for a couple days. Promise me, please."

"Nora!" Quinn lunged up and jogged beside the car, her hand on the plane of the half-open window. "Please don't do this to me. I don't know anything about kids. She's clearly terrified. I don't even know her name!"

"It doesn't matter," Nora called through the open window. And then, changing her mind, she said, "Lucy. You can call her Lucy. Take care of her, Quinn. She's one of us." Tapping the gas a little harder than necessary, Nora resolutely looked away from her sister and rolled up the window. She left Quinn, and Lucy, in a billowing cloud of dust.

# Day Two

———

## Thursday

# LIZ

MACY EVANS CALLED their little exercise group the Walkie-Talkies, and every time she did Liz had to repress the urge to slap her. It was so tasteless. So obvious. But Liz hadn't been crowned Miss Congeniality in the Miss Teen Minnesota pageant for nothing. Instead of scowling like she wanted to, she patted her neighbor's bare arm and said, "Now, Macy. We're just some friends out for a little fresh air."

And gossip. But apparently only Liz was classy enough to keep that particular to herself.

It was just the two of them this morning, a pair of ladies pushing sixty who were regularly mistaken for much younger at a distance. Macy wore spandex capris that hugged her every slightly sagging curve (Liz wouldn't stoop so low as to call the leopard print trashy, but it was just a hair's breadth shy) and a tank top that tied with a bow at her waist and concealed the little tummy bulge that her twins had left behind. Of course, the boys were grown now and long gone, but they had been gracious enough to bequeath reminders of their existence: several college loans, a hole in the basement wall where one of them had once thrown a cue ball in anger, and the gray hair that Macy regularly colored a deep brown several shades darker than her natural, mousy gray.

Liz's own almost shoulder-length saltwater-taffy-blond hair (compliments of a subtler stylist than Macy's) was pulled back by a pale pink headband, and she was dressed in a modest white tennis dress. It was a bit of an unusual choice for the four-mile walk that they took along the lake every morning. But Liz liked to be able to move freely, and to pop in for a coffee at Sandpoint Cafe mid-workout if she felt so inclined and not stand out like a sore thumb among the summer tourist crowd. Not that spandex ever stopped Macy from also sidling up to the bar and ordering a venti skinny white mocha with an extra shot of espresso. Venti. As if Sandpoint were a Starbucks instead of a refurbished bungalow with home-made lemon meringue pies and a plump proprietor who had to be told, repeatedly, exactly what *venti* meant.

Sometimes Liz wondered why she and Macy were friends at all.

Macy was particularly skittish this morning, as high-strung and spirited as a newborn filly, and as they started down the hill where they both lived at the end of a cul-de-sac overlooking the water, she could barely contain herself. "You are never going to believe what I found out," she gushed, huffing just a bit as Liz had, somewhat perversely, set a pace that agreed with her long legs and forced Macy to all but jog.

"I'm sure I won't," Liz demurred, dipping her head in acknowledgment. Normally she would be very interested in what Macy had to say, but everything felt off this morning. She had meant to stay up and watch for Quinn's late-night return to the A-frame across the lake, but she had fallen asleep instead. When she woke at sunrise, Liz was irritated with herself and prickling with something weightier than idle curiosity. She had tried to call Quinn's cell, but there was no answer.

"It has to do with Lorelei Barnes," Macy continued, unperturbed by neither the speed at which they clipped along nor Liz's brittle manner. In fact, she seemed not to notice. "Remember her? She was the guardian of that girl in JJ's class."

That girl. Of course Liz remembered her. But she wasn't in JJ's class. She was in Nora's. Liz didn't bother to correct her.

"Well, she passed away last week," Macy whispered reverently, and she started to cross herself before she remembered that she hadn't gone to Mass since she was twelve. They were Reformed now.

Liz wanted to say, "So what?" They hadn't been friends with Lorelei Barnes, close or distant. Liz wasn't sure that she had ever uttered ten words to the woman in all the years that the girls were classmates. Maybe a cursory greeting at a school event, but she couldn't conjure the memory. Instead of rebuffing her friend, Liz reined in her rebellious decorum and played along. "I'm sorry to hear that."

"Did you know she was rich?"

That gave Liz pause. The Lorelei she remembered farmed and worked the night shift at the Summer Prairie Brewery bottling small-batch artisan beers that Jack Sr. had once loved. He was particularly fond of their winter ale, a dark, thick concoction that the label assured Liz contained notes of toffee and chocolate. She had never tasted it. And neither, apparently, had Lorelei, for the woman had been as slim and lithe as a willow switch. Long auburn hair, troubled brown eyes. Liz had found her unsettlingly striking.

"Don't spread rumors," Liz said, slowing just a bit because Macy was starting to wheeze. "That poor woman went through enough."

It was true. Lorelei was a single mom living in one of the shabbier farmhouses several miles out of town. A diagnosis of ALS a few years ago had landed her in the nursing home. She wasn't even fifty. Such a tragedy, made even more wrenching because she didn't have family nearby. Or at all? No one really knew her situation. Of course, there was *that girl*, who wasn't actually Lorelei's daughter but her niece. And it was anyone's guess where she ended up.

"It's not a rumor." Macy shook her head and a dark curl stuck to the thin film of sweat at her temple. "Kent went for a run with her lawyer last night. She inherited farmland when her father passed several years ago—a hundred acres in all. It's not much, but it's valued at over a million."

"A million," Liz mused, and wasn't aware that she had said the words out loud until Macy laughed.

"It's nothing, I know. But still. Who knew? She didn't live like she had money in the bank."

Of course, it wasn't exactly in the bank, was it? And really, *nothing*? Liz swallowed hard. There was a time when she would have considered a million not *nothing* but a modest nest egg. That was before Jack Sr. passed and Liz got her first good, hard look at their finances. Her husband had made more than one terrible investment. Thankfully, they owned their home outright and Jack had put a chunk of money in a 401(k), but Liz would have seriously struggled without the rental properties. And those she would soon have to start selling. Discreetly, of course. Her bank account was nobody's business.

Liz felt a familiar twinge of bitterness at the reminder that her financial situation was nothing more than a pretty illusion. Her friends still thought that the almost-new Cadillac in the garage (she had sold Jack's) and the sprawling house in the swankiest neighborhood in Key Lake were indicators of Jack Sr.'s robust career in real estate that would ensure a comfortable retirement. Macy and Kent were already snowbirds, flying south for the winter to Arizona or Florida, wherever struck their fancy that particular year. Beverly and Peter preferred European vacations. So far, Liz had been able to decline their invitations by citing a desire to stay close to family. She wasn't sure how long they'd believe it.

Macy kept the one-sided conversation going, supplying Liz with all the tales that were fit to repeat and a couple that were not, until the lakeside bike trail merged with the quaint Main Street sidewalk of Key Lake proper.

"Sandpoint?" Macy asked, already slipping her credit card from the little clip on her cell phone.

"Not today." Liz smiled as she breezed past. "I promised Quinn I'd stop by this morning."

"Oh?"

And because Macy was standing on the sidewalk looking perplexed and rosy cheeked, Liz hurried back and gave her a hug and a breezy kiss. They were friends after all, best friends, and for all her blustery ways Macy was loyal and eager and funny. A winning combination.

"I'm sorry I haven't been myself this morning," Liz said. "A bit of indigestion, I'm afraid."

Macy perked right up. "I've been taking probiotics! I can't tell you how much they've helped . . ."

But Liz was already walking away, arms swinging purposefully. "Tell me about it tomorrow!" she called over her shoulder.

Liz had most definitely not promised Quinn she'd stop by, and she doubted that her younger daughter would be happy to see her. Quinn had been a degree short of hostile since the day she and Walker pulled up a couple months ago in that ghastly purple import. Hadn't Jack and Liz taught their children never to buy foreign? Her mind slid to thoughts of other things foreign and Liz had to hold herself in check. Walker had been born in the United States, she reminded herself, though he certainly didn't look the part. But Liz was no racist—she just didn't think that Walker Cruz (with his long mop of black, curly hair and unnaturally smooth skin) was right for her baby girl.

Their marriage papers were legitimate, though, signed by a justice of the peace in La Mirada, where Quinn was studying secondary education at Biola. Liz had seen them. And to think, Jack had only agreed to let her go to California because she was attending a conservative Christian college, and how much trouble could she get into there? More than enough, it seemed. Did the Reformed church offer annulments? And if so, was there a statute of limitations? Like, say, after three years of marriage? Liz made a mental note to check.

Main Street wasn't long, but it was lovely. For a single block the shops were pristine, hanging baskets spilling from porticos and long planters filled with geraniums so lush they looked fake. One side of the street backed onto the water, and there was a wide boardwalk that made the shops accessible from both the street and the docks.

When Liz advertised the renovated A-frame where Quinn and Walker were currently living, she always pointed out that it was "secluded, but within a short, picturesque walk from downtown Key Lake." It sounded better than it was. Though pretty, downtown wasn't exactly a bustling center of trade and commerce. There was Sandpoint, where you could get a decent latte, and Malcolm's on the Water, where you could buy something harder and a burger to go with it. Malcolm's had a sunny patio and a small boat dock, and served a famous mixed drink in a fish bowl during the summer months—which Liz thought was lowbrow, but the tourists certainly seemed to enjoy it. Other than that, there was a Hallmark, a boutique called The Bright Side that carried mostly swimming suits and cover-ups, and Louie's, a drugstore where you could purchase milk, bread, and eggs. For everything else, you had to drive to the Walmart in the newer part of town. Tourists tended to stock up at Walmart on their way into Key Lake and then leave their cars parked for the remainder of the week.

At the corner, Liz veered off the sidewalk and joined the boardwalk that led out of town. The slated boards arched over the water for a ways and she had a perfect, sprawling view of the lake in all its glory. The sun glinted off the surface and made it shimmer like spun gold, and Cardinal Island rose up from the warm glow like a tower. Once, when her children were smaller, Liz had settled them all in the canoe and paddled out to the island for a picnic. Quinn was only three and whined the whole way, and a bird had pooped on JJ. The entire thing was a bust. Liz couldn't decide if she hoped her children remembered her effort or not.

It was still early, not quite eight o'clock, and the only sign of life on the water was a smattering of lazy fishing boats. Liz waved at

Arie Van Vliet, recognizable by the abundance of white hair poking out from under his ever-present Vikings cap. He waved back a little too enthusiastically, and she was grateful that he wasn't close enough to hear her chuckle.

Jack hadn't been gone for two years and already she had had suitors. Not officially, of course. One didn't date past college in Key Lake. After that, people were more or less paired, and those who weren't knew their prospects were grim. Some moved away. Some embraced the single life. And those who found themselves widowed and alone after being a happy (or unhappy) couple for more years than they ever imagined possible learned to speak volumes with mere glances. Arie, a widower for over a decade now (he lost his wife to cancer; Liz couldn't remember the type), would have scooped her up so fast it would have made her head spin.

Liz didn't much want her head to spin.

Where the boardwalk ended, a gravel path began to wind through the trees near the water. Liz stepped into the dappled shade of gnarled oaks and drew close to the edge of the trail to let a jogger pass. She was almost halfway around the lake at this point, two and a half miles from home and another half mile to go before the A-frame. Liz didn't regret her decision to pop in on Quinn, but the day was already warming in that slow, burning way of August. She could feel the heat beginning to descend through the cooler morning air. It was going to be a scorcher. Maybe she would ask Quinn for a ride home.

The thought made Liz's stomach flutter, and she didn't know if it was because she was nervous about inconveniencing her daughter or if she was hungry. Liz had planned on stopping at Sandpoint for a coffee and a scone until she was seized with the desire to be far away from Macy. And close to Quinn. Her longing for her daughter was a layered thing, and she wasn't quite ready to examine it.

The front door of the cabin was locked, but Liz kept a spare under the lip of the flowerpot on the little front porch. She debated a moment whether to knock or quietly let herself in, and decided that if she poked her head inside and all was quiet she would just slip away unnoticed.

Renters sometimes complained that the key stuck, but the lock was butter in Liz's hands. She eased the door open and stopped just over the threshold, noting instantly that the windows were open and it was definitely not seventy degrees in the house. Walker and Quinn had turned the air-conditioning off again. She repressed a little sigh and determined to bring it up with Quinn again. Just maybe not today.

Were there lights on? Sounds in the house? Liz couldn't tell. So she took a few more steps and scanned the great room. The sitting area to her right was empty, but as her gaze flicked over to the kitchen, Liz found herself staring directly at Quinn. Her daughter was leaning against the counter, tank top bunched up in one hand and a small pen in the other. No, it wasn't a pen. It was a syringe. And Quinn was giving herself an injection.

Liz didn't mean to make a sound, but she must have done exactly that. Quinn's head whipped up.

"Mom?!" She dropped whatever she was holding and hastily tugged her top down. As she kicked the vial beneath the edge of the cupboards, anger began to mingle with the shock already coloring her pretty face. "What in the world are you doing here?"

And just like that, Liz couldn't think of a single reason for coming. A part of her wanted to scurry across the space between them and take her daughter into her arms. She looked so vulnerable in her pajamas. The girl wasn't even wearing a bra, and because she was so young and lovely and perfectly perky she didn't need to. Liz felt an ache in her heart that was exactly Quinn-sized. But another part of Liz was already pulling herself up, straightening the skirt of her tennis dress and lifting her chin a fraction of an inch.

"The renter's agreement specifically states that the windows are to remain closed," Liz said. She hadn't even known the words were going to come out of her mouth until she uttered them, and though she wanted to take them back, to ask Quinn about the syringe and the sad downturn of her sweet mouth, something stubborn and unbending and distinctly Midwestern prevented her from doing so. One didn't talk about such things.

"Oh, Mom." Quinn put her forehead in her hand and took a deep breath. When she looked up she said, "You scared me half to death. I could have sworn I locked the door last night."

Liz didn't bother to tell her about the key. "Just out on a walk and thought I'd stop by."

"You could have called first."

"Family needs to call first?" Liz began to straighten the knick-knacks on the end table beside her and then reached to square a picture on the wall that had slipped a bit crooked. "Now that I'm here, how about we have breakfast? I could take you to Luverne's for pancakes."

It was a spur of the moment offer. A stroke of brilliance, if Liz said so herself. Luverne's had been Quinn's favorite when she was a little girl, but her daughter's eyes didn't brighten at the idea like Liz had hoped they would. Instead, her gaze darted to the spare bedroom just off the kitchen, and for a moment a look of something like panic shadowed her face.

"No, thanks," she said too quickly. "Walker's working on a project. I promised I'd make him breakfast. In fact, I'd better get started." Quinn turned to the cupboard beside the stove and pulled out a frying pan, banging it onto the gas range with a bit more force than necessary.

"I could whip up—"

"No, Mom, really," Quinn interrupted. "I'm fine. We're fine. Just need a little time alone."

Liz wanted to argue that all they had was time alone. But she bit her tongue and gave her daughter a narrow smile. "Well, have a good day then, darling. Let me know if you need anything at all." She considered mentioning the windows one last time, then decided against it.

"Goodbye," Quinn called, but her back was already turned and the word was muffled and weak.

Liz let herself out, heart pounding wildly in her chest. She was hurt and embarrassed, sure that there was something going on but helpless to do anything about it. The chasm between her and her child felt enormous. The syringe was mildly terrifying—Quinn wasn't diabetic, at least not that Liz knew of. She was aware that the condition could develop later in life, and she no longer had access to Quinn's medical files, but her daughter and Walker practically ate paleo and exercised all the time. Swimming and jogging and yoga on the lawn . . . who knew what else? Type 2 diabetes at twenty-five would have been a shock.

But that mystery could be solved at a later date. Liz was far more worried about the fact that when Quinn felt backed into a corner, she didn't look toward Walker and the gorgeous master suite that they shared.

What was she hiding in the spare bedroom?

Liz couldn't even begin to guess. She wasn't sure she wanted to.

## QUINN

THE TILE WAS COLD beneath her bare knees as Quinn fumbled for the discarded syringe. She hadn't had time to release the little mechanism that covered the needle post-injection, so when her finger met with a sharp poke, she knew she had found it. Perfect. Nothing like adding insult to injury.

Quinn put her finger in her mouth and sucked the drop of blood that formed at the tip. Shuffling over to the cupboard on her knees, she tossed the syringe in the sharps container under the sink and straightened up right into Walker's chest. She stifled a gasp of surprise.

"Good morning," he murmured into her hair. His arms went around her waist from behind and she stiffened for just a moment before relaxing into them. Or trying to. Her heart was beating a staccato rhythm that refused to slow. "I thought I heard voices. Were you talking to yourself again?"

"My mother." Quinn was grateful that she could chalk up her racing pulse to the fact that Liz had just walked in on her dosing herself. She had jumped when she realized she was being watched, and the last burn of medication had pooled too close to the surface of her skin. She could already feel the itch of a bruise forming.

"Your mother?" But Liz was gone and therefore not something Walker needed to be concerned about. His hands slid beneath Quinn's tank top, finding all the places where her stomach was puffy and tender. His touch was gentle, knowing, and he asked, "Last dose, right?"

Quinn was supposed to have given herself the injection last night, but she had forgotten. In the shock that marked the minutes after Nora sped away from Redrock Bay, Quinn had forgotten nearly everything. There was a child before her. A little girl who was a complete and total stranger.

But Nora had said, *She's one of us.*

As the dust from Nora's tires settled around them, Quinn went to her knees in front of Lucy. The child was slight, her shoulders delicate and rounded in fear. Despair? She looked so tiny, so fragile. Quinn wanted to hold her. But there was something in the set of that narrow jaw that warned her away.

*Furious*, Quinn decided as she leaned back on her haunches and blew a strand of hair out of her face. She was furious at her sister. *Damn it, Nora.* She could be such a drama queen. A black hole of a woman, the kind of person who drew people to her dark gravity and sucked them in before they realized what was happening. Everything mattered to Nora, from global warming to civil rights to animal cruelty. And she expected everyone around her to care just as much as she did.

Who was Lucy? Another cause? But she was a *child*. Quinn felt a fresh wave of rage wash over her. Why had Nora abandoned a little girl?

Lucy was a dilemma in and of herself, but Quinn was livid when she realized that Nora hadn't even attempted to ease her transition. Lucy had absolutely nothing with her. No bag, no clothes, not even a stuffed animal that she clutched beneath the standard issue car blanket that Nora had so unceremoniously draped around her. Quinn would have cursed her sister to kingdom come if Lucy weren't nearby. It was just like Nora to make a mess and then leave Quinn behind to pick up the pieces. How did her sister expect her to keep a little girl a secret? Even more important, why?

Answers or no, they couldn't stay in the parking lot at Redrock

Bay all night. Somehow, Quinn had managed to convince Lucy to crawl into the back seat of her car. Really, what choice did she have? They drove back to the A-frame in silence, Quinn nursing a tension headache that made her vision blurry and worrying about how in the world she was going to explain to Walker what had happened. But he was still in the boathouse studio when they arrived home (a detail that both relieved and devastated Quinn). So she ushered Lucy into the house and decided that sleep was the only, albeit temporary, solution.

"I don't have a nightgown for you," Quinn faltered when they were finally in the great room together. It felt as if a year had passed since she had grabbed her car keys off the end table and blithely left to meet Nora. Since then, her world had been upturned.

Lucy was staring at her shoes, blanket still wrapped tight around her shoulders. Tears would have been understandable. Even a tantrum. But the little girl was just standing there, breathing shallowly with her gaze fixed on the floor. She was as stoic and unmoving as a porcelain doll. A Shirley Temple doll with her cropped red curls and creamy skin, but the similarities ended there. Lucy's mouth was quivering, her eyes so troubled that Quinn was overcome with a desire to hug her. But she didn't dare.

"No pajamas," Quinn repeated weakly. "But I do have a T-shirt that might work. It has a clover leaf on it . . ."

The girl's fingers went to the skirt of her cotton sundress, bunching the fabric as if daring Quinn to try to take it off.

"Okay. You can sleep in your dress," Quinn quickly amended, and then added, "but maybe not your shoes."

Lucy bent down slowly and began to work the double knots in her pink laces. Her tennis shoes were old and scuffed, so worn at the toe that Quinn was sure she could see a hint of flesh peeking through. For some reason, that more than anything tugged at Quinn's heart. Dirty child, tangled hair, tattered shoes.

"Can I help?"

Lucy didn't say anything, but neither did she pull away when Quinn sank to the carpet. They each worked on a different shoe, struggling with laces that had clearly been tied by someone with a sadistic streak. *Thanks, Nora*, Quinn thought. But as the back of her hand grazed Lucy's, it struck her that this was the first time they had touched. Lucy didn't pull away. It gave Quinn a crumb of hope.

She settled Lucy into the spare room off the kitchen. The bed was queen-sized and it seemed to gobble Lucy up, making her look like a tiny baby instead of a five-year-old. Six? Nora hadn't told her how old Lucy was and Quinn didn't consider herself competent enough to accurately guess. It had been years since she had been the Key Lake resident babysitter extraordinaire, and all Walker's siblings were older. There were a dozen questions on her tongue, but she ignored them all and asked, simply, kindly, "Is there anything I can do?"

Lucy turned her cheek into the pillow and squeezed her eyes shut as if she could wish Quinn and the unfamiliar cabin and the entire experience away. Quinn's heart seized. She wanted to do something, anything, to comfort her. But the girl was stone.

"My bedroom is just down the hall," Quinn offered quietly. "And the bathroom is right beside it." Should she have made Lucy pee before bed? Brush her teeth with one of the extra toothbrushes in the convenience drawer that was stocked with single-use toiletries? But there was nothing to do for it now. The girl was curled inside of herself. Inviolable. Not wanting to make the situation worse, Quinn backed slowly out of the room. She left the door open several inches and the light above the stove in the kitchen on. It cast a band of light straight into the spare room and onto the bed where Lucy lay. She hoped it was enough.

She poured herself a glass of wine and intended to wait up for Walker. It was no use texting him, he wouldn't pick up his phone when he was working, and she didn't dare to leave Lucy alone in the cabin. But by midnight, Quinn had moved to their bedroom, door thrown wide so she could listen for any hint of movement in the house. Of course, she fell asleep. She knew this about herself, that lying horizontal for any amount of time would result in a deep and dreamless slumber no matter how stressed or preoccupied she was. But Quinn didn't imagine she could rest with Lucy nearby. A living, breathing child who she was suddenly, unfathomably, responsible for.

When she woke, sunlight was streaming in the window and Walker was sprawled beside her. Most mornings Quinn rolled over and welcomed her husband to bed. He often worked into the wee hours of the morning, and his presence beside her when she opened her eyes was always a bit of a surprise. She liked to wrap her arms around the hard plane of his weary body and press kisses onto his shoulders and back, but he rarely accepted her early morning invitations. He was too tired.

This morning, Quinn had sneaked out of bed. No kisses. Instead, she had hurried to the spare room with her heart in her throat. The reality of Lucy was an astonishing thing, like pain that hit when the morphine wore off. It felt like a bad dream, but Quinn knew it was real. Worst of all, she felt guilty for falling asleep, for not keeping vigil. What if . . . ?

Lucy was there. Sleeping or faking it, Quinn couldn't tell. But she pulled the door shut quietly and stood in the kitchen with her head in her hands.

"You seem upset," Walker told her, breaking her reverie by kissing the curve of her ear. Quinn hadn't realized that her whole body was tensing, remembering, and she tried to relax her shoulders as Walker's mouth trailed down her neck. But when his hand slid into the waistband of her shorts she pulled away and turned to face him.

"We can't."

"Why not?" Walker's eyes twinkled mischievously. "The timing is perfect, right?"

What could she do but tell him? And yet, there were no words. Instead, Quinn took him by the hand and led him to the spare room. She put a finger to her lips and eased open the door. Walker stared for a moment, his face expressionless, and then he turned to her with a look of pure bewilderment.

"Who is that?"

"Lucy," Quinn said, because it sounded better than "I don't know." She carefully edged the door shut again.

"Who's Lucy?"

"Nora's friend."

"What?" Walker looked so disconcerted that Quinn made him sit down on one of the barstools while she started boiling water for a cup of his favorite pour over coffee. She told him the story in starts and stops, searching for words, for explanations to fill in the many gaps. All the same, she had told him everything she knew long before the kettle on the stove began to whistle.

"She's one of us," Quinn said, repeating Nora's cryptic revelation.

"What's that supposed to mean?"

"I don't know."

Walker just shook his head. "This is insane."

"I know, but—"

"What do you know about kids?"

*You*, because Walker was the oldest of six (ranging in age from twenty-seven to eleven) and Quinn had heard many times how he had practically raised his younger siblings. How he helped them with their homework and made them oatmeal for breakfast and could tell if his sister had had a bad day just by the way she dropped her schoolbag by the door. Walker had assured her that children were far more complicated than she imagined them to be. Quinn bristled. "I'm great with kids."

"Well, yeah, for an hour or two, but, Quinn, this is different."

"How?"

He ignored her. "Where is her mother? Her father? She didn't just appear out of thin air. I think we should check the news for a report of a missing child."

"Walker!" The entire situation was difficult enough, but Quinn was starting to get angry. She trusted Nora, and even if Walker couldn't understand her confidence in her sister, he could at least try.

His family was paramount to him. Loud and raucous, Cruz family gatherings were a riot of languages, laughter, and food. Tamales and Antonio Cruz's famous beans that had been slow-cooked for hours and then refried with garlic and lots of queso fresco. But Walker's mother, Ama, made sure there was plenty of dried cassava chips, *kokonte*, and her favorite fried plantain cakes. There was no such thing as a dinner around the table; instead meals were served buffet-style, standing up and sitting down, draped over counters with half-shouted conversations volleyed around the small eat-in kitchen of the Cruzes' modest Murrieta home. And, unlike the Sanford family, no topic was off-limits. They argued about religion and politics, music and art. Once, Quinn had watched as her father-in-law smacked Ariel, Walker's sixteen-year-old sister, upside the head for coming home with a hickey. It was good-natured, more or less, but Quinn had blushed crimson at the fact that Antonio had drawn attention to it at all. The Sanfords would *never*.

Quinn worked hard to accept and understand her in-laws. She wished sometimes that Walker made more of an effort with her family.

"Are you accusing Nora of kidnapping?" she asked quietly.

Walker reached for the mug of coffee that Quinn was cupping absently between her palms. She handed it over and passed him the cream. He gave her a hard look, his jaw set in an uncharacteristically stern line. "We need to call the cops, hon."

"*No.*" Quinn was surprised by her own vehemence. "I promised Nora I'd keep her safe. That I wouldn't tell anyone Lucy was staying with us." Her mouth hadn't promised anything, but her heart had.

Walker shook his head.

"A couple days. Give me a couple days to sort this out."

"Have you called Nora? Demanded more information?"

Quinn had dialed her number a dozen times, maybe more. Nora refused to answer. And she wouldn't respond to Quinn's texts, either. "Of course," she said. "Nora's not a bad person. She would never do anything to harm Lucy, or any child for that matter. I'm sure of it. I trust her, Walker. She wouldn't do something like this without a very good reason."

"I'm not so sure of that . . ." Walker trailed off, eyebrows arching slightly as he gaped over Quinn's shoulder. Then he smiled wide. "Well, good morning, sunshine."

Quinn whipped around. Lucy was standing in the doorframe of the guest room, her mop of bright hair exploding from her head as if she had stuck her finger in an electrical socket. She was trailing the car blanket behind her and dancing lightly, hopping from foot to foot.

"Come on," Walker said, sliding off his chair and motioning that Lucy should follow. "The bathroom is this way."

She dragged the blanket after her as she ran, scooting into the bathroom and slamming the door behind her without a backward glance.

Walker spun toward Quinn. "Who is Lucy?" he asked quietly.

She rolled her eyes. "I've already told you what I know."

"Have you looked at that child? *Really* looked at her?" Walker crossed the space between them in a few strides, his stare direct, insistent.

"It was dark." Quinn fumbled over her words. "Last night, I mean. And she wouldn't look at me."

"Quinn, look again."

"What are you getting at?"

Walker ran a hand through his hair and caught it at the top of his head. It would stay like that if he let it, a 'fro so impressive he sometimes got a thumbs-up from strangers on the street. But the movement made Quinn's breath catch because his knuckles were white, the line between his eyebrows deep. "What?" she asked again.

"Her eyes," Walker said, almost apologetically. "They're kind of unmistakable."

The truth was so simple and so devastating that Quinn felt her knees buckle. "But . . ." But what? It was astonishing. Unforgivable. A miracle. A blow. How could Nora keep such a secret?

Betrayal was a blade so thin it pierced Quinn clean through. She was hurt and angry and awed all at once, but what threatened to undo her was the way that her life was about to shift on the sand of Nora's lie.

Lucy changed everything.

*Thursday*

*8:17 a.m.*

**QUINN**
*I know who she is.*

**NORA**
*Just keep her safe, Q.*

**QUINN**
*How could you?*

**NORA**
*Promise me.*

**QUINN**
*I don't know if I can ever forgive you.*

# NORA

NORA HAD DRESSED the part. Her pixie cut was freshly washed and smoothed away from her forehead, her long, angled bangs sleek and tucked neatly behind one ear. But there were already wisps escaping her careful combing and her makeup looked as if she had put it on in the dark. Faint smudges under her eyes hinted at the fact that she had pulled up in front of her apartment at just past 2:00 a.m. and spent the remainder of the night (morning?) pacing the floor. She was wound so tight she feared her ribs might snap beneath the pressure.

Throwing her phone into the depths of her messenger bag, Nora tugged the strap over her jade-colored silk blouse. Then she took a deep breath and stepped out of her car, locking the doors behind her with a decisive click. Her heels and pencil skirt were uncomfortable and unfamiliar. She stumbled a little on the curb and teetered as she tried to regain her balance. It felt glaringly obvious that she preferred Chucks and thrift store T-shirts. That she had recently cut her hair to remove the tangled dreadlocks she had spent three years growing. Nora felt like a bad actress playing a part so poorly it was downright painful to witness.

But what choice did she have? She and Tiffany had intentionally flicked the cornerstone in their house of cards and it was falling down all around them. The only thing they could do now was try to run for cover. And that's exactly what they were doing.

The morning sun was warming the pavement as Nora wound

her way past patio tables under a cheerful yellow awning and around the arching bird fountain at the center of the plaza. She was grateful that she only had to walk a block and a half to the cafe near the edge of the pedestrian park in her heels. They were already pinching her toes.

When she and Tiffany had first moved to Rochester, they used to drive downtown just to walk around. It was all so unfamiliar to them, so urban—though the Midwestern city they now called home was hardly a cosmopolitan destination. But there was always something going on, something to do. Once they happened upon an orchestra concert with crowds of people lined up in lawn chairs. Another time they discovered an old painted piano propped up against an unassuming brick wall. It was in tune, sort of, and they had laughed as they played "Chopsticks" together. Badly. Bea's Cafe became a favorite when a local told them it had the best root beer in town. Obviously, they would have both preferred a real beer, but they followed his directions out of the city proper. The place seemed like a dive, but after one visit they agreed that the little retro diner had the friendliest owners and the best root beer floats in all of Minnesota. Maybe the world. Because, of course, they had never seen the world.

Everlee loved those floats.

That was later, much later, and the years between seemed like pearls on a strand to Nora. She and Tiffany had treated Everlee as almost an accessory in the beginning. She was so small they could swaddle her in a long, stretchy cloth like a papoose and carry her strapped to their chests or backs wherever they wanted to go. As she got older, the girl toddled along beside them, holding Tiffany's pinky in one hand and Nora's in the other. She was more often than not suspended between them on her tippy toes as she babbled and giggled and loved everything life had to offer with an abandon that seemed at once reckless and gorgeous.

But those were the good times. Nora didn't have to remind herself of that. The shadow of their lives together was always there, black and brooding, peeking out from behind every corner. There were just as many afternoons that Nora got off work and went home only to find Everlee alone in the yard, barefoot and dirty, hungry because she hadn't eaten all day. Nora would take her inside, bathe her in the kitchen sink because the bathtub was chipped and disgusting, and make her pancakes. Only after the little girl was settled on the couch watching *Frozen* for the fiftieth time would Nora go in search of Tiffany. Often she was passed out in her room. One time, she was nowhere to be found at all.

Donovan had come into their lives when Everlee was four. And at first, Nora rejoiced. Now the thought chilled her to the bone. In spite of the heat and the sun warming her back, she stifled a shiver.

The cafe was tucked between a steakhouse and a bank, a narrow building that overlooked a tiny slice of the promenade. It was the sort of "blink and you miss it" place that was well known by the locals and overlooked by visitors. In other words, it was the perfect place to meet. It didn't hurt that the bank was right next door.

Nora bought a sparkling water at the counter and took a menu, ostensibly to pick out the perfect breakfast item, though she had no intention of staying that long. Even if she did have time to order something, she'd never eat it—her stomach was clenched like a fist. Easing onto a bench near the end of a row of small tables, Nora tried to look calm as she prepared to wait.

She had hardly crossed her legs when someone leaned over her.

"I thought you'd never come."

Nora jerked at the sound as Tiffany whipped herself onto the bench beside her. Their hips bumped and Nora could feel the nervous energy flash between them like a spark. They had always been intense. Thelma and Louise, Laverne and Shirley, Elsa and Anna. BFFs forever and honorary sisters whose bond was thicker than blood. Why did some relationships feel inevitable? Inescapable? Nora's love for Tiffany defied description, but it was layered with history, secrets, and something that felt almost maternal. Nora knew that Tiffany *needed* her. It was a powerful, humbling, devastating truth.

"You scared the shit out of me," Nora whispered. "Where did you come from?"

Tiffany motioned toward the back of the cafe. "I've been waiting."

"You're never on time."

She laughed at that, a deep-throated, unhappy sound that made a few people glance up. Tiffany's long dark hair was down around her shoulders and she was wearing a pair of artfully distressed jeans, the holes so gaping they were almost indecent. Her tank top was bohemian, her bra strap bright orange. Even without the siren call of the tan curve of her thighs or the traffic-cone-colored strap that kept slipping off her shoulder in warning, Tiffany was arresting. Angular and attractive in a disconcerting way. Nora had put her finger on it years ago—it was the way that you could not tear your eyes away from Tiffany even as you felt that you should. That you *must*.

"Stop drawing attention to yourself," Nora whispered, flicking Tiffany's arm in warning.

"That's a little melodramatic, don't you think?" Tiff sounded bored, but her leg was twitching up and down, swishing against the fabric of Nora's skirt. "As if anyone here would give us a second look." She paused for a moment, soaking in Nora's outfit and her carefully coiffed hair. Her nose wrinkled as if she smelled something stale. "What's all this for?"

"To blend in." Nora lifted a shoulder self-consciously. "I didn't want to stand out."

"You stand out wherever you go," Tiffany told her. She assessed the pencil skirt, the heels, nodding as she did so. "It works for you. I'd buy it. Though I have to say, you look an awful lot like JJ with your hair slicked back like that."

Nora recoiled as if she had been slapped. Was Tiffany trying to hurt her? To throw who they were and what they had done in her face? "How could you—"

"Nora Sanford," Tiffany cut in before she could go on, sweeping her hand in front of her to indicate Nora's enticing future, "high-powered lawyer for the people, taking up the cause of the poor and disenfranchised. You'll have judges eating out of your hand."

"*Would* have," Nora said quietly. She didn't miss the flash of hurt in Tiffany's brown eyes. They could be like this sometimes. Biting. Harsh. So real with each other it felt almost cruel. Nora had learned early on that compliments and kindness made Tiffany flush, and not in a happy way. She found warmth deeply alarming. And Nora had adapted over the years to be exactly the sort of friend that Tiffany needed her to be. Not many people would understand the way they loved—gritty and jagged and without artifice. But this was different. Their lives were about to forever change.

"I'm sorry." Nora expelled regret with a hard breath between her teeth. It wasn't fair to remind Tiffany of all that she had given up—that *they* had given up. Not now. "I know you're—"

"Let's get this over with," Tiffany interrupted.

Nora wanted to talk, to ask Tiffany why she had brought up JJ after all this time. It had been years since Tiffany had said his name, and wasn't that something? But they didn't have time. It would have to wait. "Okay," Nora said, shelving her questions for later. "I've been thinking about it. Two thousand isn't nearly enough. It's not going to get you very far and—"

"It's fine." The words were crisp, final.

"But—"

"Come on." Tiffany was already walking away, the glances of cafe patrons trailing in her wake.

Nora gathered her bag and her untouched bottle of Perrier and followed.

Tiffany had stopped just outside and was rooting around in her purse as if looking for a pack of smokes. She had officially kicked the habit a couple years ago, but it didn't stop her from buying the occasional pack and stress smoking. "Some people eat their feelings," she once told Nora. "I smoke mine." But Tiffany must have run out because she came up empty-handed and scowling.

"I'm out," she said. "Why don't you make the withdrawal? I'm going to hit up the corner store. Meet you there in ten."

"I thought we were going to do this together."

"We don't have to. It's a joint account, but we can make deposits and withdrawals independently." Tiffany buzzed with irritation, with a sense of urgency that Nora didn't understand.

"I know, but . . ."

"We're in a hurry, right?"

For some reason, Nora's stomach lurched. Her palms were clammy, her heartbeat weak and fluttering in her chest like a moth. Something was wrong. Terribly wrong. "What happened?" she whispered.

"Nothing happened."

"Are you sure?" Nora reached out to Tiffany but let her hand drop before she could make contact. Tiffany had never been much for physical contact.

"Just get the money, okay? I'll see you soon."

"Fine." Nora agreed because she didn't know what else to do. She would wait until they met up at the corner store to pepper Tiffany with questions, to insist that her friend share why she looked so haunted. But when Nora turned away, Tiffany stopped her with a hand on her shoulder.

The embrace was fierce and awkward, and Tiffany held her just a heartbeat too long. "Everlee is fine, right?"

"Yes, she's with my sister," Nora said reassuringly, though she had texted Tiffany no less than three times over the course of the long night to tell her so.

"Thank you." Tiffany's words were muffled and faint. "For everything." And then, before Nora could say anything more, Tiffany spun on her heel and took off down the sidewalk.

Nora wavered for a moment, torn between the desire to follow Tiffany and the necessity of their errand. In the end, she decided to do what they had come to do. A few minutes wouldn't change anything.

The door to the bank was ten feet tall and solid glass, but it swiveled open at the lightest touch. Nora tensed as the air-conditioning washed over her sun-warmed skin. She stood for a moment in the foyer, taking in the marble floors and perfectly appointed black walnut counters where attractive tellers in sharp suits waited to assist customers. Most were busy helping other people, but one woman caught Nora's eye and smiled encouragingly.

"Hello," Nora said, striding forward with more confidence than she felt. "I'd like to make a withdrawal."

As the teller counted out the bills, Nora couldn't help feeling like she was doing something wrong. But that wasn't true at all. She and Tiffany had opened the joint bank account all those years ago for one reason and one reason only: Everlee. This was where they squirreled away all that they could spare: the change they collected in a plastic ice-cream bucket (it always amounted to much more than they guessed it would), every paltry Christmas bonus, and what little they managed to save from their paychecks. Tiffany was unemployed almost as much as she was able to hold down a job, and Nora suspected there was probably some drug money hidden in their modest bank account, too. Nothing terribly serious. Usually prescription pills for ten bucks a pop that Tiff peddled to harried moms at the park. And that was Tiffany Barnes in a nutshell: trying to be a good mother but unloading Vicodin while her daughter squealed in the baby swing. Then saving that very money for Everlee's future. Or a portion of it, anyway.

Nora pretended not to know. And what did that make her? An enabler. But more than that, too, and her mouth went dry at the thought of just how much guilt rested on her shoulders.

*We tried*, she told herself. *We tried so hard*.

At least they had the account.

Somehow, it had all added up. They had saved just over $2,000, and though Nora knew that amount was peanuts, she was proud of what they had done. She dreamed about using it someday for Everlee's college tuition. Or to help her put a down payment on a home. God forbid they ever needed to tap it for emergency reasons or were tempted to withdraw just to help make ends meet. That's exactly why they had set up the account in downtown Rochester instead of the little hamlet fifteen miles out of the city where they found the farmhouse to rent. Because it was harder to access; it required intentionality. And they had refused to link any cards to the account. Deposits and withdrawals all had to be made in paper and in person. Until today, there had never been a withdrawal.

Today marked an emergency altogether different than the relatively benign ones they had imagined all those years ago. A fender bender. A busted water pipe. A fall. It was downright laughable the things they had once considered disastrous.

Nora tucked the wad of cash deep in the recesses of her messenger bag. It was smaller than she imagined it would be, a slim stack of hundred dollar bills that seemed too spare to offer the sort of new beginning they dreamed of. But it weighed heavy against her shoulder as she left the bank and hurried back through the plaza, down the sidewalk, and across the street.

Nora didn't realize she was rushing until her heel caught in a crack and almost sent her sprawling. But she didn't stop. There was a sense of urgency growing around the edges of her personal horizon, a storm cloud that swelled and billowed with each step she took. Nora ignored the pang in her ankle and picked up the pace, heels stabbing the pavement and sending a burst of pain through her shins with each quick step. She didn't pause until she stood in front of the little mom-and-pop corner shop, a store where she and Tiffany had once bought packs of gum, a candy bar for Everlee, and bottles of water on hot summer days.

The sidewalk was nearly empty. An elderly couple shuffled slowly toward Nora, smiling as if the world was filled with a beauty she couldn't see. A woman on a bike sped by. But Tiffany was nowhere to be seen.

Nora pivoted, arching her neck to peer around the corner back the way she had come. Had she missed her? Run right past? No. There was no one who could be mistaken for Tiffany.

Nora's heart pounded, pumping dread through her veins like poison. She was jumping to conclusions, assuming things that had yet to be proven, and yet she knew deep down that her fears were founded. Tiffany was not lingering in the store, pack of smokes safe in her purse while she perused the bottles of nail polish. She was not window-shopping down the street.

Tiffany was gone.

# LIZ

AS LIZ HURRIED home, irritated and glistening in the growing heat of the day (Liz didn't sweat, she perspired), she took careful stock of her children. Motherhood had come naturally to her, not necessarily as a state of the heart but as an occupation. It's what women did, back in the day. Never mind careers or life dreams or independence. A woman of a certain age found a good match and started a family. Liz had been exquisite at it. Betty Crocker home-cooked meals every night and charming Christmas cards each December. Liz made sure everyone was looking at the camera and smiling. None of that journalistic-style photography that had gotten so popular as of late. Faces in profile, eyes closed, still-life chaos. Liz just didn't understand.

And she didn't understand why her children insisted on being so similarly disordered.

Quinn was clearly hiding something. Never mind her unsuitable husband (who, honestly, looked Middle Eastern—and what was Liz supposed to do with that?), her unemployment, and her obvious disregard for the woman who had raised her. The woman who had changed her diapers and cleaned up her vomit and driven her to cheerleading practice and play rehearsal and, really, all over creation. It hurt her feelings, Liz decided. She wished her youngest would let her in, would confide whatever secrets she was keeping. Liz had such good advice to give, and she longed to share it.

As for her other daughter, Nora felt like a lost cause—and that pain was chronic. Dull at times, debilitating at others. Impossible to predict. Nora had never gotten on well with her father, but that was such an understatement it was almost laughable. What was it about those two? They had been oil and water, as different from one another as Jack Sr. and Jack Jr. were alike. Jack Sr. had been straightlaced, enduringly pragmatic, unforgiving. Black and white. Nora lived in the space between. *Why?* Nora had asked. *Why? Why? Why?* It was her first word, or at least Liz thought it was. Who could remember? It certainly seemed to be so, for it was the mantra that Nora repeated from her high chair and beyond. She never stopped asking it.

Eat your peas. *Why?*

We go to church twice on Sunday. *Why?*

The Sanfords are Republicans. *Why?*

This is how it's done. *Why?*

Jack didn't feel compelled to answer other than: *because I said so*. And that simply wasn't good enough for Nora. When she graduated from high school she was ready to run. University of Northwestern St. Paul was the plan, but instead of going there to study, she disappeared. Well, not really. Nora's departure wasn't dramatic. There were no tears or missing person's reports or shouting. She simply left the house bound for college and never showed up. When she came home several months later, there was some yelling (on Jack Sr.'s part), but nothing would dissuade her. Nora was a grown-up and she had flown the coop. Liz let her go. What choice did she have?

Thankfully, Liz had JJ. And he was having a baby. Well, he wasn't having the baby, his pretty little wife, Amelia, was. Liz wasn't sure how she felt about Amelia, even after almost seven years of being her mother-in-law. But she was quite certain that a grandbaby was a wonderful idea, so it was hard not to love just a teeny bit the woman who was going to give her one.

Liz didn't necessarily think of herself as grandmother material, at least not in the traditional sense. Gray-haired and big-bosomed and perpetually dusted with the ingredients for something fattening and baked. But stereotypes aside, there was a part of her that longed for the feel of a baby in her arms, the warm, wiggling weight of a person who she could press tight to her chest. It had been a long time since Liz had held someone. Macy gave her one-armed hugs and feathery European kisses, and JJ pecked her forehead every time they met. But to *embrace*. It was a different thing altogether. Liz realized she was getting soft in her old age. Maybe that was okay? The jury was still out on that one.

Anyway, Liz decided as she rounded the corner into her cul-de-sac, she would be the cool grandma. If it was a boy, she could take him golfing. She had a wicked swing and had often beat Jack Sr. when he was alive. In fact, he quit playing because she trounced him so thoroughly one unseasonably hot spring day nearly five years ago—though he insisted it was an issue with his rotator cuff. And if JJ and Amelia's baby was a girl, then Liz and the tiny darling could get manicures together. Liz liked neat nails. Square-tipped and not too long, elegant and feminine with just enough of an edge to let people know that she meant business. There were so many things she could teach Ruby.

*Ruby*. Liz knew she shouldn't get her hopes up. The baby's name was ultimately JJ and Amelia's decision, but she didn't mind dropping not-so-subtle hints. Ruby was a family name; Liz's grandmother and mother had both been named Ruby and it would mean so much to Liz if the tradition was carried on. Come to think of it, Ruby Elizabeth had a certain ring to it.

"Why didn't you name one of your girls Ruby?" Amelia had asked when Liz first brought up the issue. The question was innocent enough, but Liz bristled.

"Jack Sr. preferred Nora, after his mother."

"And Quinn?"

"She was born via Cesarean section. When I came out of surgery, her birth certificate had already been signed."

Amelia looked troubled by this news, but Liz had long ago forgiven her husband. She just hoped her son would come through for her.

When Liz finally arrived home from her much-longer-than-usual daily walk, she scrambled herself a couple of eggs and ate them while she called Amelia. If Nora was going to run away and ignore her, and if Quinn refused to engage in even the most basic of relationships, what choice did Liz have?

"Let's have lunch," Liz said between bites. She was famished, but refused to talk and chew at the same time.

"I can't, Elizabeth." Amelia insisted on calling her by her given name. The possibility of "Mom" had never come up. "I'm working today."

At the real estate office. With JJ. In a job that was nothing more than an excuse to get her out of the house. But Liz didn't say any of that. "Sneak out a bit early. We can have a drink on the dock."

"I'm pregnant."

"A sip or two of champagne never hurt."

Amelia laughed a little too brightly. "Maybe it wasn't an issue when you were pregnant, Elizabeth, but I'm not drinking. Why don't you give Quinn a call?"

Liz felt herself deflate.

"Though maybe nix the champagne."

"Oh?" Liz perked up. "Why would I do that?"

Amelia skipped a beat. "No reason."

"Don't be coy," Liz said, and speared a nibble of her scrambled egg. Wondering.

And just like that, it hit her. She didn't need Amelia to explain, nor did she want her to. If the words were said out loud she would have to acknowledge them, and if she acknowledged them they would feel all too true. Irrevocable.

Liz didn't realize she had dropped her fork until it clattered on the table. Making an excuse about the UPS man at the door, she hung up quickly. Then she sat very still, hands folded neatly in her lap, eggs forgotten. Could it be true?

Quinn was pregnant. Or, no, not yet. She was trying to become so. The syringe, her obvious agitation when Liz showed up on her doorstep. (Okay, in her living room, but the house was Liz's, surely she was allowed to pop in.) Maybe Quinn and Walker were struggling? Liz had never had any trouble conceiving; in fact, Quinn had been a surprise. Not a mistake, mind you, but having the girls twelve months apart and only two years after JJ had made for several rowdy seasons at the Sanford home. Liz had her tubes tied after Quinn was delivered, and she never regretted it. But though she had been fertile and experienced relatively easy pregnancies, she knew that not all women had it so good.

"Oh, Quinn," Liz murmured, absently picking up her plate and fork and carrying them to the kitchen. She scraped the cold eggs into the garbage disposal and ran it while she washed her dishes. One sad little cup from when she woke up, one plate, one fork. Life wasn't meant to be lived alone, Liz thought as she toweled off the three pieces and put them away. Even her cutlery knew that one was a melancholy number.

A party. The thought came into her mind unbidden and certainly unexpected. How long had it been since she had thrown a party? Two years at least, for there hadn't been a single get-together at the Sanford home since Jack Sr. had passed away. It felt wrong somehow, too festive, too bright. How long was one supposed to mourn? There was no handbook for this sort of thing.

But, oh, did Liz know how to throw a party.

Champagne and cocktails and hors d'oeuvres that Liz had whipped up in minutes but that looked as if she had spent hours preparing. Flaked white fish with chiles and sesame, sliced zucchini with goat cheese and mint, heirloom tomatoes from her garden with a drizzle of balsamic vinegar and fresh mozzarella. Her designer talents extended to food and festivities, and Sanford parties were extravagant affairs in Key Lake. Their house was built on a bluff overlooking the water, and from the long boat dock to the flat yard above there were forty-two steps that arched up in three zigzagging staircases. All along those weather-worn boards Liz had hung Christmas lights, tiny white globes that glittered merrily in invitation whenever she was entertaining. Lights meant a gathering, but it was only a public party when the flag was flying at the end of the dock.

It used to be a rainbow flag—before Liz realized that the gays had claimed that particular symbol. "Mo*ther*," Nora groaned when she heard why the rainbow flag had ended up in the garbage. She turned Liz's title into two syllables that sounded exactly like something that should not be uttered in the presence of a lady. But Liz didn't care. She bought a new flag, one with the nautical symbol for *S*. It was neat and clean and simple: white with a blue square in the middle. And it meant *Sanford*. Because she liked to claim what was hers.

Yes, Liz decided, looking out over the lake and the handful of boats that dotted the dazzlingly blue water. She would put the flag out. Maybe the vacationers wouldn't know what it meant, but the residents of Key Lake had long memories. Liz knew that they would come. For the food, for the chance to sit in the vividly painted Adirondack chairs that lined the patio where Jack Sr. had once sat and held court with stories only he could tell.

A party would cost her more than she should spend, but Liz still had several one hundred dollar bills rolled up in her underwear drawer from the secret interior design jobs that she had taken from time to time when her husband was alive. Jack didn't like her working, but sometimes people came begging for her magic touch, the unique combination of color and contour and light that she could bring to a room. Liz had done it on the sly, hiding the money and insisting that her clients hold their tongues. After Jack passed she could have started her own little business, but it felt like an affront to his memory. She never consulted again.

Liz's underwear drawer looked like the counter in an upscale lingerie store. Her panties were carefully fanned so that she could extract the pair she wanted, her bras were laid out in order by color and style. The only thing out of place was an old Republic of Tea tin that was slid into the farthest recess of the drawer. When Liz popped the top she was disappointed to find that what she thought would be several bills was only two. But it was August, and she could lean heavily on produce from her garden. Lemonade and vodka would make an easy drink she could mix in volume. A single case of champagne and flowers from her yard arranged in vases she already owned would add a touch of flair. It would work. She would make it work.

It was a flimsy plan, as thin and fragile as gauze. But it was all that Liz had. If she was going to save her daughter from ruining her own life, Liz had to start somewhere. Best case scenario, Quinn would see the error of her ways and remember the love that she had left behind. Reclaim the life she could have had. Leave Walker? Is that what Liz really wanted? Maybe. But she hardly dared to hope. And because she was a realist, she knew that the most she could reasonably wish for was a concession or two. Maybe Quinn could be convinced to settle herself, put down some roots, return to the sweet, simple girl she once had been. At the very least, their relationship could be resurrected.

The best way she knew to begin was by reminding Quinn of the life she had left behind. Surely it hadn't all been bad.

Once, when Quinn was almost a woman herself, tall and thin and lovely in the way of all eighteen-year-olds, she had accused Liz of taking sides.

"You always put him before us!"

"Him?" Liz was only half paying attention. She was on her knees in the garden, a wire basket of green beans in the dirt beside her. The beans weren't important, and Liz didn't make a habit of disregarding her children, but Quinn had warmed recently to the role of victim and Liz wasn't about to encourage it. Self-pity was a slippery slope, and Liz considered it her motherly duty to hold her daughter's hand. Firmly.

"Dad." Quinn threw up her arms in anger or defeat, Liz couldn't tell. "He's manipulative and controlling. He's been reading my emails again, Mom. That's not okay."

"He's your father, Quinn."

"I'm eighteen years old!"

*And under our roof*, Liz thought. But she didn't say that. Nor did she bring up the supper that would be on the table in an hour, the fresh green beans and burgers from the grill and lemonade that she had squeezed that afternoon. Quinn drove a hand-me-down car from her father and charged gas to his account at the local station. She was educated and well dressed and had wanted for nothing in all her eighteen years. Didn't that in and of itself demand a little respect? It did.

"He loves you," Liz said, but something about the words rang insincere. Jack Sr. was not a lover. A provider and caretaker, a breadwinner. He kept his family safe and warm, but his affection was spare. Even toward her. And if Liz was perfectly honest with herself, there were things about her husband that made her skin prickle, too.

Really. They had nothing to complain about. The Sanfords had the sort of life millions—billions—could only dream of. And Quinn had been slow to reject it. As much as Jack Jr. loved his place in the world, Nora hated hers. But Quinn had spent the better part of her life bridging the gap between the two, wishing for peace. Liz saw a lot of herself in her younger daughter. But this? No, it wouldn't do to rock the boat now.

"Be grateful," Liz had said. And she wasn't just talking to Quinn. She was talking to herself.

Liz was no idiot. She knew that their lives were far from perfect, that things simmered just beneath the surface of their shiny facade. Shadowy things that hinted of discontent, of darkness that she could only begin to imagine. Weren't they all just a knife blade away from madness? From obsession? From giving in to every lust and desire and impulse? Or even just one. One slip would be more than enough.

But life was hard and self-flagellation was for the weak. People pitied those who refused to help themselves. Who couldn't make a mistake and then, proudly, stand back up in the middle of their own mess and smile. *I meant to do that. I knew all along.*

Liz chose dignity.

Of course, Quinn hadn't listened. Instead of falling back into line, she had run the first chance she got. Just like Nora. She had nearly cut ties with her family altogether and forsaken the roots Liz had tried so hard to cultivate. Quinn had done things that were permanent. Final. Or, almost final.

The loss of her younger daughter was the reason Liz took one small blue sleeping pill every night and a slow-release capsule for heartburn every morning. Not that she would ever admit that to anyone.

And yet. Quinn had come home. Liz intended to remind her of just how good home was.

*Thursday*

*9:22 a.m.*

**NORA**
*How's Lucy?*

                              **QUINN**
                              *Are you serious?*

**NORA**
*Has anyone called? Come by?*

                              **QUINN**
                              *No.*

**NORA**
*Don't tell anyone, Q. Swear it to
me. Please.*

*Quinn?*

*This isn't a game.*

# QUINN

QUINN BATTLED THE URGE to throw the phone across the room, but Walker was watching. He stood on the other side of the bed, half-dressed. A pair of ripped jeans was hanging from his narrow hips, but he didn't seem to notice that he hadn't zipped them as he studied his wife with a decidedly skeptical eye. He looked troubled. Wary.

"Is that Nora? Give me the phone." He held out his hand, clearly unconvinced that Quinn would comply.

She didn't. Quinn wasn't a very good liar, but this one came to her lips easily enough. "It's my mom. She's mad that I've been opening the windows."

Walker gave her a long look but let it go. "Is that why she came by this morning? To complain about the windows?"

Quinn lifted one shoulder as if to say "I guess so," and slipped her phone into the back pocket of her shorts. She wanted to respond to Nora—even better, to tap the little icon of a telephone that would ring her sister. They needed to *talk*. But now wasn't the time. Not with Walker around. And certainly not with Lucy curled up in a ball in the corner of the bedroom where she had slept. After using the bathroom earlier that morning, she had scurried back to the room just off the kitchen and hid in the farthest corner. As if Quinn and Walker were terrifying, dangerous people. As if they intended to *hurt* her.

It made Quinn shiver. What would make a child react like that?

What had happened to her? Quinn couldn't bring herself to think about specifics; instead her heart blistered at the heat and color and suggestion of unknown violence. Of terror.

*Her niece.* If Walker was right, Lucy was her niece. Nora's daughter. That meant Quinn was an aunt. She kept turning the word over in her mind, shaking it out like a garment that didn't quite fit and then trying it on again. A part of her felt stupid that she hadn't put the pieces together herself. It was true, Lucy bore some similarities to Nora. She was lean and angular, even at such a young age. And she had those distinctive Sanford eyes. But really, that didn't mean much. Quinn knew that her sister's eyes changed color depending on the weather, a shift in emotion, or the hue of the shirt she was wearing. Lucy's were equally indeterminate. Gray blue, green, hazel, even lavender. How was Quinn to know?

Oh God. The implications were unthinkable.

Quinn swallowed hard and forced herself to bend over the king-sized bed where she and Walker had been curled up only hours before. It felt ridiculous to focus on the details, but it was all she knew to do. As she untangled the flat sheet from the quilt, she wished she could rewind the day, start over and find a better way to break the news of Lucy to Walker. A way that wouldn't end with them at odds.

In the midst of this firestorm Quinn needed him beside her. But her husband's disapproval was a palpable thing—it came off him like steam and enveloped her in a cloud of guilt. Never mind that Nora was the one who should feel guilty. *How could she?* How could she drop a bomb like this in the middle of their lives? Nora had no idea of the havoc she had wrought.

Quinn surprised herself by wishing Walker would go back to the boathouse and leave her alone. She needed to think. To come up with a way to force her sister's hand. But then she heard the metallic snitch of his zipper and Walker took the other side of the sheet she was holding.

They made the bed together in silence, and Walker even went so far as to position the many throw pillows just the way Liz had shown them when they first toured the cabin. It was a peace offering of sorts, and when they were done Quinn met him at the end of the bed and buried her face in his chest. Walker's arms went around her slowly.

"Thank you," she said.

"It's just a bed."

"That's not what I mean."

"I know."

Walker put his hands on her shoulders and pushed Quinn gently away so he could see her face. "I need you to know that I hate this."

"I know," Quinn whispered. She couldn't meet his gaze.

"It's crazy. Like, *crazy* crazy. And dangerous. Something is going on here."

"But it's *Nora*," Quinn said helplessly. "And if you're right—"

"I'm right."

"Lucy is *family*," Quinn finished.

"I know. But there's more to the story, Q." Walker was shaking his head. "And right now this isn't about Nora. She's not even here. We have to think about Lucy. She's not okay."

"Who is her father?" Quinn whispered, voicing the question that had lodged like a burr in her mind. It had kept her up most of the night, tossing and turning and nursing worries like a wound.

"Some guy." Walker shrugged. "Does it matter?"

Quinn was taken aback. After all their talks about starting a family, his casual dismissal of Lucy's father felt unusually callous. But before she could protest, Quinn watched her husband realize his mistake.

"That's not what I meant," Walker said, holding up his hands in defense. "Of course it matters. But clearly the father is not involved. We can worry about him later."

"Maybe he's the reason Nora is being so secretive," Quinn said, choosing to ignore her husband's blunder. "What is she hiding? And—"

Walker cut Quinn off with a sudden, slicing gesture to his throat and she became aware of a presence that hadn't been there before. They had been talking in generalities, and suddenly the very real object of their concern was hovering in the doorframe, regarding them suspiciously. She clutched the car blanket to her chest.

"Hey," Quinn said softly, pushing away from Walker as if they had been caught doing something private. In a way, they had. "How are you doing, honey?"

Lucy didn't answer, or acknowledge that she had heard her at all.

Quinn glanced at Walker, but he was giving the girl his warmest smile. Only Quinn could tell it was a bit crooked. She loved him just a little more for putting aside his own feelings to show Lucy kindness.

"Did you get good sleep?" Quinn fumbled, trying again to get something, anything out of Lucy.

"She's hungry," Walker said. "I can tell by the look on her face."

Lucy had refused offers of cereal and toast, pancakes and eggs. Even the cup of freshly squeezed orange juice that Quinn had set on the night table beside her went untouched. At least, it had been untouched the last time Quinn checked.

But of course she was starving. She had to be.

"Pancakes?" Quinn asked, repeating the menu she had offered earlier. "Eggs and toast?" Her mind was spinning in a dozen different directions as she watched the unkempt little girl. It was obvious that breakfast was just the tip of the iceberg when it came to Lucy. She needed clothes and pajamas. A new pair of shoes. A toothbrush. Something other than the ratty car blanket to cuddle. Fish sticks and french fries. Walker and Quinn stocked their fridge with organics and farmers market fare. The closest thing to a kid-friendly option in their cabinets was a tin of the chocolate Quinn favored. It was dark and laced with flakes of chili pepper.

"How about some hot chocolate?" Quinn blurted. She had almond milk and Dutch-process cocoa powder. Surely she could concoct something warm and delicious from that. "And . . . blueberry muffins?"

"Grilled cheese," Walker said definitively. "Lucy loves grilled cheese. I can tell."

The child ignored his statement. But she did open her mouth. "I don't know you," she whispered. Her voice was hoarse and unused.

Quinn's throat tightened. She had wondered if Lucy could speak at all. The few husky words were a gift.

"I don't know you, either," Walker said carefully. "But Quinn told me that your name is Lucy and that you're going to stay with us for a while."

Lucy held her tongue.

"Well," Walker went on, "we sure are glad to have you. My name is Walker."

Nothing.

Walker didn't skip a beat. "How about it? Grilled cheese?"

Lucy nodded once.

"I've got this." Quinn felt a twinge of jealousy at Walker's easy way with Lucy and instantly hated herself for it. Embarrassed, she added, "Are you planning on working today?"

"Leaving now." He bent to give Quinn a kiss on the cheek. As he neared the bedroom door Lucy backed quickly away, recoiling from both his tender look and his outstretched hand. It was obvious that Walker had hoped to touch her in some reassuring way, but Lucy would have none of it. To his credit, Walker let it go. "Quinn, can I talk to you a minute?" he called over his shoulder. The look he gave her was ripe with meaning.

Quinn followed, shooting Lucy an apologetic look as she passed. But Lucy wasn't paying any attention to her anyway. She was staring at the wall, her slender jaw set in a hard line. The irony of the situation—of being rejected so soundly by a child Quinn should know intimately and love completely—was just more salt in her already gaping wound.

"What?" Quinn whispered as she joined Walker in the entryway, acutely aware of Lucy's presence just around the corner.

"Lock the door behind me."

"During the day? Are you serious? This is Key Lake, not California." She didn't tell him that growing up they hadn't even known where the house key was. Even when the Sanfords went on vacation they left the garage door unlocked so that Macy could slip in to water their houseplants.

"Don't be so stubborn," Walker said, gripping her shoulders a little tighter than strictly necessary. "If Nora told you to keep Lucy hidden, to keep her safe, she's obviously protecting her from something. Or someone."

Quinn couldn't help the tremor that passed through her. "Okay."

"And don't answer calls from any number you don't recognize."

"Walker . . ." she protested weakly.

"Promise me."

"I promise. But . . ." She shrugged, dislodging his hands. "We don't know what's going on here."

"Exactly. And we're not taking any chances. I have my phone. Call or text if you need anything at all and I'll be here in ten seconds flat." Walker pressed a kiss to her cheek and then brushed the spot with the back of his knuckles as if to wipe the evidence away. "I love you."

Quinn squeezed her eyes shut for just a moment after Walker was gone. Her heart felt like a battleground—and the fight was far from over. But she couldn't think about any of that now. There was a child who needed her.

Reaching for the door handle, Quinn set the lock with a definitive click. She couldn't decide if she was locking the proverbial bad guys out or locking herself and Lucy in. Neither thought was very comforting.

Lucy was still in the hallway where Quinn had left her. Still staring at the wall. Quinn knelt down to her eye level and gave Lucy what she hoped was a genuine smile. "Do you remember me? I'm Quinn, Nora's sister . . ." She faltered.

Lucy didn't answer and she wouldn't look at Quinn. But she did wander over to the long kitchen counter. She climbed onto a stool, gaze still stubbornly fixed on her feet, the blanket, anything and everything but Quinn.

Giving up for the moment, Quinn strode to the kitchen and turned her attention to finding something she could feed a child. There was Gouda and some leftover focaccia, a far cry from white bread and processed cheese, but it would have to do. She set the ingredients out on the counter and then pulled a saucepan from the cabinet beside the stove. She set it on a burner and poured in some milk, adding a couple tablespoons of cocoa powder and an equal amount of raw sugar. When it was simmering, she tipped in a dash of vanilla and gave it a quick whisk. She sipped a bit of her homemade concoction from a teaspoon. It was good. Not exactly Swiss Miss, but wasn't that the point?

There wasn't much Gouda left, so Quinn shredded it and spread two slices of focaccia with salted butter on one side and a thin layer of Neufchâtel cheese on the other. The butter side went down in a frying pan and she sprinkled Gouda on top of the cream cheese. Two more fat slabs of bread on top, then she left it to melt.

Quinn poured the mugs full of steaming hot chocolate and gave them a stir. Lifting two plates out of the cupboard, she set them on the counter and turned a bubbly sandwich onto each. She put one in front of Lucy. Thinking better of it, she grabbed a knife and halved one sandwich, then quartered it so that the pieces were finger-food sized. Just right for little hands.

Or was she being patronizing? Quinn studied Lucy as the girl continued to determinedly avoid her gaze. She was so thin her collarbones poked from beneath the stained dress that hung off her slight frame. No baby fat to speak of, not even in her narrow face. Lucy was all brittle angles: sharp chin, jutting elbows, ears pointed at the tips as if she were a fairy. No, a changeling, a sprite left in the place of a child. Maybe she was older than she looked. Seven? Eight? As Quinn watched, Lucy snuck a quick peek at her benefactor. She looked down, but Quinn had caught her gaze. Lucy's eyes were blue or hazel or gray, strange and bottomless. The eyes of someone who had been forced to grow up too fast. Nora's eyes.

Quinn tucked her hair behind her ears and struggled for something to say around the lump in her throat. "Can I help you with your blanket?" she finally asked. "We can put it over the couch while you eat."

Lucy didn't respond, but she let the blanket drop to the ground. She sat with her hands in her lap, head bowed over the food that Quinn had placed before her. Shouldn't she be devouring it? How long had it been since she had last eaten?

"It's not too hot," Quinn encouraged her. "I think it should be just right."

Lucy didn't move.

Exhaling loudly, Quinn bent over the counter and put her chin in her hand. "What can I do for you, Lucy?"

Seconds ticked by and Quinn felt tears sting her eyes. She wasn't sure if she was upset because of the situation or because there was a cocktail of manufactured hormones running through her veins. She was mad at Nora, arguing with Walker, and perplexed by Lucy. Still coming to terms with the fact that the child before her may very well be her flesh and blood. She couldn't begin to mine that unnerving thought. Of course, she was also frustrated by Liz's unexpected in-trusion, saddened by her own discouraging situation, and troubled by the fact that the front door was locked against the unknown. The list went on, and that scared her more than anything.

Quinn blinked hard and straightened. "Okay," she said. "You don't have to eat, but I'm certainly going to."

She yanked open the fridge and grabbed the one guilty indul-gence that had survived her clean-eating purge. Walker teased her about it all the time, but Quinn didn't care. She could get into quinoa and flaxseed and green smoothies, but nothing could make her give up ketchup. Squirting a big dollop of it on the edge of her plate, Quinn picked up her gourmet grilled cheese sandwich and dredged it through the sauce.

Lucy kept her eyes hidden behind thick lashes, her face angled more at the countertop than Quinn.

It was hard not to be the tiniest bit angry.

Wrong emotion and Quinn knew it, but she was trying. She was trying *so hard*. She felt helpless and inadequate. Like a complete and utter failure. And Lucy's silence was downright oppressive. Quinn heaved a sigh and popped the last bite of her sandwich into her mouth sloppily. A dab of ketchup missed the mark and began to slip down her chin. Quinn could only imagine what she looked like. A petulant child herself. She reached for a napkin and then stopped. This was whimsical, right? Childlike? Maybe it would make Lucy laugh? Maybe . . . ?

"Look what I've done!" Quinn forced herself to laugh a little, but it came out hollow and insincere.

All the same, Lucy couldn't help it. She peeked up.

But when she saw the mess that Quinn had made of herself, the trail of red that ran from lip to chin, Lucy didn't laugh.

She screamed.

# NORA

THE PARKING LOT was empty at the Grind when Nora pulled up at nearly 10:00 a.m., which meant that the morning rush was already over. There would be a lull for a quarter hour or so, a handful of drive-through customers as they waited for the young mothers' crowd to start trickling in after the top of the hour.

Nora pressed her lips into a thin line and squeezed the steering wheel until her wrists ached. Everlee was so far away (three hours!) Nora could feel the distance in her bones. And Tiffany was . . . where? Suddenly, it was hard to breathe. Nora was being choked by her blouse and she reached with numb fingers to undo the top button. But it was already undone. She floundered for a moment, fingers at her throat.

There was nothing okay about their current situation. It felt so wrong to be traipsing into the Grind as if all was right in the world, but what choice did she have? She was anxious and angry, edgy and—if she was honest with herself—scared. But she had to behave as if nothing was amiss. *Normal*, she told herself. *Just act normal.*

Ethan was rearranging chairs and restocking the napkins when Nora slipped in the back door. If she knew him as well as she thought she did, he had also pulled a test shot for her and adjusted the espresso machine after the early crowd. Nora hated to admit it, but Ethan made better coffee than she did. Even though he was just her assistant manager and she had more experience and a bigger paycheck.

89

"Hey," Nora called as she tucked her wallet into a desk nook in the back room. The wide swinging door between the office/kitchen combo and the coffee shop was propped open with a five-gallon bucket half-filled with used grounds, and she saw Ethan nod a hello. She forced herself to say: "Thanks for covering for me this morning. Everything go okay?"

Ethan pointed to a cup of steaming coffee that he had set on the front counter. He must have made it when he saw her car drive into the lot. Nora knew it was an Italian-style cappuccino, no flavoring, with a thick layer of foam and a light dusting of cinnamon, just the way she liked it. "It's going to be a good day for a coffee," he said. No mention of the fact that he had single-handedly kept the store running since six. He wasn't the type to keep score. "You look fantastic, by the way."

Nora glanced down and realized that she was still wearing the pencil skirt and heels, the shiny blouse. It was all completely inappropriate for a coffeehouse. And ridiculously un-her. She had a change of clothes in the back seat of her car, but when Tiffany disappeared she had forgotten all about the blue jeans and vintage Guns N' Roses concert tee. The worn, comfy tennis shoes.

"I had a meeting this morning," she managed, her voice only a little unsteady. Ethan would never know her heart was beating double time. Would he? "It's why I was late."

"Nothing serious, I hope?" Ethan looked genuinely concerned, but Nora shook her head to stop that line of questioning immediately. "Thanks for the coffee," she said, changing the subject.

Because it was exactly what she was supposed to do, Nora grabbed a clean apron off the hook and knotted it at her waist. Then she set to work. She took a tray of stuffed croissants out of the refrigerator and turned the oven to 350 degrees. The box of yesterday's muffins was waiting on the kitchen counter, and she hauled it to the front to arrange day-olds in the basket by the till. The stay-at-home-mom crowd was crazy for cheap muffins. Nora priced them at a dollar and a half and watched them disappear.

Ethan's gaze was a tangible thing, and Nora felt a prick of anxiety. She had forgotten something, but what? The oven was on, she was wearing her apron, the muffins were in her arms . . . The coffee. Setting the box of muffins on the counter, she reached for the cup he had poured her and took the first scalding sip. It was perfect. "Thank you," she said, but it came out in a whisper.

"No problem." Ethan shrugged. "Everything okay?" He was focusing on positioning the chairs just right, making sure that the corners were squared and neat, the tiny space arranged to maximize movement, though the cafe would be crooked and cluttered soon enough.

No, everything was not okay. Nora's ankle rolled yet again as she stretched to arrange the muffins, and she puffed a hard breath between her lips. Stepping out of her heels, she felt the bite of the cold, polished concrete floor of the coffee shop. The decor was all restoration hardware: thick barn-wood beams, chunky iron, chipped paint. It had once seemed too trendy to her, too hipster, but Nora was suddenly grateful for the cool, smooth cement beneath her toes and the rugged wood where her fingers found purchase.

"I'm fine," Nora said, forcing a smile. "Those heels were killing me."

Ethan gave her a sideways glance that was equal parts watchful and teasing. "You took them off? It might be against code to work barefoot."

"Too bad."

Ethan was a good guy; a friend, in fact. They had once tried to be more than that, but it hadn't worked out very well. Nora was over it; she suspected Ethan not so much. But he was trustworthy. Earnest and wholesome in a boy-next-door sort of way. Brown hair, blue eyes, and an aw-shucks, all-American demeanor. A little plain, but that only added to his charm. She wanted to trust him.

But she couldn't trust anybody. Not anymore.

Nora put the last muffin, banana nut, on top of the artfully displayed stack and disappeared into the kitchen. She was sliding the tray of croissants into the oven when Ethan came to lean against the doorframe and regard her with his mouth quirked in a half smile. He was forever smiling, always happy. A terrible fit for Nora in every possible way. What had she ever seen in him?

"You forgot these." Ethan had her shoes hooked over his fingers.

"Sorry." Nora stretched out her arms and gathered up the nude stilettos. She dumped them onto the desk unceremoniously.

"I won't make you wear them," Ethan said. "Stay behind the counter. Your secret is safe with me."

If only.

Nora pushed down a ghosting cloud of fear, but she couldn't stifle the shiver that made her shoulders tremble for just a moment.

"Are you sick?" Ethan took a step toward her, reaching out as if he would put his hands on her arms. He stopped himself.

"I'm fine."

"You don't look well."

"Just tired." Nora tried to give him a convincing nod, a confident, reassuring smile that communicated that her late arrival and uncharacteristic preoccupation were nothing more than a little sleep deprivation. And a mysterious appointment. Nora realized with a jolt that Ethan thought something was really wrong with her. For all he knew, she had just come from an oncologist. "I'm fine," she added. "Really. Nothing to worry about."

Whether Ethan believed her was irrelevant. The front door chimed just then, summoning him to the counter.

"Go flirt," Nora blurted, trying to regain some of the lightness that marked their relationship. Trying to be normal. The young moms couldn't help but crush on Ethan, and when they lingered in the coffee shop they tended to keep making purchases. First a coffee and muffin, then a strawberry-banana smoothie to appease a little one. Next a pound of whole beans or a box of the pretty tea sachets in flavors like Moonlit Path and Birdsong at Dawn. Nora knew it was because they liked the excuse to talk to Ethan, not because they were so enamored with the coffee.

He saluted her and left through the swinging door, edging the bucket out of the way so that the kitchen was no longer visible from the shop. Nora wasn't sure if he was giving her a little privacy or making it easier for himself—not too long ago, a petal-cheeked college student had slipped him her number. It didn't bother Nora, but Ethan was clearly, inexplicably embarrassed. Because he was in his early thirties and a good decade older than the coquettish coed? Or because he was still hoping things would work out with Nora?

Either way, Nora didn't care. She released a shuddering breath, weak with gratitude that she had been granted a moment alone. She couldn't do this. She was a terrible actress.

"Stop it," Nora hissed at herself. This was ridiculous. She was a Sanford, after all. Stiff upper lip and pull yourself up by your bootstraps and never let them see you cry. Her childhood had been all those clichés and more rolled into one. Hadn't she learned a single thing in the years under her father's roof? Nora tightened the knot of her apron and put her hands on her hips. Of course she could do this.

Reassuring herself that the croissants were browning nicely, Nora slipped her phone out of her purse and keyed in the passcode. Quinn had texted her—again—and after verifying that it wasn't an emergency, Nora deleted it without responding. She chose to believe that Everlee was safe with Quinn—and right now, that was all that mattered.

But there was another text, another number, and this one made Nora's skin prickle.

*Bye, Nora.*

Nora felt the blood drain from her face. For just a moment her vision blurred and she had to grip the side of the prep table to stop herself from falling as the floor seemed to tilt. Tiffany wouldn't. Would she? No. As quickly as the thought crossed Nora's mind, she dismissed it. Tiffany wasn't the sort to take her own life.

But she was the sort to get going when the going got tough.

Nora decided she wasn't sad. She was *mad*. Hissing, spitting, throwing things mad. This was not what they had planned. It wasn't supposed to shake down like this.

The scent of warm pastry wafted through the kitchen. Surprise took the edge off her rage, and Nora dropped her phone on the table so she could lunge for the oven. The flaky croissants burned easily, but she had caught them just in time. She was grateful that Ethan wasn't around to witness the tremor in her hands as she slid the baking tray onto a cooling rack.

Ethan poked his head in the back room as Nora was trying to plot her next move. If Tiffany was gone . . . ? Nora was plagued with doubt, queasy with worry, and she could see concern instantly register in Ethan's kind face.

"Seriously," he said, pushing into the back room. "You're pale as a sheet, Nora. Go home."

"I'm fine," she insisted. She shoved her phone into her purse and began transferring the croissants to a narrow serving tray. "Thanks anyway."

"I can handle the shop today."

"Midmorning rush is about to begin."

"Nah, the summer crowd is always a little thin and—"

Nora forced a laugh, but it was brittle and joyless. "I'm *fine*."

Ethan sighed, giving up. "Whatever. There's someone here to see you."

"What?" Nora's hand froze in midair, fingers still tight around the spatula. Maybe . . . ? She tossed the utensil on the counter and edged past Ethan, not even bothering to be polite as she did so. Pushing through the swinging door, she steeled herself for a quiet confrontation. "We can do this," she would say. "Stick to the plan. Be strong."

But Nora never had the chance to whisper ultimatums.

He was picking through the muffins, turning them over in his hands one by one before discarding them. But when she appeared, he dropped the last one on the counter and with a smirk watched her come. Nora knew that many would consider him attractive, with his dark hair and brooding gaze, the hint of a tattoo peeking out of the collar of his shirt, but he was repulsive to her. Terrifying.

"For God's sake, Nora. What did you do to your hair?"

If she faltered, it was only for a second. A flicker of panic in her eyes, a rigidity in her jaw that betrayed just how deeply she loathed him. But she sped right through the shock, her course not wavering as she went to the counter and stood opposite the man she loathed with a hatred so powerful it seemed to be a living, breathing thing. Nora wanted to throw herself across the counter and take him by the throat. Instead, she smiled. Dug her fingernails into the palms of her hands and pulled herself together.

"I combed it," Nora said. He liked her sharp and sassy, the bitchy, girl-power best friend of his lover. It was a role Nora had learned to play—not because she felt the need to acquiesce to him, because it was the easiest way to control him. Or, at least, his opinion of her. "What are you doing here, Donovan?"

"Isn't it obvious, Nor? I came to see you." He leaned on the counter, giving her a wolfish smile that was supposed to be sensual, coy. Donovan had done more than flirt with her over the years. An errant hand, a wayward touch, a look that spoke volumes. And Nora had never, not once, been tempted.

Nervous and needing to do something with her hands, Nora grabbed the bag of dark roast beans and poured a small amount into the grinder. "Mocha?"

"You remembered."

"How could I forget?"

Donovan watched her as she went through the motions, tamping down the grounds and then steaming milk while the espresso filled the creamer. She wished there was a way she could slip something into his drink, but when she presented it to him in a to-go cup it was perfection, rich and chocolaty with a swirl of melting whipped cream on top. It smelled like cozy nights and long talks and comfort. He didn't deserve it, but she was desperate for him to leave.

"It's on the house," Nora said.

Donovan raised his cup to her and then set it back down on the counter untouched. "I think you know why I'm here."

"Coffee?"

He gave her a look that froze her heart. It stuttered painfully, and she forced herself to say, "She's not here."

"Clearly. The question is, where is she?"

"Tiffany's mother died," Nora said, sticking to the script they had cobbled together. It was makeshift and full of holes, but it was better than nothing.

"She doesn't have a mother."

Nora swallowed. "I mean, her aunt."

"That's the thing." Donovan reached out and put his hand over Nora's where it rested on the counter. His palm was hot, clammy, and it swallowed her hand whole. "Tiff wasn't going to the funeral. We talked about it. A lot. She didn't want to go."

"I never said she was in Key Lake. You didn't let me finish." Nora's skin flamed where Donovan touched her and she longed to yank her hand away. But she didn't dare. She straightened her chin and tried to glare at him.

"Where are my girls, Nora?"

"They're in New Ulm. Visiting family." A lie. Tiffany had no family. Besides Everlee.

"Why won't she answer my calls?"

"Oh?" Nora finally tugged her hand away, busying herself with the glass gallon of whole milk that she had left on the counter. It took her three tries to twist the lid on properly. "I don't know. Last I checked I wasn't Tiffany's keeper. You were."

A vein in Donovan's neck flushed crimson as he leaned toward her. "That's right. She chose me, Nora. She chose me over you. But I've been patient, I've let you stick around and leech off our family even though all you've done is try to poison the well."

When his fist hit the counter it made Nora jump. Her eyes shot to his and she was shocked to see bald-faced hatred burning there. Donovan wasn't hiding it; he wasn't pretending. Not anymore. "What did you do with it?" he whispered, each word landing like a blow.

"What?" Nora was so shocked she couldn't stop herself. Of all the things he could have said. All the accusations he could have made. *What did you do with it?* It didn't make sense. "What are you talking about?"

By the way he straightened, Nora knew that her reaction had been the right one. "Nothing. Never mind. It's none of your business," Donovan said, rubbing the back of his hand across his mouth as if wiping away a bead of sweat. He was done here, Nora could see that, but she didn't know what it meant. She didn't know what she had said—or not said—to make his attention shift elsewhere. To Tiffany? What had happened? What had Tiffany done? The possibilities made Nora's knees go weak.

The whoosh of the swinging door caused them both to look up.

"Everything okay up here?" Ethan asked with a smile. But Nora could feel suspicion crackling off him like electricity. He came to stand beside her, close enough that his arm grazed her shoulder.

"Perfect." Donovan grinned. And though he was handsome, though his teeth were straight and his chin chiseled, it wasn't a pretty sight. He grabbed the mocha, sloshing a bit of it on his hand as he turned to go. "See you around, Nora Jane."

She didn't respond.

When the door chimed his departure, Nora felt herself deflate a little against Ethan.

"Who was that?" he asked. There was iron in his tone, something cold and hard, and Nora couldn't help but be grateful that he wanted to protect her. Not that she was the sort of girl who needed protection. It wouldn't do her any good anyway.

"Nobody," she said, pushing herself away.

"Nobody? He certainly seemed like somebody."

"You know, I'm really not feeling very good," Nora finally admitted, grateful that she was able to keep a quiver out of her voice. "Maybe I'd better go home after all."

If Ethan was exasperated, he didn't let on. Instead, he reached out and snagged her wrist as she tried to breeze past. His touch was gentle but firm, and she had no choice but to look at him as he turned her around. He stared at Nora for a moment, searching her face, willing her to confide in him. But she kept her mouth shut tight. "Look," he said after a few seconds, "if you need anything, anything at all . . ." He didn't finish. He didn't have to.

"Thanks," Nora said. And then she tugged her wrist out of his grip and hurried away. She only paused for a moment at the back door, just long enough to tap one last desperate text.

*What have you done?*

# LIZ

"I'M THROWING A PARTY," Liz said, clipping a stalk of delphinium and adding it to the growing bouquet in her arm. She blurted it out partly to distract Macy from the pagan purples she was amassing and partly because she wanted to spread the word. Macy was forever hounding her about the unique hybrid flowers in the little garden by her front gate, and Liz wasn't about to share her secrets. The party announcement was an offering, and Macy accepted it enthusiastically. Key Lake would be buzzing with the news by dusk.

"You are?" Macy gushed, clearly forgetting the cobalt flowers with their mulberry hearts. Truly, they were stunning. People were forever commenting on them.

"Tomorrow night." Liz looped the clippers over her thumb and held the flowers before her in both hands. There were ten stalks or so, an impressive, towering display that would make the perfect centerpiece for the long table. All she needed were a few bridal bouquet hydrangeas to anchor the base. Maybe some bare branches. She wished pussy willows were in season.

"It's been ages!" Macy clapped her hands together, delighted. "Will you put the flag out?"

"Yes."

Macy sighed, smiling. "Remember the summer the boys turned ten?"

It was the same year that JJ turned eight and Nora broke her arm falling off the rope swing. A golden year in spite of the first hard cast among the Sanford children and the unusually hot summer. Golden because all the kids were out of diapers and pull-ups, capable of dressing themselves, independent. Liz felt like she could breathe again, and she hadn't even realized that she'd been holding her breath. But suddenly, Quinn was sticking her own strawberry Pop-Tarts in the toaster every morning and slipping out the back door before Liz had finished her first cup of coffee. Who knew what the other two were up to? Really, who cared?

Since all her kids knew how to swim, and since there wasn't much trouble they could get up to in provincial Key Lake, their self-sufficiency was a taste of freedom for Liz. She loved it. Her abrupt autonomy softened her edges and seemed to turn back time. After the chaos and confusion of what she began to think of as the "little years," Liz felt herself relax . . . And the clock unwound. Her twenties had been spent mixing bottles of formula and hushing night terrors. Now, at thirtysomething, she looked at herself in the mirror—really looked—and found a beautiful, capable, strong woman staring back. *I almost missed it*, she thought. *What a terrible shame.*

That summer was golden because of champagne.

Twinkling lights and stars to match, the sound of laughter across the water, and her husband's hand on her waist. Jack had the most spectacular, almost peculiar gray-green eyes and he spent much of that summer training the intensity of his gaze on her. On her sun-baked arms, her long, slim legs. On the coils of yellow hair that clung to her warm neck, and the place where her sundress gapped open just a bit when she bent over him with a bottle of ice-cold beer in her hand. It was fresh and new, a sort of falling in love all over again and for the first time because after the delirious years of making a family, her husband was a stranger. And she to him. It was intoxicating.

Almost enough to make her forgive him. But not forget. Never forget.

"How are your cherry tomatoes?" Liz said, and bit back the memories with a decisive snap. She didn't have time for melancholy. Settling the flowers in a basket by her feet, she grabbed the handle and started making her way around the side of her grand two-story home. A cluster of hydrangea bushes crouched in the shade.

"Perfect." Macy hurried to follow.

"The heirlooms?"

"My Hawaiian currants are ripe and so are the black cherries. I have a few yellow pears, but they're still rather green."

"I'll stop by for them tomorrow morning." Liz didn't ask; she didn't have to.

"Want me to post the party on Facebook?"

Liz couldn't stop her nose from crinkling. She knew that nothing betrayed her age so much as her inherent dislike for all things technological, but she was finding that she didn't really care. Some things weren't worth getting her panties in a bunch over. "Sure," she said. "Go ahead."

Macy laughed, enjoying Liz's obvious discomfort. "You'd love it," she proclaimed for the umpteenth time. "Get yourself a tablet and figure it out. I'll help you! It's so fun to see everyone's pictures. Never mind the ridiculous status updates."

"Not interested." Snip. A bloom the size and color of a honeydew fell into Liz's outstretched palm.

"You should be. Amelia posts all sorts of stuff."

"Of course she does," Liz said before she could censor herself. At least she didn't roll her eyes. She didn't need Macy wondering about the state of her familial relations. Before Macy could formulate a theory, Liz added, "Amelia is a lovely girl."

"In every way," Macy agreed.

Was she being tart? For once, Liz couldn't tell.

They parted ways shortly after that. Macy headed back across the cul-de-sac to her creamy brown colonial with the wide front porch and the four hand-carved rockers. She would curl up in the sunroom with her tablet and write God only knew what on Facebook and maybe Twitter. Such an appropriate name for shrill little birdies chirping away. Liz was sure that there were others, too. Sites with names she didn't recognize and that would make Macy feel superior to announce. But Liz was determined not to care. Tomorrow wasn't about Macy or resurrecting a Key Lake tradition. It was about Quinn. About reclaiming something good and innocent and real. Liz had to focus on that.

A shelf in the basement contained Liz's flower arranging supplies, and she carefully selected a glazed clay urn in a dreamy, midnight blue. It was heavy, the sort of object she would have marked with a Post-it note and left for Jack to carry up the stairs. But she was her own woman now, self-sufficient in a way that she didn't know she could be back when her kids began to grow up. She had practically been a child bride, though twenty wasn't so out of the ordinary when she'd said "I do." Several years later she started having children of her own. And now. Who was she now? A wife, former. A mother, still. And yet.

If nothing else, she was strong enough to carry the urn.

Liz plastered it to her chest, wet foam blocks, flower wire, and a roll of green tape tucked inside. She shuffled up the stairs one at a time, straining against the weight even as she relished the tight knot of her muscles, her body performing a task that made her feel powerful. Alive. Guilty, because she was here and Jack was not. Guilty, because a part of her was glad that the roles were not reversed.

Maybe she was going through some sort of late midlife crisis.

"Buy a new car," she huffed at her reflection in the hall mirror. "Have some work done. Take a lover."

The last one surprised her. A new car was always on the table and Jack had joked on more than one occasion that he'd happily underwrite a boob job. Of course, he didn't say it like that. Jack wasn't crass. But Liz knew that his carefully timed comments and fleeting glances at her less-than-perky barely C cups were wistful. She'd be a liar if she said she hadn't entertained the thought herself. But, a lover?

Liz laughed.

She was more interested in Quinn's love life than her own.

There was newspaper on the kitchen table, spread out and ready for the heavy urn and the rough bottom that might scratch the hand-scraped hardwood. Liz hefted the container onto an article about one local woman's exquisite quilts and set to work. She soaked the wet foam in water from her rain barrel and trimmed the stalks of delphinium. Stripping the stems of leaves, she placed them one by one into the foam, enjoying the sharp snitch of sound as each flower found its place. Even before it was finished, the centerpiece was artful, gorgeous. The sort of arrangement that could be featured on the cover of a decorating magazine. Sometimes Liz wondered if she could still do that sort of thing. Mark the world in some way more significant than the thin and fleeting likeness of herself in her children.

They didn't want any part of her, anyway.

It was a hard knot of feeling in the center of her chest. A tangle of emotion that had been pulled tight with time, stony and dense and silent. As cool and bittersweet as the spice of damp air in her grandmother's root cellar. Liz blinked away sudden tears, furious at herself, at how ridiculous and sentimental and *old* she had become. She had done well by her children. There was nothing to be ashamed of.

So why were they ashamed of her?

No matter. She was still their mother and she would fix what she could fix. Whether they liked it or not.

Maybe she should have done this years ago. Taken the bull by the horns, so to speak, and steered it in the right direction. As it was, she had no choice but to interfere now. And if things got messy? Well, it was true what they said about love and war. And whoever coined that particular phrase wasn't a lover—she was a mother.

When the arrangement was *Better Homes and Gardens* center-fold worthy, Liz grabbed her purse off the hook in the entryway and let herself out the door. She had been raised well, and she knew how to right a wrong. A good old-fashioned "I'm sorry" went a long way, but a gift certainly didn't hurt. Liz knew just what to do.

She cut another armload of delphiniums, a bouquet almost as impressive as the one that would soon adorn her banquet table. Wrapping the stems in newspaper that she dampened with the garden hose, she laid them carefully on the floor of her back seat. Then she was off to the liquor store, where she spent a good ten minutes reading wine labels. What was good? Jack Sr. had liked his whiskey expensive and his wine cheap, so Liz had never really learned to pick out a bottle of wine. She finally settled on a French Chenin Blanc with a label that looked like old sheet music. Pretty, even if the wine turned out not to be to Quinn's liking.

Sometimes Liz felt like she had spent her whole life keeping the peace. Settling disputes between her children, running interference between Jack and his daughters. Well, mostly Nora. And swallowing disappointment like bad medicine because what other choice did she have? To call out her husband—to name the lies they both knew he told—what good would that have done? It would have split up a family. Left her destitute, abandoned, alone. Nobody would have won. Least of all Liz.

She was a good peacekeeper. Shush now, be content, let it go. Peace*making*—now that was a different thing altogether. That was bombs and battles, wars waged for the sake of starting over, from the scorched earth up, on something pure and worthy. Peacemaking meant casualties, and Liz was all too willing to fall on a sword of silence if it meant life could go on the way it always had.

* * *

The sun was slanting high overhead when Liz arrived at the A-frame for the second time that day. It was time to start thinking about supper, to maybe take a pound or two of ground beef out of the freezer to start thawing for burgers on the grill in just a couple hours. Beer thirty, Jack Sr. had called midafternoon in summer, and it struck Liz that maybe she and Quinn could resurrect an old tradition and open a bottle of wine on the dock.

She knocked on the door this time. A quick, happy, four-note rap that sounded to her like, "Honey, I'm home!" Then she stepped back and waited with a smile on her face.

"Mom?" Quinn opened the door slowly, peering through a crack less than six inches wide. "What are you doing here?"

"Apologizing." Liz thrust the flowers at her daughter so she had no choice but to swing the door wider. "I'm sorry I burst in on you today. Please forgive me. I brought wine." Who could resist?

Quinn hemmed and hawed, pausing with one hand loose on the door. It was obvious she was torn between wanting to hold a grudge and struggling to resist the lure of the flowers, the wine. The unvarnished "I'm sorry." How rare were those? She just needed a little push.

Liz took a confident step forward, handing Quinn the bouquet so that she had to accept it or let the gorgeous blossoms fall. As Quinn wrapped her arms around the flowers, the door swung wide and Liz eased herself in. She gave her daughter a soft, knowing smile. *It's okay*, she said with her eyes. *We can forgive each other. We can be close like this.* Out loud she said, "The wine should be chilled, but if we stick it in the freezer for fifteen minutes or so it should be just perfect. What do you say? Shall we have a glass on the dock? It's such a perfect night."

"I don't know, Mom."

"We have lots to talk about." Liz gave a little wiggle of excitement. "I'm having a party! A big Sanford party. Remember how much fun we used to have? It's tomorrow night and you just have to come. In fact, I was hoping you could help me . . ."

Liz left the comment hang hopefully between them, but before Quinn could answer, there was the sound of a door opening and closing somewhere in the cabin. Then footsteps, fast as running, and suddenly, impossibly, there was a child standing in the hall. She was slight as a shadow and just as unassuming. A ghost, a whisper, a figment of Liz's imagination.

"I have to use the bathroom," the girl said. She kept her head down but stole one furtive, repentant glance at Quinn. Her lips were pursed, her eyes wide in apology as if she knew that heeding nature's call would undoubtedly get her in trouble. Then she hurried off toward the bathroom and slammed the door behind her.

"Mom," Quinn started, the word sounding thick and uncooperative in her mouth, "that was my friend's little girl . . ."

But Liz wasn't listening. She felt chiseled from marble, lips parted in shock. She couldn't move, couldn't breathe, but as she stared at the closed bathroom door she managed to whisper, "Who is that little girl, Quinn?"

"She's—"

Liz interrupted her before she could utter another word. "Don't you dare lie to me. God knows I can't stand to hear another lie."

# QUINN

QUINN TRIED TO TALK her mother into a cup of coffee or tea, one of Walker's scones, anything. When none of those suggestions elicited a response, she reached for the bottle in Liz's hands and said, "Here, let me uncork the wine." Quinn had to wrest it away; Liz had an iron grip on the smooth glass.

"I'm not thirsty," Liz said. Her jaw was lifted, her eyes narrowed. Quinn knew the look well. It was power and authority, a call to obedience. When Quinn was a child, all Liz had to do was tilt her chin just so and her kids scrambled. But Quinn wasn't a little girl anymore. She wasn't sure how to respond to her mother like this.

But whether she wanted it to or not, the truth spilled out. "We think she's Nora's," Quinn said quickly. There was no point in pretending. Liz was sharp and inquisitive. Unexpectedly bright. She often knew things she couldn't possibly know: who Quinn had secretly loved in tenth grade, where she hid the pack of cigarettes she once bought to feel rebellious, when Quinn snuck out of the house to meet up with friends on the beach.

"Of course she is," Liz said. "She's the spitting image of your sister at that age. Minus the hair, of course. Who . . . ?" But she let the question hang heavy in the air between them. Who, indeed.

Quinn realized that she was holding a wine bottle in one hand and an armful of flowers in the other. "Come on," she said, motioning that her mother should follow. "I'll put these in water and we'll sort this out."

"I don't think so." Liz unzipped her purse and poked around

inside for a few seconds before closing it without taking anything out. "I have to go."

"But—"

"We'll talk later," Liz said decisively. And then she left without a backward glance.

Quinn faltered in the entryway for a moment, flowers sagging in her arms, and felt a surge of annoyance. No, she was more than just annoyed. She was *angry*. Wasn't this just like her mother? Liz was tough and demanding, quick to fix whatever surface-level problem cropped up. Messes and arguments and skinned knees were all treated with the same quiet calm. She was judicious in her prudent administration of palliative care, but she was no heart surgeon. Anything deep or hurtful, truly difficult or dirty, was ignored.

"Fine," Quinn muttered to herself. "I'll handle it on my own."

But she grabbed her phone off the counter and texted her mother a single cryptic message: *Don't you dare tell a soul. I mean it.* She hesitated, wondering how much to say. Enough to ensure Liz's silence but not enough to unnerve her. Quinn finally settled on one last word: *Please.*

There was no response.

Nora had made it clear that no one was to know about Lucy, but her secret hadn't lasted a day. Quinn might as well call JJ and fill him in on the family news, too. "Nora has a secret daughter. JJ, you're an uncle!" Just the thought made her queasy. In Quinn's mind, JJ was still the disinterested and slightly menacing teenager that she remembered from her youth. He had been arrogant and moody, convinced of his own importance and appeal. Who could resist Jack Sanford Jr.? Who would want to?

JJ had always been a part of her personal landscape, but Quinn hadn't given her older brother much thought until she had a sleepover her freshman year in high school. JJ had been a senior and would barely acknowledge her existence, but when he'd walked through the living room near midnight and found her curled up on the couch with a handful of girls, he had paused to lean in the doorway.

"You going to introduce me to your friends, Q?" One corner of his mouth twisted up in a half smile that Quinn all at once realized most girls would find sexy. She could feel the way her friends shifted on the couch, leaning toward JJ almost imperceptibly.

"No," she said. "Go away."

But somebody invited him to sit, and he did, right on the arm of their father's favorite chair, where he distracted Quinn's friends to the point of giddiness. She was so angry she could feel her blood begin to fizz.

It took Liz wandering into the living room bleary-eyed and still cinching her robe to finally convince the girls it was time to retreat to Quinn's bedroom. But sleeping bags on the floor and fingernail polish didn't stop them from filtering in and out on their way to the bathroom, the kitchen. And when Quinn learned through the rumor mill several weeks later that Sarah had made out with some older guy, she wasn't surprised to find out it was JJ.

No, Quinn had never been close with her brother. And she wasn't about to try to change that now.

She placed her mother—and her brother—firmly out of her mind and tried to focus on caring for Lucy. It proved much more difficult than Quinn imagined it could be.

It wasn't just the screaming over breakfast. That had been terrifying enough, but Lucy refused to thaw even a little in spite of what Quinn hoped was her attentive warmth. It was no good. Lucy wouldn't let Quinn touch her and tried more than once to leave the cabin when Quinn wasn't looking.

"No!" Quinn finally shouted when Lucy tried to wrench the front door open and escape for the third time. She stood in the doorframe, arms stretched wide to block the little girl from escape. "Stop it, Lucy! You're stuck with me!"

They both cried.

But something seemed to break in Lucy. She slipped into quiet compliance—which Quinn decided was, in some ways, worse. Lucy's deference was almost creepy.

They spent the rest of the day circling each other, wary, reluctant. Quinn didn't want to admit it, but it crushed her a bit that she wasn't able to break through the little girl's steely defenses.

It wasn't for lack of trying. The cabin was equipped with a game cupboard, and Quinn's first tactic involved Candy Land with a side of cheerful banter. Even when the board was set up and Queen Frostine was doing her sparkly best, Lucy remained unmoved. Maybe she was too old to enjoy Candy Land? Yahtzee was next, but the din of dice in the red plastic cup only gave Quinn a headache. When the games proved ineffective, she moved on to puzzles (a thousand pieces of a lake sunset—Quinn didn't get very far), bubbles (they were favors leftover from an outdoor wedding), and finally, a dance party thanks to Spotify and the portable Jambox that projected "Uptown Funk" throughout the entire cabin.

Lucy didn't so much as crack a smile.

"What do you want, Lucy?" Quinn asked as she powered off the Bluetooth speaker. The melody of horns and bass cut abruptly, and in the ensuing stillness the cabin seemed unnaturally quiet.

*Nothing.*

The little girl was sitting on the sofa, her back straight and ankles crossed primly. As Quinn watched, she smoothed her dirty dress over her knees and picked at a loose thread with an almost alarming intensity. She was, without a doubt, the most focused child Quinn had ever met. Preternaturally good at playing hard to get. Lucy was flat-out ignoring the woman in front of her—even though Quinn had done everything but swallow flaming swords while standing on her head.

"I'd love to take you outside," Quinn faltered, gazing longingly at the sun as it glinted off the water. They would make a little sand castle in the tiny beach beside the dock and then dip their toes in the water when the afternoon got too hot. Maybe Lucy didn't know how to swim. Maybe Quinn could teach her.

But that was an idle wish. Quinn couldn't take Lucy outside. Not with the dozens of boats circling in and out of the bay. Small-town curiosity was a powerful force and Quinn knew exactly how it would go: a local would spot her with a pint-sized companion and cut the engine, tossing the dock line to her as they puttered through the water. "Now, Quinn, my girl. Who do we have here?" And she would have to talk and entertain, pull a couple of drinks out of the cooler that was conveniently hidden in the bench seat at the end of the dock. Snapple and straight-talk, that was how the fine folk of Key Lake liked to spend a summer afternoon. And when the sun began to set they traded in iced tea for Coors Light. Cans, of course, because they were safer than glass on the water.

No, Lucy couldn't go outside.

They were at an impasse. So after hours of trying and failing, Quinn finally gave up and let Lucy click through stations on the flat-screen TV. And that's exactly what the child did: flip, flip, flip. Past *Wheel of Fortune* and MSNBC and *Ellen*. Home improvement shows and *Say Yes to the Dress* and reruns of *The Big Bang Theory*. Whenever Curious George ambled across the screen or Princess Sofia made an appearance, Quinn held her breath. But Lucy never stopped.

Quinn was grateful when the sun began its slow descent and she could bundle Lucy off to bed. The child didn't make so much as a peep.

"She's in bed?" Walker asked when he came in past dark.

Quinn was curled up on the couch, a magazine in hand though she hadn't read a single paragraph. "Of course she's in bed. She's not a teenager."

"That bad?" Walker plopped down on the couch and grabbed Quinn's ankle, settling her foot in his lap. He ran his finger lightly down the curve of her arch. She squirmed.

"You know I hate that."

He smiled, pressing his thumb into the soft spot beneath the ball of her foot and circling slowly. "But I know you love this."

Quinn sighed and tipped her head back against the couch cushions. She had always considered herself a kid person; she'd loved babysitting in high school and couldn't wait to be a mom herself, but an entire day with Lucy had thoroughly scuffed the patina on those shiny dreams.

Walker moved his hands over Quinn's foot, gently cracking each bone in her pretty little toes. She stifled a shiver.

"I think . . ." Quinn wasn't sure she dared to voice what she really thought.

"What?"

"I think there's something wrong with her."

Walker exhaled through his nose and fixed Quinn with an arch look. "You've just figured this out?"

Quinn reached over and punched him on the shoulder. "I mean, besides the obvious."

"Let's see," Walker mused as he put his shoulders into massaging Quinn's heel. "She was abandoned—"

Quinn tried to protest but Walker talked right over her.

"—with a stranger—"

"Hey!"

"—in a strange place. She's lonely and frightened and confused. And who knows what she endured before she was dropped in our laps."

"I'm not sure she was dropped in *our* laps." Quinn sounded accusatory, which was an accident. She was going for lighthearted. With an edge. The truth was, she had felt alone all day. Abandoned in her own way.

Walker stopped rubbing her foot. "Excuse me?"

Why did she push him away when what she really wanted was

to hold him close? *I wanted you here*, is what she meant. *With me*. Quinn crawled across the couch and straddled her husband's lap, cupping his face in her hands. But he didn't melt like she hoped he would. Walker held himself still, aloof. "I didn't mean that," she whispered. "Not that way. It's just that you've been so busy lately."

"Working," Walker interjected.

"I know. But . . ."

"No buts, Quinn." He lifted her easily and set her aside, then strode into the kitchen, where he yanked open the door of the cupboard above the refrigerator. "We need the money and you know it. I don't need a guilt trip from you."

His words stung. They had only been in Key Lake for two months—not even—and Quinn had sent out a dozen resumes. The one job she really wanted at the preschool had fallen through, but she couldn't bring herself to fill out an application for Walmart. Not yet. How could Walker throw that in her face?

Quinn was equal parts miffed and contrite. Well, not quite equal. She was spoiling for a fight and found herself wanting to hiss across the space between them that Walker's piece wasn't sold. But she managed to control the urge. Accusations would accomplish nothing except for pushing him further away. Instead, she warned: "Shhhh!" Quinn pointed at the closed door to the spare room where Lucy was, ostensibly, asleep. She hoped.

If Walker heard her he didn't let on. Instead, he grabbed a bottle of Crown Royal and a highball glass and poured himself a double shot, neat. He took a few sips before splashing in a bit more and leaving the bottle uncapped and sitting on the kitchen counter. He returned to perch on the arm of the couch. Far from Quinn.

"You know how I feel about this," he said quietly.

"I know."

"I really can't handle you complaining about it."

Quinn dipped her head in acknowledgment. "You're the only

person I have to talk to." She didn't mention her mother and the fact that there were now three of them who knew Nora's secret. She wasn't ready to tell Walker that. "It's just a lot to deal with."

When Walker softened it was a visible, tangible, obvious thing. Like butter melting. Like ice transforming to a puddle on a sun-warmed picnic table. To Quinn, it was hope itself, and she lifted her face to him now, expectant.

"I'm sorry," she said.

"For what?" He looked at her warily, as if her answer mattered much.

"For everything. All of this. For Lucy. For making you do something you don't want to do."

"It's been a rough summer," he admitted.

"Do you regret coming here?"

He tipped his glass, watching the dark liquid inside. "I'd go any-where with you," Walker said eventually. He meant it, Quinn knew he did. He told her they were one in a million, a love story for the ages, and she believed that it was true. Usually. He was a lot to con-tain. Too much to know. There were things about her husband that were still a mystery, and Quinn feared she'd always follow a step behind. Forever reaching for him.

"I'd go anywhere with you," she said.

"I know."

Walker gave her a stiff smile, but he slid off the arm of the couch so that their knees were touching. On again, off again. Hot and cold. Lust and love and desire and longing and all the things that she could put a name to plus several that she couldn't.

"I love you," she said, because it seemed like the only thing that she could say.

"I know."

"My mom's having a party tomorrow night," she blurted when the silence between them began to turn stale. A classic Quinn move.

Distract. Redirect. Anything to keep the peace. Of course, her attempts to pacify sometimes backfired. Quinn didn't quite understand the difference between keeping the peace and making peace. One required diversionary tactics. The other, battle plans.

But Walker was willing to play along. "Ah." He smiled and tossed back the last of his drink. "A legendary Sanford gathering, I presume?"

"Of course. My mom is begging us to come."

"Us?"

"Of course."

"It's an event." Walker nodded sagely. "How many years has it been?"

"Lots. I don't know. I hated them when I was a kid. All those adults with sour breath and wrinkled clothes. My mother is the picture of propriety, but those parties always had a slightly desperate air to them."

"Those are some pretty profound thoughts for a kid." Walker put his empty drink on the table and Quinn restrained herself from slipping a coaster underneath the glass.

"I was a teenager when it hit me that they were playing at youth," Quinn said.

"What do you mean?"

"I walked past a group of my mom's friends and they started commenting on my skin, my hair, my legs. They thought I couldn't hear them, but . . ."

"But what?"

"I know now that they were jealous. Of a seventeen-year-old."

"I imagine every woman you meet is jealous of you." Walker's hand was on her bare leg, his thumb tracing the arc of three small freckles on her thigh.

Quinn's skin tingled where he touched her. This was different from the foot rub, different from the way he reached for her throughout the day as if she were a lodestone and he simply needed to be grounded. She loved it when he touched her like this. With intent. With desire.

"I don't know about that," Quinn managed as Walker's fingertips brushed beneath the hem of her khaki shorts. They were so short he didn't have to reach far to graze the lacy edge of her hip-hugging panties.

"I do." Walker pushed her back gently into the pillows and kissed her slow. His mouth was fire and longing. Warm and insistent. Quinn both loved and loathed the way he made her feel consumed. As if she were drowning, but instead of gasping for air she let herself be pulled under, deeper still.

There were things that they should talk about. Realities to face. But Quinn was in no state to address them. She gave in and kissed him back, her hands twisting in his hair, holding tight.

"Go to your mom's party," he told her, nibbling at her bottom lip.

"Lucy . . ." she whispered, but the girl was little more than a ghost of a thought.

"I'll stay with her." Walker's hand was under her shirt now, following the line of her hip, her waist, the fine bones of her arching rib cage.

"But—"

"Go. I've got this covered."

And then, suddenly, Quinn didn't care about anything but his body above her.

# NORA

THE DOOR WAS OPEN, the narrow gap dark as a wound, and that scared Nora even more than the silence. It was eerie, the quiet. The night was hot and sticky, stagnant when it should have been alive with the chirp of crickets, the low whine of cicadas in the trees. But the world seemed to be holding its breath, waiting for the first few raindrops of the storm that swelled on the horizon. Even the house was still, the shades pulled, the windows black.

Nora had stood on these steps dozens of times. More. But she couldn't shake the feeling that she was in the wrong place. Where was the tinny soundtrack of a show turned up too high on the TV? Sometimes the radio played tug-of-war with sitcom stars, and sometimes Tiffany's voice drowned it all out. The bark of her laugh or belted show tunes that filled the farmhouse with a warm luster. Tiffany loved to fill up space with sound, to talk, laugh, sing, and Nora was used to hearing the muffled noise through closed doors. Tiffany believed in shutting the world out. In padlocks and chains. And she never turned from a door without securing it behind her.

Not this time.

Nora put her palm on the door and squeezed her eyes shut. She wanted to walk away, to call 9-1-1 and let the authorities handle whatever had happened inside. But she couldn't. The tug of responsibility—and something much more complicated—forced her to swallow a steadying breath and call through the crack: "Tiffany? Tiffany, honey, are you in there?"

Nothing.

The door creaked when Nora pushed it open, a scream that split the night so violently her heart thudded in her chest. She felt sure that Donovan was gone—he spent most evenings at the Cue and his car was nowhere to be seen—but if anyone was inside they would surely come running. Nora held her breath for a heartbeat or two, but nothing interrupted the sleep of the decaying farmhouse.

Nora was surprised at the sudden stab of anger that caught her square in the chest. When she found Tiffany she was going to smack her.

Nora balled her fists. She was jumping to conclusions. Tiffany would be okay. Everything would be just fine.

Her sneakers squeaked on hardwood as she walked fully into the house and fumbled for the light. "Tiffany?" she called again. "It's Nora. You haven't responded to any of my texts . . ."

She trailed off as her fingers found the switch. The bare bulb in the living room sputtered to life and Nora blinked in the dim half-light.

The house looked as if the storm had blown through already. Chairs were overturned and the television screen smashed to blistering spiderwebs that glittered strangely in the dull light. Nora stepped over an old pizza box with only one slice missing and righted a lamp that had been knocked off a scarred end table. But the bulb was shattered, and Nora's heart splintered like the jagged edge of glass when she realized what was dusting the worn tabletop. It was nothing really, a fine sprinkling. The residue of dirty white powder.

Tiffany hated needles, wouldn't have anything to do with them, but the powder was powerful enough to send her on a trip for nearly a day. Once was never enough. She binged when she started and tweaked hard when she came down. Nora had raced Tiffany to the hospital on more than one occasion, raw from the drag of her own fingernails and convinced that Nora, her only friend in the world, was a demon sent to torture her.

But that was then. Nora shuddered and tried to push down memories that were so close to the surface they bled through all her defenses. It was too late. Her nostrils filled with the scent of old eggs and cat urine, the telltale signs that Donovan was cooking meth in the kitchen. Nora pushed down a wave of revulsion at the memory. That had been the worst. Rock bottom. Tiffany had forgotten to eat for nearly a week, at least nothing of substance, and the skin beneath her cheekbones had caved until she was shadow and bone, a wisp of angry ghost that grabbed at Nora with crooked fingers when she ventured close enough to touch. When Nora threatened to take Everlee away, Tiffany had agreed to rehab.

Now, Tiffany was a changed woman. Her brown eyes clear, her frame thin but not skeletal like it had been when she was so out of control her days blurred into one. Less than two weeks ago Nora had treated Tiffany to a manicure, a little happy-twenty-sixth-birthday treat, and had relished the way her friend's hands glowed smooth and whole beneath the light of the lamp. They had both gotten acrylic nails with squared French tips and felt so elegant they spoke in bad accents all the way home.

"How are you?" Nora had asked, twisting in her seat when they pulled up to the farmhouse and Tiffany reached for the door handle. "I mean, really. How are you doing?"

Tiffany couldn't hold her gaze, but her eyes flicked to Nora's and she smiled self-consciously before staring out the windshield. "I'm fine. Really."

Nora studied her profile, the sharp angle of her slender jaw and the way her skin looked scrubbed clean. Tiffany seemed much older than her age, her eyes and mouth crisscrossed with lines too deep for someone so young. But there was an innocence about Tiffany, too, a vulnerability that always made Nora want to shield her from the world. To protect her.

Nora had failed. On more than just this occasion.

She tripped on an overturned laundry hamper, its dingy contents spilled across the living room floor, and knocked her knee on the edge of an antique chest. The lid was open, the hinge ripped and hanging crooked from the rotting wood. There were toys inside, a stained Raggedy Ann doll and a deflated purple ball amid a rainbow of colors and plastic. "Tiffany?" Nora called again, the name fracturing on her lips.

Maybe Tiffany was gone. Maybe she had left in search of another hit. But Tiffany's rusty Ford truck was parked where it always was in the gravel drive beside the house. And the little farmstead surrounded by cornfields was too far away from anything for Tiffany to take off on foot. Especially on a night like this. A night with clouds roiling in a slow boil, the radio broadcasting a tornado watch. Tiffany would be tucked in her house, the doors locked tight around her.

Adrenaline was a drug, too, and Nora found herself stumbling through the detritus of the living room with a panicked urgency. She flicked on the lights in the kitchen. Cupboards were open, soiled dishes piled so high in the sink that half of the window was obscured. Something smelled overripe, sickly sweet and nauseating, but in spite of the mess and the stench, Nora felt a pang of relief that Tiffany wasn't sprawled facedown on the floor. The room was empty of everything but the rebellious artifacts of her sad life.

The rest of the house was equally wrecked, a labyrinth of discarded magazines, toys, clothes. There was a serving bowl in the upstairs hallway, a little striped sock hanging from the banister. A window air conditioner hummed in the dim light, drops of condensation making dark Rorschach blots on the pale carpet. *An angel.* The thought flicked through Nora's mind so quickly she had to glance back at the wet spot to orient herself. It did look like an angel, the stain, and Nora prayed it was an auspicious sign.

She wasn't looking for Tiffany anymore.

Closets. Corners. Under the queen bed where Tiffany's unwashed laundry had been scattered across the faded sheets.

There wasn't a proper bed in the little closet under the eaves that Tiffany had turned into the prettiest nook in the house. Walls the color of cotton candy, a twin mattress on the floor covered with a quilt in hues of the softest green. Nora had refinished a squat bookshelf for a birthday present and it contained a treasure trove: the entire collection of Olivia and all the original Curious George, Richard Scarry with his willowy Lowly Worm and a hidden Goldbug like a secret on every page. Nora's favorites were the dog-eared procession of Anne of Green Gables paperbacks, but they were simply biding their time, waiting on the bottom shelf for the day when the picture books would be set aside.

Thank God the little girl was gone. Thank every celestial creature in heaven and on earth and under the earth that at least she was safe. As for Tiffany . . . ?

Nora put a finger on the spine of *The Lion, the Witch and the Wardrobe* and slipped it from the bookshelf. They had chosen the book purposefully, deciding that a trip through the wardrobe was exactly what they needed. A fresh start, a clean break, a new beginning. But when Nora felt for the manila envelope they had hidden, it was gone. She started yanking books, dropping them to the floor as she searched for the packet. It was no use.

Nora sank to her knees on the floor and forced herself to breathe. To think. But her mind was blank and aching. She didn't know what to do or where to turn. She had never felt so betrayed in her entire life.

Why? Where was she?

Suddenly, it hit her with the force of a lightning bolt. *She knew.* She knew what Tiffany had done. Nora scrambled to her feet and raced back through the house, down the stairs, and out the back door where she slipped across the wet grass on her way to the leaning detached garage. It had started to pour, thunder rumbling in the distance and promising that there was so much more to come. Nora shielded her face from the fat drops with her hand, but by the time she hit the shelter of the garage she was soaked.

Nora had left her phone in the glove compartment of her car, but she knew that there was a Maglite on the workbench. It was thick and heavy as a billy club—it had occurred to her more than once that it could be used as a weapon. But now, she just needed it for light.

The board she was looking for was beneath the workbench and half hidden by the support beam for the long counter. Tiffany had shown it to her long ago, back when she was still trying to prove that Donovan was a good man. The sort of man who could make an honest woman out of her and be a loving daddy to Everlee.

"See?" Tiffany said, wedging back the board and shining the flashlight into the depths of the recess beyond. Nora could just make out a brown paper bag folded up inside.

"What is it?"

"Money." Tiffany sounded smug, *I told you so* ringing in that one simple word. "I counted it a couple days ago when I knew he would be out for hours."

"And?"

"There's got to be over ten thousand dollars there."

"You said you counted it."

Tiffany laughed. "I gave up! There were too many bills."

Back then, Nora hadn't asked all the questions that were burning on the tip of her tongue. *Where did it come from? Why is he hiding it in the garage? Who else knows about it?* She didn't trust herself to because she knew that she'd start to yell. To tell Tiffany what to do and how far to run. Tiffany never responded well to demands. Instead, Nora just pushed herself up and walked away, swinging Everlee into her arms as she left the garage.

But now. Now Nora wished she knew the answers to all those questions. She wished that she'd screamed at Tiffany, told her to get out before it was too late.

Because all at once her every fear was justified.

I'M A FLIGHT RISK. Always have been. Things get heated and instead of sticking around to figure out if there's going to be a hot-dog roast or a natural disaster, I assume the worst and split.

Don't hate me for what you can't possibly understand.

I feel like I've always done my level best with what I've been given. Or, at least, usually. But sometimes life doesn't hand you lemons—it throws a snake in your lap. And what are you supposed to do about that? Before my grandpa died he taught me that you take its head off. Clean, with one sure chop of a sharpened hoe.

But I've never been good with garden tools. I prefer to run.

Usually straight into the arms of exactly the wrong man. Funny thing is, I fell for a good man once. Or someone who I thought was good. Stable, safe, familiar. But he turned out to be all soft inside, and not in a sweet way. He was rotten to the core. Nora tried to warn me, just like she has every single time. And I don't deserve her no-strings-attached friendship, because I'm about the worst listener alive.

I traded my truck for a two-door Corolla and a quarter gram of glass. My last. Can you blame me? But then, you don't know who he is. What he's done.

Believe it or not, it was the things that I couldn't put a label on, things he could never be convicted for, that seeded my imagination with violent thoughts. Those incidents made me understand with almost sickening clarity how satisfying it would be to claw his eyes out with my bare fingers. That's an expression, you know, but it's more than that, too. It's the very core of each layered feeling I have for him: the lust masquerading as love, the dependence, the need.

The way he made me feel wanted in a way that I had never been wanted before. As if I were air and water and light and life. As if he needed me for his very survival. Once, I believed he would die without me. But none of those things were real. And when it was all peeled back and I saw what he really was? It was too late. Almost.

We had been together for over a year when I glimpsed the truth. Of course, I'm no saint myself. Never have been, probably never will be. I met him in another man's bedroom, and if that doesn't tell you something, I fear you lack imagination. There were drugs and far too much alcohol. Rehab, sometimes. It didn't do much good.

He only hit me once. We were fighting about something. Maybe rent (it was his turn to pay?). I don't remember. But I do remember that I was, as my auntie would say, sassing. I have a sharp tongue. I use it. And why not? He wasn't my father, my elder. I thought we respected each other.

I was wrong. Without even giving it a thought, he hauled off and smacked me across the face. It was vicious, backhanded, and the class ring he still wore on his third finger split my lip like a piece of overripe fruit. I was too shocked to react. As the blood spilled warm and quick from the corner of my mouth I just stood and stared. Of course, my mouth throbbed and a headache was sparking behind my temple like a struck match, but I barely registered those things.

It was the betrayal that hurt. No one had ever hit me before. Not even my auntie, who chased me with a wooden spoon and pretended like she'd paddle me purple. She never did. If she caught me—which was rare—she pulled me to her scrawny chest and held me so tight I wondered if she had decided to suffocate me instead of beat me.

"Good God in heaven," she'd whisper over my dark curls. "You are ten handfuls, Tiffany Marie. And I only have two."

But wasn't that a good thing? An abundance. An overflow. It sounded perfect to me. I didn't know what it was like to have too much of anything.

I thought of that as the first drop of blood hit my white blouse and ruined it. Finally. Extravagance. It wasn't what I'd always hoped it would be. And even though I knew I could soak my pretty shirt in ice water, try to erase the dark blot with stain remover and sunshine, I'd always know that beneath the line of turquoise embroidery there was a smudge of evidence. Proof that I wasn't the woman I believed myself to be: wanted, safe, loved.

Maybe everything would have been different if we had been alone that night. I've already admitted I'm prone to escape. What's the point in fighting when you can walk away? But we must have woken her with our arguing, and when she stumbled bleary-eyed and half-asleep into the kitchen to find me bloody, she screamed.

Her fear was primal, a dark and wild thing that made her cling to me like a spider monkey. She was all arms and legs, sinew and terror wound so tight that I ended up bleeding all over her, too. The next morning I didn't even try to wash her Dora pajamas or my flowing peasant shirt, even though they were both favorites. I just crumpled them in a ball and pushed them to the very bottom of the garbage can beneath the sink. Out of sight, out of mind.

We used the same tactic to divert her attention. A half-eaten bag of M&M's calmed her down while I dabbed at my face with a dish towel. She rested her cheek on my shoulder and ate the candies one by one from his outstretched hand, saving the green ones for last because I had once told her they were my favorite. When the only chocolates left were green, she snagged the bag and handed it solemnly to me.

"For your owie."

"I fell," I told her, and had to suppress an inappropriate, crazed giggle because it was so cliché. A bad after-school special. I determined right then and there that we were gone, baby, gone. Forget the farmhouse I thought I loved and the way that he ran his calloused hands over my bare skin. Forget that strong chin and the look he gave me when he wanted me. My auntie always told me there were plenty of fish in the sea and maybe this time I would find one worth keeping.

But when I dared to sneak a glance at him, he was *crying*. Real tears on his cheeks and a line dashed across his forehead that proclaimed his guilt, his never-ending regret for what had happened.

"I'm so sorry," he mouthed to me. And when I gave an almost imperceptible nod he made a quiet, strangled sound like a sob.

"Why are you crying?" she asked him. "Mommy's hurt."

"Your momma's hurt makes my heart hurt," he said, avoiding my eyes. "I'm just so sorry that it happened."

"She fell," my little girl said sagely, and though a little burr of disgust caught and held in the pit of my stomach, I let her go to him when he reached out his arms.

"We have to take good care of her, you and me," he said, pressing her head into the crook of his neck. "You and me . . ."

She was asleep in no time.

And I, foolish fairy-tale-believing simpleton that I was, didn't run.

I'm running now.

# Day Three

---

## Friday

# LIZ

WHEN YOU LIVED in a town like Key Lake (population 6,567, give or take a few), Walmart was a necessary evil. It was the only chain store that would set up shop in such a little haven, never mind that businesses boomed during the summer as vacationers gleefully stocked up on everything from sunscreen to cases of Pabst Blue Ribbon. Always PBR. Because: small-town America.

The truth was, like it or not, Walmart was the only place in all of Key Lake where Liz could buy the essentials. Makeup and the dish soap that didn't make her rags smell musty and cheap birdseed for her collection of feeders. And, of course, party supplies.

Liz grudgingly made a list because it was better than dwelling on the fact that her granddaughter (sweet Mary and Joseph) was asleep across the lake. She had learned long ago that sometimes getting lost in the details was better than stepping back to look at the whole, ugly picture. So rather than deal with the dull ache in her heart that made it difficult to breathe, Liz took out a pen and paper.

*Napkins (the nice thick ones)*
*Citronella oil*
*Strands of white LED lights*
*Vodka (cheap)*
*Baguette*
*Mozzarella pearls*

*Prosciutto*
*Limes*

Walmart would provide. But Liz didn't have to like it. Thankfully, she also didn't have to go when she risked being seen by someone she might know.

It was after midnight when Liz pulled into the oversized parking lot. She marveled at the number of cars at such a late hour and the myriad out-of-state plates. Mostly Iowa and South Dakota. But she spotted an SUV from Michigan and a motor home that hailed, impossibly, it seemed to Liz, from Florida. *Why?* she wanted to ask the driver. You're surrounded by sea. Key Lake was, in comparison, an embarrassment. A dirty little mud puddle.

Liz slipped her purse strap crisscross over her chest and prepared herself for the worst. Drunk teens. Or—please God, no—drunk adults who should know better. Who would crack jokes and slur their words and flirt badly. There was nothing Liz hated so much as a bad flirt, the kind of man who damned a woman with faint praise or downright insulted her in a weak attempt to be charming. Liz had learned that even at fiftysomething she wasn't immune to that sort of vague humiliation. But even corny pickup lines were preferable to idle chitchat over the watermelons with Agnes from the church's Ladies Aid. Or Helen or Mira or Josephine. Liz was a good, God-fearing woman and a regular at the First Reformed Church of Key Lake, but she wasn't the quintessential parishioner. She was fond of Jesus, not so much his people. And they seemed to love Walmart more than seemed strictly conventional.

For all her idle fears, Liz found the aisles of the store to be almost completely vacant. There was no greeter at the door at such a late (early?) hour and the customer service counter was abandoned. The gardening section echoed with her footsteps, and as she drew close to the darkened corner of the store the motion-sensor lights hummed to life in greeting. Clearly she was the first person who had wandered this far in a while.

There was a feel of apocalypse in the air, as if the Rapture had happened and Liz had been left behind. It felt inevitable, desolate, and she sank onto a gingham patio set display couch and put her head in her hands.

Grief was sudden and inescapable, a wave that engulfed her so thoroughly she felt like she was drowning in it. Where had she gone so wrong? What had she done to alienate her children so thoroughly? Liz had a *granddaughter*. She couldn't get her mind around it even as her hands trembled at the thought. The child was her own flesh and blood. The earth should have moved when Lucy was born, Liz should have felt the universe shift. Instead, she had lived all these years never knowing, never even suspecting. What was she supposed to do with that?

Liz took a shuddering breath and reached to tuck her hair behind her ears. She was surprised to find her cheeks were damp with tears, the little wisps of face-framing bangs tangled instead of smooth. What a mess. She was a wreck in every way and that only added to her heartbreak.

Wiping the dampness from her cheeks, Liz straightened her spine and looked at her shopping list. There would be time to deal with the secrets and lies, the little girl who shared Nora's stone-gray eyes. But weeping in the garden section at Walmart would accomplish nothing. Liz did the only thing she knew how to do: she powered through.

Her cart was stocked with party fare and she was just about to check out when it struck her that she wouldn't have time for a cut and color before the soiree tomorrow night. No, *tonight*, she realized. Soon there would be the sound of laughter over the water, lights twinkling in the trees as the sun set, long toothpicks layered with cherry tomatoes, fresh mozzarella, and basil from her garden. Determinedly focusing on the things she could control, Liz decided she would wear that cobalt sundress she loved and the strappy sandals with the kitten heels. When she pictured her hair pulled back, her roots showed. How long had it been since she had colored her hair?

Scolding herself roundly for her oversight, Liz steered in the direction of the personal care and cosmetics section. She would never color from a box, but her stylist had once told her that she could refresh the bubbles in her champagne blond with a hair gloss. And yes, Maureen had actually said that: *refresh the bubbles in your champagne blond*. It had taken all Liz's self-control not to gape. She was not a mean person, but some people should come with warning labels.

Outrageous claims notwithstanding, a gloss sounded doable.

Liz found the aisle marked *Hair Color* and was so busy scanning the displays for a box marked *gloss* that she almost bumped right into the first person, besides a half-asleep cashier, that she had seen on her midnight Walmart excursion.

"Oh!" she cried, surprised, worrying that her eyes were red-rimmed and puffy. "I'm sorry! I almost ran you over."

The girl barely flinched. Nodding slightly, she continued to study the packages of permanent color.

Well, that was rude. Not even a proper hello. They were in Walmart, but it was the Walmart Supercenter in Key Lake, Minnesota, a place where the one-finger wave reigned supreme and everyone was friendly—even out-of-towners. Often, *especially* out-of-towners. Vacations had a soporific effect on people. Out came the Hawaiian shirts, the laid-back attitude, the expansive friendliness that made them yak for fifteen minutes with a perfect stranger in a shopping store aisle. Apparently, the girl hadn't read the unofficial handbook.

"You have lovely hair," Liz told her, trying to see past the curtain of chestnut-colored waves that obscured the stranger's face. She was determined to eke at least a smile out of her. "I hope the dye isn't for you."

She made a noncommittal grunt.

"I've always wanted to be a brunette." Not true. But whatever. Liz was making friends here. Drowning the girl in a little Midwestern nice. Maybe she was the one with the motor home from Florida. Liz had been expecting a couple with gray hair and matching jogging suits. "So, what do you think?" she fished shamelessly. "Could I pull off Dark Golden Mahogany Number 4?"

The girl had no choice but to glance at the box that Liz held in her outstretched hand. Her eyes flicked to Liz's and she nodded once, a small, curt movement that seemed more like a tic than an expression of her approval. In that moment, Liz realized two things: the girl was older than she had imagined and she was no stranger.

The coltish lines of her body and the length of her thick, dark hair were reminiscent of a teenager, but the woman before Liz was fast approaching thirty. She knew that for a fact.

"Tiffany Barnes," Liz said slowly. "It has been a very long time, honey."

Tiffany's head whipped around and she stared at Liz—for real this time. It was obvious she hadn't recognized her teenage best friend's mother. Or, at least, she hadn't looked closely enough to peg her. And what was that emotion bubbling just below the surface? Fear? Well, that didn't make sense at all. Liz and Jack Sr. hadn't exactly embraced the wild child Nora attached herself to like a sister, but she had always been welcome in their home. Even if the welcome was tepid and Tiffany rarely accepted it.

"Well, now, you're about the last person I expected to bump into tonight," Liz said. She marched over to where Tiffany stood, cowering, it seemed, and gave her a stiff Sanford hug. The younger woman didn't return the embrace. Her arms were pinned to her sides, hands still clutching the boxes of permanent hair dye. "How have you been, honey? I don't think I've seen you in . . ." Liz tried to do the math and failed. "Well, it's been a long time."

"It has." Tiffany seemed to have found her voice, finally.

"What have you been up to since high school?"

"Waitressing," she said without conviction.

"That sounds nice." It didn't. Not at all, but then Liz couldn't exactly cast stones. Nora was a barista, after all. And, apparently, a single mom who thought little of abandoning her child in the care of her somewhat-estranged sister. (A stranger?) Good God in heaven, how long did these girls plan to drag out their adolescence? To make bad choices and force other people to deal with them? By their age Liz had been a married mother of three. And if she hadn't been mixing bottles of formula and potty training toddlers she would have been an administrative assistant in some respect-able office. She had a two-year degree and a long list of excellent referrals to recommend her. Of course, she had never needed them. Mothering and housekeeping and *husband*-keeping had kept her more than busy. Liz barely had time for her garden and her fabrics and her designs.

"Do you keep in touch with Nora at all?" Liz asked, wondering if maybe there was some private pact these days between women of a certain age to underachieve.

Tiffany just shrugged. "I really should go," she muttered, shov-ing the boxes back onto the shelf all helter-skelter. One fell to the ground and she didn't bother to pick it up.

Liz's skin prickled with annoyance and she almost told Tiffany to fix her mess. But then she remembered. It came in a rush and she felt herself thaw with shame. "Oh, Tiffany! You're in town for the funeral, aren't you?"

Lorelei's funeral had to be soon. Or had it already happened? Was it only yesterday that Macy was telling her about that poor woman's passing? Whatever the case, Liz was convicted by her own insensitivity. She was being stingy and small. Here she was judging Tiffany when the clearly grief-stricken girl had just lost her aunt, the closest thing to a mother she had ever known. What was the story again? Lorelei's sister was Tiffany's mother, but she had skipped town when the child was barely out of diapers. Something like that. Sad, sad, sad. Liz's heart melted for the young woman in front of her. She reached out and hugged her again, and this time, she put some feeling into it.

"I am so sorry."

"Thank you," Tiffany whispered.

"Do you need a place to stay? Is there anything I can do?"

"No. I'm fine."

"Are you sure? I don't know if you heard, but Jack Sr. is gone and I have that whole big house to myself . . ." Liz trailed off when she caught sight of her own grocery cart and the bottles of booze and festive packages of tiny paper umbrellas. How mortifying. How inappropriate.

But Tiffany was shaking her head, excusing herself feebly as she backed out of the aisle. "Thank you, Mrs. Sanford. I really have to go."

Liz struggled for something to say, anything that might offer a little comfort or at least communicate that Elizabeth Sanford wasn't the thoughtless, bumbling idiot that she had just appeared to be. She settled on: "You're in my prayers."

Which wasn't true. But it would be now. And as Tiffany walked away Liz made good on her declaration and whispered: "God bless that poor, sweet soul."

Then she decided to order flowers for the funeral. A huge bouquet with lots of roses.

Liz was no-nonsense. A fixer and doer and stiff-upper-lipper. She believed in pulling herself up by her bootstraps and would swear until her dying day that the glass was always, and always would be, half full. But she was also a mother. A grandmother?

If she thought of it, which she tried not to, Liz might consider that secret part of her soul a sort of robin's egg. Fragile, mysterious, lovely. Delicate and prone to brokenness, but containing all that was vital and life-giving. Holy. Sometimes, at moments like this, when she was raw and aching in a sudden, unexpected way, Liz wondered at the many fissures that had splintered across her heart. The fault lines matched the wrinkles around her eyes, the telltale creases that had set deep in her forehead and around her pretty mouth. She had lived. She had loved. But she was lonely. She was alone. It kind of made her want to sit down in the middle of Walmart and cry.

But then she spotted it out of the corner of her eye. Shine gloss. The package proclaimed: *Crystal Clear Shine System. For all types of hair.*

Perfect.

Liz Sanford snagged that box off the shelf and set her shoulders. She would go home. Pull off the party of the year. Figure out why Nora kept Lucy a secret and reunite her family.

Fix everything.

# QUINN

QUINN WOKE FROM a nightmare, a silent scream clawing at her throat. She bolted upright, frantic and panting, and gathered the blankets around her as if the cotton sheets could protect her from whatever had scared her awake. They were in danger, she could feel it, but the worry that troubled her sleep vanished the moment she opened her eyes. Quinn squinted in the early morning light. Nothing was amiss. The room was empty, even Walker was gone—no doubt to his studio. Quinn was alone and the terror that had yanked her from sleep was just that: a bad dream.

"You're being ridiculous," Quinn said just to hear the sound of her own voice.

She glanced at the clock and discovered it was a few minutes after six. Much earlier than she normally woke up, but the nightmare felt grim and dirty against her skin and her T-shirt was damp with sweat.

Quinn scrambled out of bed, eager to wash her fear down the drain. She took a cool shower and then made quick work of her morning routine. Curtains thrown wide, bed made, teeth brushed. Clipping her bangs back with a pair of bobby pins, Quinn studied herself in the mirror. She was pale, almost gaunt. An uncharacteristic look for August and it made her shiver a little. *Stress*, Quinn decided. *This whole Lucy thing is making me crazy.*

The thought of Lucy sent a jolt of worry through Quinn. Was she . . . ? But when Quinn hurried through the cabin to Lucy's room she found the little girl sound asleep in her bed. All the same, Quinn double-checked the front door (it was locked) and the sliding glass doors (the bolt was still in place). She pressed her hand to her forehead for just a moment, unexpectedly shaky and relieved.

Quinn lifted her phone from her pocket and tried to call Nora, but the attempt was halfhearted. After several rings she gave up and tapped a text instead: *Call me.* She doubted Nora would respond.

The living room was a mess and Quinn dulled the sense of foreboding that raked bony fingers across her skin by tidying up. She folded the blanket that had been piled on the floor and straightened pillows, righted a picture frame, rescued the remote control from the couch cushions. It looked like a storm had blown through.

Last night. It came back to her in a blur of snapshots, close-ups of Walker's dark skin, white teeth, strong hands. He had been passionate, possessive, hungry. Almost angry. It was beautiful and unexpected. The tiniest bit unnerving because it felt so significant.

The thought slid through her like a specter: *I'm pregnant.*

Could it be?

Finding out that Quinn had endometriosis shortly after she and Walker were married hadn't seemed like that big of a deal. So what if her periods were heavy? But the pain could be intense, and when Walker insisted that she see an ob-gyn, Quinn relented—as much to appease him as to quiet her own misgivings. The diagnosis wasn't shocking or scary, just something she had to deal with. But when her doctor suggested that a pregnancy earlier rather than later would be wise, they took him seriously.

"I want kids," Walker had said, a mischievous glint in his eye. What he meant was: I want to try to make babies with you. But they both knew that having a family was what they always wanted, so Quinn went off birth control.

A year later, nothing had happened. And suddenly, the quiet, "let's see what happens" approach seemed paltry and trifling. If they wanted children, they were going to have to work for it.

Quinn placed her hands over her belly and said a desperate, wordless prayer. A wish, really, that she released with a sigh so soft it hardly existed at all. *This time*, she thought.

Of course, there was no way to know. Not yet. Her doctor in California warned her that the medication she was on could produce a false positive. A theory she tested more than once only to be bitterly disappointed when that hopeful pink plus sign dissolved into her period just days later. It was almost too much. Her body— each curve and angle and even scent that she had called her own for well over twenty years—was foreign soil. The hormones rendered her so strange and unfamiliar she sometimes felt as if she had experienced a sort of incomprehensible exchange. A bait and swap. Switcheroo. Who was this woman with full hips, hair so thick she could barely fit a ponytail holder around it twice, skin as smooth and flawless as molded plastic? Quinn didn't recognize herself and she certainly didn't expect Walker to.

Which was why last night was such a gift. They made love, a far cry from the clinical, scheduled sex that was supposed to result in a baby the size of a pinpoint. Walker had been so intense, so passionate that Quinn had forgotten all about her final dose of Gonal-f. But now, she knew. The timing was perfect. Or, close enough. Besides, wasn't this exactly the way it was supposed to happen? They were taking fertility treatments, but this baby had been conceived in love.

The door to Lucy's bedroom was still closed, so Quinn turned her attention to coffee. She felt as if she stood at the center of a teeter-totter, balanced between despair and hope. There was so much to long for she didn't even know where to start.

Next to the coffeepot, Quinn found a package on the counter, a clear plastic Walmart bag rolled into a tight little bundle with the receipt stuck on top. Walker had left a note of sorts on the back side of the strip of paper, an *XO* that had been quickly sketched in ink. The *O* was a mandala design, the intricate lines reminiscent of the patterns he sometimes liked to trace on Quinn's hands and wrists. Hugs and kisses in detailed art, Walker's version of a love letter.

Inside the shopping bag Quinn found an assortment of items for Lucy. Walker must have made the trip to town after tucking Quinn in for the night. Lucy had been so fragile the day before, Quinn had known there was no way she could leave her. And taking the girl along on a Walmart run to casually bump into the fine, gossipy people of Key Lake was out of the question. Quinn smiled as she marveled at her husband's forethought, his kindness, in the things he had picked out for the little girl.

A pair of plaid shorts in bright, cheerful colors, size 5/6. Holding them up, Quinn guessed they would fit Lucy perfectly. There were two shirts to match, a pink chambray and a gray baseball tee. Then, a casual, breezy mint-green sundress and a pajama set with purple hearts. A pair of flip-flops. A five-pack of Fruit of the Loom underwear printed with, of course, fruit. Dancing cherries and round-cheeked apples and smiling bananas. Finally, at the bottom of the bag there was a small stuffed fox and a pad of thick art paper with a box of rainbow pastels. Classic Walker.

Quinn grinned in spite of herself, struck by sudden inspiration. She had applied to be a teacher's assistant at the Pumpkin Patch, the only preschool in Key Lake, and during the interview the principal had waxed poetic about the role of art and play and nature in the development of a child. Quinn's degree was in secondary education and the emphasis on finger paints and pinecones seemed childish and just a bit naive. Maybe that's why she hadn't gotten the job. But now, with Walker's unblemished pastels and hope unfurling before her, Quinn decided she'd take another shot at cracking through Lucy's seemingly impenetrable facade.

. . .

Half an hour later, Lucy emerged from her room.

"Good morning," Quinn said. Lucy looked rumpled and fragile, and there were lines on her pale cheek from the creases in her pillowcase. Quinn had convinced her to wear an old T-shirt as pajamas and the hem came down to her shins. Lucy looked so lost, so vulnerable; Quinn's heart seized. She wanted to gather her niece up in her arms, study the soft lines of her face, and ask her all the questions that she should know without fail. *What's your favorite color? When is your birthday? Can you ride a bike? Do you know I'm your auntie?*

"I'm running water in the bathtub for you," Quinn said, pushing all those unwieldy questions, those tricky emotions down. She pointed toward the bathroom door. "There are strawberry bubbles and a pair of rubber ducks on the ledge. And I left a surprise on the counter."

Lucy didn't respond, but she did wander off in the direction of the bathroom and close the door. Quinn rushed over and listened for the click of the lock. It never came, but a couple of seconds later, she heard the water shut off. She assumed Lucy knew how to bathe herself and had carefully set out everything in advance. A bottle of shampoo and conditioner, a new bar of oatmeal soap. The bubble bath had come from a decorative basket and probably wasn't supposed to be used, but, oh well. There was a fluffy white towel and a washcloth folded on a stool beside the tub, and on the counter Quinn had arranged the pale gray shirt and plaid shorts. Cherry underwear on top. On the floor, the flip-flops printed with tiny beach balls were set and ready for Lucy's feet.

A part of Quinn wished that she had been invited inside. She would have gently lathered Lucy's hair, circled the plush washcloth on her back. Her own mother had been harsh and unbending at times, but baths were almost sacred in the Sanford house. Liz got down on her knees beside the tub and trailed her fingertips through the water while she listened to her kids prattle on. She washed them with care, hands gentle on velvety skin and eyes warm. At what? Their innocence? The delicate curls of their wet hair and scrubbed clean faces? It didn't really matter. It was a fond memory.

While Lucy bathed (at least, Quinn hoped that's what she was doing) Quinn pulled the wicker picnic basket from the top shelf of one of the kitchen cupboards. The hamper was fitted with a pair of wineglasses, a corkscrew, and leather straps to hold a wine bottle. But Quinn removed those things and began to layer in more appropriate goods. A gingham blanket, a small bunch of bananas. Peanut-butter-and-grape-jelly sandwiches on thick slices of Walker's homemade whole-grain bread that she had prepared and wrapped in wax paper while Lucy was still asleep. She wedged two jam jars filled with orange juice and tightly capped into the corners of the basket and topped it all off with the art pad and pastels.

"What are you doing?"

Quinn was startled by the sound of Lucy's voice and she whirled around, expecting to see her flattened hair and T-shirt. But there was a towel wrapped turban-style around her head and she was wearing the outfit that Walker had bought. The clothes were a bit too big and the boat collar of the shirt hung off her delicate collarbones. But she looked clean and bright. Really rather adorable. Quinn just couldn't understand how she had done it all so fast.

"You look lovely!" Quinn smiled, a fierce and sudden pride sweeping through her. *Remarkable girl.* "How was your bath?"

"Fine."

Her niece wasn't much of a talker, but Quinn was getting used to it. She tried to read more in the tilt of her head, the way she stood with her feet firmly planted in new flip-flops (also a tad too big). She was a strong one, this Miss Lucy. Brave and shrewd and hard as a little nut. Maybe that was a good thing. Necessary. "Were there enough bubbles?"

Lucy nodded, her eyes still on the picnic basket.

"Oh! You asked me a question and I didn't answer. We're going on a picnic." Quinn figured that if she didn't give Lucy a choice in the matter she just might go along with it. The tactic had clearly worked well with the bath and new clothes. "Do you like picnics?"

Lucy shrugged, but something in the rise of her small chin told Quinn that the child's interest was piqued.

"Well, I love them. How do you feel about peanut butter and jelly?" Quinn was rambling, fastening the clips on the picnic basket as she tried to keep the tone in the kitchen happy and light.

"Where are we going?"

"It's not far," Quinn assured her, adding: "Can I help you with your hair? I have a comb in my bathroom . . ."

Lucy paused for a moment, considering. Then she nodded slowly. It was all the encouragement Quinn needed. She rushed to her bedroom and found her wide-toothed comb in the en suite. She wished she had detangler, something that would ensure the process was painless. But she didn't have anything like that. She'd just have to take it slow.

Back in the kitchen, Quinn carefully removed the towel from Lucy's head. Where had a little girl learned to wrap a turban like that? To bathe herself so thoroughly? Quinn was close enough to catch a whiff of the sweet scent of Lucy's skin: strawberry bubbles mingled with oatmeal and shea butter and something that was simply the essence of a little girl. She breathed in deeply, her fingers working through the red strands of Lucy's cropped hair.

But as she pulled her hands away, she saw that there was blood on her palms.

Quinn gasped, a shiver racing down her spine. Had Lucy hit her head? Where was the wound? But before she could truly panic,

Quinn realized two things: the red streaks on her hands weren't blood, and someone had dyed Lucy's hair. Recently.

"What's wrong?" Lucy asked, her slight shoulders lifting toward her ears. She was retreating, preparing to protect herself.

"Nothing!" Quinn swallowed hard and reached for the towel that she had just discarded. Yes, there, on the perfect white terry cloth were rust-colored stains. She hadn't noticed the evidence before because she had been so intoxicated by the prospect of connecting in some small way with Lucy. But now her heart lurched painfully. Quinn wished she could take it back, pretend she had never seen what so surely meant that Nora wasn't being melodramatic at all. This wasn't a game.

Who dyed a little girl's hair? Why? The possibilities skittered across Quinn's mind. Wild things. Rabid and dangerous.

"What's wrong?" Lucy asked again, her voice barely a whisper.

"Nothing, honey, nothing at all." Quinn forced herself to take the comb in her hand and start again. "You just have such pretty hair." Taking a section at a time, she gently ran the comb from scalp to ends until the loose waves were smooth. Around her ears and at the nape of her neck Lucy's hair was drying in corkscrew curls and Quinn had to repress the urge to kiss the spot where the ringlets brushed her skin. Poor child.

"All set," Quinn said. She dared to lay her hands on Lucy's shoulders for just a moment and the girl tolerated her touch. She wanted to ask her questions, to somehow show Lucy that she was safe, trustworthy. But Quinn also didn't want to push her luck. Too much too soon could send Lucy scrambling. Moving away, she reached for the picnic basket as if nothing at all was wrong. "Ready?"

Quinn had decided that it would be better if she didn't wait for an answer. Instead, she headed toward the front door and hoped that Lucy would follow.

She did.

Quinn hesitated for just a moment with her hand on the door, but the summer sun was doing its sparkly best to lure her outside. It was warm and lovely and bright. What ill could befall them at eight o'clock on a gorgeous summer morning? What evil could lurk in Key Lake before breakfast? None at all, Quinn decided.

The front door of the cabin actually opened on the side that faced away from the lake. There was a small porch, a gravel drive-way, and, best of all, no neighbors. Well, they were there, but the house on the south side was obscured by the boathouse, and the home to the north was a good quarter mile away. Directly in front of the cabin was a cornfield that stretched for acres. But just to the north stood a small grove of gnarled oak trees and a swath of prairie grass so tall it swept past Quinn's waist. An abandoned shack stood sentinel on a small hill, but it was picturesque, not scary.

"Aren't we . . . ?" Lucy trailed off, and when Quinn looked back she saw the girl pointing at her car.

"Nope. We're going on an adventure close to home."

When she hit the grass, Quinn kept going, parting the swishing blades like a scythe. She glanced at Lucy just once and bit back a smile at the sight of the child pushing away the stalks of big bluestem and silky wild rye and switchgrass. Most of them towered over her head, but Lucy didn't seem to mind.

A good twenty to thirty feet into the heart of the field Quinn decided they had come far enough. Shuffling along slowly, she stomped down a clearing just big enough for the blanket she had brought. When she spread it out on the bent stalks, the haven it created was as thick and soft as a bed.

"When we were kids we used to make forts in the grass," Quinn said as she sat down crisscross applesauce. Isn't that what she and Nora used to say when they were kids? *Easy peasy lemon squeezy.* Home again, home again, jiggity-jig. But Nora had lost sight of home a long time ago. For a moment, it was all too much, and

Quinn's heart wrung in her chest. She and Nora should be here together, sitting side by side as they laughed and teased, as they taught Lucy all the things they had once loved as children. Instead, Nora had shut them out. And she had denied Lucy the right to family.

"We would take the stems like this"—Quinn cleared her throat around the tears that threatened and grabbed a handful of grass in each palm—"and twist them together. We crawled through the tunnels."

"Weren't you afraid?"

"No." Quinn passed a hand over her cheeks, hoping that Lucy didn't notice her suffering. Then she lifted a sandwich out of the picnic basket and held it out for Lucy. The girl took it and sat down gingerly on the edge of the blanket. "What would we be afraid of?"

"Spiders."

"They can't hurt you," Quinn said.

"Snakes."

"I don't like snakes," Quinn admitted, "but they're more afraid of us than we are of them."

"What are you afraid of?" Lucy had unwrapped her sandwich and she took a tiny bite.

The question caught Quinn off guard. The things she was afraid of she couldn't share with Lucy. *I'm afraid that my husband doesn't love me as much as I love him. I'm afraid I'm going to lose him. I'm afraid that if I don't get pregnant soon everything is going to fall to pieces.*

*I'm afraid of things that I can't name and don't understand. Of you. Of what you mean.*

"Mice," Quinn finally said, because she had to say something. "I'm terrified of mice." It wasn't exactly true; she wasn't afraid, just grossed out.

"But mice aren't scary," Lucy protested.

Quinn shrugged. "What are you afraid of?"

And for one of the very first times since Nora dropped her off, Lucy stared straight at Quinn. Her gaze was troubled, her eyes gunmetal gray in the sloped early morning sun. Or maybe it was just the way the color of her shirt set off her hair, her eyes, her skin. Either way, Quinn felt a chill ripple over her skin that had nothing to do with the cool morning breeze.

"Him," Lucy said simply. "I'm afraid of him."

*Friday*

*8:11 a.m.*

**QUINN**
*Who is he, Nora?*

> **NORA**
> *OMG. Did something happen?*

**QUINN**
*???*

*We're fine.*

> **NORA**
> *Stay put. This will all be over soon.*

**QUINN**
*Nora?*

*I don't know if I can do this.*

# NORA

SHE RAPPED THREE quick times on the door, and then drew back on the landing, wondering if there was time to run away. What was she thinking? What did she hope to accomplish by coming here? Nora pivoted and would have taken off down the staircase, but before she could beat a hasty retreat the door creaked open behind her. She flinched and froze midstep.

"Hello?" And, of course: "Nora? Nora, what in the world are you doing here?"

Nora exhaled sharply and then made use of her dimple, pinning what she hoped was an appropriately contrite smile on her face. But it slipped and fell away before it fully formed. She turned around and lifted one shoulder instead. "Wondering if your offer still stands?"

Ethan gave her an indecipherable look, but he held open the door and motioned her inside. "Where have you been?" he asked, plucking a leaf from her sleeve as she passed.

"Here and there."

Shutting the door, Ethan leaned against the frame and studied Nora for a few awkward seconds. She realized she was still wearing the jeans and concert T-shirt that she had changed into after leaving the Grind, and her clothes were rumpled and musty from running in the rain. Of course, she was dry now, but she hadn't bothered to look in a mirror for hours. She had no doubt her hair was stringy, her makeup smeared. Slipping her thumbs into her belt loops, she tried to stand a little taller and exude an air of nonchalance. Ethan wasn't buying it.

"Have you been drinking?"

"Really?" A spark of annoyance licked through her fear. It was, after all, just after eight o'clock in the morning, and all her nighttime worries had amounted to nothing at all. At least, as far as she knew. Nora had enough on her plate; no need to endure the Inquisition. "I didn't realize we were playing twenty questions," she said, moving toward the door.

Ethan put up his hands. "Sorry. But you have to admit this is a little unorthodox. And, nothing personal, Nora, but you look like hell. Have you slept?"

She hadn't. Well, she'd dozed a little in her car, but the truth was she had spent the entire night trying to find Tiffany. Tiff wouldn't pick up when she called or respond to any of her messages. And she had turned off the friend tracker that they had both installed on their phones. They told each other the app was so that they could coordinate Everlee's schedule seamlessly. But they had really downloaded the software so that Nora would know, always, where Tiffany was. Donovan Richter was not to be trusted.

When her phone proved to be a dead end, Nora scouted out their favorite dive bar and a park where Everlee loved to go, and knocked on the door at the trailer of an old friend. She even drove past Tiffany's dealer's place several times, an unassuming house on the edge of town where you could score not just marijuana and a little E, but things that packed a much harder punch, too. There wasn't a trace of Tiffany anywhere.

But even after she came up empty-handed, Nora hadn't dared to go home. What if Donovan was waiting for her there? What if he came? What if he demanded answers that Nora didn't have—or worse, ones that she did?

"No," she admitted. "I haven't slept."

Ethan put his fists on his hips as if he was faced with a tough decision and he wasn't quite sure what to do. Get involved? Make her leave? In the end, he gave Nora a grim smile and waved her deeper into the apartment. "Let me make you some breakfast," he said.

Nora found that she didn't have the will to refuse. She was so exhausted she was shaking, and her heart was a riot of warring emotions. Where to start? How to find Tiffany and make sure Everlee stayed safe and keep Donovan far, far away? And what about Quinn? Nora knew her sister might never forgive her for the secrets she had kept, the trust she had broken. That wasn't what Nora wanted. Quinn was innocent of any wrongdoing, and Nora had ensured she would never escape unscathed. The guilt was crushing.

"Can you stomach eggs?" Ethan asked as he rummaged through his refrigerator. "I have some red peppers and a bit of ham. Maybe an omelette?" He was wearing plaid pajama pants and an old T-shirt that had been washed so thin it was almost transparent. Nora could see the outline of his broad shoulder blades and the narrowing of his waist. He once told her that he played hockey in college, and she wasn't surprised.

Nora looked quickly away. Seeing Ethan like this felt indecent somehow. Uncomfortably intimate. But what did she expect at this hour on his day off? "Yeah," she forced herself to say. "Eggs would be great."

Ethan emerged from the fridge with his arms full of containers, but when Nora tried to help he waved her away. "Sit," he instructed. "I'll bring you a cup of coffee."

Nora realized that she could already smell it; clearly he had brewed a pot before she showed up on his doorstep. Her stomach lurched at the promise of coffee, of food. How long had it been since she last ate? Nora honestly couldn't remember.

"Please."

Nora looked up to find Ethan studying her, a line of worry creased between his eyes. "What?"

"Sit down."

She complied, sinking into a chair by the table in the eat-in kitchen.

It was round and obviously secondhand, the surface pockmarked and lined with scratches. Nora found herself tracing the grooves because it gave her hands something to do. But less than a minute later Ethan placed a mug of coffee before her. No questions, no more attempts at conversation. He just set the steaming mug down and turned back to the counter where he was chopping vegetables and whisking eggs.

They had gone on a date. Once. And Nora had liked it, had liked *him*, but things were complicated with Tiffany and Everlee, and even though Donovan had already entered the picture, Nora felt responsible for her girls. No, not her girls. Anyway, it was messy. A brief but passionate kiss had fizzled into nothingness and now they were coworkers and friends, nothing more. But, sometimes . . . Nora watched Ethan working and was startled to find that though she was falling apart at the seams, though she was dirty and weary and scared, she felt safe here. She felt safe with him.

When the omelette was done, Ethan cut it down the middle with a spatula and slid the two halves onto mismatched plates. "Salt and pepper?" he asked. "Tabasco? Salsa? Ketchup?"

"Just salt and pepper," Nora said.

"Perfect." He snagged the condiments in one hand and managed to balance the two plates in his other. "Knives and forks are in front of you," Ethan said as he put one plate in front of her.

"Thanks."

Ethan sat down and smothered his eggs in Tabasco. Reaching for utensils from the wire container at the center of the table, he fixed Nora with a level gaze. "I'm happy to make you breakfast, but I need to know: Are you okay?"

"Fine." Nora hoped she sounded breezy, casual, but her hand shook a little as she reached for her own utensils.

"You're not a very good liar," Ethan told her.

"That's funny. I've been told I'm a great liar." She took a bite of her omelette and had to suppress a moan. "This is so good."

"Thanks. And, for the record, you're a terrible liar."

They ate in silence for a few minutes, Ethan making quick work of his plate and then settling back to sip his coffee and study Nora. She felt self-conscious beneath his gaze, exposed. Running a hand over her forehead, she forced a laugh. "I'm a wreck, aren't I?"

He didn't say anything.

"Are you giving me the silent treatment?"

Ethan shrugged. "Just waiting to see if you'll come clean or if you're going to keep pretending that everything's fine." He put a wry, one-handed air quote around *fine* and took another swig of his coffee.

Nora studied her eggs, running through every possible scenario. She and Tiffany had agreed that no one could know, no one could *ever know* because it would jeopardize everything. But then, Tiff hadn't exactly stuck to the plan. And now what was Nora supposed to do? Tiffany had run off, presumably stolen Donovan's money, left Nora to pick up the pieces . . . It was more than she could handle. And, like it or not, there weren't many people Nora could talk to. Could trust. She'd given up so many things for Tiffany and Everlee—including friends.

"I'll tell you what I can," she said eventually.

"Good enough for me. You done? Let's sit somewhere more comfortable."

Taking off in the direction of a small living room, Ethan motioned for her to follow. Their brief fling hadn't brought Nora inside of his apartment, and she couldn't help but analyze it now. Ethan's rooms in an upscale, newly finished complex were neat and spare, as clean-cut and warm as he was. The couch and matching love seat were a homey corduroy in teddy-bear brown, but the rest of the decor had an exotic flair. There were carved wooden animals and a batik that set off one wall with striking primary hues. A horn of some kind. An intricately woven basket. He had told her once that he loved to travel. Nora didn't realize that he meant internationally.

"Gorgeous," Nora said, studying what appeared to be an authentic Venetian mask. "Where did you get this?"

"Venice."

"Really?" Nora was nervous, hardly even aware that she was making small talk. That they were discussing things so inconsequential they didn't matter at all. "I've never been to Europe."

"It's beautiful," he told her. "Avoid Paris, London, and Rome. You'd like Majorca. Warm beaches, blue water, friendly people." He paused, considering. "Or maybe Istria would be more your style."

"Istria?"

"Croatia."

"Oh." Suddenly Nora felt as if she were in the living room of a stranger instead of the man she spent nearly every day with. What did she really know about Ethan Holloway? Single, barista, part-time grad student. What was he studying again? Literature of some sort. She was almost sure of that. Nora felt herself warm with an uncharacteristic blush and quickly took another sip of her coffee. Clearly she was falling all to pieces. It pissed her off.

"Sorry." Ethan laughed, waving a hand in front of him as if to dismiss his own travel recommendations. "Listen to me. I'm intolerable. If I had a slide projector I'd make you sit through at least a thousand pictures."

"Sounds fascinating."

"Now you're making fun of me." But he didn't seem to mind.

"I just didn't know you were so . . ." She cast about, looking for just the right word.

"Geeky?" Ethan offered helpfully. "Boring? Banal?"

"Global."

"There's a lot you don't know about me, Nora Sanford."

And for some reason, she felt her eyes burn with sudden tears.

"Hey . . ." Ethan put down his coffee and slid closer to where Nora had sunk into a corner of the comfy love seat. There was an end table between them, but Ethan leaned forward with his elbows on his knees. He regarded her earnestly, compassionately. A part of her wished that his expression wasn't so damned fraternal. Since when had she become the damsel in distress? It wasn't her. It never had been.

Nora brushed at her eyes with the heel of her hands and forced a derisive laugh. "I'm fine, Ethan. Totally fine."

"I thought we were past that."

"It's a long story."

"I'm listening."

It was a simple enough statement, but it cut Nora to the quick. *She* was the listener. The confidante. The quiet, behind-the-scenes best friend and fixer of all things broken. Hadn't she been cleaning up after Tiffany since high school? Back then, Nora let Tiffany copy her homework assignments and cheat off her test papers. She took the rap when Tiffany's aunt found a pack of Camel Lights in the pocket of her jean jacket. And when things got really out of hand, Nora had given up everything—including her own family—to stand by Tiffany's side. To cover for her and help her, to make sure that Tiff and Everlee were provided for and together and safe. And now? Tiffany was gone.

"Thank you," Nora whispered. But she was so used to listening that she found that when the tables were reversed her tongue felt thick and feeble. What could she say? She settled for a sliver of the truth. A beginning. "I'm worried about Tiffany."

Of course Ethan knew who Tiffany was. Tiff and Everlee had come into the coffee shop regularly. He knew them so well that when her rusty red Ford truck with the white racing stripe pulled into the parking lot he started to make their drinks. A weak, white chocolate mocha with a drizzle of caramel for Tiffany and a hot chocolate, extra whipped cream, for Everlee. Nora had thought something might spark between Ethan and Tiffany—she was long and lean and angled like a runway model—but Ethan treated Tiffany with kid gloves. He was gentle with her, almost paternal in his concern for her and the girl who followed her as close as a shadow. Tiff had that effect on people.

"What do you mean you're worried about Tiffany?" Ethan asked. His eyes hardened and his fists clenched. Nora could almost hear his thoughts and they had everything to do with Everlee. If there was something up with Tiffany, what about the pretty little slip of a girl who called her Mommy? For all her fierce beauty, Tiff had the look of a former addict. Nora knew it was one of the reasons people were so soft with her. Or maybe *careful* was a better word.

"Everlee's safe," Nora said, answering the question before he voiced it. "She's okay. But . . . Tiffany's gone."

"What do you mean, gone?"

Nora laughed, but it was joyless and cold. "She left. Abandoned us. Disappeared. And I don't know what I'm going to do. How I'm going to keep Everlee away from him."

"Him?"

"Donovan. The guy who showed up at the Grind yesterday."

Ethan's eyes narrowed. "What's he got to do with Everlee?"

"He's the closest thing she's got to a dad. And if Tiffany is gone, he'll fight for her."

"And?"

"He'll win." It was barely a whisper, but Nora knew it was true. Donovan got what he wanted. And he wanted Everlee.

It looked like Ethan knew the answer before he voiced the question, but he asked it anyway. "That's a problem?"

"You have no idea." Nora squeezed her eyes shut and rested her head in her hands for a moment. And then, before she could stop to consider what she was doing, she started to talk.

She told him everything. Almost.

# LIZ

AS LUCK WOULD have it, Lorelei Barnes's funeral visitation was from three to six on Friday afternoon. Liz only knew this because she slept well past her alarm and woke with the local news setting a drowsy soundtrack for her disjointed dreams. Usually when the old clock radio clicked to life, Liz was already wide awake and watching the pastel sunrise flirt with her sheer curtains. But after her late-night Walmart run, Liz had slept through the familiar click as well as an entire hour of Hawk Country radio programming. Lady Antebellum, Sugarland, The Band Perry, and a little throwback Sawyer Brown mixed in for variety (the morning host obviously lacked both imagination and the desire to diversify).

At the top of the hour, nine to be exact, the Key Lake "Community Minute" cut through the sleepy fog and Liz heard, clear as day: "Lorelei Barnes's visitation will be at the Thatcher Funeral Home this afternoon, from three p.m. until six p.m."

Liz dragged herself out of bed with a feeling of cotton in her mouth and a knot of consternation in her chest. She couldn't decide if knowing about Lorelei's visitation was a good thing or just a stroke of very bad luck. Poor timing? It didn't really matter. She knew, therefore she felt obligated. And there was nothing so motivating in Liz Sanford's world as a healthy dose of obligation.

People would start to arrive at the house around six, but at 2:00 p.m. Liz found herself slipping into the black sheath she had worn to Jack Sr.'s funeral. It seemed indecent somehow that she was wearing the same dress to mourn both her husband and a woman she barely knew. But black wasn't a color that Liz frequently wore. It was too boring. Too drab and depressing and *dark*. Her closet was a soiree of fuchsia and cobalt, persimmon and turquoise. When it came to sober occasions, she didn't really have a choice.

The dress had three-quarter-length sleeves and an itchy lace overlay, and Liz looked longingly at her cute party sundress even as she fastened the clasp on her single-pearl necklace. "You had flowers delivered," she reminded herself. "You didn't really even *know* Lorelei."

But it was no use trying to talk herself out of going. She had bumped into Tiffany, which had set off a chain reaction that culminated with Liz believing she could right past wrongs with a suitable mix of contrition and social convention. If only she could fix the brokenness in her family so easily. The flowers she ordered were exquisite, the few lines on the card inspired. And yet it wasn't enough. Liz felt that she had to *be there*. To press Tiffany's bony hands between her own and say, with heart, "I'm so sorry for your loss."

It wasn't a lie. She was very sorry for loss of any kind because Liz Sanford knew what it meant to lose something. Each loss was a thorn in her flesh, a wound that pierced like a needle at first then faded to a blunt, insistent ache. When Liz was little, her mother taught her to cover up her wounds with a Band-Aid and a smile, and though such shrouding worked to hide pain from the rest of the world, it only taught Liz how to live with the hurt. Sometimes, when she was tired or sick, fragile or just incapable of keeping her smile sweet and straight, Liz was stunned by just how much her heart throbbed. She was the walking wounded.

Oh no. Speaking of misty eyes . . . Liz snatched a tissue from the bathroom counter and dabbed carefully beneath her eyelashes. She didn't have time to redo her makeup, and it wouldn't do to host a party with blotchy skin and puffy eyes. No time to cry. And certainly not about Lorelei Barnes. Or Tiffany or whoever or whatever had set her off. Liz had things to cry about, but strangers were not one of them.

*Put the tomatoes on the counter*, Liz texted Macy as she hopped into her car. *The door is unlocked. I have to run an errand.*

*Today?!?!?!*

Macy was all about lavish punctuation. And emojis. Liz particularly hated the one with the little yellow face grinning and crying at the same time. She couldn't think of a single instance in her life when she had laughed so hard she cried. Did people actually do that?

*Yes, today. There's basil on the counter and mozzarella in the fridge if you want to be helpful.*

*I'm on it!!!!!!*

Although Macy's culinary expertise was limited to grilled foods and particularly adventurous salads with quinoa and pomegranate seeds, Liz doubted her friend could screw up caprese skewers too badly. In her limited experience, overuse of exclamation marks was rarely a barometer of competence in the kitchen.

Thatcher Funeral Home was located in the heart of Key Lake. The tree-lined streets were wide, the houses old and, for the most part, lovingly restored. The funeral home was one of the largest, an impressive Victorian with crenellated trim and lush hanging baskets that made it appear almost storybookish. From the front, the only indicator that the home was anything other than a particularly exquisite family residence was a tasteful brass plaque by the front door. Of course, in the back, the yard had been turned into a small paved parking lot and an oversized garage had been attached to the house. It accommodated the hearse and, Liz assumed, the rooms where they prepped the bodies. It gave her a little chill, both the thought of the burial preparation process and the parking lot in the middle of such a lovely neighborhood. Clearly the city council had been asleep at the wheel when that building permit had been approved.

Liz avoided the lot and parked on the street in front of the funeral home. There were no other cars around, and, shouldering her purse, Liz congratulated herself on beating the rush as she hurried up the front walkway. She let herself in the carved antique door with a thin-lipped smile of satisfaction.

Thatcher's had handled Jack Sr.'s funeral, but Liz hadn't stepped foot over the threshold since the day she saw her husband's lifeless face for the very last time. And she hadn't paused to consider how it might make her feel. Consequently, she wasn't at all prepared for the barrage of memories.

The entryway was close and warm, the heady aroma of lily-scented candles overpowering. Heavy rugs muffled sound and a crystal chandelier sparkled overhead, though the fixture wasn't even turned on—the light was refracted from the high transom window above the front door. The prisms winked and danced so furiously Liz had the impression of being thrown underwater. She squinted at the onslaught, her throat constricting as if she were drowning.

Liz had stood in this exact spot while Christopher Thatcher (not the original Chris Thatcher, but his thirtysomething grandson who was as wobbly chinned and pasty white as a corpse himself) explained the finer details of the family visitation process. The funeral would happen at the church, but the viewing was here, in a large room that took up most of the main floor of the converted house. "People will file in through this door," Christopher had told her. And she hadn't heard much else. Stand, sit. You will be there. The body will be here. I'll put tissue boxes on every available surface should you need them.

*I need you to blow out those damn candles*, Liz had thought, rather ungraciously. *It smells like a funeral home in here.* And, *I need a stiff drink.*

Rum. She would have sold her soul for a tumbler of good, dark rum in that moment. On the rocks. Please, oh please, the rum that Jack Sr. had spent a small fortune on one year when they were in Jamaica. A teardrop bottle of liquor as thick and rich as caramel. She could almost feel the burn of it sliding down her throat.

It was so unlike Liz to crave something like that, to *long* for it, that she tucked her hand through her son's arm. Jack Jr. mistook her gesture as sorrow and patted her hand clumsily, a moan catching in his own throat. *No, no*, she wanted to say. *You have it all wrong.* But she didn't say anything at all. How could she begin to explain the way she felt for her husband? The pretty layers that peeled back to reveal something dark and rotting beneath? They had lived a good, solid, respectable life. But that didn't mean that she loved him. That she would mourn his loss. And yet.

Good God in heaven. What was she doing here?

Liz swayed a bit in the foyer, her heels missing the rug and clicking on the restored wood floors as evidence of her presence. She could feel the door handle at her back, and she steadied herself, taking the crystal knob carefully in her fingertips. If she turned it softly, if she tiptoed, it might be like she had never come at all. No one would ever have to know.

"Mrs. Sanford?"

She squeezed her eyes shut for a moment. Swallowed a sigh. A sob? "Christopher Thatcher," Liz said, pulling herself up to her full height and extending her hand to the funeral director who had appeared from somewhere deep inside the house.

Christopher stepped from the shadow of the hallway and took just her fingers, touching them lightly as if in another era he might have raised them to his lips. Liz hated limp handshakes. "It's a pleasure to see you," he said. But it was obvious to Liz that he was more surprised than pleased.

"I suppose I'm a bit early, aren't I?" Liz checked the delicate face of the watch on her left wrist. It was a quarter to three. Fashionably late wasn't a thing in her books. If you wanted to be fashionable, you were punctual. Early, even. Liz had always considered herself a trendsetter. "I can wait," she assured him. "Or maybe if I could just have a moment with Tiffany? I'll be gone before a crowd starts to gather."

"Tiffany? I'm not sure . . ." Christopher fumbled, glancing over his shoulder as if an answer might emerge from the hallway behind him.

In that moment, Liz realized several things. First, and most important, that the funeral director was wearing a T-shirt and jeans. Not a black suit and tie. The candles weren't lit. The door to the chapel where the viewings were held was bolted shut with an antique latch and catch, and there wasn't even a sliver of light seeping from the gap between the floor and the bottom of the door.

"I have the wrong day," she whispered, mortified. "The visitation for Lorelei Barnes isn't today, is it?"

"Oh!" Understanding settled on Christopher's sallow face. "I'm so sorry, Mrs. Sanford. It was an error on the community events sheet. Our secretary does all the scheduling and she didn't realize . . . I didn't think it would be a problem. I mean, I didn't think anyone would notice." He blushed as he heard the words come out of his mouth, an unattractive pink that put Liz in mind of Silly Putty. "I'm sorry, I didn't mean—"

"Lorelei was a lovely person," Liz said, offended for a woman she barely knew. "I'm sure *everyone* noticed."

"Yes, of course—"

"When exactly *is* her visitation? I, for one, will be here with bells on." Too late, Liz grasped just how stupid that sounded. Bells on? For a funeral visitation?

But she didn't have time to be embarrassed. Christopher was still waffling.

"Well?"

"There isn't a visitation for Lorelei," he finally managed.

"What do you mean?"

"She didn't want one."

"When is the funeral?"

Christopher's chin sagged even farther toward his chest. "No funeral either. She was cremated several days ago."

Liz wasn't sure why she felt so indignant, but she battled an almost overwhelming urge to slap Christopher Thatcher's droopy face. "That's ridiculous. Is that what Lorelei wanted? What about Tiffany?"

"Who's Tiffany?"

Now Liz was just plain mad. "Her daughter!" she said, throwing up her hands. It wasn't accurate, not quite, but she didn't want to nitpick with him, to waste time explaining what she knew (and didn't know) about the situation between Lorelei and the girl who had been, for all intents and purposes, her only family.

But Christopher wasn't paying attention anyway. He was shaking his head slowly. "There is no daughter," he said. "Besides her caretakers at Pine Hills, no one has inquired about Lorelei at all."

For once, Liz was speechless. She was angry and confused and sad. A sadness that settled deep down in the marrow of her bones and made her feel like she could sit on the ugly rug in the foyer and weep. "That's terrible," she whispered.

"It is," Christopher agreed solemnly. And then after a moment he added: "And we still have her ashes."

Liz didn't say anything.

"I, uh . . ." Christopher cleared his throat. "I don't suppose you would like to take them with you?"

Because he looked so hopeful and because the whole situation made her so very outrageously angry, when Liz drove away from Thatcher Funeral Home, the remains of Lorelei Barnes were buckled into the passenger seat beside her. It was absurd. Bizarre. A completely preposterous situation that would require her to single-handedly track down Tiffany, shoulder the young woman's grief, save the day. It was exactly the sort of thing that Liz excelled at.

In some ways, it was the least that she could do. She owed it to Tiffany. A little recompense for the way her husband treated Nora's best friend. Although Liz tried to pretend otherwise, the truth was Jack Sr. had been downright nasty to the girl. Stony silences, a cold, hard stare that seemed to have been created for Tiffany alone. Liz had never seen her husband respond to someone the way he reacted to Tiffany Barnes.

"What is your problem?" she hissed one night when his icy dismissal of Tiffany—and the casual demand that Nora give up their pathetic friendship—had sent Nora out the door into a building snowstorm.

"She'll be fine. She's going to *Tiffany's* house." Her name sounded ugly on his lips.

"I'm not talking about Nora," Liz said. "What is your problem with Tiffany? She's just a kid."

Jack Sr. snorted. "She's no kid. She's a slutty little thing. I don't want JJ anywhere near her."

The memory made Liz's fingers tighten their grip on the steering wheel. That word in Jack's mouth made her want to slap his face—and she prided herself on the brisk surety of her own self-control. But, of course, she did no such thing. Instead of hitting her husband for his filthy language, his callous treatment of a teenage girl, Liz set her jaw so tight her teeth ached. She turned and walked away.

"I'm sorry," Liz said, to no one in particular. Or maybe she was talking to the memory of Lorelei, whether or not the poor woman could respond and absolve her from a sin long forgotten.

Of course Lorelei's ashes were in the ugliest urn imaginable. A brassy gold thing that Christopher Thatcher had undoubtedly chosen and Elizabeth Sanford would definitely replace.

It galvanized her, the urn and the experience. The memories. She slid her phone out of her purse at a stop sign and dialed 4-1-1. If he worked for the city of Key Lake, she would have had him on speed dial. As it was, she knew the receptionist, but not the seven digits that would patch her through. She waited for the operator.

"Marla?" she said, pressing the phone in between her shoulder and her cheek as she clicked on her blinker. "Connect me to the police department, will you?"

And when he answered, she knew his voice. Even after all these years. If anyone could offer a little perspective, change the game, it was him. "Bennet? Honey? I need to ask something of you."

*Friday*
*2:59 p.m.*

**LIZ**

I need to talk to you.

           **NORA**

           Now's not such a good time.

**LIZ**

I never ask you for anything. I'm
asking now.

           **NORA**

           What is this about?

**LIZ**

We should talk in person. What
if I drove up to Rochester on
Sunday?

           **NORA**

           I don't know, Mom.

**LIZ**

I'm not sure you have a choice.

# QUINN

WALKER WASN'T RESPONDING to her texts. True, Quinn had been subtle all day. Nothing too insistent or alarming. Nothing that really required a response, now that she considered it. But she was starting to get stir-crazy. Her thoughts and the ever-intractable Lucy made for troubling companions. She craved a little adult conversation. Someone stable and supportive and warm. Someone who would listen to all her crazy theories about just who "he" was and why Lucy was so scared of him.

"I think it's time to start cleaning up," Quinn said. They were sitting at the round dining room table, the pastels Walker had brought arranged in a cup between them. Paper was scattered across the glass in a carousel of color and would-be art. Among the sheets were Quinn's feeble attempts at a tree, a sunset in blended hues of red and yellow, and a rainbow-petaled flower.

Lucy's work was, in Quinn's opinion, much better—and more disturbing. The little girl had also drawn a tree, but hers was black with spidery, leafless branches. Another piece boasted her own small hand, traced and shaded entirely in a dark, shocking red. But what worried Quinn the most was the picture of Lucy's family. At least she assumed that's what it was; the pastel drawing had all the trappings of a child's homemade family portrait. There were four people scattered across the page, each character drawn separate from the others. Solitary and alone.

Quinn reached for that picture. "Is this your family?"

A shrug.

"Let me see . . ." Quinn studied the drawing carefully, giving it her full, flattering attention. When she was a kid, that kind of fawning made her purr like a kitten. "This is just lovely, Lucy. I'm going to guess that this girl by the fence is you?"

It was little more than a stick figure, but it was smaller than the rest and clearly feminine. But she didn't look at all like Lucy. The caricature had long yellow hair that hung all the way to the hemline of her purple skirt.

Despite the obvious physical differences, Lucy had nodded almost imperceptibly at Quinn's assessment. *Yes*, she tacitly agreed. *That's me.*

Quinn felt a burst of triumph as a small piece of the puzzle clicked into place. Lucy's hair had definitely been dyed. A few short days ago it had been long and blond. And the change had happened recently enough for Lucy to forget as she was drawing that her curls were now Shirley Temple short and ginger.

"How about this handsome fellow?" Quinn pressed. "Who's this?"

There were two men in the picture. Or boys, it was hard to tell. They both had short hair and pants in contrast to the long hair and skirts of the girls. Lucy had drawn them on opposite corners of the page, as far apart as she could possibly space them. One looked like he was flying away. The other, grounded.

"Wait." Quinn was struck with sudden inspiration. The grounded character had yellow hair, green eyes. "Is this Nora?" Why had Lucy drawn her mother so far away?

But Lucy clamped her lips shut tight and focused instead on rubbing her thumb and forefinger together. Her fingertips were coated in pastel dust and she smudged the whorls together until they were a dingy cardboard brown.

"What about this one. Who's this?" Quinn tried again, tapping the only other female figure in the picture. This one had squiggly cocoa-colored hair and stood in the middle of the paper beside Lucy. Definitely closer to the girl than her own mother.

Quinn was eager to know more, to crack Lucy open like an egg so she could begin to understand what was inside. But Lucy persisted in ignoring her questions, so she gave up and started to collect and stack the papers.

"Want to watch a little TV?" Quinn offered, sighing inwardly. So much for her feeble attempt at art therapy.

Lucy slid off the chair and wandered toward the living room without a backward glance. From where Quinn was sitting, she could see the child locate the remote control on the end table and turn the TV on. Before she even sat down she began her methodical click-click-click through the stations.

It was unsettling how vacant she could be. How flat. *Flat affect*, Quinn thought, recalling the term from one of her developmental psychology classes in college. If she remembered correctly, flat affect was usually a symptom of schizophrenia. She highly doubted that her niece was schizophrenic, but her dulled expressions and lack of emotion were worrisome. Maybe she was in shock as the result of some unidentified trauma. Quinn wasn't very familiar with the features of shock, but if crime dramas could be believed, Lucy certainly seemed to fit the bill.

Where were the tears? The anger? The indiscriminate rebellion that seemed the most logical reaction to the sort of reckless abandonment Lucy had recently experienced? Quinn tried to put herself in Lucy's shoes and knew that if the roles had been reversed, her younger self would have ranted and railed, thrown things and bitten people. But even after Lucy shared her fear with Quinn in the field, she went on to nibble at her sandwich as if nothing had happened. It was starting to creep Quinn out.

*What have you been through?* She wanted to gather the girl

in her arms and force attachment. To take back all the years that Nora had stolen from them. It made Quinn so mad she could've screamed. But instead of pitching a fit, she carefully stacked their artwork and pastels on the kitchen counter and went to stand near the arm of the couch. Lucy was perched on the edge, staring at the progression of daytime shows as they flicked past on the screen.

"I have to run out to the boathouse," Quinn said. "You know, that building just down the hill? Near the water? I won't be gone long."

Lucy didn't seem to care whether Quinn stayed or left.

"I need you to promise me that you won't go anywhere."

No answer. No acknowledgment that Quinn had spoken at all.

She moved in front of the TV. "Lucy," Quinn said, "I need you to promise me that you won't go anywhere while I'm gone. I'll be right outside. But you have to stay here."

"Okay." Lucy's eyes were trained on the narrow segments of screen that she could see around Quinn's waist.

"Fine." Quinn tossed up her arms and let them fall back to her sides, the sharp smack of skin on skin punctuating her frustration. "I'll be right back."

Quinn slipped on her flip-flops by the door and stepped out into a brilliant summer afternoon. It was hot and dry, the sun on the water so lovely she could feel the beauty like an ache in her chest. She complained about Key Lake, but there were moments like this—when it was clean and lovely and pure—that still took her by surprise.

Or maybe she was just sick of being cooped up with Lucy.

The boathouse was down a gentle slope and close to the water. In fact, there was a wide front porch and a short dock that arched out over the lake. It was shady and private, protected by a service-berry tree that had grown askew but that no one wanted to cut down because of the way it shielded the porch. Quinn and Walker had made love on that porch when they first arrived. It was the middle of the night and even if Liz had been peeking through the lens of her telescope she wouldn't have seen a thing. The memory gave Quinn a little thrill, and she felt her heart go warm and liquid, melting through her limbs like a drug.

*I'm pregnant*, she told herself, and the hope was so incandescent she was sure it smoldered in her cheeks. This was what she had always wanted. A happy family. A family filled with laughter and marked by openness. Forget the secrets and lies, the hiding and gritty scum of things that she could never quite put her finger on but that always lingered.

Quinn was so caught up in the moment that she grabbed the door to the boathouse and tried to wrench it open. But it was locked with a hook and latch from the inside, and her shoulder jerked painfully. It was a bit of a wake-up call.

Walker had never expressly forbidden her from entering his workspace when he was creating, but she knew that he needed privacy and time and room to dream out loud. His art was public and accessible—just not until the moment that he declared it done. His critics called him moody and temperamental, the sort of self-absorbed, self-proclaimed genius who expected the world to wait with bated breath for his next inspired offering. But Quinn knew that Walker was actually painfully insecure when it came to his art. Terrified that another person's approval or disapproval might pop the fragile soap bubble of his artistic revelation.

She should have knocked.

Quinn was rubbing her shoulder and chastising herself when Walker lifted the hook from the latch and opened the boathouse door. "What are you doing here?" he asked, squinting in the sunlight and peering around Quinn.

"I came to see you," she faltered.

"Where's Lucy?"

"In the house." Quinn crossed her arms over her chest. "She's watching TV, Walker. She's fine. It's broad daylight."

"I don't think you should leave her alone."

"What's she going to do? Burn the house down?"

He gave her a hard look but then softened a little and held out his arms. "Sorry. Nora's got me spooked, I guess."

"I've missed you today," Quinn said, stepping into his embrace. She lifted her face to kiss the curve beneath his sharp chin. He smelled of spice and peppercorns, wood and something industrial that she couldn't identify. Steel? No matter. She suddenly wanted to lick his skin. To eat him up.

"This isn't new," Walker reminded her as her teeth grazed his collarbone. "This is how I work, Quinn. You've known this for years."

It was why there was always a secondhand couch and a mini fridge in his studio space. A place to sleep and a place to keep the chopped salads that Quinn made for him cold. Walker refused to drink alcohol when he was working, but he was rather addicted to a carbonated kombucha that he had to order in by the case. His studio was his own makeshift apartment, complete with a Bluetooth speaker and, if he was lucky, a bathroom where he kept several essential toiletries: toothbrush, toothpaste, deodorant. The boathouse was equipped with a toilet and an old rusty sink, but no shower. Walker made do.

"I know," Quinn said. "I didn't mean to interrupt you, but you weren't answering my texts."

"Sorry, my phone is dead."

"Have you been working nonstop?"

"I napped for a while early this morning. I got in a few hours." Walker rubbed her back, pushing the heels of his strong hands into the tight muscles beside the ridges and valleys of her spine. Quinn moaned, and she could feel the pleasure rippling off her husband in waves. "Feel good?"

"You know it does."

"Good."

They stood like that for a moment. Quiet. Holding each other. But Quinn couldn't stop herself from breaking the silence. There was so much to say, she didn't know where to begin. Lucy, her eerie detachment, the man she was afraid of. And a thank-you for the clothes, the art supplies, the little acts of kindness that made it possible for her to begin to scratch the surface of the child who was living with them.

The baby.

"I think I'm pregnant," Quinn blurted out.

"What?"

Tears burned hot and sudden and she blinked them back furiously. "I'm not. I mean, it's only been a couple hours, right? I'm just . . ."

"It's a lot." Walker took her by the shoulders and pushed her back so he could study her face. "There's a lot going on right now. But I need you to just let this go for now, okay? We have to focus on Lucy and—"

"Let this go?" The anger she felt was a bolt of lightning, a gunshot. Quinn was surprised by how quickly her attention shifted, but she was deep, drowning, and she couldn't rationalize her way out. She shrugged off Walker's arms and backed away, her blood boiling, sizzling and popping in her veins as if she were on fire. "I can't just 'let this go.' We said this was our last chance. If it doesn't work this time . . ."

"That's not what we said," he reminded her. "This isn't our last chance; we just agreed to take a break if it doesn't work. Step back. Regroup."

"I don't want to step back."

"I know, but—"

"I don't want to regroup."

"Quinn—"

"I want a baby."

There was an almost tangible pause, a beat of time so small and yet so significant that Quinn felt it as a tremor in her bones.

"Me too," Walker said.

Too late. It was a lie or a half-truth or just something to say to placate his crazy wife. And Quinn could see that now: that she was acting crazy. Irrational and hormonal. This wasn't her, not at all. Not the way her emotions could turn on a dime. Not the way she struggled to see the silver lining. Usually, Quinn was the queen of silver linings, the eternal advocate for the theory that when God closed a door he opened a window.

But she felt trapped inside a house with no windows at all.

"I want this, too, Quinn. I want a family with you. But the family we have right now is pretty messed up. Maybe the timing just isn't right."

Quinn drew a shaky breath, surprised that she wasn't crying. But her eyes had dried up; her heart felt shriveled and empty in her chest. "Go back to work," she told Walker. But when she glanced at his face, expectant and fearful of how he would receive her dismissal, she realized he was looking past her toward the house. His brow was furrowed, and as she watched, he pushed past her and began to jog up the hill toward the cabin.

Spinning around, Quinn saw Lucy coming toward them. She was barefoot and wild, her shock of hair tousled by the wind and clinging to her mouth, her eyes. She looked like an apparition in the wavy light of the humid afternoon, and she was holding something in her hands. The telephone?

Quinn raced up the incline, only a few steps behind Walker, and reached the two of them just as her husband sank to his knees in front of Lucy.

"Hey," Walker said gently. "You're supposed to stay inside, honey."

Lucy shied away from him, backing up slowly even as her eyes found Quinn's. There was a smattering of freckles across her nose that popped in the bright sunshine, but the set of her face was grim. She seemed so much older than her age.

"What is it?" Quinn asked, reaching for her.

"He called," Lucy said, backing away from Quinn, too. She was holding the handset from the landline in the cabin, and she clutched it to her chest as if it were precious. Or terrifying. "My daddy said he's coming for me."

# NORA

THE BAR WAS DIM after the glare of the bright summer sun and Nora blinked in the entryway as her eyes adjusted. The air smelled of popcorn and old fryer grease, but instead of turning Nora's stomach, the scents reminded her that she hadn't eaten anything since Ethan's omelette that morning. She made her way to the commercial popper in the corner of the bar and helped herself to a cardboard container and a generous amount of stale, buttery popcorn. Not exactly nourishing, but it would do.

The Cue was mostly empty at four thirty on a lazy August afternoon, but it was Friday and the sticky booths would soon fill up with workers from the window factory down the street. The day shift was over at five, and the crew usually celebrated with a cold one or two. Nora knew many of them by name, mostly because the majority of the men who frequented the Cue had tried at one time or another to buy her a drink. She always refused. Accepting a drink from a man was an open invitation for said man to flirt. Nora had no desire to chitchat with half-drunk perennial adolescents who were only interested in one-night stands and NASCAR. Okay, maybe they also liked football. Nora hadn't really taken the time to find out.

She picked a booth near the front of the bar and directly across from the cash register. There would be lots of traffic, lots of people stopping by to say hi and shoot the breeze, if only for a moment or two. Nora wanted that sort of visibility.

"The usual, Nora Jeane?" Arlen had come out of the kitchen and spotted her. He called her Nora Jeane, not because her middle name was Jane but because he said she reminded him of Norma Jeane. Which was ridiculous. She looked nothing like Marilyn Monroe. Quinn, maybe, with her curves and full lips and periwinkle eyes. But not spare, angular Nora, whose razor-sharp jawline matched her personality. A guy in high school had once called her the Ice Queen. A far cry from the Blonde Bombshell.

"Actually, no," Nora said. "I'll take an Arnold Palmer."

Arlen gave her a bit of a sideways look as he took his hand off the sleek Guinness tap. But he poured the iced tea and lemonade mocktail without question and came around the bar to deliver it to her table. He was humming "Candle in the Wind."

"Thanks, Arlen."

Nora sipped the drink—too sugary—and bounced her knee as she settled in to wait. After the shock of Tiffany's betrayal and the fruitless search of all their former favorite haunts, Nora needed something much stiffer. But she couldn't risk dulling her senses with alcohol, no matter how much she would have liked to.

Ethan had let her crash on his couch for a couple of hours and then insisted she take a shower. While he was out. Nora locked the doors to both his apartment and the bathroom, and stood for far too long under the lukewarm spray. She wished she could wash her problems away as easily as she lathered the grime off her body. But even after she had toweled off, the sickening miasma of the trouble she was in would not dissipate. Nora didn't dare go to her apartment alone. She didn't dare contact Quinn or call the cops or do anything to upset the delicate balance of the precarious situation in which she found herself.

But as she slipped on the jade blouse she had worn to the bank and her now-rumpled pair of jeans, her phone pinged with a text.

*We need to talk.*

It was Donovan's number.

*Meet me*, he wrote. *The Cue.*

She had only agreed to meet him because she was afraid that if she didn't say yes he would hunt her down. That was a bit melodramatic, but he did often remind her of a bird of prey. Hawkish features; slick dark hair; thick, weightlifter arms that were intimidating, to say the least. Nora could still remember the first time that she ever met him on the porch at the farmhouse she shared with Tiffany and Everlee.

"I've heard so much about you," he said, extending his hand toward her as she walked slowly up the front steps. She was still wearing her apron from her evening shift at the Grind (she had just started), and before that she had worked eight hours at the car dealership, where she washed and detailed the trade-ins and got them ready for the lot. Nora had been weary and irritable, not at all in the mood to meet Tiffany's boyfriend du jour. But from the moment her fingertips touched Donovan's—no matter how reluctantly—she knew that there was something different about this one. Instead of shaking her hand, he pulled her into an uncomfortable embrace. Too close, too intimate for a stranger. As he held her too tight, he whispered in her ear, "We're going to be one big, happy family, aren't we?"

Everything inside her screamed *no*.

But less than two months later she moved out and Donovan moved in.

*I should have fought harder*, Nora thought. But what could she have done? The spell had been cast and Donovan was suddenly a part of their lives. Well, he was a part of Tiffany's and Everlee's lives. Nora found herself being slowly but surely edged out. Once it had been her job to wake Everlee and get her ready for the day. To dress her in the frilly pink ensembles that she and Tiffany bought on the clearance rack at Shopko. Nora made most of the meals and bathed Everlee and often put her to bed, too. But when Donovan moved in, Nora was lucky to see her patchwork family once a week, and though Everlee complained at first, though she cried and clung to Nora when she visited, the little girl was young enough to begin the guileless process of forgetting. It wasn't her fault, but it broke Nora's heart.

Her pulse quickened and her palms went clammy just thinking about it. It was a conditioned pain response, the only way she knew to deal with the hurt that came with knowing that she had been replaced. Breathe through it. Try to forget.

It had been so difficult to let Tiffany and Everlee go. Tiff was her best friend, but Everlee was altogether different. She wasn't just Nora's friend's daughter or a girl she cared deeply about. Nora loved her more than that. More than anything, really. Sometimes she had to remind herself that Everlee wasn't hers and never had been.

Nora checked her phone and was surprised to see that it was nearly five. Donovan was late. She wasn't sure what to think about that.

Of course, she was terrified to see him. She and Ethan had worked on a script, a series of things that she could say that were safe, benign. And though Nora doubted they would be effective, she had to try. *Tiffany is gone. I don't know where she is. Everlee, too. Let them go, Donovan. Just let them go.*

But he wouldn't. He wasn't the sort. Obsessive, addictive, controlling, manipulative—never mind the money that Nora was sure Tiffany had taken. He was dangerous. It was enough that he considered Tiffany his possession. Unconscionable that he called Everlee his daughter. His girl. *His.* How dare he? After what he had done?

Nora squeezed her eyes shut and wished on every golden thing that Everlee was safe. But how could she be? She was hidden in plain sight—with Quinn, who was both long-suffering and relentlessly curious. It wouldn't take her long to start digging for answers on her own. And what would she find? What was Everlee—Lucy—

sharing about her past? About her mother, her relationship with Nora, where she came from? Thankfully, Everlee didn't know much. Her real name was a hint, but even Quinn couldn't put those pieces together. Or could she?

The front door whooshed open and Nora looked up, her heart tight as a clenched fist. But it wasn't Donovan. Just a group of rowdy guys from the window factory. Nora knew them by the embroidered name patches over the pockets of their navy shirts. They gave her appreciative looks as they entered, and one of them waved, but no one wandered close or offered to keep her company. Word about her had gotten around. Perhaps a single glance in her direction was enough to warn them that she wasn't in the mood.

Nora watched them laughing at the bar for a while and battled nerves when the door to the Cue opened three more times. It was never Donovan.

Finally, at five thirty, the door opened and Ethan was standing there.

The Cue was bustling and he had to scan the room to find her. Nora was jittery and exhausted; she barely had the energy to lift her fingers in greeting. But he found her easily enough and wove through the crowd to slide into the booth across from her.

"How'd it go?" he asked, unsmiling.

"He never showed."

"What?"

"I don't know what happened." Nora held herself taut, stifling a tremor that threatened. Where was he? Why would he set up a meeting and then not show?

A waitress who Nora didn't recognize sidled up to their table and gave Ethan a pointed look as if to say, "I'm busy, make it fast."

"I'll have whatever she's having." Ethan nodded at Nora's still-full glass.

"It's an Arnold Palmer."

"Clearly it's going to be a wild Friday night." Ethan smirked.

"Is that all you want?" The waitress looked unimpressed, but her smug expression didn't seem to bother Ethan. When he nodded, she shrugged. "Whatever."

"You could have ordered something stronger," Nora told him when the waitress was gone. "Just because I'm not drinking doesn't mean you can't."

"I happen to love a good Arnold Palmer."

"This one's terrible."

Ethan grimaced. "I'll try to choke it down." He reached for a handful of her untouched popcorn and tossed the whole bunch into his mouth.

They were quiet for a few minutes, the noise and laughter of the bar crowd washing over them. Conversation would be difficult, and Nora couldn't decide if she was grateful for the chaos or discouraged by it. She had hoped that Ethan's appearance would temper things with Donovan, but now that Donovan hadn't showed, Nora felt vulnerable and awkward. Scared of things she couldn't name.

"What now?" Ethan said, angling himself across the table.

"I don't know," Nora said again. "He won't stop until he finds them."

The waitress appeared at Ethan's elbow and plunked down an overfull glass. Iced tea and lemonade sloshed on the table, sending syrupy rivulets across the worn wooden boards. Both Nora and Ethan scrambled for napkins while the waitress walked away unconcerned.

"Well, let's do something about it," Ethan said.

She had done something about it. Or tried to. Only a few days ago, on a lazy Tuesday morning, Nora showed up at the farmhouse. It was Nora's day off and she had a date with Tiff and Everlee, a morning of antique store shopping followed by a trip into Rochester for a root beer float at Bea's Cafe—Everlee's choice. But when she knocked on the door at ten, no one answered. The cars were in the yard, the shades drawn as if no one was up even though it was the middle of the morning. Even though Everlee was a habitual early riser and an enthusiastic door opener. Usually all Nora had to do was walk up a few of the porch steps and Everlee would come running, alerted by the high-pitched cry of the creaky stairs and so eager for company Nora couldn't help but feel like the Publishers Clearing House Prize Patrol. If only she carried an oversized check for a million dollars.

A ripple of concern made Nora shiver, and she knocked again—harder this time. The doorbell had never worked, so she jogged back down the stairs and made her way around the house to the door that opened onto the mudroom and the dark little kitchen at the rear of the house. She knocked again, banging her hand on the wooden frame until it was red and aching. And then the door swung open.

It was unlocked. It was an invitation.

Nora crept through the dirty kitchen, dishes abandoned on the table, Donovan's gray socks lying limp across the radiator as if he had thrown them there to dry. The house smelled at once stale and sharp, the acrid tang of something chemical and elemental making Nora's nose wrinkle. Her heart dropped like a stone and settled deep in the pit of her stomach. She was nauseous, terrified.

"Everlee?" Nora called, bypassing Tiffany entirely. There were times her friend made her so angry she wanted to throw things. To punch holes in walls and swear until her mother's ears burned from hundreds of miles away.

Tiffany was brash and foolish, selfish and immature. But she was also a woman who had never really had a fair chance in life, who had been abandoned and forgotten and cast aside. Nora had seen that deep hurt the moment she laid eyes on Tiffany Barnes in first period English their freshman year of high school. The girl was all arms and legs, too much makeup and too much hair. She was raw and hurting, and doing a poor job of covering it up in a tank top that she kept yanking down to expose her nonexistent cleavage and jeans so tight Nora spent the majority of the period worrying that the girl with the long brown waves wouldn't be able to stand up again when the bell rang. She pictured the stiff lurch of a Barbie doll and determined that when the class was over she would be there to help lift her up. Turned out that Tiffany could indeed stand on her own, but over the years there were many other instances when the job fell to Nora.

Was that what had drawn Nora to Tiffany? Her need? Maybe, in the beginning. But it wasn't long before Nora began to see her not as a project but as a friend, a girl with a killer sense of humor and a sarcastic streak that never failed to make Nora laugh so hard her sides hurt. And all those things, those good, kind, *real* things inside of Tiffany only added up over the years. She wasn't perfect, but she was Nora's best friend. Everlee's mother. For better or worse, they were bound together.

But there were times, like that morning, in a house that was dark and forbidding and filthy and cold, that Nora wanted to take her by the shoulders and shake her until her teeth rattled. *What were you thinking? What in the world were you thinking?*

Tuesday morning, when Nora found Donovan, he was passed out on the couch in the farmhouse. He was wearing a pair of pajama pants and nothing more, his thick, hairy chest naked and shiny as he sweat off the high. Both of his arms were full-sleeve tattoos, sexy if not for the fact that pressed beneath one of them, pinched tight between the back of the couch and the crush of his rank body, was Everlee. Her eyes were huge and frantic, her cheeks crimson from the heat of his burning skin and the fear that choked her. And she *was* choking. Nora could see that the second she laid eyes on the child—mouth wide, lips thin and bluish, tearstains tracking from lash line to chin.

Nora was across the room in seconds, hands under Everlee's arms, lifting her up and away with no regard for Donovan as he slept. No, he wasn't sleeping, he was unconscious, and he didn't so much as twitch when Nora wrenched the little girl from beneath him. She gathered the child close and left the house without a second thought about his well-being. Or Tiffany's, for that matter.

It was hatred that bubbled up in Nora's chest. Thick and viscous and black as bile. She wanted to take Everlee far away, to call child protective services or maybe the cops. But even as she buckled her into the back seat (no car seat, no booster, nothing at all), Nora knew that getting law enforcement involved wasn't an option. It never had been.

Instead, Nora texted Tiffany one word: *Now*. It looked innocent enough glowing on the screen of her cell phone, but it meant so much. Everything they had planned for, all the weeks of watching and waiting, of scrabbling together money for papers and possibilities, had come to this. They couldn't wait any longer. It was now or never.

Now what?

Tiffany was gone. She had abandoned their plan and her daughter.

"We need to find her," Nora told Ethan, her throat aching. "Donovan's obsessed. He makes Everlee call him Daddy." Nora didn't realize she was white-knuckling the edge of the table until her fingers turned numb.

"I think it's time to call the cops, Nora." He said it gently, but the words sounded dangerous in Nora's ears.

"No, that's not an option."

"Why not?"

She paused for a moment, considering. But what did she have to lose? Quietly, urgently, Nora told Ethan about the hiding place at the farm. The detached garage and the loose plank beneath the workbench. Ten thousand dollars was missing. More? It was everything Tiffany needed for a clean break.

Without Everlee.

Nora's stomach flipped. Tiffany was stupid. Foolish and short-sighted and selfish. Had she paused, even once, to consider what leaving would mean for her daughter? Donovan wouldn't stop. He wanted his money and he wanted his girl.

"Worst case scenario, she'll go to jail. Best case, who knows?" Nora said. "And what will happen to Everlee? We have to find Tiffany."

Ethan was quiet for a long time. He templed his fingers together in front of his face, holding Nora's gaze as if the answers resided there. After a couple minutes he asked, "Where would you go if you wanted to feel safe?"

"Away," Nora answered without pausing to think about it. "As far away as the money would take me, and then I'd hitchhike. Walk. Swim. Whatever it took."

Ethan nodded. "Where would Tiffany go?"

Just as easily, Nora said: "Home."

Nora hadn't even considered the possibility because it was the last place on earth she would go. But to Tiffany, Key Lake was everything she had left behind. It was stability and family, a fractured sort of love. *Home.*

"I think that's where you'll find her," Ethan said. "And Donovan, too."

# LIZ

THE HOUSE SEEMED quiet enough, but Liz cracked open the door that led from the garage to the entryway and called through the narrow gap: "I'm home!" She waited, straining to hear any hint of movement—the shuffling of feet, a knife thumping against the cutting board, anything. There was nothing. Thank goodness. When she texted Macy she hadn't paused to consider what she would do if she came home to find her friend skewering mozzarella pearls and cherry tomatoes in her kitchen. How would Liz explain away the funeral dress? Even worse: What about the urn? Liz could hardly leave poor Lorelei's remains buckled in the front seat of her black car. It was a furnace in the summertime. No pun intended.

Since it felt wrong, downright disrespectful, to simply abandon Lorelei's ashes, Liz hurried over to the passenger side of the car and grabbed the urn. She clutched it tight to her chest and slammed the door with her hip. In the entryway, she stepped out of her heels and kicked them under the bench where she sat every morning to lace up her tennis shoes. The house was empty for now, but Macy could pop in the door at any moment. Liz rushed to the bedroom on bare feet, breathless because the situation was just so ridiculous. Her life had suddenly become a daytime soap opera complete with all the usual intrigues: a secret granddaughter, a mysterious threat, and the ashes of a beautiful woman in an ugly urn.

Liz placed the urn in the center of her armoire to serve as both a reminder and a reprimand while she changed for the party. She shimmied out of the black sheath and into the blue sundress, then loosened her neat chignon so a few strands framed her face. Peering into her lighted makeup mirror, Liz added a layer of mascara and smoothed on a plum-colored lipstick. The nude gloss she had worn to Lorelei's nonexistent visitation was the furthest thing from festive. But the plum was particularly flattering, and when Liz surveyed herself in the full-length mirror on the back of the bathroom door, she had to admit that she looked good. Sun-kissed and elegant, her dress tasteful and her hair really quite striking. Very shiny. The kit from Walmart had worked.

When Liz left her bedroom she felt like an actress. She had donned her costume and was preparing to play a role that felt completely detached from who she really was. Quinn was across the lake. Lucy, too. And Nora lingered at the edges of her consciousness, entangling Liz in uncertainties without end. Throwing a party was the last thing she wanted to do, but the scene had been set and she had no choice now but to rise to the occasion. If nothing else, the evening would be a chance for Liz to ask Bennet some delicate but pointed questions. She wanted to see his face, track each expression and reaction. Bennet had never been very good at hiding his emotions.

Liz had tucked the urn beneath one arm, the other hand supporting the flat bottom. She knew exactly what she would transfer the ashes to: an antique Egyptian box inlaid with mother-of-pearl. It was approximately the size and shape of a tissue box, a perennial favorite of hers and a gift from a friend who had traveled the world instead of marrying and having children. It would hurt to pass Tiffany her aunt's ashes in such a treasured heirloom, but that was kind of the point. It couldn't be considered a sacrifice if it didn't sting a little.

Liz was so focused on her plan, so intent on transferring the ashes quickly and then painstakingly, believably performing the role of hostess, that she didn't realize Macy was in her kitchen until she rounded the corner.

"Well, don't you look gorgeous!" Macy gushed, turning from the sink, where she was rinsing tomatoes in a white enamel colander. "But what is that hideous thing you're carrying?"

Liz felt a quick burst of justification. She wanted to say: "See?" She wanted to jab her finger at Christopher Thatcher. "This is the ugliest urn on the face of the planet. You should be ashamed of yourself." But she forced herself to shrug, trying to be nonchalant as she deposited the urn on a side counter where it would be out of the way. "It's nothing. I found it in storage and I'm going to get rid of it."

"It's hard to believe you ever bought something so vile." Macy quirked an eyebrow as if her confidence in Liz had been shaken to the core.

"It was a gift."

Macy turned off the tap and began to gently dab the tomatoes with paper towels. "I'll have the skewers done in no time," she said cheerfully. "Is there anything else we need to be doing?"

Liz paused, trying to sift through her thoughts and find the only thing that she could bring herself to focus on right now: her to-do list. "I set up the tables this afternoon," she said. "And the chairs have all been wiped down."

"The flag is out?"

"Of course."

"I bet nobody knows what that means anymore."

But Macy obviously remembered. Liz's friend was wearing a long, creamy maxi dress and sandals. Her dark curls were loose and mussed in a style that was just enough bedhead to be sexy. It made Liz nostalgic for the days when beauty came so effortlessly. Messy ponytails and no need for makeup because their skin was silk itself. The long nights when the kids played Kick the Can around the cul-de-sac while the adults sipped wine spritzers and believed themselves to be kings and queens of their own little kingdom. How simple life had been back then.

Nothing felt simple anymore.

Liz grabbed a wide, handled tray and began stacking paper goods on it so she could easily transport everything outside. Napkins, thick plates, the small tags that she had printed in swirling text to set by each dish. She liked to know what she was eating and assumed everyone else did, too. "It doesn't matter," Liz said, picking up the thread of the conversation. "About the flag, I mean. Word of mouth is enough. And maybe an intimate, local party would be nicer than a big bash with strangers anyway. You look lovely, by the way."

"Thank you!"

"Be right back," Liz said, balancing the tray on one arm so she had a hand free to open the French doors that led to the patio. Out back, tables had been set at the four corners of the sweeping pergola. The wisteria that twined around the cedar beams had stopped blooming months ago, but the trumpet vine was dappled with flowers the color of ripe tangerines. Or maybe blood oranges; the heart of each cone-shaped flower looked as if it had been dipped in wine.

Liz worked on autopilot as she went around to each table, depositing some of the napkins and plates at every one. She intended to serve the way she always had: buffet-style. But instead of having all the food and drink in one place, she liked to offer different things at each corner of the patio. As people walked and talked and mingled they could try something unique at every location. The lawn was reserved for small circles of Adirondack chairs, two fire pits that she would ask some of the men to light later in the night, and the occasional pick-up game of bocce ball. Sometimes Liz regretted that they had never put in a pool, but the requisite fence would have impeded their view of the lake, which was gorgeous.

When her hands were empty, Liz stood for a minute at the edge of the brick walkway and tried to enjoy the lake spread out before her. It was a gem, a shimmering jewel cut into the earth, and it sparkled so bright she had to put up an arm to shield her eyes. There were boats on the water cutting white arrowheads in their wake, sometimes pulling a skier or wakeboarder but just as often not. Back in the day, Liz had skied herself, and well. She knew she made a pretty silhouette on the water, legs long and tanned in a slalom ski as she jumped the wake and leaned so low her fingertips trailed the water. It was like touching glass; the water was so smooth, so hard beneath her.

"Hello? Mrs. Sanford?"

Liz whipped around as if she had been caught doing something indecent. What time was it? It couldn't be six, not yet, but there was a man walking toward her from the side of the house. Liz smoothed the skirt of her dress and flashed him a smile that she knew could dazzle, even at a distance. Even though it was forced.

"You're early!" she said, but she had no idea who he was. Tall, dark, handsome. Late twenties, maybe early thirties. The kind of man who would have made her pulse flutter if she were a few years younger. Okay, several. "A quality I admire."

They were close enough now for Liz to see that his grin was crooked and utterly disarming. "I'm glad to hear it," he said. "But I'm afraid I don't know what you're talking about."

Liz's smile flickered. "You're not here for the party?"

"A party sounds incredible. Here?" He looked around and gave a low whistle. "You've got a great place."

"Thank you." Liz's hand went to the nape of her neck, where she wound a stray hair around her index finger. It was a nervous habit and something she hadn't done in a very long time. Jack Sr. used to take her hand in his own when he caught her doing it. He said that anxious tics were unbecoming. Which was true. But why was she on edge?

"I'm sorry," the man said, obviously sensing her discomfort. "The lady who answered the door said you'd be back here. Clearly you're expecting guests—just not me."

"Everyone is invited," Liz said. "You're welcome to stay."

"Thank you, but I don't have much time. I'm actually looking for a friend of mine."

"I'm not sure how I can be of any assistance."

"It's a long shot," the man said, shrugging. "And a bit of a crazy story. You see, my fiancée is missing."

Missing? What was that supposed to mean? She ran away? Was abducted? Got lost? Liz didn't know what to say so she settled for "I'm so sorry."

He stared at the ground for a moment, and when he looked up his eyes were filled with something that Liz couldn't define. She didn't know whether to hug him or take a step back from him. Either way, she was surprised when he said: "She's a friend of your daughter Nora."

"Nora doesn't live here anymore," Liz said carefully. "She hasn't for years. How did you know where to find me? And what exactly do you think I can do for you?"

He shrugged, sheepish. "You're listed in the Key Lake phone book. This is Nora's hometown, her last name is Sanford, there are only two Sanfords: Jack Sr. and Jack Jr." He ticked off each fact on his fingers, and though it made sense, it unsettled Liz that he had gone to such trouble. "I'm sorry. I shouldn't have come. I'm just"—he held out his hands, palms up—"desperate."

"I suggest you get a hold of Nora." Liz took an almost imperceptibly small step back. "I don't keep track of her friends for her."

"Of course not." He shook his head as if chastising himself and then pressed his palms together and gave her a half-bow of sorts. "Thank you for your time, Mrs. Sanford. I hope you have a lovely evening."

"Thank you."

He turned and began to walk away, and Liz realized for the first time that he was wearing jeans and a long-sleeved shirt. It was easily ninety degrees. She crossed her arms over her chest, disquieted, though she couldn't put her finger on why. He never told her his name. That was part of it, though it was no use chasing after him now; he was almost gone.

But at the corner of the house he turned back. Called over the distance between them: "If you see Tiffany Barnes around, would you tell her that I'm looking for her?"

In spite of the heat, Liz's blood turned to ice in her veins.

Not just because Nora and Tiffany hadn't seen each other in years or because a strange man had just stood on her property and made her feel weak-kneed and queasy. What shook her to the core was that she had bumped into Tiffany only hours ago. For the first time in almost seven years. Coincidence? And when she had seen the girl her daughter had once considered her best friend, there was really only one word that could summarize the look in her eyes: *hunted.*

*Friday*

*7:03 p.m.*

**LIZ**

*You have to come tonight.*

                       **QUINN**

                       *You're kidding, right? I can't leave Lucy.*

**LIZ**

*This is about Lucy. Leave her with Walker.*

                       **QUINN**

                       *I don't think that's such a good idea.*

**LIZ**

*Half an hour. That's all I'm asking.*

*Bennet will be here.*

195

# QUINN

LUCY WAS NOT IMPRESSED by Quinn's announcement that she was going out.

"Why?" she asked, her voice so tiny it was barely a whisper.

Good question. Quinn slipped a pair of delicate gold hoops through her earlobes and touched her neck to make sure she was wearing the right necklace. She was stalling, trying to come up with an answer that would explain why she was shirking the duty Nora had so thoughtlessly—so belatedly—thrust upon her. But *I'm punishing my husband* and *I just have to get out of here* weren't exactly kid-appropriate answers. Neither was *We have to discuss what to do with you.*

And Quinn absolutely couldn't speak the truth that was making her heart beat high and just a little too fast in her chest: *I'm dying to see him.*

She pushed the thought out of her mind with a savage thrust and said: "My mom needs me."

It was an explanation that seemed to resonate with Lucy. She nodded in resignation, as if she knew what it was like to be beholden to her mother. *Why?* Quinn wanted to ask. *What happened to you?* But prying had proven to be an exercise in futility before. Little Miss Lucy-Lou was a riddle with layers that had to be slowly, carefully peeled back.

"I won't be gone long," Quinn assured her. "And Walker will be here with you."

That didn't seem to offer Lucy much comfort. She was wedged into a corner of the couch, and at the mention of Walker's name she drew herself into a tight little ball: knees tucked snug beneath her chin and arms wrapped around her legs. Lucy was wearing the pajamas that Walker had bought her and she balled the excess fabric in her fists.

"Hey." Quinn sank to the floor in front of the couch. Her dress was a soft, silky material and it pooled around her thighs as she knelt. Tentatively, Quinn reached out a hand and placed it over Lucy's bare foot. Besides brushing Lucy's hair, it was the only time that Quinn had touched her, and she was grateful that the child didn't jerk away. They were making progress at a snail's pace, but at least they were moving in the right direction. Were they bonding? Or starting to? A part of Quinn wanted to stick around and find out, but she was committed now. Her mother had texted no less than four times and Walker was in the shower, prepping himself for a night on the couch and a *House of Cards* Netflix binge.

But they both knew he had no intention of watching TV. Walker would spend the evening listening, watching, waiting. After Lucy's unnerving phone call, Walker had abandoned his sculpture for the day. Instead of working, Quinn watched as he fished a tire iron out of the trunk of his car and unearthed an old metal baseball bat from the shed.

"What are you doing?" Quinn whispered when she saw him carrying the tire iron in one hand and the bat in the other.

Walker didn't look at her as he passed. "She's afraid. I'm going to keep her safe."

From what? Her father?

"This is ridiculous," Quinn said, following him.

Walker wheeled on her. "You saw her. She's scared to death, Quinn. I don't know what's going on here, but there's something terribly wrong—and if your sister won't tell us what it is, the least we can do is make sure Lucy's okay."

"Nora—"

"I don't want to hear it." Walker stormed past. "Stop covering for your sister. Lucy is the one who needs our protection."

They had hardly spoken the rest of the day. What was there to say? Walker wasn't a violent person. As far as Quinn knew, he had never even been in a fistfight. If something actually happened—if someone came for Lucy—what would he do? But the whole situation still seemed ludicrous to Quinn. Impossible. This couldn't be their lives. All the same, she agreed to go to her mother's in the hope that Liz would be ready to join the cause. Whatever it was.

Quinn sighed and tried to give Lucy a reassuring smile. She squeezed her foot. "I'm going to tuck you in," she said, "and when you wake up in the morning it will be as if I was never gone at all."

"It's not my bedtime."

"It's eight thirty," Quinn said, glancing at the clock on the wall. "When I was your age I had to be in bed by seven thirty." It was true, or at least close enough. Quinn still wasn't exactly sure how old Lucy was. She had asked, but the number changed. Six? Seven? Was it common for children not to know their age? Quinn just wasn't sure.

"I'm not tired." But Lucy's eyes were heavy, her arms loosening their grip on her skinny legs. She was clearly exhausted.

"I'll carry you to bed . . . ?" It was an offer that Quinn wasn't sure the girl would accept, but after a moment of consideration, Lucy held out her arms.

She didn't weigh much. Or maybe she just held herself carefully. Either way, in one quick movement Lucy was pressed against Quinn. Her legs went around Quinn's waist and her arms circled her neck. Quinn stood still for a heartbeat, two, as she held the girl close and breathed in the scent of her hair, her sun-warmed skin. It was impossible not to love a child, and Lucy's innocence was an arrow that pierced Quinn. *I think I love you*, she thought, *and I don't even know you*. The thought surprised her. And scared her.

Quinn carried Lucy to the bedroom and tucked her in, tugging the sheets up to her chin and offering her the stuffed fox that Walker had bought. Lucy took it and pulled it close, then rolled onto her side so that her back was to Quinn and the bedroom door. She cut such a sad silhouette that Quinn faltered, ready to break her promise to her mother and forget the whole evening out. But then she had an inspiration.

"Wait a sec," she said, and disappeared into the kitchen. Grabbing a pen and the handset of the telephone off the wall, she hurried back to Lucy. "Give me your hand, honey."

Lucy rolled over, a skeptical look on her face. But she held out her hand anyway.

Writing carefully, Quinn traced her cell phone number onto the smooth skin of Lucy's palm. "This is the number to my cell," she said. Passing Lucy the handset she added, "And here's the phone. If you need me for any reason at all, you call that number and I'll be here so fast your head will spin."

Lucy stared at the numbers, her face blank and unreadable. But then she curled her fingers over her palm as if protecting a precious secret. With her other hand she took the phone and hid it beneath her pillow. She settled back, wrapping herself tight in the covers.

Quinn watched the curve of her back for a moment, the rise and fall of her steady breath. "Do you want me to lock the door?" she asked, wondering what Lucy would say.

She nodded.

"Okay." Quinn touched her shoulder and wished she dared to brush a kiss across the shallow divot of her temple. "Good night, Lucy."

Quinn locked the door from the inside and pulled it shut behind her, hoping that the phone and the closed door made Lucy feel safe.

"Did you just lock that door?" Walker asked. He was standing in pajama pants, drying his unkempt hair with a towel. His narrow chest was bare and though it made Quinn's stomach knot, she was thankful that Lucy hadn't seen him half-dressed and lean, masculine and intimidating. Walker had the body of a runner, lithe and spare, but he was all man. *I'm afraid of him*, Lucy had said. And though Quinn had no idea who he was or what he looked like, she could ballpark a few generalities.

"Yes, I locked the door," she said. "Lucy felt safer that way. There's an ice pick in the utensil drawer if you need it. Just stick it in the hole in the center of the knob and it'll pop open."

"Sounds like you've done this before. Is there anything you'd like to confess?"

"Just that I liked to borrow my sister's clothes when I was a teenager. She locked her door; I broke in."

"I like this side of you, Mrs. Cruz." Walker arched an eyebrow, but it was a feeble attempt at flirtation.

Quinn looked away quickly, afraid that he could see the truth written across her face. That when they fought sometimes she wondered: *Do we belong?* Of course, she knew the answer to that question. Yes. Yes, forever. But sometimes . . . "Call me if you need anything," she said, and was surprised by how her voice fell limp and weak between them.

Walker didn't seem to notice. "I think I can hold down the fort for a couple of hours."

"Just promise me you'll let me know if she needs me."

He slung the towel across his shoulders and put his hands on his hips. "Be careful," he said.

"Yeah. You too."

. . .

When Quinn pulled up to her mother's house, the cul-de-sac was full of cars. The vehicles stretched around the circle and down both sides of the street, but no one had dared to park in Liz Sanford's stamped concrete driveway. Well, Quinn had no problem doing so.

She pulled in and turned off the car, then sat behind the steering wheel for a minute, watching the sun set in her rearview mirror.

How many times had she lingered on this driveway, wishing she didn't have to go in? The tension between Nora and her parents was often thick and suffocating and JJ's superiority was unbearable. Quinn had longed for happiness, for peace. For banter around the supper table and maybe the odd family movie night with popcorn and laughter. But the Sanfords had always spun just a little off-center, the wobble imperceptible to anyone who wasn't on the inside. Weren't they lovely in Christmas cards? Attractive and smiling? Weren't they sociable and accomplished and model students and citizens of Key Lake? Well, for the most part.

Sighing, Quinn finally stepped out of the car and made her way to the back of the house. Her dress swished against her hips, her hair loose and wavy across her shoulders. She had spent an inordinate amount of time getting ready, making sure that she would leave Walker wanting when she walked out the door. Now she realized that her mother's backyard was filled with strangers, people she didn't know or acquaintances she had all but forgotten about in her five-year exile. Quinn felt their eyes on her, their attention direct because they were tipsy. Each gaze was a brushstroke against her skin, an almost tangible thing. All at once she felt conspicuous, exposed.

"Quinn!" Liz broke away from a group of people near the small fountain that flanked a rose garden and swayed toward her daughter, arms spread wide. "I'm so glad you came," she said, gathering her daughter into a loose hug. Then, a whisper: "You're late."

"I'm here," Quinn said. "Can we—"

"Hi, Quinn." Amelia appeared at Quinn's elbow and put a stiff arm around her sister-in-law. Her belly was so huge they couldn't properly hug, and she gave up, resorting to rubbing her tummy absentmindedly.

"You look beautiful," Quinn told her, and though she meant it, there was a thread of jealousy woven through her words. The truth was, Amelia looked like she belonged on the cover of *Parenting* magazine. She was diminutive, dark, and shapely, her lips full and her thick, shoulder-length hair held back with tortoiseshell clips. There was something indefinably wholesome about her, as if pregnancy had conferred a sort of purity on her that canceled out what Quinn knew of her sister-in-law's partying days. Despite being five feet two and barely a hundred pounds—pre-pregnancy, of course—Amelia used to be able to shotgun a beer in three seconds flat. Now her tummy was almost exactly the size of a mini-keg, but instead of Bud Light it contained Quinn's soon-to-be niece or nephew. Well, Quinn's *other* niece or nephew. She swallowed. "How are you feeling?"

"Big, fat, tired . . ."

JJ came up behind Amelia and offered her a small plate filled with hors d'oeuvres. "Hungry," he added. "Often, hangry. Hi, sis."

Quinn didn't move to hug him, but she forced a smile. JJ was dapper and charming as always, resembling a model in a Polo Ralph Lauren ad in a slim-fitting jean shirt and plaid shorts. He even had the quintessential cleft chin and dazzlingly white smile—never mind the prep school attitude. Quinn often longed to remind him that he had been born in the provincial backwater town of Key Lake, Minnesota, not upstate New York. She suspected that he'd be genuinely surprised at this news. "It's good to see you guys," she said, grasping at normalcy. "We haven't gotten together much this summer."

It was true. JJ and Amelia had their own social circle, their own carefully constructed lives. JJ had taken over his father's real estate business and Amelia worked as his secretary. Nepotism be damned. It was his company and he could do what he wanted with it. Besides, they made a pretty couple, and no one ever seemed to question things that were lovely.

"This is exactly why I decided to throw a party," Liz interjected, slipping one arm around Quinn and the other around Amelia. "Here we are, all living in the same town, and we never see one another. It's a tragedy."

JJ and Amelia exchanged a look, one that clearly said less family time was hardly a tragedy in their books.

"I suppose I'm feeling a little nostalgic these days," Liz admitted. "And you will *never* guess who I ran into yesterday."

"I'm sure I have no idea," JJ said, taking a pull on his beer and looking past his mother. He was clearly bored, and Amelia tucked her hand into the crook of his arm and pinched. Quinn could tell by the way he winced and gave his wife a sharp look.

But Liz seemed unaware of his disinterest. "I ran into Tiffany Barnes," she said with relish.

It was a name that Quinn hadn't heard in years. Nora's high school best friend? So what? But the air between them was suddenly brittle, chilly. Amelia dropped JJ's arm and looked away, the set of her jaw hard and angry. JJ moved to put his hand on the small of his wife's back, but she shifted toward Quinn and his fingers brushed empty space.

"She was at Walmart," Liz said, apparently oblivious to the effect of her words.

But studying her mother, Quinn realized that Liz knew exactly what she was doing. She had brought up Tiffany on purpose.

And then Quinn remembered. Another night. Another party like this. Nora was looking for Tiffany, asking everyone where her best friend had disappeared to. She eventually found her on the dock with JJ. Tiffany's hair was mussed, her lips flushed pink from kissing, and when she chased after Nora to try to explain, Quinn could see that her shirt was buttoned wrong. JJ? It was inconceivable, the worst kind of betrayal, even to Quinn, who at fourteen knew very little about the rules of love and friendship.

It came to nothing, as far as Quinn knew. Tiffany chose Nora, or something like that, and her fling with JJ was nothing more than fuel for the gossip mill. It had all happened before Amelia, before they were of an age where they could make decisions that weren't primarily based on hormones. A lifetime ago. What did it matter? And why would Amelia care now? She was clearly stunningly pregnant with JJ's baby.

"Well." Quinn clapped her hands together, suddenly eager to get away. What was she supposed to do? Pretend that she was close with JJ and Amelia? That this bizarre conversation made sense to her? Quinn was still angry at her mother for other reasons. She hadn't forgiven Liz for bursting in on her the morning before and was downright livid at her casual disregard of the fact that she had a *granddaughter.* It was unnatural. They were too far apart and far too close all at the same time. Perpetually missing each other. "I, for one, would love a glass of wine."

The proclamation was an excuse to leave, but it was also a bit of a jab at Amelia in her current state. And, if Quinn was perfectly honest with herself (why the hell not?), a challenge to her own womb and the life she hoped was taking root inside. A glass of wine would be a gauntlet thrown, an "I dare you" to her own broken body.

Quinn was suddenly, irrationally angry. At Walker, at her brother and his blossoming wife, at Nora and Liz, at her out-of-control life. Her mother was saying something to her, but it didn't matter, Quinn was already gone. Off in the direction of the nearest table where she could see a profusion of bottles. Her mother always mixed a drink or two for these occasions, but guests usually came bearing wine or fine whiskey, sometimes cheap tequila with a bag of key limes. There was never a shortage of options.

But, apparently, there was sometimes a shortage of cups. There wasn't a paper Dixie cup in sight, and Liz's plastic reusable wineglasses (the ones she liked to stack in towers like champagne flutes) were clearly long gone. For a moment, Quinn stood at the table, contemplating whether she would stoop so low as to swig straight from the bottle of pinot grigio only inches from her fingertips. But before she could take the plunge, Quinn felt someone touch her elbow.

She turned from the spread before her, thirsty and irritated and vulnerable, her composure thin. It was the worst possible state for her to be in when she spun around to find Bennet Van Eps standing before her. Of course, she knew that he was coming, but his proximity was still a shock. Quinn hadn't seen him in five years, but he hadn't changed a bit. Same quirky smile, one cheek creased as if he were laughing at a private joke. Same ashy blond hair, cut marine close and perfectly edged, a striking complement to his broad features. He would have looked dangerously handsome in fatigues, but instead of joining the military like he always said he would, Quinn had heard years ago that he became a cop.

Bennet was tender and soft-spoken, skilled at long silences and careful listening. He had been quiet when Quinn was loud, steady when she was tossed in a troubled sea. Bennet was the opposite of Walker in so many ways that Quinn found it jarring to see him now, to be reminded of who he was and what he had been, when her life had taken such a different path.

"Bennet," Quinn said, and wasn't sure if she was surprised or happy or just a little bit heartbroken. He had always been so patient with her, so quick to forgive. Quinn wondered if he had forgiven her betrayal. No, she didn't have to wonder. There was no excuse for what she had done.

"Hi, Quinn."

There was no playbook for this, no rules she knew to follow. Should she shake his hand? Laugh? Cry? It was more than Quinn could handle, and the chaos of her life in that moment tipped her toward him. It was the slightest hint of movement, just a shift in his direction, but Bennet fell a little, too. For just a heartbeat the world seemed to pause in its orbit, a fraction of a second that spun back the clock to a time when this was all that had mattered. Them. Together.

When his arms went around her, the thought that wisped through Quinn's mind quiet as a wish was: *home*.

# NORA

"IT'S NOT A ROAD TRIP until there's junk food." Ethan swung into the car and tossed an armful of brightly colored packages at Nora.

"I'm not sure I'd call this a road trip, exactly." Nora shook her head, sifting through the detritus in her lap. "Doritos, Mike and Ikes, Slim Jims . . . Seriously, Ethan, what's wrong with you?"

"Hey, I got two Slim Jims. One for me and one for you."

"What in the world makes you think I eat beef jerky?"

"It's dried sausage," Ethan corrected her as he put the car in drive and pulled out of the gas station. "And you don't strike me as the Slim Jim type. That just means more for me."

When he wiggled his eyebrows at her, Nora couldn't help but laugh. It was dry and short-lived, but it felt good to smile, to feel the weight in her heart lighten, even if it was only for a moment. "You should weigh twice as much as you do."

"I know, right? Good thing I work out."

"Are you trying to be funny?"

"I'm trying to make you laugh," Ethan said. "Clearly I'm not very good at it."

Nora shrugged, but she felt a warm little rush in the center of her chest. She wasn't used to Ethan's brand of attention. It had been a long time since someone had cared about whether she was happy.

They drove in silence for a few minutes, watching the traffic as Ethan merged onto I-90. It would take them just over three hours to get to Key Lake, which meant they would arrive after midnight. *Then what?*

If Nora had felt almost normal a minute ago, her fear redoubled as she considered what might happen when they arrived in her hometown. A wave of nausea turned her stomach and her palms went cold and clammy. What if Tiffany was nowhere to be found? What if she didn't want to be found?

Never mind the fact that Nora would have to contend with her own family in Key Lake. And she owed them more than just an explanation. She owed them an apology. But how could she ask for forgiveness? There could be no absolution for what she and Tiffany had done.

And Ethan. What was she going to do with him? Like it or not, she was stuck with him now—and torn between relief that he had offered to come (and that she had impulsively accepted) and irritation that he was in the driver's seat. Literally, of course. They both knew exactly who was in charge of this particular rescue mission. But Ethan had heard the whole sordid tale, and after he realized the kind of danger that Everlee was in, he refused to back down. *I'm coming*, he said. And then he cleared both of their schedules at the Grind and steered Nora toward his car. She let him.

"I kind of can't believe I'm going to see where you grew up," Ethan said, either oblivious to her inner turmoil or intentionally trying to distract her. Nora couldn't tell. He had set cruise control at seventy-five miles per hour, five miles above the speed limit but five below Nora's preferred speed. She mentally recalculated their arrival time and forced her hands to be still in her lap.

"Don't get your hopes up," she said. "Key Lake isn't much to write home about."

"That bad?"

Nora shrugged, looking out her window at the green expanse of fields beside the interstate, and willed her heart to slow its manic pace. "It's not bad, I guess. If you're into walleye fishing. And small towns. And . . ."

"And what?" he prompted.

"And not much else. I'm trying to think of more ways to describe Key Lake and I can't. It's a cliché. Everything you've ever thought about sleepy little lakeside towns is true."

Ethan didn't say anything and Nora could feel him looking at her. She whipped her head around to meet his gaze. "Watch the road!"

He smiled and dutifully turned his attention to driving.

"What?"

"I just find your angst amusing. We're twentysomething, you know."

"I happen to know you're thirtysomething," Nora interjected.

He nodded. *Touché*. "Whatever. The point is, we're past hating our hometowns and rebelling against our idyllic childhoods. Right?"

"You had an idyllic childhood?"

"You didn't?"

"No."

"Me neither."

Nora threw up her hands. "Then stop giving me such a hard time!"

Ethan smiled, but it wasn't patronizing. "We get older. We soften. You just seem so touchy about your past."

"Touchy."

"Yeah."

Nora bit her lip, considering. "I suppose I have some bad memories that are tied to Key Lake."

"And Tiffany is a part of them."

"Among others."

"Who else?"

Nora didn't know whether to be annoyed or amused. "You're very persistent."

"We have a long drive ahead of us," Ethan said as he turned on the radio. He found a preset station and smoky jazz created a muted backdrop in the car. Yet another side of him that took Nora by surprise. "Might as well get to know each other."

She was under the impression that they did know each other, but Nora was beginning to realize that her definition of friendship was rather insubstantial. What did she really know about the people she claimed to care about? Even Tiffany had disappeared on her without a word of warning. There was very little left for Nora to lose.

"Fine," she said, relenting. "I'll tell you a story."

"I love stories."

Nora slapped his arm in warning. *Be quiet.* "When I was ten years old, my family went to Chicago for a week."

"I thought this was a story about Key Lake?"

"Shut up. I'm talking."

Ethan gave her a grave two-fingered salute.

Nora started again. "We stayed downtown in this huge high-rise with a view of the lake. And every day we went somewhere new. Shedd Aquarium, Navy Pier, the Art Institute, the Field Museum— that one was my favorite." Nora paused, waiting for Ethan to insert a quip, but he didn't. His hands were loosely gripping the steering wheel, his eyes trained on the taillights of the car in front of them. He was relaxed, at home in his own skin, and *listening*. Nora opened up the Mike and Ikes and tapped a few out into her palm, then passed him the box.

"So, it was a really great vacation. I mean, we all had fun. It was exciting to stay in the big city and walk in the shadows of all those tall buildings . . . I think we were too tired and happy and overwhelmed to fight."

Ethan nodded.

"I mean, not that we ever really fought. Sanfords don't yell or throw things or anything like that. At least, not usually. We were pretty buttoned up." She slid him a wry look. "And don't bother telling me I still am." Why did she want him to understand? Why did she care what he thought about her family, her upbringing?

"So what happened?" Ethan asked.

"The last day that we were there, we passed this homeless girl in the street. Don't get me wrong, we had passed dozens of homeless people over the course of the week, but she was different."

"Why?"

"She was my age. Or not much older. She was holding a piece of cardboard that said: *Today is my birthday.*"

Nora was watching Ethan's face and felt relieved to see his jaw clench. "That's awful, right?" she said. "My dad had given each of us kids ten dollars to spend on a souvenir and I had saved mine. I wanted to give it to her. But he wouldn't let me."

"Why not?"

"He said it was probably her birthday yesterday and the day before and the day before that. I said I didn't care. He told me she was manipulative and a liar and that she would likely spend the money on drugs anyway."

"That's harsh." Ethan had a handful of Mike and Ikes, but instead of eating them he shook them around in his palm. The soft clicking was comforting, somehow.

"That was my dad. Pull yourself up by your bootstraps, get a job, no free handouts. But to me, she was just a kid. I didn't care if it was her birthday or not. I wanted to help her."

"Didn't your mom say anything?"

Nora pushed a hard breath through her lips. "Are you kidding? My mom was a pushover. She never stood up to Jack Sr. a day in her life."

"What did you do?"

"Nothing," Nora said, and for some reason the memory still stung. "I walked away. My brother laughed, my sister was clueless, and I walked away."

"You were just a kid, too, Nora."

"I know that," she said quickly. "It's not a big deal. You just wanted to know about my idyllic childhood. I think that pretty much sums it up."

"It certainly helps me understand you more."

"Oh really." Nora forced a laugh. "Enlighten me."

"How about I save my observations for the end of the trip? And how about you pass me those pork rinds?"

Nora wanted to ask him about his own childhood, and she did, but she couldn't help feeling like she had revealed much more than Ethan did when he answered her questions. He was born in Washington State, moved to Minnesota when he was twelve, played hockey on scholarship in college. He was a defenseman with a pretty stellar slap shot from the point. His words. Ethan had graduated summa cum laude with a degree in engineering but decided after he had his diploma in hand that what he really wanted to do was study neoclassical literature.

"That's insane." By this time, Nora had ripped open the bag of Doritos and they both had orange fingers.

"That's exactly what my parents said. Thanks for your vote of confidence." Ethan stuck a Mike and Ike in his mouth and glared at her. Nora smiled primly back. He deserved it. Who drank water with Doritos? She was craving a Coke.

"How did I not know these things about you?" she asked, popping the last Dorito in her mouth.

Ethan lifted a shoulder. "You never asked. We talk mostly about specialty roasts and whether or not the new kid you hired for the after-school shift should be fired."

"We're so boring. At least, I am," Nora said. "You travel, study *neoclassical* literature, play hockey . . ."

"It's just a rec league."

"Still."

She didn't mean to be so pensive, but what in the world had she done with her life? The sun had set long ago and Nora could see at least a few of the stars in the sky. If they were on a dirt road, or out in the middle of Key Lake, there would be a thousand points of light, but speeding down the interstate she could only make out a few major beacons. The Big Dipper was just visible out her window, and a little to the left, Polaris. If it were earlier in the summer she knew she could star hop from the outer stars of the Dipper's bowl to Leo. Nora had never been the sort to wish on stars, but she had once liked to chart them. And to hope that somewhere out there, in the midst of all the inconsistencies and little hurts of her life, someone cared enough to listen to the dreams of her lonely heart.

Lonely. As if.

"Where are we going?" Ethan asked, and Nora turned from the window quickly, caught in the act of . . . what? Daydreaming? In the darkness, she could see the corners of his eyes crinkle into a smile. "I'm not being existential, Nora. I think we're close to the turnoff."

"Oh." Nora looked around, taking in the landscape. The hours had flown by, and Ethan was right—the turnoff for Key Lake was only miles ahead. Of course, they would wind on country roads for a while, but this was the homestretch. The point in the trip when most people would lean in, feeling the pull of the familiar as steady as a magnet. Nora pressed herself deeper into her seat.

She navigated easily, telling Ethan which direction to turn and when, but she didn't elaborate on their surroundings or narrate through the small towns they passed. Truth be told, Nora was exhausted. She had traveled these very roads only two nights ago, and it was hard to grasp just how much things had changed in the time between. Her life was unraveling around her, the snag a seemingly fatal flaw in the fabric that was everything she knew.

"Welcome home," Ethan said quietly when they passed the Welcome to Key Lake sign. "Are we going to your mom's house?"

"No." Nora glanced at the dashboard clock. It was just before midnight. They had made better time than she anticipated, but she still wouldn't think of knocking on Liz's door. And Quinn and Walker's cabin was out of the question. "How do you feel about roughing it?" Nora asked.

"I have my camping badge if that's what you're asking. Boy Scout Troop 211. 'On my honor, I will do my best—'"

"Good enough."

They drove straight through the edge of town, skirting the heart in favor of the truck bypass and the few commercial imports Key Lake had to offer: Walmart, a Shell superstation, McDonald's. Nora half expected Ethan to make some crack about craving french fries and a Big Mac, but he was comfortably silent.

"Turn here," Nora instructed one last time, and they pulled onto a gravel road several miles past town.

"I didn't bring my tent, though."

"No need for that. Tiffany's aunt passed away not long ago."

"Oh. I'm sorry."

Nora bit her lip. Tried to make her words sound normal, light, though she felt anxious. "It's okay. She'd been sick for a very long time. But she owned some land."

"Okay . . ."

"A farm, actually. The main house has been rented out for a couple of years, but there's a second place on the property, a little cabin that hasn't been used in ages. Tiff and I used to hide out there." She felt a smile crease her face in spite of everything. There was some beauty in the ashes of her past. "Her grandparents lived there up until the day they were moved to a home. They left everything the way it was."

"What makes you think it's still empty?"

She shrugged. "No one wants it. There's nothing of value there. But if Tiffany came back to Key Lake, it's where we'll find her."

Nora's heart juddered at the thought and she squeezed her eyes closed. *Be there. Please, be there.* She wished she had paid more attention in Sunday school so she could wrap a prayer around her hope. *You can't leave me like this, Tiffany. I don't know what to do.*

Ethan must have sensed the way Nora was feeling, the way her soul lifted as they rounded the final corner. He reached across the space between them, and when he found her hand, she didn't pull away.

# LIZ

"SIT DOWN," Macy said, taking Liz by the elbow and steering her in the direction of the nearest circle of Adirondack chairs. Liz had no idea what time it was. Midnight? Later? It didn't matter; the night had been a smashing success. The bottles were nearly empty and the raucous din had gentled into the intimate conversations and quiet hum of the twenty or so remaining guests. It was lovely, but Liz was a wreck. Perfectly put together and benevolent on the outside, a tangled mess on the inside. And though her heart was pulled in a dozen different directions—from her daughters to her granddaughter to fears about her own future—at the center of it all was one person. Jack.

*Life goes on.* The thought flitted through her mind, unwelcome, unbidden. What the hell was that supposed to mean anyway?

Of course Liz had known that her heart would keep beating after Jack Sr.'s body had been laid in the ground. She would weed the gardens and vacuum the carpets in the living room and even go on walks with Macy when the sun was rising and the morning was shimmering and surreal, impossibly beautiful. But these were her things, the world she inhabited with or without her husband. A Sanford party was altogether different. Or so she had believed.

But Liz had been wrong. There was laughter and fine food and music that floated out over the water and into the air where a riot of stars pricked holes in the night sky. *How can it be?* Liz wondered.

Even though it was she who had planned all this extravagance, she herself who had made it so, she didn't realize until Macy pushed her into a brightly painted chair—canary yellow—that it would work. She corrected herself: that it *had* worked. Gorgeously. In spite of everything. In spite of the fact that Liz's life was crumbling around her.

"Oh my goodness," Macy said, falling into the chair beside her (it was painted Caribbean blue, though Liz noted in some small, rational part of her mind that it could use a fresh coat). "We did it!"

Liz tried to muster up a smile but she was too blurred at the edges to care. How many glasses of wine had she had? Just one, she was sure of it. But there had been that hard lemonade, and someone had placed a glass of peach sangria in her hand. She didn't remember drinking it. "I suppose we did," Liz said.

"Well, I mean, this was really all *you*." Macy laughed lightly. "I just posted the event on Facebook and made a few caprese skewers."

"Don't sell yourself short." Liz was on autopilot, saying the things that should be said, though they made little sense to her. "They were delicious."

"You had one?"

"Several."

"And a few glasses of wine, I'd wager."

"Just the one."

But Macy winked at her and dissolved in a fit of giggles. Impossibly, illogically, Liz found herself joining along. They were almost hysterical, their outburst more appropriate for teenagers than women of their age and sophistication. Macy liked to say, "We're not old, we're elegant." Elegant indeed.

Liz dabbed at her eyes with hands that, though strong and familiar, were covered in skin like crepe paper and lined with pale blue veins. When had that happened? When had everything started to unravel? Liz felt like her life was a tapestry that was unwinding all around her. Who had pulled that first thread? How could she ever weave it all back together?

"You okay?" Macy asked, leaning forward.

*No*, she was decidedly not okay. But admitting that had never been an option. Liz took a deep breath. Forced a smile. "Fine. I'm fine."

"Are you sure?"

"Yes." And because she willed it so, it was. There was no handbook for this. Liz Sanford would have to write her own. If she wanted to, she could reach out and snag a star from the sky. Stand beneath the twinkling lights and sing a lullaby in her more-than-passable husky-sweet voice. Kiss a stranger.

"What is that look for?" Macy reached over and slapped Liz's bare knee.

Liz crossed her legs primly, sweeping her ankles to the side so that her calves were accentuated. Jack Sr. had always told her she had gorgeous legs. Her stomach lurched at the thought and she uncrossed them again. "Nothing at all."

"Oh, come on. I saw the way that Arie looked at you all night."

It was true. Liz had felt his glances against her skin like a sigh. He had sipped wine from one of her stemmed glasses and tossed back his head to laugh at her jokes. There was something downright attractive about him in a pair of linen shorts and a white buttondown shirt. Cuffed at the elbows, untucked. And no Vikings cap. Liz had hardly recognized him. Now she wondered absently where he had gotten off to.

"He left," Macy said as if reading her mind. "But he didn't want to go. You just didn't give him a reason to stay."

"I'm a recent widow," Liz told her.

"Not that recent. You're young, Elizabeth. You're allowed to love again."

"Arie Van Vliet?"

"Not necessarily." Macy tapped her lips with her fingertips, considering. "You know, lots of people meet each other online these days."

"Not a chance!" The thought lit a match in Liz's chest and the flame licked clean any normalcy she had fought to attain. Suddenly she felt off-balance again.

"Fine, fine. It was just an idea."

"A bad one." No, Liz wouldn't consider using a matchmaking service, and, come to think of it, her little buzz was really just the beginning of what would undoubtedly be a mild hangover. How long had it been since that happened? "I'm tired," Liz said, pushing herself up.

"Leave it," Macy instructed as she watched her friend survey the damage. The chairs were helter-skelter across the yard, dragged into small groupings and circled close to the two fires that were starting to burn low. The tables that Liz had set up, her careful presentation of food and drink and vases of flowers, were a war zone of tipped-over bottles and half-empty glasses, nibbles of endive stuffed with goat cheese and blood oranges wilting on napkins. While Liz was watching, one of the strands of lights flickered in warning and then went out with a dull pop.

"Lovely party, Lizzie." Kent came up behind them and slipped a familiar arm around Liz's waist while curling the other around his wife. He had been almost paternal since Jack Sr. had died, sweet and protective in a brotherly way that Liz in turn loved and hated. Tonight, she loved it and laid her head on his shoulder.

"Thank you," she said, and felt her throat tighten as she tried not to cry. Cry? For the love. What in the world was wrong with her? Clearly a single glass of wine was her new limit. She really was getting old. But that thought only made her have to blink more furiously.

"Remember that night when all those college kids joined the

party?" Kent laughed low at the thought, but his words jarred an unexpected memory loose in Liz's heart.

"I had forgotten all about that."

"Me too," Macy said. "I think I was too worried about the boys to properly enjoy myself."

Kent guffawed. "No need to worry about them. They were the troublemakers back then, not those sorority girls."

"That's exactly why I was worried."

It had been a rowdy night from the beginning. Maybe it was the fact that it was summer solstice, the longest day of the year. Maybe June had just been long and languid and slightly boring, and they were eager for something out of the ordinary to break the routine. Whatever the reason, when Liz had put up the flag at the end of their dock in her bikini that afternoon, there had been a boat full of unfamiliar coeds floating by. She had felt lovely, brave, and called the news across the water: "Everyone welcome!" Her invitation spread like wildfire around the lake.

"It was really more like a frat party than a Sanford affair," Kent said, but there was still a hint of a grin in his voice. It was a fond memory for him.

Not so much for Liz. She slipped out from under his heavy arm and bent to pick up a beer bottle that was lying in the grass. There were several other pieces of garbage close at hand and she gathered them up in her arms, irritated at the stink and the mess and the sudden understanding that nothing quite turned out the way a glossy *Better Homes and Gardens* spread promised it would.

"Here," Kent said. "Let me do that." He took the trash from her and wandered off in the direction of the nearest garbage can. Liz had placed them at the corners of the house, out of the way but still easily accessible. Clearly people didn't know how to throw things away. What was the world coming to?

"I didn't like that party either," Macy said, placing a hand on

Liz's back and giving her a familiar little rub between the shoulder blades. "Those kids were out of line."

They had danced on tabletops and played an elaborate game of long jump over the fire. Nobody got hurt, but they just as easily could have. Liz hadn't felt like a gracious hostess enjoying her own gathering, she'd felt like a babysitter who was woefully out of her depth as her charges became increasingly uncontrollable. When one of the girls did some sort of half-drunk striptease down to the string bikini she was wearing under a T-shirt and a pair of way-too-short cutoffs, Liz had had more than enough. But her proclamation that the party was over was met with indifference. They either didn't hear her or didn't care. So Liz went in search of Jack Sr. and the authority of his booming voice to back her up.

"We're too old for this," Liz said, waving away the awful memory with a flick of her slender wrist. She stepped away from Macy's touch and sighed. "I don't know what I was thinking."

"Don't be like that. It was a great party."

"Don't try to cheer me up."

"Come on, everyone had fun. You're just feeling let down now that it's over. It happens every time. You know that."

It was true, but it didn't make anything better. Liz's emotions were out of control, a train of roller-coaster cars that had jumped the tracks and were careening wildly. Up, down, inside, out. Arch, contrite, exuberant, desolate.

"Thank you," Liz said. "For everything. I think I will take care of this in the morning. Take Kent home. Get some sleep."

"We'll be over first thing," Macy told her. "Garbage bags in hand. Oh! And coffee. I'll swing over to Sandpoint and pick up a toffee latte for you."

"Perfect."

"Hang in there, kiddo." Macy caught Liz's hand and gave it a squeeze.

"Of course."

When Macy and Kent said their goodbyes, the remaining guests took the hint and began to comment on how late it was. Liz put on her consummate hostess face, complete with a charitable half smile, and accepted the hugs and warm wishes her friends and acquaintances had to offer. She deflected a dozen saccharine compliments that left her feeling coated in a thin layer of scum, and then she said, firmly: goodbye.

The yard was empty when she remembered the reason she had thrown the party in the first place. It came as a jolt, a reminder like a splash of ice water against her warm skin. *Quinn*. What had happened to Quinn? And Bennet? Liz had seen them talking. The shock on Quinn's face, the hug. Then they had disappeared.

Alone. There was really only one place for privacy on the expansive yard and it was the same place that made Liz's heart twist painfully when she thought of that out-of-control party so many years ago. When she had gone looking for Jack Sr., she had found him in the small garden beyond the rose arbor. It was a secluded corner of the yard, hemmed in by a willow tree and a smattering of forsythia bushes that glowed golden in the spring. Beyond the narrow arbor, Liz had painstakingly laid flagstone in a nautilus pattern, the dark gray stones swirling in closer and smaller until the final slab was just the size of her fist. She had positioned a pair of benches in the private heart of it all, white wrought iron that felt light and airy, whimsical.

Jack Sr. had been there, sharing a single bench with a girl who was not much older than their Nora. Twenty-one? Good God, Liz hoped so. Otherwise they were contributing alcohol to a minor. Otherwise her husband was leaning over a child, a look of wanton lust in his eyes. Was he going to kiss her? Had he already done so?

Maybe Liz imagined it all. The girl popped up at the sound of footsteps on the stone and teetered, giggling. "You have a great place here, Mrs. Stamford." Stamford? It could have been worse.

It could have been so much worse.

Liz hurried to the garden, heart thumping high and wild in her chest. What was she hoping for? She knew what she wanted when she set her plan in motion. When she spooned chicken salad with apples and walnuts onto tiny wheat crackers and stood on her A-frame ladder to hang Christmas lights in all the trees. But now. What had she done?

Voices. There were words slipping through the night air, catching on the thorns of the roses that covered the arbor. And yes, in the soft moonlight Liz could see Quinn and Bennet together, on the same white bench but at opposite ends, knees close to touching but not quite.

"Mom." Quinn stood up, but not quickly, not guiltily.

Bennet stood up, too. "Great party, Mrs. Sanford," he said, clearing his throat. "Thanks for inviting me."

"You're welcome," Liz managed. "You're welcome anytime." What else was there to say? She had tied up so many hopes and dreams in Bennet Van Eps. But now she was just confused. Tired and disillusioned and confused. But something had ignited in her heart, and it was growing, building even as she stood across from her daughter and the man she once loved. This wasn't about them.

"Has Quinn told you the news?" Liz asked, addressing Bennet.

Quinn looked shocked, almost panicked. "Mom, no—"

"I have a granddaughter." The words were final. Absolute. It felt so good to say them out loud. Liz felt herself standing taller, drawing resolve around her like a cloak. "And I think we may need your help."

THEY SAY HOME is where the heart is, but I've known for a long time that it's far more complicated than that. My heart doesn't have a home, but if it did, I suppose it would be 1726 Goldfinch Lane, Key Lake, Minnesota. My auntie Lorelei's house, to be exact. White clapboard siding, diamond-patterned linoleum floors, old windows with wavy glass and a rime of frost around the edges all winter long. We lived in the same farmhouse where she and my mom grew up all those years ago, but I never stopped to consider how that must have made her feel.

Trapped. I know that now.

I don't talk about my mom often, but I find myself thinking about her a lot these days. She was the younger of the two Barnes girls, but that didn't mean much in Key Lake. Their parents—my grandma and grandpa—weren't churchgoing people and kept mostly to themselves, which is to say, they didn't have a boat. They were godless and boatless, cardinal sins both. People couldn't understand why my grandpa didn't, at the very least, own a little aluminum-sided skiff for the odd expedition. He wasn't even interested in bullheads, and that's saying something, because on warm spring days after a long, cold winter they would all but leap into your boat, stinking of mud and wet rot. I think he hated their flat, ugly faces and their stinging whips of whiskers.

I know I sure did. And believe me, I went on my fair share of fishing dates that began with hauling bullheads out of the lake (easy pickings—I once caught one without a worm on my hook) and ended with my shoulder blades cold and aching on the damp boards of many a rusty boat. But don't feel sorry for me. I was a willing participant. More often than not, the instigator.

Auntie Lorelei used to tell me that I was the carbon copy of my mom.

I barely knew her. Okay, that's not true. I didn't know her at all. She skipped town when I was four and died not much later just outside a nightclub in Detroit. Why Detroit, I'll never know, but I can tell you with certainty that she had not overdosed or been hit by a car or anything equally exciting or dramatic. It was an undiagnosed heart condition, according to the autopsy report. One second she was blowing her boyfriend of the week a feathery kiss, and the next she was dead on the pavement. Simple as that.

Not so simple for Lorelei, who had just inherited her parents' poorly managed farm (they were aging fast and barely able to care for themselves, never mind a hundred acres of soybeans and corn) and was now the legal guardian of one Tiffany Marie Barnes, illegitimate child of her baby sister and four-year-old orphan. I was a gift by circumstance and luck (good or bad, I never puzzled that one out), for there was no will that declared me her charge. I had no father to speak of—my birth certificate remains firmly blank on that matter—and nowhere else to go.

Poor Lorelei.

And poor Mary Ellen. Mother. Mom. Mama. I wonder sometimes what I would have called her had she lived long enough for me to know her as something other than Mommy. Kids grow out of the sweet mommy stage so quickly, morphing overnight into titles that sound more adult. Don't be fooled—it's a sort of letting go, that moment when the near-perfect queen of the universe becomes a little more human, a little less divine. I know this from experience, too. When my baby made the switch, it was instant. One moment I was Mommy and she had cheeks like round, ripe peaches and a lisp that made me swoon. The next I was "Hey, Mom" and she was all skinny little girl with sharp elbows and corners to match. Don't get me wrong, I like straight-up, no frills *Mom*, but knowing myself the way I do, I'm sure I would have called Mary Ellen all sorts of terrible names along the way. Like I did with Lorelei. Like Everlee would have eventually done with me.

Lord knows there are a lot of things I have to ask forgiveness for. But I think the sin that might trump them all is making sure my girl will never have the chance to cuss me out like a sailor.

That's not true. Leaving her is my redemption.

I can't even think of it or I'll fall all to pieces, lose my resolve. Maybe drive the ten or so miles to Mrs. Sanford's house and beg her to let me in. Or to the A-frame at the north end of the lake—if Nora followed our plan, then my girl is there with Quinn. I never paid much attention to Nora's little sister, but in my memory she is a smudge of light and laughter. Always happy, ever sweet. Nora assures me that she'll hold Everlee close and read her stories. I was never very good at that—the reading stories bit. I guess there are a lot of things I'm not very good at.

Like loving the people I've been given. My auntie died alone. Alone and hurting and scared, though the nurse who I called at Pine Hills every Saturday night told me that she passed peacefully.

I know enough to call bullshit when I hear it.

Maybe that's why I came here one last time. To make amends? To say goodbye? But I'm not nearly as dense as all that. I wanted to be close to my girl for just one more day. I wanted to be *home*.

I can't say that I loved Key Lake, but for a couple of years when Nora and I were teenagers I thought that my life could be something good. We were bold and beautiful, wild and free. Nora didn't know how lucky she was to have a family intact, even if it wasn't exactly what she wanted. She had big dreams and the means to make them come true. All those things Nora told me? I believed them.

The farmhouse is being rented by a couple with four kids. I know this because their little bikes are lined up in front of the attached garage. Two sparkly pink and purple ones with banana seats, and two in a bigger, more masculine design. Two girls, two boys. One dog who didn't even bother to stand up and bark when I drove past. I wish I could see the house, wander through the rooms like a ghost, but I know that's not an option. So I settle for the cabin, the four-room bungalow where my grandma and grandpa spent their final years.

Hair dye and scissors, I'm doing it again. But this time the face in the mirror is mine and even I don't recognize who I've become. Blond, wispy fringes. A messy Meg Ryan do circa *You've Got Mail*. It matches the wig I wore for the photos, more or less. A passing glance at my new driver's license will cement the truth: I'm not Tiffany Barnes anymore.

It's dramatic, all of it. Like something out of a movie or one of those fat paperback novels my auntie used to love. Real life doesn't turn out like this—with families scattered, loved ones abandoned at funeral parlors, kids scared and alone. No, not scared and alone. Everlee is far from alone.

*I* will be alone. But I don't have a choice in this, and before you think I'm making much ado about nothing, let me tell you what I know.

I know that he's a predator.

Of course, I didn't know this in the beginning or I never would have stayed. In fact, we had a happy season together—or as happy as you can be when you're juggling dead-end jobs and fighting the easy pull of bad habits. Not that we fought very hard. Life was good enough that when he suggested we make it official I actually felt like a blushing bride-to-be. No ring to speak of, but he was working on it. And even more than that? He wanted to adopt my girl. Make her his own.

We started the paperwork right away because I have a hole in my heart that's exactly the size of the blank line on my birth certificate where my daddy's name is supposed to be. And Everlee? She has the same gaping hole. Not because I don't know who her father is, but because I won't tell. I can't decide which is worse.

But Donovan? He loved her. He loved her so much that one

day when I was working at the window factory he took her on his lap and put his hand under her My Little Pony T-shirt. And up her flouncy little jean skirt with the three tiers of ruffles.

When I walked into the living room he moved quick. Nothing going on here, nothing at all . . . And because I was reeling and didn't know if I could fully trust what I had witnessed, I pretended that I hadn't seen a thing. But the next day I burned that T-shirt and the skirt in the barrel behind the farmhouse. And then I called the cops from the pay phone in the parking lot of the Hy-Vee grocery store and gave them an anonymous tip about the meth they would find in his trunk.

Once, I found the title to a car in Donovan's underwear drawer when I was putting away laundry. It wasn't in his name, but the initials were the same so I remembered it: Derick Robertson. Nora helped me look him up on her laptop and what we found is this: Derick Robertson was charged with the possession of child pornography and the abuse of an undisclosed minor less than one year before he waltzed into my life. The charges didn't stick. Well, the abuse one didn't.

But I could testify in a courtroom that he was guilty as hell and just as slippery. Thing is, I'm not a credible witness. And I don't want the world's so-called justice anyway. I just want my girl safe. The plan was always that we would leave together—we thought it would be easy when Donovan was sent to jail.

They let him off.

Sometimes I think I should just kill him. I could. I hate him enough. But whenever my vision goes black and I burn with loathing so thick and animal it scares me, I pull myself back to Everlee. Her smile. The way she bites her lip when she's concentrating. The sound of her bare feet slapping, always running, across the narrow boards of our wood-plank floor. Can you imagine? Everlee Barnes, the murderer's daughter. She doesn't deserve that.

And I don't deserve her.

# Day Four

## Saturday

# QUINN

BENNET DIDN'T REALLY have to drive Quinn home because she was sober as a kitten. In fact, she hadn't had a single sip of alcohol all night. The pinot grigio she'd contemplated guzzling was forgotten the second she turned and found her former fiancé standing before her. But she let herself be led to his car anyway (a black Land Cruiser, he'd always wanted one) and climbed in without protest when he held open the passenger door for her.

Quinn felt weak and feverish, as if her body were fighting an infection. Being with Bennet was so strange, so painful Quinn could hardly bear the ache. It was foreign and familiar, bitter and sweet. Her mouth stung with the taste of metal and lemons, acid and burnt sugar. The second she laid eyes on him she realized the truth: she loved him still, and always had.

Or maybe she just loved what might have been.

Bennet swung into the driver's seat and asked, without looking at her, "You're living at the château, right?"

Quinn cringed a little at the nickname she and Bennet had given the cabin she and Walker now called home. She stole a glance at her former fiancé in profile and wondered if he remembered that they had once dreamed of living there. Of course he did. When her dad bought the dilapidated A-frame and her mother began restoring it, they snuck into the construction zone one night and made love in the loft. Daydreamed out loud about how they would decorate the rooms and the number of children who would fill them. Three, at least. Maybe four. They both wanted a big family.

"Yeah," she said quietly. "How did you know that?"

"Your mom told me. And"—he paused, seemingly hesitant to say her name—"Lucy is staying with you?"

"Yes." It was barely a whisper.

Bennet knew about Lucy. Quinn still hadn't decided whether she was horrified by this or relieved. If they needed help, Bennet could very well be the person to provide it. But what if the police were exactly who Nora was hiding from?

Quinn was just as perplexed by her mother's motives. It wasn't like Liz to call things out, to invite scrutiny. She wanted Bennet involved for some reason, but Quinn had yet to puzzle out why. It was enough to give her a migraine.

"Want to tell me what's really going on?"

"I don't know." It was the truth. Liz had summed up pretty much everything that Quinn knew. Nora had dumped Lucy in Key Lake without so much as a hint about why or where she came from or what she needed protection from. "Nora didn't tell me anything."

Bennet stopped at an intersection for three full seconds and looked both ways before continuing on. So straightlaced, even past midnight. Even on empty country roads where the only light was cast by the moon and the glow of his own headlights. "I'm going to have to check the missing and exploited children's database," Bennet told her quietly.

"Bennet, please—"

"If Lucy is in danger, and if you don't know who she really is, I don't have a choice."

"She's my niece," Quinn said with more conviction than she felt.

"Did Nora tell you that?"

Her silence was answer enough.

"I'm going to need to talk to her. Nora, I mean."

"Good luck," Quinn muttered, turning her head to look out the window. A part of her wanted to lay her cheek against the glass and cry. And another part wanted to bridge the gap between them and make Bennet remember that they had been more than this once. More than strangers.

How many times had she sat like this, beside Bennet as he navigated the same dark roads they now drove? She used to reach across the console and take his hand, trace patterns in his palm like a love story in a sign language all their own. In some ways, it would feel natural to do so now. Her heart cartwheeled at the thought, but instead of thrilling her, Quinn felt nauseous.

"You shouldn't get involved," Quinn said. "Please, just forget that my mother said anything at all."

"And if something happens?" Bennet slid her a sideways glance. "That's on my head, Quinn. If I knew about Lucy and didn't look into the situation, I could lose my badge."

Was he punishing her? Quinn couldn't tell. She knew she deserved it. If the roles were reversed, Quinn would want her pound of flesh. Recompense for the way they had been torn apart. Who wouldn't? In some ways it felt like a lifetime ago that they had stopped on the sidewalk in front of Betty's Cakes, but in others it was only yesterday. The wound was fresh, seeping.

"I can't do this," she had said. She was standing in the shadow of a sweeping lilac bush in late May, the fragrant purple blooms just a little fetid and a week or so past their prime.

"Forget your mom," Bennet said, lacing his fingers through hers and giving her forehead a chaste kiss. "If you want chocolate cake, let's have chocolate cake. So what if white is traditional?"

But Quinn wasn't talking about the cake. She was breathing quick and shallow, her lungs pinched tight as she struggled beneath the wave of panic that threatened to consume her. It was all too much, too fast, and their whirlwind engagement (less than three months from proposal to wedding day so they could take advantage of married student housing in the fall) had left her dizzy and heartsick.

"I don't care about the cake," she choked.

Quinn could see in the way his heart shattered before her eyes that Bennet knew exactly what she meant.

It wasn't supposed to be forever. Just a little break while Quinn set herself in order. But then she found the acceptance letter from Biola when she was cleaning out her backpack, and suddenly the option she had already discarded seemed her only saving grace. She was gone.

For all Quinn knew, the simple solitaire with a diamond the size of a grain of rice was still in the top drawer of the bedside stand in her childhood room. Bennet had refused to take it back. She could hardly stand to think of it.

"I still can't believe you're a cop," Quinn said, just to fill the silence. The stillness felt thick and threatening, but what was she trying to do? Distract him? Flatter him? Quinn didn't even know her own mind. She just felt the need to talk, to keep talking. They had wasted an hour, two, at her mother's party by carefully reminiscing, laughing modestly about old friends and reliving the sort of safe stories that would keep them balanced on a tightrope where they were suspended above reality. It was a diversion. But now the night felt urgent.

Bennet shrugged.

"Do you like it?"

A grunt. "I guess. Everly is a much bigger town than Key Lake, so there's always something going on. I don't spend my day writing traffic tickets, that's for sure."

Quinn was quiet for a moment, trying to imagine what sort of savagery he faced. Drugs? Domestic abuse? Murder? In their little corner of Minnesota? She decided she didn't really want to know. "Do they still have the grad dance?"

"Of course." Bennet smiled, but it was tight and unamused. "This year may have been the last. Too many minors drinking."

"We were minors drinking at the Everly dance."

"That was different. I swear, teenagers get younger every year."

Quinn hummed her assent.

"There was a fight this year. Someone was thrown off the bridge."

"You're kidding."

"He landed in the shallows. Nothing more serious than a broken leg, but we were never able to prove that he was helped over the edge. A half-dozen boys swore he was drunk and tripped. We're pretty sure they tripped him—the railings are four feet high—but what can you do?"

"He's not talking?"

"Would you?"

Quinn glanced out the window. She could picture it: the end of the year grad dance on the old bridge to Everly. Or the bridge to Key Lake, depending on where you lived. It was the only time the two rival high schools came together for a reason other than competition. Though there was plenty of preening and posturing, petty jealousies, and girlfriend stealing that transcended the festivities.

"No," she finally said. "I wouldn't say a word."

"Me either."

Because the trestle bridge was on a gravel road, the county police closed it off for one night in early June and let a DJ set up speakers on the wooden deck between the first and second beams. It was a BYOB affair, but of course, beer was prohibited. So there were two-liters of Coke and Mountain Dew, boxes of pizza on the open tailgates of the trucks that backed onto the entrance of the bridge. Half the bottles of Pepsi were filled with rum. Vodka mixed well with Sprite. And a few kids could be relied upon to smoke up in the trees along the sandy beach between the trestles. The woods around the little tributary of the Cottonwood River were thick and mysterious, perfect for secrets and things people would rather keep hidden.

"It used to be the cops would cruise around once or twice but mostly leave everyone alone."

"That's not the case anymore," Bennet told her. "It's just too dangerous. We're all afraid that someone is going to get really hurt."

What did her mother say? The more things change, the more they stay the same? Quinn was quite sure that many people had already gotten hurt on the Everly bridge—just maybe not in the way that Bennet and his cop friends expected.

"Quinn?"

Something about Bennet's voice was off and Quinn pulled her attention from the stars so she could study him, a wisp of anxiety rising in her like smoke.

"What's going on?"

She followed the path of his finger through the windshield to the black edge of the horizon beyond. At some point he had turned down her road, the gravel ribbon that wound around the farthest curve of the lake. Quinn knew the serrated edge of the landscape around her, the familiar trees, rolling hills, and sleepy homes that looked two-dimensional, cut from black cloth against the backdrop of the equally dark night. But instead of peaceful shadows, the silhouettes were alive and writhing, dancing against a curtain of orange.

Quinn couldn't make sense of what she was seeing and she leaned forward, clutching the dashboard in her sweaty palms. But even as she wondered at the spectacle before her, it became suddenly, terrifyingly clear. Something was *burning*.

"Oh my God!" Quinn fumbled for the door handle, Walker's name on her lips.

*Lucy.*

But Bennet was quicker, and stronger. "Quinn, no!" He snagged her by the arm and hauled her back, bruising the skin with a grip that brooked no argument. "Shut the door!"

She obeyed, but just long enough for him to drive the final stretch past the boathouse and the A-frame, which, *thank God*, was not on fire. When Bennet pulled to the side of the road just past her home, Quinn yanked her arm out of his hand and threw open the door while the car was still coming to a stop. She ran up the same short hill where she and Lucy had picnicked, tripping and stumbling through the tall grass, and stood at the top of the rise, panting.

The little abandoned shack was aflame, each board cast into bright relief as a roaring fire blazed through the dry wood. The heat singed her face and Quinn had to shield it from the lick of the scalding air. As she watched, a beam gave way and the fire soared even higher. It was vicious, hungry, lapping up the night sky in greedy, violent mouthfuls that made Quinn fear for the field, the cabin, the boathouse, and beyond.

"Are you insane?" Bennet's voice in her ear was accompanied by his arms around her waist. He hauled her unceremoniously away from the spectacle, down the hill a ways where they could still see the flames but were no longer scorched by the heat.

Quinn spun on him. "What is this?" she sputtered. "What happened here? Cabins don't just spontaneously combust!"

"The fire department is on their way," Bennet said. He emanated a cool, professional calm that only made Quinn feel more crazy. "They'll put it out. The shack was abandoned, right? Everything is going to be okay."

"What if . . . ?" But before Quinn could articulate all her fears, a shape emerged out of the darkness from the direction of the A-frame.

"Quinn?"

"Walker!" She rushed at him, uncertain until the last second whether she was going to throw her arms around him or beat his chest. In the end, he caught her up.

"Are you okay?"

"I'm fine." Quinn wiggled out of his embrace and searched his face. "Lucy?"

"Asleep in her room. I had no idea this was going on until I went to close the bedroom window a couple minutes ago."

"What happened?"

"I don't know." Walker ran one of his hands up and down her arm. Quinn didn't realize until she looked down that his other hand was locked tight around the handle of the baseball bat. "It's probably nothing, Q. Just a fluke thing."

But they both knew that wasn't true.

"The fire department is on their way," Quinn said, motioning toward the spot where Bennet stood talking into his phone and openly examining the two of them. "That's Bennet. He's a cop." She ignored the question in Walker's eyes. "I'm going to check on Lucy."

"Not without me." He gave the bat a little swing as if testing its weight, and then laced his fingers in hers.

The house was just down the hill, but Quinn couldn't shake the feeling that they shouldn't have left Lucy alone for even a few short minutes. She found herself racing, clinging to Walker's hand for purchase as they hurried toward the open front door.

The cabin was dark. Quiet. Almost hysterical, Quinn ran across the floor and wrenched open the utensil drawer to dig around for the ice pick. Then she raced over to Lucy's door and popped the skinny metal rod into the hole in the door handle. She wiggled the ice pick until she heard and felt a tiny click.

Deep breath. Lights off. Quinn squinted, waiting for her eyes to adjust to the dark and hoping with every fiber of her being that Lucy would be safe and sound. Asleep. She was, and when Quinn saw the little comma of Lucy's body curled beneath the blankets, all the air went out of her in a rush. A tear slipped down her cheek and she pressed her knuckles to her mouth. Walker squeezed her shoulder and backed away so that he wasn't framed in the doorway with a bat in his hand.

"The doors are all locked," he whispered. "If there's a cop on the hill and the fire department is in transit, I can't imagine that anyone would dare to try anything."

"Go," she told him. "Go figure out what's going on."

"I won't let the front door out of my sight." Walker picked his phone out of his pocket and made sure the volume was turned all the way up. "Call me if you need anything at all."

She nodded.

Walker brushed the back of his hand against her cheek, wavering, but Quinn gave him a little push. He turned and disappeared down the hallway, shutting the door carefully behind him. A second later Quinn could hear the key in the lock, sliding the dead bolt home. She couldn't decide if it made her feel safe or terribly alone.

Quinn would have closed Lucy's bedroom door and spent the night with her back against it, but as soon as Walker was gone, Lucy stirred in her bed and turned over.

"Quinn?" Her voice was small in the shadowy room. Tremulous. It was the first time Lucy had called her by name.

"Yes?" Quinn sniffed and ran a hand beneath her nose. She took a small step forward.

"Nothing."

"Are you sure, honey?" Quinn struggled to make her voice sound normal, comforting. She cleared her throat and tried again. "Do you need a drink of water? The bathroom?"

Lucy was quiet for so long that Quinn thought maybe she had been asleep the whole time. Sleep talking. Quinn herself had been an epic sleepwalker back in the day. She'd once unlocked the front door and taken off down the driveway before her mother caught up with her. Quinn was about to back out of the room, but as she edged toward the door Lucy pushed herself up on her elbows. She said, "Would you lay with me for a while?"

"Of course," Quinn whispered, her voice breaking.

Lucy pushed back the covers and slid over to make room in the queen-sized bed. If she cared that Quinn was still in her party dress, that she smelled like smoke, she didn't let on. Instead, she blinked in the darkness as Quinn crossed the room and climbed in beside her. Then she rolled onto her side and pressed her back into Quinn, yawning as she settled her cheek into the pillow.

Clearly, blessedly, Lucy knew nothing of what was going on outside, the fire and the fear, the huge trucks that would come racing down the gravel road. Quinn could already see the flicker of their lights between the blinds and was grateful that the fire department had a policy of not using the sirens in the dead of night. Grateful that Lucy was beside her, already more than half-asleep.

"Good night," Lucy whispered.

It was so natural, so sweet. In the midst of the madness that roiled outside, Quinn automatically put her arm around the little girl and tucked her in close. She was bone and muscle, sinew and air. But her skin was creamy soft and warm, and Quinn traced circles on the back of her hand that held the stuffed red fox. Lucy's breathing was deep and steady in no time, but Quinn kept rubbing, smoothing her curls away from her face and running her palm along the curved line of Lucy's spine.

Quinn fell asleep like that, one arm snug around Lucy as her silent tears dampened the pillow they shared.

# NORA

"SHE MUST HAVE USED the hand pump in the yard." Nora plucked the box of hair dye out of the dry sink and held it between her fingers as if it were something filthy. Vile.

"If the water and electricity are turned off, why would the yard pump work?" Ethan swept the beam of his iPhone flashlight app around the tiny bathroom, illuminating the gossamer strands of broken cobwebs and highlighting the years of dust that had settled on every flat surface. Mirror frame, bathtub ledge, shelf. Nothing had escaped the thick, gray film except the sink where Tiffany had obviously changed her appearance. Dramatically. Beneath the cardboard box, the bowl was filled with long dark hair.

"Because it draws from a cistern. We used it when we were kids to put out bonfires. Lorelei used to hang a five-gallon bucket from the handle. It might still be there."

"Nobody cared that you had bonfires out here? This place is a tinderbox."

"Obviously we didn't have fires in the house." Nora rolled her eyes, but Ethan's back was turned to her.

"Still."

"It probably bothered Lorelei. But it wasn't like she could stop us. Besides, out of sight, out of mind. There's half a mile and an old oak grove between the farmhouse and this shack."

Ethan spun toward her and smiled. In the slanting, shadowy light he looked slightly maniacal. "You're such a badass."

"Were," Nora corrected. She tossed the empty box of dye back into the sink and left the bathroom. "I'm straight as a pin these days."

"Oh, I don't know." Ethan followed close behind, illuminating her path as she led him back to the abandoned living room. It was just as tiny as the rest of the house, with barely enough space for a sagging couch and a plaid La-Z-Boy. "This whole situation is a little off the grid."

"What's that supposed to mean?"

Nora had stopped abruptly, and Ethan walked right into her. "Sorry," he said, catching her about the shoulders. But Nora didn't want to be touched. She pulled away. "I didn't mean anything by that," Ethan said, holding up his hands. The light from his phone glowed white on the water-stained ceiling.

"No, you did mean something by that."

"I'm sorry." Ethan searched her face, his gaze earnest. "Bad joke. Nerves. I don't know. I've never done anything like this before."

"Neither have I."

But that wasn't entirely true. Hadn't the last several years of her life been one giant lie? A game of hide-and-seek—except the people who were supposed to be seeking her never came. Until now. And Donovan was the last person she wanted on her trail.

"I don't understand," Ethan said slowly. Carefully. "Why can't we go to the cops for help?"

Nora brushed past him and sat down on the couch with a sigh. A cloud of dust puffed up around her and she sneezed. Twice in quick succession. "Because they'd take Everlee away. Tiffany is not exactly the mother of the year now, is she?"

"But—"

"No buts. We can't lose her."

"You've lost her now."

"She's *safe* now," Nora said, rubbing her nose with the back of her hand.

"With Quinn?" Ethan put his phone on the table between them, then sat down in the La-Z-Boy. Another explosion of dust. They both sneezed. "That's not a permanent fix, Nora, and you know it."

Did she ever. "That's why we're going to find Tiffany."

"What about Everlee's birth father?"

Nora froze. Breathing shallowly, she attempted a joke. "She was immaculately conceived." It came out brittle.

"Tiffany never struck me as virginal."

"He's not in the picture, okay?"

"Why not?" Ethan pressed. "Seems to me we could use this information against Donovan."

"It's complicated. Look, you don't understand. It's been over six years. We worked so hard to keep Tiffany and Everlee together that—"

"He doesn't know, does he?" There was no judgment in the question, just a calm statement of the truth, but Nora's blood fizzed just the same. She shivered.

"If I have my way, he'll never know."

"Why not?"

"He doesn't deserve her. He never did."

Ethan didn't ask any more questions after that. He sat on the edge of the rocking chair, elbows on his knees, and stared at Nora across the dim room. She couldn't see his eyes.

"Sometimes you have to take matters into your own hands," Nora said quietly, as if in explanation. She felt the need to make him understand that whatever they had done was for love. "Tiffany and Everlee are supposed to be together—and far, far away from here."

"But Tiffany took off. Without Everlee."

"We're going to fix that."

He didn't say anything, but Nora could almost hear the questions swirling in the air between them.

"There are a couple of motels in Key Lake," Nora said, changing the subject. Her tone carried a note of finality, but it was diminished when she broke into a wide yawn.

"I thought we were roughing it."

"This is definitely roughing it. The house is dingier than I remember," Nora admitted. "Tiff and I used to keep the place in decent shape. We shook out the cushions in the spring and swept the floors . . . We spent the night in the summertime when we could open the windows to catch a breeze."

"This place is a museum, Nora." Ethan looked around, taking in the velvet print above the couch and the crocheted doily on the end table.

"When Tiff's grandparents moved out, they only took a few things with them. They were . . ." She fumbled. "*Unique* people. Kept mostly to themselves, didn't much care for the stuff most people get all caught up in."

"I can tell." Ethan leaned over and tapped the face of his phone. "It's one thirty," he said. "Are we going to stick around and see if Tiffany comes back?"

"She won't."

"But Donovan?"

Nora glanced around and felt the skin prickle at the back of her neck. She felt like someone was watching her, just outside the room, and she wrapped her arms around herself to ward off the sudden chill. "He's already been here."

"What?" Everything in Ethan tensed. He perched on the edge of his seat, vigilant. "How do you know?"

Nora pointed to the front door, clearly visible from the tiny living room where they sat. It was hanging open a couple of inches, the bolt still protruding from the casement. "I have the key," she said, holding up the set that she had taken from the piece of loose siding next to the tiny front porch. She hadn't needed it because the lock had already been popped, forced open by a blunt instrument that hacked away at the soft, moldy wood. Tiffany would have used the key.

"Why didn't you say something?"

Nora shrugged. "You were walking around the perimeter of the house when I let myself in. It didn't seem relevant until now."

"Relevant?" Ethan was visibly upset. "It didn't seem relevant to share that someone had already broken in? You're insane, Nora."

"I just know Donovan. It's not like he's going to walk in here and kill us both with a chain saw." But her words, so blithely spoken, made her stomach somersault. What did she know about Donovan Richter? How could she claim what he was and was not capable of? She said, with more conviction than she felt: "If he was here and she was gone, there's no reason for him to come back."

Ethan looked skeptical, but he asked: "Can you sleep? Here?"

Nora folded her arms behind her head and closed her eyes. "Can you?"

"I can sleep anywhere."

"Me too," Nora said. But that was a dirty lie.

"And tomorrow?"

"We find Tiffany."

But Nora wasn't sure what they were going to do. And she doubted she'd be able to sleep, but Ethan tactfully pretended not to notice her distress. He pushed himself out of the chair and cracked open the double-hung window on the wall behind him. Then he grabbed a straight-backed chair from the kitchen table and shut the front door as firmly as he could, securing the chair beneath the wrecked handle. As if that would save them.

"Thank you," Nora said softly.

Ethan just eased back into the La-Z-Boy with an elaborate sigh. Yanking up the footrest, he crossed his arms over his chest. "Good night, Nora."

"Night."

Within minutes, he was snoring lightly. Or pretending to.

There wasn't really a breeze, but the cool night air ghosted into the room and raised goose bumps on Nora's arms all the same. She felt clammy and restless, haunted by memories of this place and the friendship that had taken her so far from herself. Tiffany was more than a friend to her, more than a sister even. They shared a secret, and in some ways a little girl.

It seemed everyone wanted to stake their claim on Everlee.

.  .  .

Nora thought she wouldn't sleep, but when Ethan touched her shoulder she bolted upright and realized that the sun was streaming through the windows of the old Barnes house.

"Good morning," he said with a smile. "I hate to wake you, but I was afraid you were about to fall off the couch."

The cushions had slipped sideways in the night and Nora was indeed teetering on the edge. She must have had a rough night. She hoped that she didn't call out in her sleep or do something equally embarrassing.

"Hi," she said, running her hands through her short hair. No doubt she was a walking disaster. Mussed and wrinkled, bleary-eyed and in desperate need of a shower, a toothbrush, a fresh start. At least Donovan hadn't come back to the house. But, then again, neither had Tiffany. "Have you been up long?"

"Nah. Fifteen minutes or so. I grabbed my bag and cleaned up by the pump outside." Ethan smiled crookedly at her and Nora realized that he looked exhausted. He clearly hadn't slept a wink all night long. But his teeth were white and he smelled of peppermint and soap. Irish Spring, if her nose could be trusted.

"I'm a wreck," she said, standing up. She was a little unsteady, but Ethan didn't reach to right her. Instead, he handed over her backpack.

"Take your time," he said.

The water was icy, but the morning was already warm. Nora scrubbed her teeth first, brushing away the film of the night and the fear that had turned her tongue sour. Then she began to wash her face, but, thinking better of it, dunked her whole head under the stream of well water. Short hair, don't care. She finger-picked it out and shook her head. It would settle into a tousled, beachy style that would fit in perfectly in Key Lake. Not that it mattered.

While Nora changed her clothes in the bedroom, Ethan straightened out the house and erased the signs of Tiffany's presence. Donovan had already seen the evidence (or maybe he had witnessed the transformation?), but it seemed imperative that they destroy any trace of what Tiffany had done. Her hair and the box of dye went into an old grocery bag that Ethan stuck in the trunk of his car. Then they tried to lock the damaged front door of the shack and replaced the key in the hiding spot.

"Where to?" Ethan said, rubbing a hand over his face.

"Why are you doing this?" Nora asked suddenly. She was surprised by her own boldness but compelled by the guilt that she felt. It hurt to see Ethan like this. To know that she was the one who had etched lines across his usually smooth, carefree forehead. "Seriously. I don't know why you're here."

But rather than trying to defend himself, to offer up some trite, made-for-the-movies answer, Ethan just gave her a small smile. Something about him softened. Fell away. For just a moment he looked younger than he was. And scared, too. "You need me," he said simply.

It was true. It was so true Nora didn't know what to say. She swallowed hard. "You need to eat," she finally offered. "Cinnamon rolls? Coffee?"

"Sure."

"I'd like everything to-go. I don't really want to bump into anyone I know today."

"Small-town life, huh?"

"Something like that."

"I'll pop in. You can wait in the car. Just give me directions."

The clock in Ethan's car read 8:07. Nora was sure the people she wanted to talk to would be up by now, but it was Saturday morning. Estes Law Offices would be closed for the day, but that didn't mean she couldn't look up Roger Estes's number in the white pages and knock on his front door. Thankfully Pine Hills was always open. They could start there.

Ethan picked up a pair of giant cinnamon rolls and two cups of coffee in paper cups from Luverne's, then followed Nora's instructions to one of the lesser-known beaches along the south side of Key Lake. Redrock Bay, with its long expanse of sifted sand, was a favorite among locals and vacationers, and there was the Key Lake public beach along the west side that attracted families with younger kids because of the playground equipment, shallow waters, and gradual drop-off. But Pocket Beach was exactly that: a little pocket of land hidden by weeping birches. The beach itself was shaped like a diamond and too stony to make sunbathing an option. They would be alone, Nora felt sure of that.

She was right. The slip of rocky sand was deserted. A stiff summer wind stirred up chop on the water that spread out blue and foamy from the small headland. There were boulders along the south edge of the secluded beach, and Nora headed there, coffee in one hand as she shielded her eyes from the glare of the morning sun with the other.

"Key Lake's best-kept secret," she told Ethan as she settled cross-legged on one of the wide rocks. "Nobody ever comes here."

Nora expected him to at least try to chatter back and pepper her with questions or comment on the unexpected beauty of the alcove in the trees. His personality mandated it. But when Nora turned to face him, she found that Ethan was holding something out for her—and it wasn't the bag of cinnamon rolls.

"I found this on the bulletin board at Luverne's."

"What is it?" she asked without reaching for it.

"Just take it." Ethan took a step forward, the set of his jaw uncharacteristically grave, and pushed the paper toward her. Nora had no choice but to accept it.

How could a sheet of white printer paper be ominous? Even terrifying? But as Nora unfolded the page her heart shuddered and stopped, if only for a moment.

It was a picture of Everlee.

The photo had been snapped a year or so ago, her head tilted to the side, her eyes wide and reflecting twin points of light. She was smiling, but it was a closemouthed, hesitant smile, as if someone had instructed her to do so and she'd obeyed. Good girl.

Nora had never seen the picture before.

And she was so intent on studying the curve of her cheek, the way Everlee's long blond hair fell past her shoulders and beyond the frame of the photo, that she almost missed the text beneath the portrait.

*Missing Child*
*If you have any information, please call the number below.*

# LIZ

BY THE TIME KENT AND MACY wandered over, Liz was nearly done cleaning up the evidence of her party. She woke at dawn, weary and confused but certain that she had been wrong about some things. Okay, a lot of things. Obviously, the hangover that never materialized, but about bigger matters, too. More significant ones.

The party had been her attempt to ease the symptoms of a disease that Liz was starting to believe she could cure. Why pop a Tylenol if she had access to the antidote? Even if it was a tough pill to swallow. But things had spiraled out of control and she had been left raw and aching, convinced of her own complicity in sins of the past. Sins of omission—ones she once hoped she would never have to atone for.

Now what? At the very least she had set the ball rolling. Bennet Van Eps knew that she had a granddaughter. A granddaughter who was shrouded in mystery and secreted away like something filthy, obscene. It made Liz sick to her stomach. But, damn it, something would *happen*. Liz had spent too much time letting other people chart the course of her life to settle for the back seat now.

"I think I have a God complex," Liz said when Macy handed her a to-go cup with a stamped Sandpoint sleeve. She sipped it immediately. Still piping hot, just the way she liked it. But she wasn't comforted. Liz was convinced she didn't deserve even the littlest of pleasures.

Kent laughed, oblivious to her mood. "You're just figuring this out?"

"Don't be mean." Macy smacked his bottom good-naturedly.

"I'm serious." Liz took another sip of her toffee latte and fixed Kent with a grave look.

"Me too."

Macy swung at him again, but he twisted away from her and grabbed a full garbage bag in each hand. "I think I'll leave you ladies to it," he said. "Looks like Liz has this thing in the bag."

Kent laughed at his own bad pun all the way around the side of the house and until he was out of earshot. Liz had no doubt that he would continue to cackle over his quick-wittedness for the rest of the day. How exasperating. For once, she didn't envy Macy and her whole, hale husband.

No, Liz poked at that idea, worrying it like a loose tooth. She had *never* envied Macy and her living, breathing spouse. Not even in the immediate aftermath of losing Jack Sr. Being alone wasn't so bad; she rather liked the independence. In fact, saying goodbye to her husband had been a *relief*.

But what a terrible thing to think! Liz would have gasped, but there was hot coffee in her mouth and she ended up swallowing it too fast. It burned all the way down and she coughed and sputtered, her eyes watering.

"You okay?" Macy thumped her friend on the back, then took her by the elbow and led her to the low brick wall that flanked one edge of the patio. "Sit down, I don't think you're quite yourself."

"I'm a monster," Liz managed when she had caught her breath. Her throat stung and she had to dab at the wetness that had gathered in the corners of her eyes.

"That's ridiculous! You're perfectly lovely, Liz. In every way."

"You have to say that. You're my best friend."

"I am?"

"Of course you are. See? How could you not know you're my best friend?"

"Well, it's just—"

"Clearly I'm a terrible person." Liz didn't realize she was fling-ing the cup around until a little splatter of camel-colored coffee ex-ploded on Macy's white blouse like an act of violence. "Now look at what I've done!"

Macy ignored the stain, wresting the cup from Liz's grip and placing it carefully on the ground behind her. "What in the world has gotten into you?" she asked, taking Liz by the arms. "Pull your-self together!"

But Liz found she didn't much want to pull herself together. She felt off, to be sure, but it wasn't as bad as she imagined it would be. It was actually rather freeing. A bit intoxicating. She felt the need to con-fess, to unburden herself of some of the many ways in which she tried to play God. The ways she had covered up and pretended and down-right lied. "I watch people through Jack's old telescope," she blurted.

"Is that what you're upset about?" Macy pursed her lips, mak-ing her laugh lines deepen. "That's hardly a secret. Everyone knows what Jack really bought it for. And your windows aren't as opaque as you think they are."

Well, that wasn't nearly as satisfying as Liz had hoped it would be. She tried again. "One of the reasons I threw the party last night was because I hoped that Quinn and Bennet would reconnect. I thought that maybe . . ." She couldn't finish. Apparently she had al-ready exceeded the limits of her newfound boldness.

But Macy wasn't fazed by this either. She pulled Liz's hands into her lap and patted them soothingly. "Bennet is a good boy and it broke your heart when Quinn left him. Those kids don't stop to think about how much we come to love their circle of friends. Ben-net was like a son to you. For years."

Liz blinked. "He was."

"I know he was, honey. And then he was just gone. It was prac-tically like a death in the family."

"It *was*." Liz's eyes filled with tears and she didn't even bother to whisk them away. They hovered, heavy and indulgent against her lower lashes. Thank goodness her mascara was smudge proof and waterproof.

"And then Quinn took off to California and came home with a new husband . . ." Macy tsked, shaking her head. "A stranger."

"Walker *was* a stranger!"

"How were you supposed to feel?"

"Betrayed," Liz confided. "I thought of all my kids Quinn would stay in Key Lake and marry someone local and get regular manicures with me at Halo."

"I know." Macy nodded. "But he's very handsome, isn't he?" She tipped her head and looked away, a thoughtful expression settling over her features.

Liz could almost see the wheels spinning in Macy's head, and it suddenly made her feel defensive. Almost possessive. She felt her emotions spin on a dime. "*Very* handsome," Liz confirmed, sniffing away her tears. "He's an artist, you know."

Where had that come from? Jack didn't like artists. He said they were freeloaders and hacks; that a five-year-old with finger paints could do a better job than most of the famous prints that hung in the Art Institute of Chicago. They had gone at her insistence during a long-ago family vacation and stayed for less than an hour. His sneer had come as she had studied one of Van Gogh's bedroom paintings. Blue walls, red bedspread, hat hung askance on a hook. The windows were cracked open and the sun was shining. For one sparkling moment Liz could imagine herself sweeping the shawl that hung near the door over her shoulders and stepping out into a world all green and gold. It seemed both a fairy tale and a distinct possibility. She could *live* in that painting.

"Let's go," Jack Sr. had said. And though they had barely scraped the surface of the treasure that was the Institute, they went.

"I love art," Liz said, more to herself than to Macy. "I *love* it."

"Good for you," Macy said, still stroking Liz's hands like a lap dog.

Liz pulled away and sat up straighter. Jack Sanford had not been a good man. True, he was steady and levelheaded and hardworking. He had made a way for himself in a world that favored the lucky, the people who were born with privilege and a place at the table. Jack Sr. had none of those things. But he took a small farmer's inheritance and made something of it, built a legacy for his wife and kids and fought for it every day of his life. If he argued the validity of a bootstraps philosophy, it was only because he pulled himself up by them. A success story.

But for all his vim and vigor (piss and vinegar, as Liz's father always said), Jack had not been a man who recognized beauty. Who loved deeply. Who gave extravagantly. When Liz thought of him, she thought of his big hand swallowing hers. Pinching. She thought of his arms around that teenager, the look in his eyes. Most of all, her heart seized at the memory of his confession, so many years ago, and the way that it wasn't a confession at all: it was a proclamation that things would remain exactly as they had always been. Period.

And she had let it be so.

"I have to go," Liz said, standing up. She was being abrupt, obtuse, but she couldn't bring herself to care. "Thank you for your help."

"I didn't do anything." Macy followed her lead, but she rose slowly, confused.

"Yes, you did." Liz turned to go but thought better of it at the last moment and spun to envelop Macy in a hug. A real hug, not the halfhearted, light-fingered, skimming caress that they had perfected over the years. That so-called embrace was anemic and ineffectual. Liz squeezed Macy until she felt the air go out of her lungs. And then she backed away as tears filled her eyes. "Go for a walk with me later today?"

Macy's eyebrows seemed permanently knit together. "But it's Saturday."

"So what?" Liz choked.

"Where are you going?" Macy called as Liz strode away.

"I have to talk to Quinn."

"You might want to call her first. Or text?"

"Not this time."

"Oh! Liz!"

She turned at the French doors to see Macy still framed in the shadow of the pergola, the trumpet vines arching over her in a chorus of green and orange. Her friend was digging in the back pocket of her white Bermuda shorts, reaching for something that she had tucked there. It was a piece of paper, folded several times over until it was a fat little rectangle.

"Here," Macy said, walking toward Liz and waving it in front of her. "I almost forgot. Kent and I found this stapled to the light pole in front of your house."

"What is it?"

"A flyer."

Liz took the paper and unfolded it quickly. There was no sense of foreboding, no premonition that alerted her to the fact that everything was about to change. The truth was, Liz was as buoyant with a fierce, defiant hope as she had ever been—and spreading out that innocuous sheet was little more than an indulgence. She didn't want to be bothered by minutiae right now, but because she loved Macy she decided to acquiesce. What could it possibly be? A page of coupons? A notice for an upcoming concert? An advertisement for a local boy who hoped to procure some summer lawn-mowing jobs?

It was a picture.

A little girl with long blond hair and eyes the color of sandstone and moss. Of Key Lake before a storm. Of the buds on Liz's hydrangea bush on the day before they unfurled in full bloom.

Liz knew those eyes.

She felt her heart flutter and fail, the oxygen leaching from the tips of her fingers and the furthest edges of her toes so that she was faint and unstable.

*What now?* she thought. But the only thing that she could do in the moment was sink to the ground in front of her French doors, her back pressed painfully against the cool glass.

# QUINN

"WHAT'S YOUR FAVORITE COLOR?" Quinn reached across the counter and drizzled syrup all over Lucy's blueberry pancake.

"Pink. No, green."

"Tough choice. You can have more than one. I do." Quinn couldn't believe that they were talking, *really* talking, but her quiet joy had a shadow side. Walker was outside with the fire chief, answering questions about the shack and the fire. Answering questions about their very lives. *Do you own this land? Who is your insurance provider? Where were you last night?* As if he was a suspect. A criminal.

It had burned to the ground. A pile of smoldering ash was all that remained of the little building where Quinn had once posed for senior pictures. The peeling paint and rustic boards had made a perfect backdrop for her white lace dress, the long flow of her strawberry-colored hair. Quinn would never look at that picture the same way.

"Would you like me to cut up your pancake for you?" Quinn asked, forcing herself to focus on the task at hand. On the child before her.

"In strips," Lucy said. "I can do the little cuts."

"Of course."

"What's *your* favorite color?" Lucy had no idea what had happened outside the walls of her bedroom only hours before. It was hard for Quinn to reconcile the girl's innocence, the tender way she

257

was starting to unfurl, with the violence they had experienced last night.

*It wasn't an accident.*

Walker told her the truth in the wee hours of the morning after Quinn woke and crawled from the bed she had shared with Lucy.

Quinn had nodded, resigned. She knew there was no way the old building could spontaneously ignite.

"They found evidence of accelerants," Walker said. "And there were multiple points of origin."

"Now what?" Quinn didn't know if her question was rhetorical or if she actually hoped for an answer.

"They're investigating."

"That's it?"

"It could take weeks." Walker reached out and tried to pull Quinn close. She resisted at first, but he folded her into his embrace. Her hands went around him reluctantly. Not because she didn't want his comfort, but because she didn't believe she deserved it. Wasn't she the one who had gotten them into this mess? Who insisted that they keep Lucy a secret? The sudden appearance of her niece in their lives, the phone call, the fire . . . surely they were all connected. And this was all her fault.

"Bennet promised me they would leave you alone for a while. And there's been no mention of Lucy," Walker said. "At least, not yet."

A scrap of grace in this whole frightening mess. "For how long?"

"Awhile." It was the best he could give her.

"Do they really think . . . ?" She couldn't finish her thought.

"We're not suspects, Quinn. Just witnesses. They have to ask questions, they have to find out what, if anything, we know."

"Okay."

Walker kissed the top of her head, breathing in the scent of her smoky hair. "Everything is going to be just fine," he said. Quinn wished she could believe him.

A little huff of disbelief pulled her from her reverie. "Don't you have a favorite color?" Lucy asked, incredulous, impervious to Quinn's growing anxiety. Walker had been gone for over an hour.

"Colors," Quinn corrected, forcing herself to focus on the child before her. "I have more than one, remember? Blue and turquoise."

"That's kind of the same thing."

"I don't think so." Quinn finished slicing the final strip and pushed the plate toward Lucy. "Orange juice?"

The girl nodded, a big bite already stuffed into her mouth.

Quinn grabbed the carafe of orange juice from the refrigerator and poured a glass half full. "Turquoise is a bright blue-green, like water in the Caribbean Sea or a peacock's feathers or the sky at sunset after a thunderstorm. Have you ever seen a turquoise stone?"

Lucy shook her head and took a sip of her orange juice.

"Here." Quinn slipped a finger beneath the silver chain that hung around her neck. After they whispered together in the kitchen as dawn spilled light across the horizon, Walker had led her to the bathroom. He slid the dress off her shoulders and let it fall to the floor, then turned on the shower and made her stand beneath the cool spray. When she stepped out, he was gone. But her clothes were laid out for her. She had added the necklace as an afterthought.

"I've had this for years," Quinn said, standing on tiptoe and leaning over so that Lucy could admire her pendant. It was about the size of her thumb, an irregular orb cut through with dark veins and flecked with bits of copper.

"Pretty," Lucy said, turning it in her fingers.

"That's turquoise." Quinn pulled back and turned to the stove so she could flip a pancake that was turning golden in the frying pan. "Not the same as blue at all."

Lucy murmured her assent gravely and popped another bite in her mouth.

"Favorite food?" Quinn asked, still standing at the stove. It seemed almost ridiculous to act as if nothing was wrong, but what else could she do? So much better to keep Lucy in this sweet, curious state than worry her with all the ugly that waited for them outside.

A beat of silence and then: "Blueberry pancakes."

"Oh really?" Quinn twisted, the second pancake balanced on a spatula. She flipped it expertly onto a waiting plate and slid Lucy a tired smile. "That wouldn't have anything to do with the fact that you happen to be eating the world's best blueberry pancakes at the moment, would it?"

Lucy giggled. It was a rapid burst of sound, a gravelly rasp in the back of her throat that was over before it even began. But it was music to Quinn's ears. She schemed, trying to come up with a way to make the girl laugh again. She could never tell a joke properly; she screwed up the punch line every time. And slapstick just wasn't her thing. She'd have to simply keep talking—and hope.

"Okay," Quinn said. "My favorite food is maple-glazed dough-nuts, with bits of crispy fried bacon on top." She almost added, "Don't tell Walker," but realized at the last second that the mention of him might send Lucy into an emotional scurry.

"That's a thing?" Lucy asked, wrinkling her nose. "I don't think you can put bacon on a doughnut."

"Oh, but you can. And you should. Everyone should. It's the most delicious thing in the world."

Lucy was still unconvinced. "I would try a little bite."

"You're very brave." Quinn smeared a pat of real butter on her own pancake and drenched it in syrup. Walker would probably have a heart attack just looking at her breakfast. The butter melted and pooled on her plate, and she cut a big bite and dredged it through the glistening goodness. "And if you don't like it, I promise to finish it for you."

"You're very brave, too," Lucy said sagely. "Two doughnuts at once is kind of a big deal."

So she had a sense of humor! "It's true." Quinn nodded. "But then I'm kind of a big deal."

"Me too."

"Yes, you are." Quinn could feel her cheeks glow warm and was pleased in spite of the situation. In spite of everything. *Darling girl*.

When the doorbell rang, Lucy froze, a forkful of pancake halfway to her mouth. "Who's that?" she asked carefully, setting her utensil down on the side of her plate. Such manners for someone so young. Such vigilance.

"I don't know," Quinn said. She didn't know what to do. Walker had said they would be left alone for a while. Long enough, hopefully, to formulate a plan. To talk to Nora. What now? Should she ignore whoever was at the door? Ask Lucy to hide? Or pretend that the little girl in her kitchen was the child of a friend and she was simply babysitting for an hour or two? Each option seemed flimsy and fraught with risk. "Maybe you'd better . . ."

But Lucy had already climbed down from the stool and was making her way to her bedroom. She shut the door, without once looking back at Quinn.

The doorbell rang twice more as Quinn walked toward the entryway. "Hold your horses," she muttered, attempting irritation, though what she really felt was a ripple of fear. *You can do this*, she told herself. *Be firm. Send them away quickly.*

But when she turned the handle on the door, the person on the outside pushed it wide open.

"Quinn!" Liz burst through the door and grabbed her daughter by the upper arms as if she intended to shake her. "I've been texting you and texting you!"

"I think my phone is in my purse," Quinn said, trying to pull away. Liz only held on tighter. "I haven't checked it lately."

"That's ridiculous! Who doesn't check their phone? How are people supposed to get in touch with you?"

"I've been a little preoccupied."

"What *happened*?" Liz looked frantic, downright disheveled. It was such an unusual state for her that Quinn wasn't quite sure what to make of it.

"Is everything okay?" Quinn asked. A drop of panic seeped into her stomach and blossomed like blood in water.

"Clearly not. What is going on here?"

Over Liz's shoulder Quinn could see an unmarked car still parked by the side of the road. Nearby, a small circle of men hovered over the crime scene. Two in uniforms. They were no longer combing the site of the fire, sifting through the ash as if it contained the secrets of the universe. Instead, they were talking determinedly, comparing notes, and apparently continuing to question her husband. Walker stood in their midst, sandals planted firmly on the scorched earth, arms folded across his chest.

"There was a fire," Quinn said. She reached around her mother and shut the door. Locked it.

"At the shack? But there's nothing there. No electricity, no wires, nothing."

"I know."

"Do they think . . . ?" Liz left the question hanging and Quinn nodded, against her better judgment.

Liz rummaged around in her purse for a moment and handed Quinn a folded piece of paper. "This was stapled to my light pole this morning," she said.

Quinn knew it was Lucy the second she looked at that grainy photo on the flyer. No matter that the picture quality was poor (obviously taken on a cell phone and blown up) or that it was wrinkled and creased with folds. Lucy's hair was long and silvery blond instead of short and red, but those eyes were unmistakable. "What are we going to do?"

"Where's Lucy?"

Quinn shook her head as if to clear it and then tucked the flyer into her pocket. "She's right here. She's fine." Quinn walked over to the guest room and opened the door. She gave Lucy what she hoped was a warm smile. "My mom is here. Remember her? You met her the other day."

Lucy looked skeptical, but she came out of the room and reclaimed her place at the counter. It seemed the pull of the pancakes was too much to resist.

There was an awkward moment or two as Quinn watched Liz study Lucy. They were mother, daughter, granddaughter caught in some strange, bewildering rite. It shouldn't have to be like this, the three of them circling one another like strangers, and Quinn felt a stab of anger at her sister. *Nora*. Sometimes it felt like everything came back to Nora. But she didn't have time for spite.

"Would you like a pancake, Mom?" Quinn wasn't aware that she was going to say the words until they were out of her mouth. But the look of surprise on Liz's face, and the accompanying half smile, made Quinn's heart stutter. Such a simple kindness, and yet her mother looked as if Quinn had offered her the moon.

"I'd love one."

They were silent as Quinn poured the batter into the frying pan and Lucy continued to make short work of her breakfast. By the time Quinn turned the pancake onto a plate for her mother and passed it over, the room was crackling with tension and unanswered questions. Quinn was sure she could feel them spark against her skin like living things. But she didn't dare to talk about anything that mattered in front of Lucy. Not here. Not now.

"Thank you," Liz said quietly.

Quinn watched as her mother poured the syrup and took a tentative bite of the warm pancake. It must have earned her approval because she cut off three squares in quick succession and lined them all up on the tines of her fork. "These are delicious," she said, and for some reason she looked as if she might cry. "Did you make them yourself? I didn't know you could cook!"

"Of course I can cook. Very well, actually."

"But Walker's the baker in the family."

Quinn felt like throwing her hands up in the air. When she had first told her mother about Walker's aptitude with bread, Liz had smiled thinly and made a comment about how she had never before known a man who *baked*. As if baking bread was akin to collecting porcelain unicorns. "I'm not sure you've ever even tasted his bread," Quinn managed, fighting to keep her tone civil.

"And that's *wrong*." Liz's eyes flashed with uncharacteristic fervor. "I would *love* to taste his bread."

Quinn was so taken aback her tongue was cemented to the roof of her mouth.

"I'm sure he makes *delectable* bread. Can I buy some from you? Maybe a loaf a week or something like that? I'm not really supposed to eat carbs, but . . ." She trailed off.

"Mom." Quinn gave her head a little shake, trying to regain some of her composure. "Are you sure you're okay?"

"No, I'm not okay. I told you that already."

Quinn leaned her forearms on the counter so she could be face-to-face with her mom. "You need to tell me what's going on. You're not having a stroke, are you?"

"Absolutely not! That's a crazy thing to say."

"You're not exactly acting like yourself." Quinn searched her mother's pale blue eyes. What were the ABCs of a stroke again? Wait. That was the acronym for a suspicious mole. FAST? Yes, that was it. Face drooping, something about the arms . . . Quinn couldn't remember the rest. But it didn't seem to matter anyway. Apart from acting like she had been the victim of the body snatchers, Liz looked perfectly fit and healthy. As always.

"We need to talk," Liz whispered. As if Lucy was deaf. As if she couldn't hear the woman who was sitting right next to her. "*Alone*."

"Mom." Quinn shot Lucy a quick, nervous smile. "I think that—"

"You don't understand," Liz said, ignoring her. She looked pained, her eyes red-rimmed and puffy as if she, too, had hardly slept. "Honey, there are some things I need to tell you."

*Saturday*

*10:12 a.m.*

**QUINN**
Mom knows about Lucy.

> **NORA**
> How could you let that happen?

**QUINN**
It doesn't matter. He's here.

> **NORA**
> What? Now? Is Lucy okay?

**QUINN**
We're all fine. But we need you.

Now.

# NORA

PINE HILLS WAS a squat, uninspiring building in desperate need of a fresh coat of paint. It had once been white but was now a dismal, dirty gray that would have made even the most cheerful person question her sunny disposition. Nora was by nature more prone to doom and gloom, and even driving past Pine Hills was often enough to make her mouth sag at the corners. She steeled herself as Ethan put on his blinker and turned into the mostly empty parking lot.

"Why do old folks' homes always have to be so depressing?" he asked, pulling through the roundabout in front of the main doors. "I hope I'm shot. Or die in a fiery blaze. Anything would be better than ending up in a place like this."

Well, Ethan certainly wasn't helping matters. "That's morbid." Nora turned to him, her brows in a hard line over her narrowed eyes. She didn't know it, but angry was one of her best looks. She was resolute and ethereal, remote and untouchable. *Gorgeous* was the term that an ex-boyfriend had once used as she was flaying him alive with her keen tongue.

"No offense." Ethan lifted a hand in surrender. "I didn't realize you were so attached to the Key Lake convalescent home."

Nora waved her hand dismissively. "I'm on edge," she said. But that was more than an understatement. Quinn's text had unnerved her—all she wanted to do was get this over with and race to the A-frame, where she knew Everlee was waiting. And Quinn. And her *mother*. Nora resisted the urge to groan. How had Liz gotten involved? More important, what was Nora thinking? Why had she dragged her family into all of this? She sighed and gave Ethan what she hoped was an apologetic smile. "Don't mind me."

"Do you want me to go in with you?"

"No."

"I'll be right here."

Nora didn't bother responding.

It was only a few paces from the car to the main entrance of Pine Hills, but the automatic doors swooshed open a bit late and Nora was left standing in front of the glass for a few seconds longer than was strictly comfortable. She could see the welcome desk and the receptionist who sat behind it, and as she waited for admittance they stared at each other. Nora thought she recognized the woman, but she couldn't quite place her.

"Hello," she called in greeting when Nora was finally admitted. "I think you're about the last person I expected to see walk through those doors today, Nora Sanford."

Nora waffled for a moment, slowing her steps as a generic smile spread across her face. *Who?* she thought, riffling through an outdated Rolodex in her mind. She could almost smell the dust of disuse. Memory lane wasn't a place that she frequented these days.

"Anika." She came up with her name at the last second. They had attended Key Lake High for a couple of overlapping years, but Anika was almost unrecognizable. Frizzy hair pulled back in a tight ponytail, anemic scowl, unflattering scrubs printed with baby-blue squares that made her look washed out and pale. Nora swept a hand through her own short hair and wished that she had taken the time to apply a little makeup or at least work some mousse into her limp strands. Anika probably thought she had aged just as poorly. "It's nice to see you."

They didn't shake hands, but Anika did give her a small smile. "I can't imagine what you're doing here, Nora. We don't have any of your friends or relatives in residence and you never struck me as the charitable type."

On second thought, Anika hadn't smiled. She'd bared her teeth.

Because Nora was in a hurry and not much in the mood for social convention anyway, she followed Anika's lead and got down to business. "I'm actually here to ask about Lorelei Barnes."

"You know she's gone, right? She passed early last week. I'm afraid you're too late."

"I know." Nora was suddenly overwhelmed by the scent of antiseptic and boiled eggs, chlorine with an undercurrent of staleness. It made her unaccountably sad. Lorelei had died here. Alone. The thought was enough to make her want to throw things, to pick up the heavy vase of silk flowers on the corner of the reception desk and hurl it at the Pollyanna-perfect Thomas Kinkade print behind Anika's head. She imagined the sound it would make, the way the glass would shatter and rain down in a thousand pieces.

Nora had loved Lorelei in her own way. She had been a strong woman. Brave and quiet and unflagging in her devotion to Tiffany. It wasn't Lorelei's fault that her niece was detached and desperate, defined by the death of a woman that she had barely known. Tiffany prickled at affection. Rebelled every chance she got. Marked Lorelei's life with worry and disappointment. It wasn't fair.

Nora set aside her respect for Tiffany's surrogate mother and offered Anika a half smile. She leaned forward, trying to seem conspiratorial. "I'm actually just wondering if Tiffany has been by to collect her mother's belongings. Or maybe I could talk to one of the nurses who was here? Could you tell me who was with Lorelei when she died?" Apparently Nora wasn't very good at separating her emotions about Lorelei's passing from the task at hand. She wanted to know *everything*.

"Did you stay in contact with Tiffany Barnes after high school?" Anika asked, ignoring Nora's questions. "I didn't think you two were friends anymore. Not after that fight."

Nora resisted the urge to groan. She had almost forgotten how small towns worked. The rumors and narrow-mindedness. The way that everybody knew everything about everyone. Who cared? Lorelei was gone. And all that nonsense had been a lifetime ago. "Yeah," she said, trying not to be snide. "We're still friends. Have you seen Tiffany lately?"

"Nope." Anika popped her lips on the word, the sound an indictment of Tiffany's inherent defects. *We always knew she was a bad apple*, Anika's look implied. *Which means, by association, so are you.*

"Look, it's kind of important. Can I talk to whoever was with Lorelei at the end?"

"No one was with her." Anika examined the chewed ends of her ragged fingernails. "She died in the middle of the night and the night nurse didn't realize it had happened until her body was starting to cool."

Nora's mouth felt stuffed with cotton. What a terrible thing to say. What a god-awful way to die. But she pressed on. "And Tiffany hasn't called or anything?"

"She called every Saturday," Anika said.

"And who did she talk to?"

"Me," Anika said, sniffing a little as if the answer should have been obvious. "It's Saturday today, Nora. Clearly I work the weekend shift."

It was all Nora could do not to launch herself over the counter to take Anika by the throat. She didn't remember her being so bitchy. So bitter. But attacking Anika was hardly the way to get the information she wanted. She took a deep breath and tried a different tack. "What did you and Tiffany talk about?"

"You might as well ask me to violate my Hippocratic oath."

"You're a doctor?"

"No," Anika said almost petulantly. "But a private conversation is still a private conversation."

"Fine." Nora rubbed her forehead with her hand and squeezed her eyes shut. She turned to go, adding as an afterthought: "Thanks for your help." But, of course, Anika hadn't been helpful at all.

"Wait."

Nora could hear the shift and shuffle as Anika came from behind the counter. She faced her former classmate slowly, uncertain whether she had experienced a change of heart or was going to offer some rude parting shot. But Anika's face was set and unreadable when she took Nora by the arm and pulled her outside. There was a stone bench near a dried-up fountain and Anika hurried there, taking a pack of smokes out of her pocket and lighting up as she walked.

"I'm not allowed to talk about the patients," Anika said quietly as Nora sat down beside her. She held out the cigarettes and Nora took one even though she didn't want it. "But it's just about time for my smoke break."

"Thanks," Nora said, because it felt like the right thing to say.

Anika reached over to light Nora's cigarette and they were quiet for a drag, two, while Anika inhaled deeply and squinted out over the parking lot.

"Tiffany came about two weeks ago."

"She did?" Nora was incredulous. "You said she hadn't been by!" She had no idea that Tiffany had made the drive, that she had managed to visit Key Lake without Nora realizing it. Had Donovan known?

"I said *lately*. Depends on your definition of *lately*." Anika blew a perfect ring of smoke and turned to regard Nora. "She knew that Lorelei didn't have long. Her blood pressure was dropping, her breathing was erratic . . . she had days. I told Tiffany so."

"And she came to say goodbye?"

Anika fixed Nora with an indecipherable look. "She had a little girl with her."

*Everlee.*

Nora didn't know whether to laugh or cry. They had kept Everlee a secret from Lorelei because they thought the truth would be more than she could handle. It had the potential to undo everything they had worked for. But something inside of Nora splintered at the knowledge that Lorelei had met her granddaughter—if only once. She took a long drag on the cigarette in her hand to stop herself from completely breaking down. They hadn't meant for it to be this way.

"She's the daughter of a friend," Nora improvised, her voice cracking.

"Give me a break, Nora. The little girl is Tiffany's kid. Anyone could see that. Cute as a button, too."

"Why are you telling me this?"

Anika looked around, leaned in. Jabbing her cigarette at Nora, she said: "Because they didn't come alone. A lawyer met them and closed the door to Lorelei's room."

"Roger Estes?"

"That's the one."

"Why?"

Anika shrugged. "Only one reason you need a lawyer when you're dying."

*So stupid.*

Nora could have screamed. Could have kicked herself. Lorelei Barnes wasn't a rich woman, but she had land. Enough of it to set Tiffany and Everlee up for life. Enough of it to make them a target for someone like Donovan Richter.

He didn't care about his $10,000. He cared about Tiffany's million.

"I have to go," Nora said, dropping her cigarette and grinding it out with her heel. Her pulse was galloping, pounding so hard and heavy in her chest she could hardly breathe. She was already several steps away when she remembered that against all odds, Anika had helped her. Had made her realize that nothing was quite what it seemed. Over her shoulder, she said: "Thank you."

"You're not the first person to come around asking about Lorelei," Anika called.

Nora stopped dead in her tracks. "What?" she whispered, turning slowly.

"Yesterday. A man came in. Good-looking, tall. Tattoos peeking beneath the cuffs of his sleeves." Anika snuffed out her own cigarette and stood up. "You know, Tiffany's type."

*No.*

When Nora wrenched open the car door and threw herself inside, Ethan reached for her. "What's wrong?" he asked, searching her face. "What happened?"

"Just drive."

He steered away from Pine Hills but paused at the intersection, waiting for her to give him directions.

"I don't know!" she shouted, casting about. "I don't know where to go, I don't know what to do . . ."

Ethan put on his blinker and turned on a side street. He drove halfway down the first block and pulled close to the curb, then put the vehicle in park. "Okay," he said, swiveling to face her. "Tell me what happened. What's wrong, Nora?"

"Tiffany came here a couple weeks ago."

"So?"

Nora put her head in her hands and tugged her short hair as if trying to draw the truth from her own mind. She was putting the pieces together, filling in the blanks, but the situation was so surreal she didn't know if she could trust herself.

"Talk to me," Ethan said.

"She came with Everlee."

"And?"

"And they met with Lorelei's lawyer."

"So?"

"Lorelei was worth a lot of money. Land rich. If I remember correctly, she had a hundred acres."

Ethan tapped the steering wheel, calculating. "What's an acre of farmland worth? Six thousand? Seven?"

"More."

"That's almost a million bucks."

"Don't forget the acreage and farmhouse."

Ethan whistled low.

"But Lorelei didn't know that Tiffany had a daughter. If she left everything to Tiffany—"

"And Tiffany was going to run—"

"Where would that leave Everlee?" Nora finished. What was Tiffany thinking? She had a false identity and enough money to disappear, but she went back to Key Lake all the same. And then she left Everlee behind. Why? Did she have any idea how much danger she had put her own daughter in? Herself? Lorelei's land was no secret, and Nora felt like an idiot for not considering the possibility sooner. Of course Lorelei would leave everything to Tiffany. And of course it would leave Tiffany agonizingly vulnerable to a man like Donovan. Especially now that—Nora could only assume—Everlee was named in the will.

"She's gone," Nora whispered. "We'll never find her."

"What do you mean?"

"Tiffany wore a wig for the driver's license photo. That's why we found her hair in the sink at the farmhouse. She has a new name, a new identity . . ."

"You're not kidding."

"No, I'm not."

"What's her new name?"

But Nora shook her head. "I can't tell you. A Jane Doe name.

Not so generic that it's obvious, but common enough that there are hundreds who share her name across North America. Maybe thousands."

"Okay. So if she runs using her new identity, it'll be hard to track her down."

"Nearly impossible," Nora moaned. "Especially if she doesn't want to be found."

"But if you had a plan, surely you knew where she was going."

"Tiffany kept that detail to herself, but there were possibilities." Nora ticked them off on her fingers. "New York City because: of course. Washington State because there was a poster of Mount Rainier in her childhood bedroom and she loved it. Arizona because Lorelei had taken her there one spring and she said the whole state smelled like orange blossoms. And Detroit because it's where her mother died."

Ethan pushed a hard breath through his nose.

"Impossible, right? And Tiffany's nothing if not unreliable. For all I know she's headed to Salt Lake City or Charleston or Orlando."

"Her car?"

"She'll switch the plates a couple times, sell it, buy a new one."

"What about titles?"

Nora gave him a withering look. "You're so naive."

Ethan just stared at her. After a moment he said, cautiously: "What about her father?"

Everlee's father. The great mystery, though, of course, Nora knew the truth. But that line on Everlee's birth certificate matched her mother's: blank. It would take a lot to prove what Nora knew to be true. Never mind the fact that she doubted anyone really *wanted* the truth. The closest thing Everlee had to a dad was Donovan Richter, and Nora was sure that he would stop at nothing to bring home his girl. He had so many reasons.

*What was Tiffany thinking?*

Nora turned away and studied the street outside her window, the neat homes that seemed to sit cheerfully behind the long stretches of idyllic sidewalks. Key Lake really was a pretty community, a slice of the American dream right down to the stars and stripes hanging from an eagle-topped flagpole attached to a pristine front porch. The annual Key Lake Fourth of July parade went right down a street like this, and she and Tiffany had gone every year, perching on the edge of the painted curb and pretending to hate it but secretly loving every minute. Especially the marching band. For some reason the marching band always made Nora's heart feel swollen and tight.

"I love her," Nora admitted quietly. The tears on her cheeks were sudden, unexpected, and she swallowed against the knot of hopelessness in her chest. "But Tiffany's the opposite of dependable. If she gets spooked, she runs. I just never imagined that she'd leave Everlee behind. What are we going to do?"

Ethan was still for a long time. But when he spoke, a part of Nora wished he would have just kept his thoughts to himself. "Maybe we're not supposed to find her," he said carefully, slowly. "Maybe Everlee would be better off if we didn't."

The only reason his words hurt so much was because they were Nora's dirty little secret. The idea that plagued her. She had spent the last seven years of her life fighting to keep Tiffany and Everlee together. What if, after all they had been through, she had been wrong? About everything?

Nora wasn't sure she could ever forgive herself if the world they had created turned out to be a lie.

# LIZ

"NORA IS IN KEY LAKE," Quinn said, staring at the screen of her phone.

"What?" Liz looked up from the sink. "She can't be."

"She just texted me."

Liz didn't know what to say. How to feel. Such secrecy, and from the woman who had once been the very center of Liz's universe. When Nora was born she was just over six pounds, but by the time Jack and Liz took her home from the hospital she'd lost a couple of ounces. One afternoon, on a lark, Liz wrapped her baby girl up in a blanket and tucked her in an old Louis Vuitton shoe box. She was a perfect fit. Downy head, petal pink cheeks, rosebud mouth pursed in a tiny pout. Her whole life contained in a small, neat rectangle. It was hard to believe that once upon a time, Liz had known all that there was to know about her daughter. The sprinkling of freckles across her shoulders, the way her nose crinkled when she was upset. Who her best friend was and how she liked her eggs cooked (scrambled with cheddar cheese) and that any problem could be fixed with a gingersnap cookie and a glass of cold milk. Who was this stranger? What had she done?

"Is she coming here?" Liz asked, turning back to the soapy water, the final sticky dish.

"I think so. I don't know." Quinn put her phone down on the counter and reached for a towel. "She has to, right? I mean, I haven't even told her about the fire."

"Or the strange man who stopped by my house last night," Liz added.

"What?" Quinn spun on her, shocked.

But Liz just reached for the towel in Quinn's iron grip and dried off her hands. "It's him, right? It has to be." But the thought didn't make her scared, it made her angry. Gone was the woman who teared up about things she couldn't control anyway. Liz could *do* something about this, and heaven help her, she would. "Now tell me everything you know."

"Nothing." Quinn shook her head almost furiously. Liz wanted to grab her by the chin and tell her to knock it off. "I swear, absolutely nothing. Nora brought Lucy to me a couple of days ago and asked me to look after her. No, she *told* me to. She didn't give me a choice."

Liz peered over her shoulder at the closed bathroom door. Quinn had drawn Lucy a bath and brought her an old ice-cream bucket filled with cups and plastic containers, an old spray bottle and some sponges. Hopefully that would keep the girl occupied for a while. Breakfast had been abandoned. Even Liz couldn't stomach the blueberry pancakes anymore.

"Okay," Liz said, all business. "Clearly we know who she is, we just need to figure out why Nora is trying so hard to keep her a secret."

"You said we need to talk." Quinn crossed her arms over her chest, regarding her mother with a skeptical look. "Do you know something about this?"

Liz sighed. "No," she said. "Not about this. Not about why Lucy is here now and seems to be in some kind of danger." She thought about the missing child poster and stifled a little shiver.

"But . . ."

"But I think I know why Nora ran. Why she never told us about Lucy." Liz came here for this exact reason, to share this knowledge with Quinn, but at the moment of revelation she found herself wavering. Really? Did Quinn need to know? What good would it do now? But the set of her daughter's jaw told Liz that it was too late. She sighed. "Let's sit down."

"I don't want to sit down."

"Fine." Liz put her hands on her hips. Took a deep breath. "Years ago I overheard your father having a conversation with someone."

"Go on."

"He was in his office, on the phone. And I didn't mean to eavesdrop, but he was obviously very upset. I was going to step in, but then I heard what he was saying."

"Mom?"

Liz pressed the heels of her hands to her eyes for just a moment. Gathered enough courage to say: "He was telling someone to 'take care of it.' He said: 'If you don't get rid of it now, I'll ruin you.'"

"What was 'it,' Mom?"

"Lucy. I mean, I think." Liz was overcome with the need to explain, to wipe away the look of horror on her daughter's face. Of course Quinn looked like she was going to be sick! What did she know of the things Liz had worked so hard to keep hidden? Nothing at all. And now, for it all to come out like this. It was almost too much. "The conversation could have been anything, right?"

"But you think Dad knew Nora was pregnant and he was threatening her. Telling her to get an abortion. Why?"

"Because he was afraid."

"And ashamed," Quinn said bitterly. "You hide things you're ashamed of."

Liz didn't argue. Especially because she intended to hide her own shame—at least for a while yet. Right now, Quinn didn't need to know about her father's multiple affairs, about the way that he stopped pretending when his kids were older because the ruse was too complicated to maintain. "I have needs," he had told Liz. Blithely. As if he were confessing to a craving for brownies when she had instituted a weeklong sugar fast. What was she supposed to say? Do? She had two choices: endure or leave. And leaving wasn't really an option at all.

"It makes sense," Quinn said finally. Fatally. But then she looked up, her eyes flaming with fury. "He *stole* her from us. He did this."

"Quinn, there's obviously much more to the story than just this. I think—"

They were interrupted by the squeal of the bathroom door. Lucy stood in the opening, wearing a pale green sundress. Her hair had been toweled dry but not combed, and as Liz watched, Quinn walked over and straightened the girl's dress where it was bunched on one shoulder.

"You look lovely," Quinn told her. "Let me get the comb and we'll go through your hair, okay?"

While Quinn was gone, Liz studied the child. It hurt to admit, but she didn't feel anything, not really. Even though she knew that she should—even though she wanted to. This little girl was her granddaughter. Of course, she had been hoping for exactly this with JJ and Amelia's firstborn—a little girl, a daughter once removed. But the sudden arrival of Lucy—of this half-grown child who had unexpectedly been thrust into their world already living and breathing and embodying her own memories and personality and a life that was completely separate from Liz—was unsettling. *Granddaughter.* The word felt complicated and heavy on her tongue, overripe with consonants. *I'd like to buy a vowel*, she thought. Something to make this word—this reality—more palatable.

She wondered what would have happened if she had walked into the office that night so many years ago. If she would have confronted her husband. Thrown things. Yelled. What would their lives look like now?

"Who are you?" Lucy asked after a few moments. She didn't seem scared, just hesitant, curious. And oh, but she was adorable. Slight and wispy, big familiar eyes, thin shoulders, sweet mop of hair that, though unnatural, suited her remarkably well. She would have fit in perfectly with the childhood version of Nora. And JJ. They took after their father—and Liz's stomach coiled at the thought. It was Quinn who favored her mom.

"I'm Quinn's mother," Liz said, taking the safest route possible. "Remember? And Nora's, too. My name is Liz."

If she expected some bolt of recognition to flash across Lucy's face, it didn't come.

"I own this house," Liz said. It was a foolish thing to say. What did Lucy care? But Liz wasn't sure how to relate to a six-year-old anymore, and she had grasped at the first thought that flitted through her mind. "I did all the decorating."

Lucy looked around as if taking it in for the first time. "I like the pillow on the couch," she said eventually.

It was a bold print, one Liz had created with oil paint and an old canvas that she'd had to scrape. The texture had created strange shadows on the strike-offs that the mill had sent her, but instead of correcting the tones, Liz had decided to print the fabric as is. She loved it more than one should love an inanimate object. "Thank you," she said, pleased. "I designed it myself."

"The pillow?"

"The fabric."

Lucy wandered into the living room, picking up things as if looking at them through new eyes now that she knew Liz had pulled all the pieces together.

"Did you design these, too?" Lucy asked, her fingers raking through a small bowl of smooth glass shards.

"No." Liz left her seat and went to join the child near the window. "That's sea glass."

"That's not the sea," Lucy said, pointing at the lake.

"No, it's not. But a long time ago a ship sank in Key Lake and sometimes the glass from all the windows still washes up on shore."

"What kind of a ship?"

"It was a steamboat. A boat with a big paddle on the back. Have you ever seen one of those?"

Lucy shook her head.

"Sometimes they're called riverboats, but Key Lake isn't a river so we just called it a steamer. It had two decks and a big red wheel on the back that rotated through the water to make it go." Liz used her hands to demonstrate. "It took people on tours of the lake. And do you know what they called it?"

Lucy shrugged.

"The *Queen Elizabeth*. It was painted on the side in the same red paint they used for the paddle."

Lucy seemed unimpressed.

"My name is Elizabeth," Liz said, prompting. "I loved that boat when I was a little girl because I believed that it was named after me."

"Your name is Liz."

"That's short for Elizabeth."

"You were named after the boat, not the other way around," Quinn reminded Liz, coming out of the bathroom with a wide-toothed comb in hand.

"Well, you didn't have to tell her that part," Liz said. "It kind of ruins the story, don't you think?"

"Not really." Quinn took Lucy by the shoulders and steered her in the direction of the sofa. She set her on the arm and began the slow process of untangling her shock of red curls.

Liz watched her daughter work in silence for a moment (brushing her *granddaughter's* hair) and felt an ache so deep her breath caught in her throat. Had she done this? At the very least, had she been complicit?

No more pretending.

"I'm sorry," Liz whispered. "I'm so, so sorry."

Quinn heard her, but she shook her head urgently. *No. Not now.* But Liz never had a chance to explain what she meant because the sound of a key in the door made them all look up. A few seconds later Walker stood in the entryway, a grim look on his face.

"They want to talk to you, Quinn."

She faltered, the hairbrush still in her hand.

"I've got this." Liz stepped forward and carefully took the brush. "We'll be fine," she said, giving Quinn what she hoped was a fortifying smile. "We're all going to be just fine."

But the words were thick and heavy on her tongue. Bitter.

# QUINN

"I WON'T BE GONE LONG," Quinn said after she had collected her sandals and cell phone. She ruffled Lucy's still-damp hair in good-bye. "My mom will take good care of you."

Liz had finished brushing out Lucy's tangles and had already commandeered the tote of Quinn's fingernail polish. She was setting out the bottles in a rainbow on the counter. Why hadn't Quinn thought of that? Lucy was mesmerized, picking up each little glass jar and studying the glossy contents so seriously Quinn wondered how she would ever decide.

"We won't even know you're gone," Liz said, waving her away. "We're having a spa day, aren't we?" But her eyes were dull, worried.

"Well, have fun." Quinn stalled for just a moment, then reached for the bottle of cotton-candy pink. "I think you should go for this on your fingernails," she told Lucy. "And"—grabbing a polish in a pretty shade of mint green—"this for your toes."

Lucy gave her a shy smile. A "You remembered!" smile that made Quinn so brave she gave the girl a quick peck on the forehead. "Be back soon," she said. Over Lucy's head she mouthed to her mother: "Lock the door." They had already determined that Liz would call her cell at the slightest hint that anything was amiss. All the same, it felt wrong to Quinn to just leave her mother and her niece.

Walker was waiting for her on the front steps, his hands on his hips as he surveyed the scene before them. The shack was really and truly gone, the only evidence that it had been there at all was a circle of charred earth and a mound of cinders that still emitted a faint and stammering smoke. A puff of gray. Then nothing. A wisp of vapor that made Quinn think the ruins were sighing in defeat.

But the unmarked squad car was gone. The men, too.

"Where is everyone?" Quinn asked, casting around for her interrogators. They were nowhere to be seen.

"We're going into town," Walker told her. "I thought it would be better that way. So did Bennet. We're trying to draw everyone away from Lucy. For now."

Quinn wasn't sure how she felt about that. "Are we going to the police department?"

"Nah. The fire house." Walker gave his keys a shake and then headed in the direction of their car. "It was arson, but nobody was hurt. Nothing was really damaged. It's not like the shack was worth anything. They think it was a bunch of kids being stupid."

And yet: arson. Quinn remembered the crackle of the fire, the intensity of the heat. The thought that someone could do that on purpose, could inflict that sort of destruction, was leveling.

When they were safely buckled in and heading down the road, Walker cleared his throat and Quinn knew exactly what was coming. "So," he said, staring straight ahead, trying to act casual, "that was Bennet."

She looked out the window and pinched the bridge of her nose, willing the sudden headache that had materialized to dissipate. "Yeah," she said, because what choice did she have? "That's Bennet."

Of course Walker knew about her former fiancé. About the way she had once desperately loved him. And how she had walked away. He had never seemed too traumatized by the story, adopting a cavalier attitude about her past that sometimes made Quinn wonder if he cared at all. Shouldn't he want to punch her past lovers in the face? But she was being needy. Dramatic. However, it was obvious by the way he strangled the steering wheel that Walker wasn't quite as nonchalant about the former love of her life after meeting Bennet Van Eps. He was rather impressive.

"And you were with him last night?"

"We haven't seen each other in years," Quinn said. "My mom invited him to her party."

"Why?" The word was stiff with emotion.

"I don't know." Quinn shrugged, but she had her suspicions. "Because she wanted to talk to him about Lucy, I guess."

"Or orchestrate a meeting between you and Bennet."

"To what end?" Quinn asked.

Walker was silent for several miles. But when he pulled up in front of the fire department, he left the car running and swiveled to face Quinn. "He's a great guy, Q."

"I know."

"I don't have to . . . I don't . . ." He couldn't finish.

Quinn unbuckled her seat belt and slid across the space between them, catching Walker's face in her hands and kissing the hollow beneath his ear, his jawline, his mouth. When their lips touched, it was electric, consuming. And by the way his tongue found hers, hot and insistent, Quinn knew that he was just as desperate for her as she was for him. In just as many ways. "It's you," she whispered against his mouth. "It will always be you."

Walker let her go reluctantly, and when Quinn was halfway out the door he snagged her hand and leaned across the passenger seat. "Be careful," he said. "Try not to mention Lucy. This will all be over soon."

"Okay." She nodded. But her pulse was high and fluttering in her chest.

Quinn didn't recognize anyone who had gathered in the fire chief's office. Bennet was nowhere to be seen—presumably because Key Lake was out of his jurisdiction. But a man with salt-and-pepper hair and a faint, jagged scar on his cheek turned and gave her a warm smile as she entered the building.

"Crazy business, this," he said, extending his bear paw of a hand. The back of it was furred with white hair. "We haven't dealt with an arson in a long while . . ."

The interview was brief, to the point, and Quinn was in and out in a matter of minutes. The fire chief seemed more amused than concerned, grateful that nothing valuable had been damaged and quite convinced that the same people who were responsible for the graffiti that they were forever scrubbing off the band shell in the park could be blamed for this.

"Call me if you think of anything else," he told her, handing over his card as Quinn prepared to leave. But it was obvious he didn't expect anything to materialize. And Quinn had no intention of telling him about Lucy, the phone call, Nora's insistence that they be careful, wise.

"Of course."

The sun was directly overhead and beating down with a merciless zeal as Quinn jogged across the sidewalk. How many minutes had passed? How long had she been gone? Her distance from Lucy felt like an itch she couldn't assuage.

"You all right?" Walker said, searching Quinn's face as she slid into the car.

"Fine."

"What now?"

"Have you talked to my mom?"

"She texted a minute ago. All is well."

"Then I want to see Nora," Quinn said, already tapping on the screen of her phone.

"What?" Walker sounded shocked. "She's in Key Lake?"

"Yes."

"Where?"

"That's what I'm going to find out."

Nora responded to Quinn's text immediately and suggested they meet at Malcolm's.

*Why?* Quinn typed.

*Mom. Lucy. Walker.*

Three reasons. And because Quinn wanted answers, she complied. "Can you drop me off?" she asked Walker, worried that he would balk.

"Sure," he said, giving her a sideways glance. "I want to pick up some locks from the hardware store anyway."

Malcolm's on the Water was hopping on a late-summer Saturday afternoon, and the only table available was in the far corner of the patio. The lunch crowd—all dressed in swimwear and cover-ups, sundresses and board shorts—seemed to prefer the air-conditioning or the shade, and the little table the hostess led Quinn to was the only one bathed in a wide swath of direct sunlight.

"Is this okay?" she asked Quinn with an air of defeat. It seemed the table had been turned down by more than one party already. But it was perfect as far as Quinn was concerned. Private, out of the way, situated next to a speaker that was crooning the Beach Boys. It was all so cheerful, so normal. Quinn felt conspicuous as she jittered and bobbed with nerves.

"It's fine," Quinn told her, all but collapsing into a seat.

"Great." The hostess dropped a stack of menus on the wrought iron table and left without another word.

When the waitress came by, Quinn ordered a sparkling water and the tower of onion rings. She wasn't much in the mood for fried food, or any food for that matter. But one didn't take up a table at Malcom's in the summer without ordering. And onion rings had once been Nora's favorite.

She put on her sunglasses and scanned the crowd for any sign of Nora. A part of her wanted to slap her sister. To throw herself into the fray when Nora arrived and make a horrible, ugly scene. There would be tears and shouting, accusations of the reality TV sort. But beneath her anger and confusion, Quinn mourned the loss of her sister. The hurt that had brought them here. If their *father* had turned Nora away . . . It was unthinkable.

When Quinn opened her eyes to find Nora weaving through the tables as she made her way toward the corner, what was left of her composure crumbled to dust.

"Nora," Quinn said, standing as her sister approached. Her voice trembled even as she fought the urge to reach for Nora and pull her into a crushing hug. Anger and affection made awkward dance partners, and Quinn couldn't decide whether she loved her sister in that moment or hated her just a little.

"Keep your voice down." Nora's sunglasses obscured her eyes, but the set of her mouth was grim. "What happened? You said he's here?"

"I don't even know who *he* is, Nor. But there was a fire—"

"What?" Nora looked shaken and leaned forward to grab Quinn by the arms. "Is everyone okay? Is—"

"It was the shack just up from our cabin," Quinn said quickly. "We're fine. Everyone's fine. But we think he did it. Whoever's after Lucy, I mean."

"Oh my God." Nora whispered. She sank into the chair next to Quinn's and pulled it close. She said, "Sit down."

Quinn complied, but as she did so she realized that there was a man standing just behind Nora. He was broad shouldered and pleasant-looking, his tawny hair just messy enough to be natural and not the result of careful styling. His smile was small and serious as he pulled out a chair and joined them. "Nice to meet you, Quinn," he said. "I'm Ethan."

"Nice to meet you, too," she managed, but her mind was racing. Was this Lucy's father? Impossible. Ethan wasn't someone that Quinn remembered—definitely not from Key Lake—and Nora had to have gotten pregnant right after her senior year of high school. During? Close enough. The timing explained so much. Why Nora withdrew from the family. Why she abandoned her scholarship and ran away. Why she had never really come back.

Quinn shot Nora a look that begged for a few more details, but they were all wearing sunglasses and her attempt at sisterly ESP was lost in the space between them. Questions burned on her tongue, making her feel tingly and just a little delirious, but she settled for: "I ordered onion rings," because she didn't know what else to say. *Stupid*.

Nora didn't seem to hear. "How could you?" she asked, pulling off her sunglasses to fix Quinn with a look of deep betrayal. "How could you let Mom know about Lucy?"

As if Quinn was the one who needed to beg forgiveness in this impossible situation. "I didn't *let Mom* know anything," Quinn said. She felt a stab of righteous indignation and it was a thousand times better than the anxiety she had almost grown accustomed to. "She barged in the other morning and Lucy was there."

"Lucy?" Ethan asked softly, but both Quinn and Nora ignored him.

"What was I supposed to do?" Quinn asked. "Lock her in a closet? This is ridiculous, Nora. Who is she?"

But Nora just shook her head as if she regretted ever trusting Quinn with a secret so monumental.

It made Quinn furious. "Fine. Don't tell me. What is *this* all about?" She reached into her back pocket and yanked out the flyer that her mother had given her.

Nora snatched it away and studied it with her bottom lip between her teeth. Quinn was surprised to see that the emotion that registered on Nora's face wasn't annoyance or even anger. It was fear.

"Where did you get this?" Nora asked, crumpling the paper in her hand.

"It was stapled to the pole of the streetlight outside Mom's house.

There are more. I saw another one on the side of the picnic shelter when I parked across from the public beach."

Nora put her forehead in her hand. She was still for so long that Quinn pulled off her own sunglasses and tried to catch Ethan's gaze. He was having none of it.

"If Tiffany is gone, would the courts just give her to him?" Ethan asked quietly, tucking close to Nora as if Quinn wasn't even sitting there.

"He's the only father she's ever known," Nora whispered, still cupping her head.

"But that doesn't make him her legal guardian."

"Wait," Quinn cut in. "What are you talking about? Who is 'he'? Is someone trying to adopt Lucy? Why?"

But Nora ignored her. She kept her voice so small Quinn had to lean in to hear her say: "If anything ever happened to Tiffany, I don't know where things would land."

"*If anything ever happened,*" Ethan echoed. "You don't think . . ."

Quinn grabbed Nora by the sleeve and gave a quick jerk. "What in the world are you talking about?" she said, her voice far louder than she intended it to be. "What does Tiffany have to do with this? Are you talking about Tiffany Barnes? From high school?"

There was a moment or two of stillness as Nora glared at her sister, but Quinn was just as annoyed and glared right back. She opened her mouth to unleash more questions, but before she could voice so much as a syllable a shadow fell across her face.

"I couldn't help but overhear a bit of your conversation."

Quinn let go of her sister and shielded her eyes to look up at the newcomer. He was midthirties, smirking and arrogant, handsome in a sleek, strangely artificial sort of way. His hair was as oiled and immovable as Superman's, and he was overdressed for the casual patio, where flip-flops reigned supreme—downright out of place in his dark pants, black shoes, and long-sleeved button-down shirt.

*He's hiding something*, Quinn thought. Tattoos or scars or something else that he didn't want people to see. It was so obvious Quinn almost felt sorry for him.

"Donovan." Nora's voice was reedy and thin, and she had sunk back from him as if he emanated an odor she found repulsive. "What are you doing here?"

"I wanted to see where Tiffany grew up," he said, grinning. But the cheer didn't reach his eyes—Quinn realized with a start that he looked predatory, hungry. Was this *him*? Phone calls and flyers and matchsticks. *Lucy*. What was he doing here?

"Imagine my surprise when I heard her name across a crowded patio," he continued. "And then looked up to see you. Small world. I'm assuming you think Tiff's still in New Ulm?"

"Yes." Nora's admission was quiet, defiant. Quinn realized that Donovan had phrased the question strangely, but before she could wonder at it Nora went on. "Visiting family."

"Hmm," he said, considering. "Mind if I sit down?"

Quinn had watched their exchange suspiciously, but when Donovan asked to join them she felt a chill race down her spine.

"Sure." Nora motioned to the empty seat across from her.

"And what are you doing in town?" Donovan sat down and leaned back, stretching his legs out languidly as he studied Nora's face.

"Visiting family," she said again. "I'm from Key Lake, too, you know."

"Of course." Donovan's eyes fell on Quinn. "And who is this?"

"My sister," Nora said woodenly. "But I'm afraid she was just saying that she has to go."

Quinn felt Nora's hand fall on her arm. Her big sister squeezed almost imperceptibly, but there was a note of desperation in the air around her. A plea to be quiet, don't push, no more questions. Leave *now*.

"Yes." Quinn fumbled for her purse and rose awkwardly. "I have to go. It was, uh, good to see you, Nora. Ethan."

"I'm Donovan Richter, a friend of your sister's," the man said, stopping her. He leaned forward and stuck out his hand to make it official.

*Yeah right*, Quinn thought. *Friend, my ass.* But she took Donovan's hand anyway. It was cool and dry, oddly smooth and uncalloused. It gave her the creeps. "I'm Quinn," she said, even though she hated sharing her name with him. It made her feel dirty, exposed. Being near him made her long for lovely things: the tang of a sour lemon drop, the summery, coconut scent of suntan oil, a thick book. She pulled her hand away as quickly as she could.

"I can't shake the feeling that I've seen you before," he said, and gave her a wink that shot straight through to her bones.

# NORA

QUINN WAS GONE, and for the moment, that was all that mattered. The thought that Donovan was *here*, in Key Lake, that he knew her sister's name, had touched her skin, made Nora's vision blur at the edges. If he had started the fire in the shack—and Nora had no reason to doubt that he had—Donovan knew what type of car Quinn drove and where she lived and what exactly she looked like when her guard was down. When she was alone. Never mind that Quinn was decades older than Donovan's preferred type. She was young and lovely, still softly round in the way of someone much younger than her years.

Nora had seen the way he looked at her.

"I have an order of onion rings and a mineral water here." A waitress hovered at Nora's elbow, eyeing the empty seat where Quinn should have been.

"Yeah," Nora said, grateful for the brief interruption. Her mind was spinning. How had Donovan found them here? It wasn't a co-incidence. Nothing with him was a coincidence.

The waitress plopped down a green bottle of Perrier in front of Nora and stuck the metal tower of onion rings in the middle of the table.

"Thanks, Nor." Donovan plucked the top ring and dredged it through the little cup of sauce.

Nora didn't know what to say.

"Your sister's a real looker. How old is she?"

What was he trying to do? Scare her? Make her angry?

Unnerve her.

After Tiffany found Donovan touching her daughter in a way that no grown man should ever touch a child, she tried to find as many excuses as possible for Everlee to have sleepovers at Nora's house. She didn't dare to just *run*; their lives were too entwined, her dependency on Donovan and his paycheck absolute. Her surrogate mother was dying, her lover was terrifying, and when she gave the cops an anonymous tip in an effort to get Donovan out of the way, nothing came of it. What was he capable of? They just didn't know.

So while they laid their plans, Tiffany started bringing Everlee over to Nora's apartment. Hours at a time. Sometimes overnight. Nora gave the child warm baths and toast for breakfast. Peanut butter and Nutella, milk with so much Nestlé's Quik she could practically stand a spoon up in it. But bubble baths and food couldn't erase the things Everlee had seen. The things that had been done to her? Nora couldn't bear to think about that.

One night when Everlee was supposed to be sleeping over, Donovan had shown up at Nora's door. His eyes were rimmed in red and watery, but his hands were almost preternaturally steady. And his intent was clear. "Hey there, big girl," he said, pulling Everlee into his arms. "Time to come home." She was exhausted, already in her pajamas and on her way to bed, but she didn't protest. Donovan held her close, arms wrapped full around the child, and he fixed Nora with a look that told her clearly: *Know your place. She's mine.*

"You can't have her," Nora said suddenly, louder than she meant to on the patio where everything seemed sunny and bright.

"Excuse me?" Donovan had a mouthful of onion ring but that didn't stop him from talking. And though the food in his teeth took the edge off his words, his entire countenance shifted at Nora's proclamation. He arched like an animal catching a whiff of his prey. "What's that supposed to mean?"

"Her birth father hasn't signed away parental rights." It wasn't something Nora and Tiffany talked about. Ever. At least, not since Tiffany told her the truth about what happened that night. And they had promised each other never to speak of it again. To pretend that Everlee was immaculately conceived and wholly theirs. They were stupid, young. They had made a decision that would affect the rest of their lives when they were emotional and irrational and barely nineteen years old.

"She doesn't have a daddy," Donovan said, picking at one of his teeth with a fingernail. "At least, not yet." He gave her a Cheshire grin, but it was menacing.

Nora felt Ethan's hand brush against her leg beneath the table. If he was trying to comfort her or warn her, she couldn't tell.

"I know who Everlee's real father is."

"You do." It was a statement, not a question, and Donovan sat back again, folding his hands behind his head as if preparing himself for a good story. A funny one.

"Yes, I do."

"So what?"

"So I'm going to tell him the truth."

"You think he'll believe you? You think he'll care after all this time?" Donovan sneered at her, warming to his own narrative. "I think he'll slam the door in your face. You can't prove a thing."

"DNA."

He waved his hand, dismissing her. "Consent, sweet cheeks. DNA tests require a signature from the person whose samples are submitted." It sounded rehearsed, memorized.

"He'll consent."

"I'm not sure he can." Donovan leaned forward, hands flat on the table, and glared at her. But there was an emotion behind his eyes that Nora couldn't place. Glee? He was delighting in this, but she couldn't figure out why. "It's been a long time, Nora. Things have changed."

"Listen." Nora angled forward, too, erasing the space between them until they were nearly nose-to-nose. "I know exactly what you are. And if you think I'm going to let you have Everlee, you're dead wrong."

"No need to be so nasty, Nora. I thought we were friends." He reached out and ran a finger along her jawline before she could jerk away. "Besides, I don't think you have a choice in the matter."

She knew she shouldn't take the bait, but Nora couldn't help it. She felt like she was careening out of control, fierce and dazed as she spun round dizzy corners and tried to chart a new path, though the terrain was unfamiliar. Savage. "Of course I do. Everlee is my—"

"What?" he hissed. "Everlee is your what? I'll tell you what. She's not yours and she never was. You have no claim to her—or Tiffany. Tiff is that girl's mother and *she* will call the shots."

"Yeah, well, Tiffany's not here right now, is she?"

Donovan pushed himself back roughly and stood, tugging the sleeves of his shirt as if he had just been in a fight and needed to right himself. "Funny you should mention that." He smirked. "Turns out she's not in New Ulm at all. Turns out Tiffany *is* right here."

As Nora watched, he pulled a phone out of his back pocket and unlocked the screen. It was an old smartphone with a hot-pink case. Nora didn't have to see the rhinestones or the skull and crossbones to know that it was Tiffany's phone. A sense of dread slid through her, cold and sharp as a blade.

"How—"

"We're soul mates," Donovan told her, his lip pulled back in an ugly sneer. "Till death do us part."

Nora spun around in spite of herself, scanning the crowd at Malcolm's for a hint of the familiar. *Please, God*, she begged. *Let Tiffany be here.* But even before her desperate gaze had skittered over half the crowd, she knew that her search was futile.

When Nora turned back to Donovan, he was gone.

# LIZ

"YOU'RE BACK EARLIER than I expected," Liz said, not even bothering to look up from where she was bent over Lucy's little feet. She had propped up the girl's heels on a fat pillow in her lap and was holding one tiny toe between her thumb and forefinger. With her other hand she carefully applied Pixie Dust Green in quick, light strokes. Funny, but Liz couldn't remember doing this with her own girls. Probably because Nora had been such a tomboy. And by the time Quinn came around, Liz was just plain tired. But really, who could blame her? Three kids and one man-child. Sometimes Liz thought she deserved a medal for surviving those years. And sometimes, like now, when she held Lucy's perfect, miniature-sized foot in her hand, Liz worried that she had let them slip through her fingers.

"We need to talk." Quinn's voice was choked, and Liz looked up quickly, smearing polish on Lucy's toe.

"Shoot. Hand me a Q-tip, will you?" Liz asked, straining for normalcy, but over Lucy's head her eyes searched out Quinn's. Her daughter looked ragged, her face pinched and drawn.

Quinn complied and Liz dabbed at the skin around Lucy's pinky toenail. It was roughly the size of a fresh green pea and was now the same approximate color.

"There you go," she said, giving Lucy's feet a gentle pat. "All done. Just sit still while they dry for a few minutes, okay? Then you and your lucky toes can hop down."

"Look," Lucy said, swiveling her torso so she could wriggle her fingers in front of Quinn's face. "My fingers look like Princess Frostine."

"They do." Quinn tried to smile, but it flickered out before it formed. "And your toes remind me of Tinker Bell."

Liz could feel Lucy stiffen at the mention of Tinker Bell. Her slight body went still, rigid beneath Liz's hands still cupping the arches of her feet.

"Hey, you okay?" Quinn asked. But Lucy ignored her. She shook her feet out of Liz's grip and slid off the stool. Then she walked carefully toward the living room, favoring her freshly painted toenails even as she disregarded Liz's instructions to sit still. Liz opened her mouth to stop her, to tell her to be extra careful not to get nail polish on anything, but Quinn laid a hand on her mother's arm. *Let it go*, her touch warned.

"So," Liz said, picking up the bottle of green polish and twisting the cap on. She made sure it was tight and then wrenched it one more time just to be safe. Her hands were trembling. "How'd it go?"

"It was nothing," Quinn whispered, waving the question away. Louder, she called to Lucy: "You can turn the TV on if you'd like."

The four-note measure of the television powering on tinkled through the air.

"Where's Walker?" Liz asked.

"Putting a dead bolt on the boathouse."

"But—"

"He has one for the cabin, too." Quinn lifted her chin defiantly, daring Liz to object.

She didn't.

"I saw Nora," Quinn said.

"You did? When?"

"Just now. She's in Key Lake, but we didn't have much time to talk."

Liz didn't know what to think. "Did she at least admit that Lucy is her daughter?"

"About that." Quinn's gaze flicked over to where Lucy sat clicking through channels on the TV. The girl was thin-lipped, and Liz thought maybe even a bit pale. Why? What had set her off? But she didn't have time to contemplate. Quinn was talking again. "I think we were wrong."

"What do you mean?" Liz had lost the thread of the conversation.

"I think we were wrong about Nora being Lucy's mother."

Liz humphed. "That's ridiculous. It all fits. Lucy has Sanford eyes."

"Listen." Quinn seemed nervous, jittery even. "Nora made me leave, but before she did, she and Ethan were talking about Tiffany Barnes."

That name made all the fine hairs on Liz's tanned arms stand on end. But she seized the less problematic issue. "Who's Ethan?"

"A friend of Nora's. He came to Key Lake with her. But—"

"*Tiffany,*" Liz whispered. It was almost reverent. Why did that girl keep coming up? "What does she have to do with all of this? It doesn't make any sense."

"I know. I haven't seen her since the summer Nora graduated high school. I didn't realize that they kept in touch, but I think they must have."

"So what were Nora and her friend talking about?" Liz asked, her mouth unusually dry. She could feel something buzzing at the corners of her consciousness, distant alarm bells that were starting their high, insistent whine. But she had no idea what they meant.

"They were talking about Lucy, I think. And Tiffany. And some guy . . . He was there, Mom. He was the reason Nora made me leave."

Liz shook her head in an effort to clear it. "Tall, thick, built like a wrestler? Dark hair, dark eyes?"

"That's the guy."

Liz gave her hands a little shake, trying to dislodge the hysteria that was creeping across her skin. "Where does Tiffany Barnes fit into all of this?"

Quinn's attention swept to Lucy. It was an innocuous shift, but Liz followed her daughter's gaze and saw Lucy through a different lens.

The truth clicked into place like a bolt sliding home.

Liz closed her eyes very deliberately for a moment, trying to shut out her own suspicion. It was no use. She snapped them open and met Quinn's quiet gaze. "Tiffany is Lucy's mother. Then . . . ?"

"JJ."

Quinn said it so quietly Liz didn't actually hear her daughter utter the two syllables that felt like an indictment—she watched her mouth them. But, really, Quinn didn't have to say anything at all. Liz knew. Maybe she had known all along.

JJ had been obsessed with Tiffany. A crush, Liz had thought. And why not let them give it a try? Go out on a few dates so JJ could get her out of his system? Tiffany wasn't right for him at all and everyone knew it. If he could only realize that obvious truth for himself, the strange, almost magnetic pull she had on him might be broken. But Nora forbid it—and Jack. Sr., too. For once, they were aligned on something, and Liz didn't stop to wonder at the motives behind their sudden alliance. She just relished the fact that her husband and their firstborn daughter had finally found a square inch of common ground. JJ, on the other hand, was outraged.

If Liz remembered correctly, and she knew that she did, Tiffany was just as enamored with JJ as he was with her. Classic good boy, bad girl scenario. Or something like that. It all made perfect sense. A secret relationship? A one-night stand? Did it matter?

And did it change anything if JJ was Lucy's father instead of Nora being her mother? Liz figured she was probably being politically incorrect, but yes, this changed everything. JJ was married, expecting a baby of his own. He—presumably—had no idea that there was a gorgeous little girl who might someday call him Daddy. But what if he did? What if he had known all along?

Liz's heart sank like a stone as another detail clicked into place. The phone call she had overheard all those years ago wasn't between Jack Sr. and Nora—it was between her husband and Tiffany Barnes. He had sent her away, had *threatened* her. Jack Sr. had known all along and had done everything in his power to protect his son. *Oh, JJ.* Liz's throat tightened around tears, but she refused to let them fall. *Let him be ignorant,* she wished. *Please, let him be stupid and insensitive and immature instead of malicious and hateful and cruel.*

*Let us be a part of Lucy's life, even if that's the last thing Tiffany wants.*

Liz was surprised at the depth of her own emotion. Hadn't she been ambivalent only hours ago? But how could she be? The affection she felt for Lucy was fresh as a bud and just as precious. Blood was thicker than water, or so they said, and Liz felt like she suddenly, irrevocably knew exactly what that meant.

"What are we going to do?" Quinn rasped.

Liz tapped her lips with her fingertips, willing herself to come up with a solution, to once again step in and clean up the mess that someone in her life had made. That was her job, after all: righter of wrongs, fixer of all things broken. It was what mothers did.

"I'm going to call him," she said, finally. Her phone was on the counter and she grabbed for it, but Quinn got there first. She snatched it up and held it away from Liz.

"Really? You think a phone call is the right way to tell JJ he has a *daughter*?"

"Don't be ridiculous. I'm not going to tell him anything. I'm going to tell him we need to talk."

"But—"

The doorbell interrupted their argument before it could heat up.

"Are you expecting someone?" Liz asked warily, eyeing the hallway that led to the door.

"No. But I'm sure it's Nora." Quinn stalled for a moment, looking back and forth between her mother and the concealed entryway. "Just, listen, okay?" she urged. "Let Nora talk. Let her say what she needs to say."

"Are you implying that I don't—"

"*Please.*"

"Fine, fine." Liz threw up her hands and turned her attention to the bottles of fingernail polish that still littered the counter. She began to gather them up one by one, checking and double-checking the lids to make sure they were on securely and then depositing them back in the Rubbermaid. In order by color and shade because it was the only thing she could do in the moment to put things right in her world.

Liz was in a private place, a locked room in her mind, where everything was dark and hushed and smooth—no edges, no worries, nothing to make her frustrated or angry or sad—when the sound of Quinn calling fractured her fragile peace.

"Mom? I need you to come here."

Of course. Liz smoothed the front of her shirt and gave her hair a fluff. It had been a while since she had seen Nora and she was walking a fine line between wanting to touch her baby girl and wishing she could smack her around a little. Not that she had ever given in to corporal punishment. That was Jack Sr.'s job, and he had carried it out with a cool, detached efficiency. And a ruler. Liz had once seen the red marks on the backs of Nora's legs and it filled her with an indescribable fury. How dare he? But then, she had given him permission to do so. It was a decision they'd made together.

*Nora.* Liz practiced her name, the way she would hold out her arms and hope that Nora fell into them. But that wasn't like her eldest daughter at all, and by the time Liz rounded the corner she was confused and hopeful, scared and upset. How did her children always manage to make things so difficult?

But Nora wasn't standing in the doorway.

Tiffany was.

She looked different than the last time Liz had seen her only days ago. No, not different, necessarily; her distinctive hair was just swept up in a colorful scarf, bohemian-style. It wrapped completely around her head like a turban and hid her lovely dark waves. But somehow it worked for her. It was her cheekbones, her eyes that slanted up just a bit at the corners. She looked exotic and lovely, as if she hailed from somewhere far more extraordinary than Key Lake, Minnesota.

"Tiffany," Liz exclaimed, fumbling for purchase. What was she doing here? What now? And though it was insane for the thought to pop into her head at such a heavy moment, Liz remembered the urn. The ashes of Lorelei Barnes. "I have something for you."

"I believe that you do," Tiffany said quietly. "I'm actually here because—"

There was a quick patter of light footsteps. A little gasp. "Mom?"

Tiffany's face crumpled and she fell to her knees, arms out for Lucy as her child raced across the space between them. When the girl threw herself against Tiffany, all doubt about her lineage was erased.

"Oh, baby." Tiffany buried her face in Lucy's hair and pressed her close, hands tugging at her arms, her dress, the blunt ends of her hair. It was as if she was drinking her in, memorizing each line and curve with the urgent stroke of her fingers—a blind woman fumbling for sight. "Oh, honey," she cried. "I've missed you so much."

Lucy pushed back from her mother, small hands squeezing her

shoulders in reproach. She was sobbing, the tears sliding down her cheeks and off her chin in quick succession. "Why did you do that to me? Why did you leave me? Why—"

Tiffany put her fingers to Lucy's mouth, stopping the flow of words but not the accusation, the hurt that still poured from the child's wide eyes. "Shhhh," she said, her own lips trembling. "That's enough now."

"But—"

"Enough." Tiffany stood up abruptly and brushed her own tears away with a determined swipe. She took Lucy firmly by the hand. "We're leaving."

Liz reached out to stop her and realized at the last second that there was nothing she could do. "Wait," she said, but Tiffany was unswerving in her confidence, in the set of her jaw and the hard look in her dark, flinty eyes.

"Thank you for watching Everlee these past few days," Tiffany said, keeping her eyes trained on the ground.

*Everlee?*

But before Liz could even formulate a question, Tiffany and Lucy (Everlee? Her granddaughter?) were gone, running across the browning August grass. Lucy tried to look over her shoulder once, to catch a parting glimpse of Quinn and the house where she had been fed and cared for, where her toenails had been painted the color of spring and moss. Of hope. But Tiffany held on tight and Lucy's head snapped back around before she could make eye contact with either of the women who stood framed in the doorway.

Liz wanted to *do* something, but she was frozen, her feet cemented to the ground and her throat strangled by a nameless, faceless panic that she couldn't quite identify. This was wrong. Everything about it was horribly, terribly wrong, but she didn't know why.

There was nothing she could do. It was too late. There was a car at the end of the driveway and Tiffany yanked open the back door. She pushed her daughter inside and climbed in behind her.

In the driver's seat, the man with the square jaw and black hair gave Liz and Quinn a little two-fingered salute. And then he put the car in reverse and squealed out in a cloud of dust and exhaust that filtered slowly through the air to where Liz stood, choking.

*Saturday*

*3:47 p.m.*

**QUINN**
*They took her.*

**NORA**
*Who?*

**QUINN**
*Tiffany. And the man from Malcolm's.*

**NORA**
*Oh my God.*

*Stay there. I'm coming.*

# QUINN

THE MOMENT AFTER she read Nora's last message, Quinn texted Bennet. *I need you.*

He wrote one word in reply: *Coming.*

But the impending arrival of *help*, of people who would be able to make sense of what had just happened, didn't begin to take the edge off Quinn's panic.

"Where are you going?" Liz half shouted as Quinn shoved her phone into her pocket and took off across the yard.

She didn't even pause to acknowledge her mother.

Quinn banged on the door to the boathouse, two-fisted and frantic. Lucy was gone and Quinn was so heartsick she was weeping. When had that happened? She hadn't even known she was crying until she heard the ragged intake of her own shuddering breath.

Her palms landed on Walker's chest as he wrenched open the door. He caught her wrist in one hand and held on tight. His grip was desperate, his eyes wild. "What happened?" he barked. "Are you okay? Is Lucy okay?"

"She's gone!" Quinn shouted. "They took her!"

Walker's jaw tightened and he sprinted in the direction of the driveway, but it was too late. The car was long gone. Lucy was long gone. And they still didn't know why her disappearance was so terrifying. But it was. Quinn could feel panic roil in her stomach like acid.

"You have to tell me what happened," Walker called, hurrying back to her. He still held a power drill in one hand and it made him look slightly dangerous. Unhinged.

"Tiffany Barnes took Lucy." Quinn didn't bother to sweep the tears off her cheeks.

"Who's Tiffany?"

"Her mother." Liz was only steps away from them, striding down the incline toward the boathouse. Quinn watched her mom come, the wind whipping her white-blond hair around her face. Her expression was so frosty, her spine so ramrod straight you could practically see the fury coming off her in an icy blast. Quinn recoiled a bit.

"What is going on here?" Walker waved the drill, looking for all the world like he wanted to hurl it against a wall. It was so unlike her husband that Quinn reached out for him. Their fingers caught, held.

"We're not entirely sure," Liz said. She stopped a few feet away and put her hands on her hips. "But we do know that Tiffany is Lucy's mother. And I'm not sure her name is Lucy."

"What?" Walker squeezed Quinn's fingers. "That doesn't make any sense. I thought Nora—"

"Nora lied to us about everything," Quinn said. She passed the heel of her hand beneath her eyes, took a steadying breath.

"I don't understand." Walker shook his head, looking between his wife and his mother-in-law as if they had lost their collective minds. "Why would she change Lucy's name? Why would she lie to us about that?"

"I don't know."

"Come on." Walker tugged Quinn's hand and started leading her back toward the house. "Both of you," he said over his shoulder. Though his tone was no-nonsense and his voice carried the bite of authority, Quinn was surprised when her mother complied.

Walker led the ladies into the cabin, shutting the door behind them with a decisive snap. "Where's Nora?"

"On her way."

"Do we need to call someone else? The cops?"

"I texted Bennet."

At this, Walker nodded once, resigned. Studying Quinn, his face softened. "You look pale. Have you eaten anything today?" he asked, his knuckles grazing her cheek in a gentle touch.

"I'm pale because I'm worried." She grabbed the front of Walker's T-shirt. "We have to *go*. We have to find her."

"And do what?" he asked. "Run them off the road? We're going to wait for Nora. For Bennet."

He was so cool, so logical. Quinn didn't know whether to hug him or hit him.

"You didn't answer my question," Walker prompted.

Quinn tried to think back to the morning, to breakfast and Lucy's sweet smile as they shared their favorite things. She'd tasted a single bite of the blueberry pancakes she'd so casually whipped up. The rest had been deposited, cold and congealing, in the garbage can beneath the sink. What time was it now? A quick peek at the clock above the stove indicated it was almost four in the afternoon.

"I'll take that as a no," Walker said. Then he instructed her: "Sit."

Quinn did as she was told. Liz, on the other hand, tried to come around the island, to take her spot in the kitchen beside Walker. But he would have none of it. Without even looking properly at his mother-in-law, he put both his hands on the small of her back and ushered her out of his space. It was such a bold move Quinn caught her breath. She couldn't believe that Walker dared to touch her mother. She half feared Liz's wrath would turn him to stone. But rather than unleash on him, Liz just gave Walker a long, hard look. Then she climbed up on one of the barstools. There would be peace—for now. But Quinn knew that her mother wasn't being obedient. She was biding her time.

While Walker boiled water for coffee and removed a loaf of rosemary garlic bread from the basket on the counter, Quinn and Liz told him as much as they knew. About Quinn's meeting with Nora, the ominous poster with Lucy's face on it, and Tiffany's sudden appearance at the cabin.

"Wait." Walker stopped them at this juncture. He carefully slid a mug of hot coffee across the counter to Quinn. It was just the way she liked it: creamy with milk and just a pinch of sugar. A sip-sized comfort. "If Tiffany is Lucy's mother, what's the problem?"

"Something's not right," Liz said. "Lucy was happy to see Tiffany, but there's something else going on here."

"That man." Quinn gave a little shiver.

"I think Tiffany was being forced." Liz nodded.

Walker looked skeptical. "Against her will? By whom?"

"Him."

"Lucy's father," Walker suggested.

"No, he's not," Quinn said, repulsed by even the thought.

When the door slammed open they all looked up. Nora appeared moments later, Ethan not far behind.

"What happened?" Nora demanded. She was distraught and disheveled, spots of high color on her cheekbones. But despite the unruly sweep of her hair and the way she seemed to shimmer at the edges—trembling, Quinn realized—Nora looked unyielding, battle ready.

It awakened something in Quinn. "Hang on," she said, jumping off the stool so she could stand toe-to-toe with her sister. "*You* tell *me* what happened. What is going on here?"

"I'm not sure it's any of your business."

"Oh, that's rich!"

"This doesn't have anything to do with you."

"Excuse me?" Quinn knew she was yelling, but she didn't care. "You think you can drop her in my lap without a word of explanation, let me grow to care about her, and then just whisk her out of my life without so much as a thank-you?"

"Thank you!" Nora spat.

"I don't want your damn thank-you! I want to know who Lucy is!"

"It doesn't matter right now, Quinn. What matters is finding her. What—"

Nora was stunned out of her tirade by a hand on her shoulder. Quinn watched as her sister blinked, fumbling for purchase on something solid, steady. It was Walker. He was standing between them, a Sanford girl in each hand. "Take a breath, Nora," he said, but it didn't come off condescending. It sounded like the first sane thing that had been said since Nora and Ethan walked in.

Clearly, Nora wasn't in the market for sanity. She shook him off. "Stay out of it, Walker."

"Oh, I'm very much in it," he said, weaving his fingers through Quinn's. "We all are. And we can't do anything about it, we can't help, until we know what's going on."

"Don't be so dramatic," Liz called from her perch on the stool. They all turned as if they had forgotten she was there at all. "We know the bones of it. You've just got to flesh it out a bit for us, Nora."

"What do you mean?" she asked warily.

"Well, we know that Tiffany is Lucy's mom. And that Lucy isn't her real name." Liz pinned a stare so cool, so direct on her eldest daughter that Quinn felt herself lean back into Walker. She could feel it coming, the coup de grace: "And we know that she's a Sanford."

For a moment, Nora's face didn't change at all. She peered at her mother, unblinking, like Liz had spoken in a foreign language and the words did not compute. But then she folded a little, her shoulders sagging and her mouth, too, the wind in her sails gone suddenly still. All the hope and ferocity that had held her taut fell slack.

Quinn was there to catch her.

It was an awkward embrace, made even more uncomfortable because Nora was still fighting it, still pushing away. Still angry. "What am I going to do?" she whispered over and over, pulling back from Quinn and then clutching her wrists so hard Quinn had to stifle a cry.

"Come on, Nora," Liz said. She stepped forward and enveloped both of her daughters. They stood there stiffly for a moment, uneasy in the fragile affection that was second nature to so many. Not them. Not their family. But they were good at other things. "Sanfords get shit done," Liz said with conviction, and Quinn gaped at her mother's use of language. It was so out of character it was downright unsettling. But Liz went on: "Let's fix this thing. Just tell us what's going on so we can figure out what to do."

And Nora did. The story was halting and spartan, and in some ways brought up more questions than it answered. But Walker supplied their motley crew with tall glasses of lemonade and thick sandwiches of his homemade bread slathered with unsalted butter and roasted red pepper hummus. They ate standing up, quickly, like they were fueling for whatever awaited them outside the walls of the cabin. And though it felt strange at first, Walker kept working, kept slicing bread and spreading it thick, pressing sandwiches and coffee and tall glasses of cold lemonade in their hands. They ate. They talked. They felt stronger.

"I did what I had to do," Nora said, but it sounded more like a confession than an apology. "Tiffany said that JJ didn't want anything to do with her—that he told her to abort the baby." Nora stalled, reaching for words, for a way to explain everything that had happened and her role in it. She settled on: "It's my fault. All of it. I talked her into keeping Everlee."

"I'm glad that you did," Quinn said quietly.

"I convinced her that we could bring up a child together." Nora shook her head. "Without JJ. Without any Sanford family help at all."

"I still don't understand why you felt like you had to do it alone," Quinn said.

"Because even if JJ didn't want her, Dad would have taken control. He would have forced Tiff to take care of the problem if he didn't want the scandal, or fought to have Tiffany labeled an unfit mother and removed Everlee from her custody if it suited his purposes."

Quinn saw her mother start to say something, but she clamped her lips down tight. Nora was right and they all knew it.

"Why'd you call her Lucy?" Quinn asked. "If her name is Everlee, why didn't you just say so?"

"I was afraid it would make you curious," Nora admitted. "She's named after the bridge. It happened at the Everly dance—only a couple days after our high school graduation. JJ was home from college, remember? And Tiff was masochistic enough to want that reminder every day of her life." Nora drummed her fingers on the countertop, an indication of her growing impatience and the urgency of the situation. "I thought that if I showed up with a mysterious little girl and called her Everlee—an obvious connection to our community—you'd start wondering. You'd see hints in her mannerisms, her long legs, her eyes. She's the spitting image of JJ—down to how she hums herself to sleep—but I thought if you weren't looking for it, maybe you wouldn't see it."

"We saw it," Quinn said. "Walker knew the second he laid eyes on her."

"And now?" Walker said as he cleared away the glasses. "Who is this man? Why are you so afraid that Lucy"—he caught himself—"*Everlee* is with him?"

Nora shivered a little and Quinn felt a tremor pass through her own body. "He's evil," Nora said simply. "He's going to hurt her. And Tiffany. Both of them. I don't know."

"Why'd he show up at Malcolm's?" Quinn asked. "If Tiffany was with him, why'd he bother to track you down?"

"To let me know he won," Nora said. "He has exactly what he wants. And Tiff isn't strong enough to stop him."

"Then we'll have to." The voice came from outside of their circle, from the hallway where Quinn suddenly realized the cabin door still stood wide open. The summer sun was careening down the hallway, bouncing off the walls and illuminating the place where Bennet stood haloed in the slanting afternoon light. He was dressed in street clothes, but there was a radio on his hip and as Quinn watched him it crackled to life, spilling static and indistinct phrases into the silence. It sounded very official. Very ominous.

It made everything feel stark, surreal—and filled Quinn with an indefinable fear.

# NORA

THERE WAS AN AWKWARD beat of silence while the whole room watched Walker regard Bennet. His face was blank, impassive as he looked between his wife and the newcomer, this stranger with a slightly thickening middle and generic good looks. Bennet was neat and clean shaven, immaculate compared to Walker's ripped jeans, wrinkled T-shirt, and five o'clock shadow. Walker's rowdy hair was escaping the short, sloppy ponytail he had pulled it into at the back of his head, and the wiry curls were little exclamation marks around his smooth forehead. The two men couldn't possibly be more different.

But in the second before things got downright uncomfortable, Quinn reached for Walker and slid two fingers through the belt loop of his sagging jeans. Her touch was possessive, unmistakable, and the strange hush in the room evaporated.

"What can I do to help?" Bennet asked.

"What do you know?" Nora spun on him, wary at the sudden appearance of a cop and yet grateful for the authority in his tone.

"Not much." Bennet took a small step back and put his hands on his hips. "I take it we've got a missing girl."

"She's not exactly missing," Walker reminded everyone. "She's with her mother."

"And a man," Liz cut in. "But he's not her father."

Nora wasn't ready to go there yet. "We think she's in danger," she said before her mother could proclaim JJ the father and complicate things further.

"What kind of danger?"

Nora hesitated. It was the point of no return. If she admitted what she knew, Everlee would likely be taken away from Tiffany. And hadn't she spent the past seven years of her life doing everything in her power to prevent exactly that? Nora had given up so much to fight for Tiff and Everlee, to give them a chance at a life together. Even when Tiffany screwed up, when she failed, when they *both* struggled to make it work, Nora had believed in their little family. In the hope that everyone deserved a chance to be the person they were always meant to be. What if everything she had fought for fell apart?

Another thought struck her: If Everlee was removed from Tiffany's custody, where would she go? JJ knew nothing about his daughter. And Nora had no idea if he would deny everything and refuse contact or if he would embrace this unexpected development with open arms. No, Nora knew her brother. There would be no open arms. There would be nowhere for Everlee to land.

"They should have run away." Nora didn't realize she had said it out loud until Bennet pushed her.

"What do you mean?"

Nora had nothing to lose. "We had a plan," she said, picking at the hem of her shirt as she blinked back tears. "They were going to get out together. Start over."

Ethan's hand found the small of her back. He pressed gently. "It's not over yet," he whispered.

"Why?" Bennet asked. "Why would Tiffany need to run?"

"Her boyfriend is not a good man."

"I'm going to need more than that, Nora."

She faltered. "Drugs," she said. "Distribution. He's been charged before, but the allegations didn't stick."

"And?"

"The sexual abuse of a minor."

All the air went out of the room.

"And you feel certain she's in danger?" Bennet demanded.

"Absolutely. I'll testify. I've seen . . . things."

Something snapped in Bennet. "I need names, last known address, and any aliases. Nora, come with me. The rest of you, I want you to compile a description of the child and her mother. Do you have any recent photographs?"

Nora nodded, grabbing her own phone as she followed Bennet toward the front door.

But Liz stopped them. "Wait! I can tell you the license plate of the car he was driving if it would be helpful."

Bennet froze. "You memorized the license plate?"

"Of course." Liz looked affronted. "It's only six characters. It's not that hard to remember."

"Yes," Bennet said, and in spite of the situation, Nora could see that he had to bite back a grin, "that would be very helpful."

While her mother rattled off the letters and numbers, Nora went to stand in the yard. She needed air, space, and she wanted to go through her pictures alone. Nora flipped through her camera roll to find all the photos she could of Tiffany and Everlee. She had saved some old favorites, one of the three of them at a lake beach when Everlee was just two years old. Her legs were little sausages, rolls of skin between wrinkles that were so deep it looked as if someone had snapped rubber bands on her ankles and around her knees. She was breathtaking.

There was another picture of just Tiff and Everlee, sitting on the top step of the farmhouse porch, a litter of new kittens crawling in and around their laps. Another was slightly blurry, a still life of them spread on the couch watching something on TV. And here they were at the park. But the picture that Nora settled on had been taken only a week ago. She and Tiffany had just picked up the fake driver's license and the new birth certificates that transformed Nora's best friend and beloved niece into strangers. Miranda and Lucy Smith. There were over eighty-one million hits for Miranda Smith on Google. They had looked. Miranda Smith was every color, shape, and size. She lived in every state and every Canadian province. She was everyone. And no one.

"How will you ever find us?" Tiffany had said when they first hatched their plan, talking late into the night while Everlee was asleep and Donovan was at the bar.

"It'll take some time. You'll have to give me hints." Nora smiled. "It'll be like a game. Where do you want to go?"

"Washington," Tiff said dreamily. "I want to live in the shadow of a mountain. Or New York. Like *Sex and the City*."

"Except you have a little girl and aren't a freewheeling bachelorette," Nora reminded her. "Anywhere else?"

Tiff shook her head. "Arizona? Detroit, maybe? Anywhere but here."

When Nora snapped her last photo of Tiffany and Everlee, Tiff was clutching the manila envelope that contained their hopes for a new life. It was innocuous enough in the picture, just a big square of brown paper held shut with a brass clasp. But the look in Tiffany's eyes was transcendent, luminous with wishes that seemed to reach right out of Nora's iPhone screen and grab her by the throat. *You did this to me*, Tiffany seemed to say. *You made me believe. Thank you.* And Everlee, safe in the circle of her mother's arms, was looking up at Tiffany, smiling so big her eyes were all but winked closed.

"I've put out an APB for the license plate your mom gave me," Bennet said, joining Nora outside. He gave his head a little, admiring shake. "Props to Elizabeth Sanford for that one."

"Yeah, she's something all right."

"She is, Nora." Bennet gave her a sideways look. "Always has been. She's a strong lady; you're lucky to have her."

Nora wasn't sure what to say.

"What now?" Ethan came to stand beside Nora. "Do we wait?"

"No, let's go," Bennet said. "I don't have my cruiser and I'm not officially on duty, but we can drive around. Check out a few spots you think Tiffany might turn up at."

"Her grandparents' place?" Nora suggested.

"I was thinking of that, too."

"What are *we* supposed to do?" Quinn had come to stand in the doorway, her eyes shielded from the sun with a slender hand. "You can't expect us to just sit around and wait."

"That's exactly what I want you to do," Bennet said. "Write up those profiles and then stay put. What if they come back? What if she calls or texts?"

"Her phone!" Nora didn't mean to shout, but she couldn't believe that she hadn't realized it sooner.

Ethan caught on instantly. "Donovan had her phone," he said. "He had *her*. But how did Donovan know that she was in Key Lake? How did he find her?"

The truth clicked into place. "*She* found *him*." It was so obvious it hurt. "She called him. She had to. How else would he have known where she was hiding?"

"I don't know," Bennet said, "but if we're lucky we'll get the chance to ask her. Nora, I want you to text her. Call her. See if she answers."

"I can do better than that. We installed friend trackers on our phones. I'm sure it's how Donovan found us at Malcolm's. My phone must have pinged in the location."

Nora's fingers shook a little as she tapped into the app. But Tiffany's icon was still dark.

"No problem," Bennet said. "Try calling."

Tiffany's name was right at the top of Nora's call history, the photo next to her information as familiar as Nora's own reflection in the mirror. She held her breath as she hit Call.

It rang. Once, twice, a half-dozen times. It rang and rang, but it didn't go directly to voicemail. In fact, it didn't go to voicemail at all—even after Nora let it ring for thirty seconds, more.

"It's on, but she's not answering."

"Maybe she can't," Liz said.

The thought filled Nora with a blind horror.

"Okay," Bennet said, stepping into the fray before Nora could completely lose her mind. "Let's go. You can keep trying. In the meantime, I'm sure someone will pick them up, thanks to Mrs. Sanford."

Liz made a dismissive sound in the back of her throat.

"Unless they've changed the plates," Nora said. That was another thing they had included in the envelope—a set of license plates so Tiffany could change hers before she traded in the car she was driving for a new one. They had thought of everything, or at least tried to. New papers, a little cash, a forged recommendation letter from a nonexistent landlord.

"That'll make it harder," Bennet agreed. "But I'm hopeful. We'll pick them up soon. They couldn't have gotten too far."

But Nora worried that they wouldn't have to go far to achieve Donovan's purpose. She hadn't even told Bennet about Tiffany's inheritance, the will. The money that Tiff had taken from Donovan and the way that she knew he would never let her go—would never let either of them go—without a fight. She almost said something, almost told Bennet that there was even more to the story than she had already shared, but tucked deep in her pocket, her cell phone buzzed with an incoming text.

*Saturday*

*5:21 p.m.*

**TIFFANY**

*The corner of 338th and
Goldfinch.*

                        **NORA**

                        *What? Is that where you are?*

**TIFFANY**

*Come quick.*

                        **NORA**

                        *Are you okay?*

**TIFFANY**

*Bye, Nora. Everlee is all I ever
wanted. Take care of her.*

                        **NORA**

                        *Tiffany?*

                        *Tiff?*

                        *We're coming.*

# LIZ

NORA AND BENNET were gone in a squeal of tires and a fine cloud of gravel dust. It settled over Liz in a gritty film that coated her skin, her tongue, and tasted exactly like despair. She had wanted to go along—they all did. But Bennet had been professional, removed. He refused point-blank. No cushioning it in niceties or trying to spare their already raw feelings. It was simple, straightforward, devastating: *No.*

"Now what?" Quinn asked, voicing the helplessness they all felt. They made a reluctant quartet—Ethan, Walker, Quinn, and Liz—the tenuous thread connecting them taut and quivering like a plucked string. This concern for a little girl they barely knew was deep and sonorous, engulfing. Liz felt herself shrink before it, her shoulders caving in as if she wasn't just helpless, she was hopeless.

The texts Tiffany exchanged with Nora were nothing short of terrifying. Nora had leaned out the car window and let Liz read them while Bennet gave Walker last-minute instructions. They made her heart flutter weakly in her chest.

*Bye, Nora.*

"You need to talk to JJ," Walker said, surprising Liz with a hand on her shoulder. It was gentle, protective, and she was suddenly undone. Or, nearly.

"I do," she managed. But those two words were heavy as baggage, one in each hand, weighing her down.

"Are you crazy?" Quinn spat.

Liz very deliberately closed her eyes, shutting out the sight of her daughter and the desperation etched across her face. "He's right."

"What?"

"We have to talk to JJ."

"But—"

"Your brother has a right to know," Liz interrupted. Walker's hand was still on her and she drew strength from the unexpected connection. Who was this young man who presumed to know her? To touch her? But when she looked at him, the unraveling hem of the old T-shirt he was wearing and the beginning of a beard on his proud jaw, she was surprised by tenderness. *Thank you,* she wanted to tell him.

"I'll take you," he said. And suddenly he was more than all the fragments she had collected over the years. Skin smooth and dark as mahogany, hair wild, teeth white. The hands of an artist and the scent of a stranger. But here he was: whole. Walker.

"Yes," Liz said.

Ethan stayed so that there would be someone at the cabin should Nora and Bennet return. (With Lucy? Liz seized that hope and held it fast.) And Liz gave Walker the keys to her Cadillac and climbed into the back seat so that Quinn could sit beside him in the front.

"Should we call?" Quinn asked.

"I don't think so." There was purpose in this and Liz was clinging to it. Drawing herself up and buttressing the walls of her resolve. "There's no way to soften the blow of something like this, Quinn."

"What about Amelia?"

What about Amelia, indeed? JJ's obsession with Tiffany had only overlapped his relationship with Amelia a little—at least, as far as Liz could tell. The happy couple had met in college and fallen in love over the stacks in the library, or so the story went. Liz suspected their love story had much more to do with frat parties and beer pong— she wasn't naive when it came to the pretend purity of her slightly playboy son—but she went along with their narrative anyway.

Sadly, she couldn't feign ignorance about the fact that JJ and Amelia were definitely together the night of that Everly dance. Nora had just graduated, and Amelia had accompanied JJ to Key Lake for the celebration. If Liz remembered correctly—and the night was slowly beginning to take shape in her mind—Amelia had stayed home with Liz and Jack Sr. the night of the post-grad dance. It had something to do with "townies," and the term was not used fondly.

It fit. Everything was starting to fall into place like the tumblers in a padlock. And then what? Liz wished that some secrets could remain hidden.

"She's going to be devastated," Quinn whispered from the front seat.

But Amelia's hurt was unavoidable. And just the tip of the iceberg.

They were turning into JJ's subdivision—a shiny new neighborhood that flanked the golf course—when Quinn's phone rang.

From the back seat, Liz could see her daughter startle at the sound. Quinn groped for her phone and accepted the call, holding the device with two hands tight against her ear.

"Nora?"

And then: "What? Yes. Okay. Okay. We're on our way.

"Turn around," Quinn told Walker, a quiver in her voice.

"What?"

"We're meeting Nora at the hospital."

"The hospital?"

Liz froze, fear crackling and snapping through her veins like ice forming. "Is she . . . ?"

"They have Lucy," Quinn said. "They're bringing her to the hospital. That's all I know."

JJ would have to wait.

If Walker had taken a somber pace en route to JJ and Amelia's house, he drove like a man possessed toward the Key Lake Hospital. Liz would have nagged him from the back seat if she wasn't so heartsick, so afraid of what they would find when they arrived. She counted the blocks by praying, one word over and over again: *Please. Please, please, please.*

Key Lake Hospital wasn't large, and the parking lot beside the ER was all but empty. Walker pulled haphazardly into a spot and slammed on the brakes. He tossed the transmission into park and turned off the vehicle in one quick motion. Then they were all falling out of the doors, hurrying toward the entrance lit garish red by the glowing Emergency Room sign.

Nora was waiting there.

Hair tangled, cheeks bright and flushed. She had been crying but either wasn't aware of the dusty tracks along her skin or didn't care. Liz suspected the latter. The sight of her daughter dislodged something inside, and Liz threw her arms around those slight, rounded shoulders.

"What?" Liz snapped. "What happened?"

Nora pressed her face into her mother's shirt and said the sweetest words they could have possibly heard: "She's okay."

"Lucy?"

"Everlee." Nora pushed away. "We found her in the ditch near the corner of 338th and Goldfinch. Not far from Lorelei's farm." She shook her head. "The old Barnes place, I mean."

"In the ditch?" Quinn repeated. "I don't understand."

"She was wrapped in a car blanket. We think . . ." Nora stammered. Stopped. "We think Tiffany threw her from the car while it was moving."

"Oh no." Liz gasped.

"She's okay. We think she's okay. The paramedics just want to make sure."

"And Tiffany?" Liz hardly dared to ask.

"There's been an accident," Nora said, her mouth in a razor-thin line. She was trying to keep her lips from trembling.

Liz reached for a hand, any hand. Walker was beside her and his strong fingers engulfed her own. He had Quinn on one side, Liz on the other. He linked them all together.

"Bennet's there now." Nora drew a shaky breath. "He's going to . . ." She didn't have to finish.

"Can we see her?" Hope made Quinn's words tangible. Liz felt like she could have plucked them from the air and tucked them in her pocket. The truth that the opportunity existed, that Everlee could in fact be seen, was precious as gold.

"Yes, you can." Dr. Welch came around the corner wearing a pair of blue scrubs and a half smile. He had delivered both Nora and Quinn, and he reached out in turn to take all their hands in his own warm grasp. His presence was the perfect mix of familiar and reassuring, and Liz found comfort in the arch of his pale, bushy eyebrows as he told them that Everlee was going to be just fine. "She rolled," he said. "Just like a little sausage in that car blanket. There's not a scratch on her."

"How fast was the car going?" Walker asked.

"I don't think they know that yet." Dr. Welch shook his head and a shock of white hair flopped across his forehead.

"But the car . . ."

Dr. Welch's eyes flashed briefly to the ambulance bay. It was quiet. Apparently they were waiting for a second ambulance. How long had it been? Liz felt a shiver tremble across her skin. If they weren't racing to save a life . . .

"Come on, she shouldn't be alone." Dr. Welch motioned for them to follow, an invitation but also a distraction. The good news of Everlee's well-being was a buffer against all the things they didn't yet know.

"Go," Liz said, waving them on. "She doesn't know me."

"I'll stay with you," Walker said. "Nora, Quinn, she knows you best."

Liz nodded, encouraging them to go, and her daughters complied. They walked shoulder to shoulder behind Dr. Welch, and Liz was glad that Everlee had such strong women on her side. *Aunties.* They were her family.

They all were.

Liz and Walker didn't talk as they waited. They sat next to each other in the molded plastic chairs of the waiting room, knees touching, and listened to the clock tick on the wall. It was enough for Liz. Too much, in some ways, for she felt as if she had been turned inside out. Her skin prickled at the cool whisper of the air-conditioning, at the knowledge that everything she believed to be true only hours ago was . . . what exactly? A lie? Maybe Liz just wasn't who she always thought she was.

At one point, Walker got up and came back with a cup of coffee from the hospitality table. He handed it to her without bothering to ask if she wanted it, and Liz accepted gratefully. It was scalding and acidic, bracing.

When Quinn finally came around the corner, there was a shadow of a smile on her face. Walker put out his arms and she sank into his lap like it was the most natural thing in the world. He put his forehead against her temple and closed his eyes. "So?" he asked.

"She's fine." Quinn shook her head. "No, not fine. I mean, she's physically unharmed. She's scared. Crying for her mother."

Liz put her hand to her throat and slipped the chain of her necklace between her fingers. Quinn's words released something visceral in her, a longing to take charge, to make things right as only a mother can. But she wasn't Everlee's mother, and she had no idea if Tiffany would ever be given the opportunity to hold her baby again. The thought made her so nauseous she had to sit very still and will her stomach to obey.

"There's a social worker with her now," Quinn told them. "And they've called in a child psychologist from the mental health clinic in New Ulm."

The reality of what Everlee had endured was sobering.

"Was she . . ." Walker stalled, tried again. "Was she happy to see you? Or Nora?"

Quinn released a shaky sigh. "She let me hold her. I think she's in shock? I mean, she's really upset."

"Of course."

Walker was rubbing circles on Quinn's back, erasing the tension between her shoulders with the heel of his hand. "She'll stay the night for observation," Quinn said, leaning into his touch.

"And then what?" Liz asked.

"I don't know. I mean, we're her family, right? We might . . ." But Quinn trailed off, unable to finish.

"What about Tiffany?"

Quinn gave her head the slightest shake. *Don't ask.*

They looked up at the sound of footsteps in the hallway and watched as Nora came to join them. "Bennet's on his way," she said.

"And?" Liz was sick to death of waiting and wondering. "What happened?"

"He wants to talk to us in person."

"That's ridiculous," Liz spat.

Nora raised one shoulder as if she didn't have the energy to fire back. She looked so weary. There were purple smudges beneath her eyes and her skin was pale and waxy in spite of the warm summer sun. When she was a teenager, late August meant arms the color of toasted almonds, hair bleached so blond it was almost white. Of course Nora had always pretended not to care about her looks, but Liz knew that her daughter often felt awkward, self-conscious. Quinn was the beauty of the family and JJ was the brains—where did Nora fit? It was a question she had spent many years trying, and failing, to answer. The thought made Liz unaccountably sad, because, of course, Nora was the whole package: whip-smart and lovely, bighearted and wise. Why hadn't Liz ever told her so? Or had she? She couldn't quite remember, and in some ways that was even worse.

They didn't say anything more as they waited for Bennet to arrive. It had been almost two hours since Tiffany's cryptic text messages, and Liz marveled at how the whole world could unravel in such an insignificant amount of time. *What now?* she thought. But the future was determinedly opaque.

When he came, Bennet pulled a chair up to their circle and sat on the very edge of it so that he could rest his elbows on his knees and lean close. The set of his mouth was serious and he clutched a small black backpack in his hands as if it contained something precious. Liz wanted to shake him, to rip the bag from his hands so she could upend it on the floor and see what was inside. But she crossed her arms over her chest and forced herself to remain still, silent.

"Donovan Richter is dead," Bennet said without preamble. "There was a car accident about a mile down the road from where we found Everlee Barnes in the ditch."

Liz stole a glance at Nora. Her daughter's face was smooth as a statue and just as emotive. This was not the news she was waiting for, and she didn't so much as flinch when Bennet hung his head for a moment. The entire room seemed to hold in a frightened breath.

"Tiffany is gone," he told them, looking up. His gaze was a sword, and Liz watched as it pierced right through Nora's defenses. She crumpled.

"What?" she whispered, her lips trembling.

"No one else was in the car."

"*What?*" Nora's hand snaked out and seized Bennet's wrist. "What does that mean? Is she okay?"

"We don't know. If she was in the car, and if she was critically injured, she couldn't have gotten far."

"I don't understand." Quinn looked between them all, searching for the answer. "Where is she?"

Bennet avoided her gaze as he answered: "It has not yet been determined that a second passenger was in the vehicle at the time of the accident."

"But—"

"She's not there," Bennet said. "Tiffany was not in the car when we found it. I don't know what else to tell you."

"She's gone." The words were so absolute, so final, that Nora should have sounded devastated. But Liz could see that though her daughter looked stunned, her mouth was curving in a faint, improbable smile. "She survived, and she's gone . . ." Nora trailed off, shooting Bennet a quick, nervous glance.

"Look," he said carefully. "I don't know what happened this afternoon. But it looks like there was a rollover on a gravel road with a single fatality. If there was another passenger, we don't know why she would have run."

"Do you think . . . ?"

"We have no reason to suspect foul play."

Nora gave an almost imperceptible nod.

"Now if there was a witness, someone who was in the car at the time of the accident, that person is definitely someone we would like to have a chat with."

"Will you issue a warrant?"

Bennet pushed a hand through his hair as he gave her words consideration. He finally said, "If there was a passenger—and that's still an *if* at this point—this is a bit unprecedented. We usually deal with the other end of the spectrum. People want to sue for damages, not flee the scene."

"So what now?" Liz didn't even realize she had spoken aloud until they all turned toward her.

"The sheriff's department is processing the scene, but it looks pretty straightforward. If the investigation determines that the driver lost control and rolled, there are no charges to file."

"And Tiffany?"

"I don't know, Nora. You tell me."

"Are you suggesting that I had something to do with this?"

"I never said that." Bennet shook his head. "But I do have some questions for you."

"I have nothing to hide."

"Okay." Bennet unzipped the backpack and pulled out an evidence bag. Inside the clear plastic was what appeared to be a scrap of fabric. It was bright and beautiful, a pattern of flowers and splotches of color that looked like great dollops of fresh paint. He held it up in front of Nora. "We found this on the ground near the vehicle."

Liz recognized it instantly. It was the scarf that Tiffany had been wearing when she showed up at the cabin door and took Everlee. Liz opened her mouth to say as much but then clamped it down so hard her jaw ached. She didn't dare to sneak a peek at Quinn but was grateful that her daughter chose to hold her tongue, too.

"I've never seen that before in my life," Nora admitted, and Liz had no doubt that she was telling the truth. Nora had never been a very good liar.

"You're sure."

Nora nodded, and Bennet stuffed the evidence bag into the pack. He took out another one. "What about this?"

It was a cell phone with a gaudy pink case that was adorned with sequins in the shape of a skull.

"That's Tiffany's phone," Nora said reluctantly.

Bennet nodded. "There's an unsent text message on it." He

pushed the home button through the plastic bag and then turned the phone so that everyone could see it. "Do you have any idea what this means?"

Liz squinted as she drew close, trying to make sense of the words that glowed on the screen. And then they came into garish, shocking focus.

*You should know: JJ is the wrong Jack.*

HE FOUND ME. Or, rather, I found him.

When did I realize that this would never be over? That he would chase us and fight for us and never let us go? And not in a good way. Not in the "where you go, I'll go" way of those sappy romance novels Lorelei used to love.

The will was my insurance policy. Really, I just wanted my aunt to meet her great-niece. No, her *granddaughter*. Just once. And if we survived this thing, if we made it out the other side safe and sound, yes, I believed that my girl deserved her inheritance. When she came of age, of course. Lord knows I would have been a walking disaster with a fortune at sixteen. Fine. I still would be. But it was a template last will and testament, easy to change. Mr. Estes was happy to help.

*I direct that my residuary estate be distributed to my niece, Tiffany Barnes.* And below that we added: *And great-niece, Everlee Barnes.*

I should have known that I was painting a target on our backs. Making everything infinitely worse than it had to be.

But I took care of it. I did what I had to do. And you can think I'm evil, the worst kind of person, but I dare you to put yourself in my shoes.

The truth? I didn't think I'd make it.

I didn't want to. But I've been saved twice now, and I'd be a terrible liar if I told you I wasn't down to my bones grateful. For life. For things turning out nothing like they were supposed to.

"What did you just do?" Donovan shouted when I pushed Everlee from the car. But the door was already wrenched closed and his foot was still on the gas pedal. Surprise? Disbelief? Maybe he couldn't grasp what I had done. It didn't really matter. I ignored him and threw myself over the back of the seat to grab for the wheel.

Hands and arms. Fingers clawing. He hit my face. I tasted the sharp, salty tang of his damp skin in my mouth, my teeth grazing the bones of his thick wrist. But he was still accelerating, and when I finally held that steering wheel in my hands, there was nothing he could do. We swerved, jerked left so hard I lost my footing and slammed against the headrest.

The car flipped.

For one jagged breath I rose above it all, a spectator as the world fell away. I could see the breeze dance warm and indifferent through perfect rows of corn. The sharp glint of sunshine off the hood of Donovan's car. And then, for just a second, Everlee as she rolled down into the ditch far behind us. Of course I couldn't really see her, but in my mind's eye she was caught in the soft embrace of prairie grass and a sea of summer dandelions so bright they rivaled the sun. The perfect place to land. To rise. To be reborn. *She'll be okay*, I thought, and for just a moment it made my soul float light, lifting from a body I had already dismissed.

But then: impact. The windshield shattered into a million tiny pieces and showered down, a hailstorm of light. Hissing, popping, a metal scream, eerie and final as an unholy requiem.

What is death supposed to feel like? A sigh, a shriek, a letting go? *Nothingness*, I thought, until I realized that it hurt and that my heart still raced in tandem with the drip-drip-drip of something that I could hear but would not identify.

I wasn't dead.

I was wedged on the floor of the back seat, hip caught at an excruciating angle beneath the bench frame and the floor, legs bent unnaturally, left arm broken. It had to be, for it dangled into the empty space below me, swaying from the momentum of the crash like a pendulum that would forever keep splintered time. From where I was suspended, trapped upside down on the floor of the car that had crumpled like a tin can, I could see Donovan. Or the impression of him. My mind skittered away from recognition and reduced him to fragments. Shirt. Seat belt. Arm raised high. Torn. I didn't have to touch him to know that he was gone.

Will you hate me if I said I loved him once? That I could have wept for what I had done? All I had lost? Hope is a tenacious thing, everlasting and stubborn, refusing to give up, to let go. To stop.

And I know him better than you do. I held his face in my hands and looked so deep into those big brown eyes I thought I could see to the very bottom of who he was. I once loved to trace the scars on his back, the places where the skin was puckered and pink, exactly the size of the burning tip of a cigarette. His mother didn't love him the way that she should have, but isn't that always just a little bit true? I thought I could make up for all that pain, read those scars like a constellation and find the star that pointed home. But there were other hurts, too, wounds that dug deeper than skin. Scars aren't always visible. But I still wish I could have kissed each mark and made it new. For him. For Everlee. For me. But some hurts never quite heal.

I have a deep affection for broken things.

When the world stopped spinning like the needle of a smashed compass, I crawled out the back window of the car. It was still intact but warped and crisscrossed with cracks like a wilting spiderweb. I didn't even have to kick at it, not really. I just put both my feet against the glass and pushed. It sagged at my weight, bubbling out, and I pressed until it gave.

My own sort of rebirth.

Here is what I know: I should have died. I think I wanted to. But something threw me to the floor when that car hit the field driveway and decided to spread its wings and fly. Maybe it was a coincidence. Something that could be explained away by a crash test dummy and the quick flip of a car in some factory. I don't know. But I do know that I have now stood in an empty field twice and grasped that my life would never be the same.

And twice, I found salvation.

The first time the grass stains were on my jeans, the back of my favorite shirt. Jack Sr. wiped his hands on a handkerchief that he took out of his pocket, and then he touched his mouth real careful, dabbing the spot where I bit his lip. "Nobody will believe you," he told me. "Not a girl like you."

And he was right.

Who would believe me?

I left the dance to hook up with JJ. We'd danced that night, so close I could have flicked out my tongue and tasted the sweat in the hollow beneath his ear. I knew he was in a serious, here-comes-the-bride relationship, but what does that matter to a girl like me?

The truth? My heart ached at the thought that I was second best, that JJ's arms holding me tight were bold with whiskey and lust, nothing more. But sometimes second best is better than nothing.

JJ didn't show up at the spot we agreed on.

Jack Sr. did.

It was a practical joke. Mr. Sanford was confused at first, irritated that JJ had called for a ride (too drunk to drive) and that the only sign of life in the dark grove beside the cornfield was me. Dirty little Tiffany Barnes. Slut. Skank. White trash, cheap, easy, I've heard it all. And in the second before he realized the opportunity before him, Jack Sr. was quick to dismiss me. I could see it written all over his face: *bitch*. Because that's what men like him call women like me.

Who am I kidding? I was no woman; I wasn't even twenty years old. I was a girl.

Is it rape if you don't cry out? If you lie back and take what's coming to you?

I blame myself. I don't need your sympathy or that look in your eyes that tells me you don't just feel sorry for me, you thank God every day that you're not like me. I'd rather be despised than pitied, thank you very much.

What good is compassion if a chance at redemption is on the table?

Nora was the first to make me believe in second chances. I lied to her because I couldn't stand to tell her the truth, and though she didn't respond the way that I expected her to, she saved me from myself. Everlee is the best thing that ever happened to me from the worst thing that ever happened to me, and isn't it unbelievable that things could work out that way? My darkest hour and my saving grace were all played out on the bridge to Everly. Don't ask me to explain it. I can't.

But when I stood in that field beside Donovan's mangled car, chest heaving and shirt glued to my back from sweat and horror, it struck me that maybe we get more than just a second chance. A third? A fourth? How many times forgiven? How many new beginnings? At least one more for Tiffany Barnes, because there I stood in spite of it all: whole.

I shed myself. Phone dropped, scarf that had hid what I'd done to my signature dark waves unwrapped and left to the wind. The air raked fingers through my short hair and cooled my damp skin, and I was new. Again. In my bag: $10,000, a new life, a new me. And though leaving my girl is the hardest thing I have ever done, this is her redemption, too.

I love you, sweet girl. Love deep. Work hard. Your life is just beginning. You have to be brave.

I'm trying to be.

# After

"THIS IS A LITTLE MELODRAMATIC, don't you think?" Nora held up the bottle of champagne and needled Quinn with an exasperated look. But it was halfhearted and insincere, the smile tugging at the corners of her mouth, betraying how she really felt. Which was serene. Anyone could see that. It was in the casual jut of her hip, the way Ethan's arm wrapped around her waist as if it were the most natural thing in the world.

"Walker is nothing if not melodramatic." Quinn sighed.

"What's melodramatic?" Everlee slipped her hand into Quinn's and swung their arms together, pulling her in the direction of the boathouse door, where Walker had strung a black sheet across the worn boards.

"It means he likes to make a big deal out of things."

"It means he likes to exaggerate," Liz added.

"*You* like to exaggerate!" Everlee pointed at Liz, her eyes sparkling with the magic of a private joke.

"I do not."

"Do too!"

"Do *not*," Liz huffed.

"You said that my math flashcards were so boring you could *die*."

Liz flapped her hands at Everlee in an attempt to hush the child.

"That bad?" Nora laughed. "I didn't realize second grade was so strenuous."

"It's *every* night," Liz told them. "We have to go through the stack. Every. Single. Night. And then there's spelling words and reading—"

"Don't forget Handwriting Without Tears!" Everlee enthused.

"How could I forget?" But even as Liz complained, she shot Everlee a playful wink.

"Good thing she's so smart." Quinn turned Everlee's hand so the girl had no choice but to twirl. She pirouetted awkwardly at first, her corduroy dress and striped leggings swishing and catching as she tried to spin. But then she got the hang of it and whirled faster and faster beneath Quinn's careful hand, a rainbow blur of giggles until she collapsed onto the bed of leaves beneath her feet. Ethan kicked more on her, burying her beneath a sort of autumn confetti. Everlee didn't mind. She only laughed harder.

The late October sun was slanting across the water, glinting off the cold blue surface and casting diamonds across their shoulders. It was unseasonably gorgeous, the air crisp and tart, scented with wood smoke and earth. Quinn had forgotten how much she loved fall, the brisk, hopeful mornings and the long twilights that made the world seem golden. Key Lake felt like a well-worn picture book after a hot, frantic summer. It was comforting to lose herself in the quiet pages, soft from use and just a little tattered. But familiar, lovely. Home.

"Remind me what we're waiting for, Q?" Nora dangled the bottle of champagne in front of Quinn.

"The right light."

"The right light? Are you serious?"

"Yes." Quinn grinned at her sister. "Sounds crazy, I know, but Walker's a genius."

"That's debatable. Have you seen it?"

Quinn's eyes flashed proud and eager. "Not yet."

Nora sniffed. "You two are nauseating."

"Adorable," Ethan corrected. Deliberately changing the subject, he asked: "How's the Pumpkin Patch these days?"

"Great." Quinn couldn't help the way her smile widened. The preschool director had called her a week before classes began and offered her a job. Not as a teacher's assistant or paraprofessional, but as one of the four-year-old preschool full-time teachers. It wasn't her degree, but she had been an education major and they were desperate. So was Quinn. What started as a temporary position and a place to hang her heart for a season had become a passion she didn't expect. "I think I'm really getting the hang of it. Speaking of school . . ." She trailed off and arched one eyebrow at Nora.

"It's not school. Well, not technically," Nora sounded exasperated, but there was a spark of something fierce in her eyes. Something confident.

"It is too," Ethan cut in. "Online courses are totally legitimate. Nora's going to get a few core classes out of the way, transfer to a four-year college, ace the LSAT . . ."

"Please, I'm way too old for that." She rolled her eyes, but it was all for show.

Quinn couldn't have possibly been more pleased.

Nora and Ethan had traveled to Key Lake for the weekend partly to witness Walker's grand unveiling, but mostly to spend time with Everlee. The child was coming around slowly, learning to trust and feel safe. She saw a counselor twice a week and attended school part-time. The rest of her days were filled with Liz's—often harebrained—schemes. They took calligraphy classes in the basement of the library and swimming lessons at the indoor pool. Once they attended a French cooking seminar and made ratatouille for a small dinner party that consisted of Walker and Quinn. Liz even let Everlee have free rein with her oil paints and watercolors, and more than one fabric now bore the tiny swirling *E* that signified an original Everlee design.

Nora and Quinn were astounded to discover that their mother was the perfect place for Everlee to land—if not forever, for a season. A sweet, sunny season that could only be classified as fumbling toward happy. There were still many late-night phone calls and texts, desperate pleas for help as Liz all but sobbed into the phone. But Liz and Everlee were healing together—more than that, they seemed to be healing each other.

It was a group effort. After Donovan's accident and Tiffany's disappearance, Nora took a leave of absence from the Grind. She and Everlee moved in with Liz to begin the difficult process of learning to live in a new normal. It was supposed to be temporary, but something clicked between the six-year-old and her would-be stepmother. The arrangement was as miraculous as it was mysterious, and when Nora went back to Rochester, it was a relatively easy transition. But she and Ethan made the trip to Key Lake often.

"Can we go in now?" Everlee dug herself out of the small pile of leaves and stood to brush off her dress.

Quinn bent over and helped her out, plucking leaves from the clingy corduroy and the unruly mop of Everlee's hair. The red had dulled to a strawberry blond that almost seemed intentional—ombre coloring was all the rage. Still, they were eager for that last physical trace of what had happened to disappear entirely. Everlee's other scars were indelible. But fading. Growing faint and fine as silver.

"Good question," Liz piped up. "I think Walker's changed his mind. I think today might not be 'the day.'"

"Oh, it's the day, all right." Walker emerged from behind the black sheet and slipped his arms around his wife's narrow hips.

Quinn straightened up and swiveled to brush a kiss against his cheek. "We're a very patient bunch," she teased.

"Clearly."

"So," Liz broke in. "Are you ready? Do we finally get to see it?"

Walker shrugged, feigning nonchalance. "If you want to." He turned to squint at the angle of the sun. "It should be perfect just about *now.*"

In spite of their earlier prickliness, a wave of excitement rippled through the entire group. The past three months had been some of the hardest of their lives. Quinn came to grips with the fact that she wasn't pregnant—and might not ever be. Nora grieved the loss of her best friend and the years she had spent living a lie. Liz began the slow process of forgiving her husband—and learning to be a mother again. But no one had suffered as much as Everlee, and Quinn expected Walker to reach for her hand and lead her through the door of the boathouse first.

He didn't. Walker stepped away from his wife and stuck out his arm for Liz.

"Me?" She fluttered her fingers to her chest, surprised at being singled out, and was just a little hesitant.

"I want you to be the first to see it."

"Why me?"

Walker didn't answer her question; he just stood with his elbow out and waited for his mother-in-law to take it.

"Oh, fine, fine." Liz tried to come off gruff, but she sounded like she was going to cry, and that made her more than a little flustered. "Everlee, honey, take Walker's other arm." And because no one questioned Liz Sanford, Everlee did as she was told.

Quinn hurried ahead of them and pulled back the sheet, swinging it wide so they could enter the boathouse unhindered.

"Thank you," Walker said.

And then they were inside.

It was blinding white, and Liz blinked against the onslaught of light. She dropped Walker's arm to shield her eyes, but she couldn't stop herself from whirling around, from trying to take it all in.

Suspended from a frame high above her, a thousand pieces of glass (thousands?) shimmered in the sun. Dusk poured in through the high windows on the west side of the tall boathouse and illuminated each spinning shard of glass so that it reflected light like water. As Liz tried to absorb what she was seeing, she realized that the glass hung from silver wires so slender they were almost invisible. They were all arranged in progressing layers so that they seemed to swell and heave.

Waves. Wind. Sails.

"*Walker*," Nora whispered from somewhere behind her, and Liz was struck with the desire to catch her daughter's hand and hold it tight. "What have you done?"

"It's the ship," Quinn breathed. "The *Queen Elizabeth*."

They all looked at Walker as he nodded. "I've never seen sea glass in a lake," he said. "But the little bowl of it in the cabin and the story of the steamboat made me realize there must be tons of it at the bottom of Key Lake. I dove for it all summer."

"It's like nothing I've ever seen," Ethan said. "What is it called?"

Walker put one hand behind his neck and rubbed the tender skin beneath his ponytail. He looked sheepish, almost afraid when he said: "*Elizabeth Undone*."

It was dazzling, resplendent, the face of the sun. And the depths of the ocean when the world was filled with light. Hope and despair, for how could this have happened, how could it be undone if it had not at first been done? Making and remaking in a constant round, and as Liz spun beneath the twinkling light, the glittering, gleaming, otherworldly bright, she felt something inside of her shatter free.

Elizabeth undone, indeed.

They drank champagne beneath the upside-down ship. It was the world upended, a beautiful disaster. Worthy of a second bottle of champagne and music. Everlee danced abandoned, throwing her hands up and laughing so hard she fell down clutching her sides and howling.

At one point, Liz found herself face-to-face with her daughters, the first, the second, the unlikely third in her arms with her head on Liz's shoulder. *How can this be?* Liz thought. But it was, and it would be.

They talked of insignificant things. Funny stories and small-town gossip, a new recipe and plans for Christmas. And then, when Everlee was heavy and quiet in Liz's arms, drowsy with something that drew very near to joy, Liz told her girls: "I'm going to find her. Someday."

Neither Nora nor Quinn had to ask her what she meant. They had a scarf, a name, an antique Egyptian box with the remains of a woman who was as much a mother as any of them. Lorelei belonged with Tiffany and in some way Everlee did, too. With all of them, actually.

And the Sanford girls were fierce and determined, tenacious and brave. The sort of women who refused to give up. Who knew that all the loveliest things were broken.

And in all the broken places they were strong.

# ACKNOWLEDGMENTS

IN DECEMBER OF 2013, my husband and I stepped off a plane in Sioux Falls, South Dakota, with the newest member of our family. We had known our daughter for years, but the catastrophic event that precipitated her adoption was just beginning to rewrite our personal story. At the time, we knew just a few things: she was sick, she needed our help, and we desperately loved her. In the weeks that followed her arrival on US soil, we became increasingly aware that the trauma she had endured would shape our lives forever. This beautiful girl was wary, watchful. She didn't speak much and she held her emotions tight to her chest. We often wondered what she was thinking and feeling, because she certainly wasn't going to share those thoughts and emotions with us. I spent my days loving her and reaching for her, trying to bridge the gap between us and earn the title that the Liberian and US governments had already given me: *Mom.*

*Little Broken Things* grew out of that time. In a quiet moment as I held her in my arms and we both cried, I knew I wanted to write a story about a girl searching for home—and a woman becoming a mother in a broken but beautiful way.

My heartfelt gratitude and forever love to Eve for making me the mother of a daughter. I am so glad that you are ours and I will spend the rest of my life trying to be a good, good mother to you.

To Isaac, Judah, and Matthias: thank you. My boys have my heart and always will. I am the luckiest because I get to call you mine.

Aaron, I love you to the moon and back and I am forever grateful that we get to live this crazy adventure together. You are my favorite.

I am indebted to Emmanuel and Fatu Bimba for so many reasons, but none so much as this: you shared your lives with us. You are more than friends, you are family, and even more so because we get to walk the road of parenthood together. I thank God for you.

A small army of people have surrounded our family and shown us unconditional love and support through surgeries and trials and hardships we could have never predicted. For bringing meals and making us laugh and giving me time to continue to pursue my own dreams and write books, thank you from the bottom of my heart.

To Danielle Egan-Miller, my agent and friend, thank you for all that you do and for the many ways that you continue to fight for me. I could not ask for a better advocate in my corner. And thank you to Daniella Wexler for taking on a new author and believing in this project.

I'm a new member of the incredible group called the Tall Poppy Writers, and I find myself continually inspired and encouraged by this selfless, enthusiastic bunch of women. Thank you so much for your confidence in me and for welcoming me into your fold.

And finally to Joseph, who is not yet in my arms but already in my heart, thank you for saying "yes." I still can't believe that you are going to be our son. You are the best, most unexpected of gifts. I love you more than you will ever know.

Thank you, thank you for reading.

*xoxo,*
*Nicole*

# Little
# Broken
# Things

NICOLE BAART

*A Readers Club Guide*

THIS READERS CLUB GUIDE *for* Little Broken Things *includes an introduction, discussion questions, and ideas for enhancing your book club. The suggested questions are intended to help your reading group find new and interesting angles and topics for your discussion. We hope that these ideas will enrich your conversation and increase your enjoyment of the book.*

---

## Introduction

From author Nicole Baart, whose writing has been called "gorgeously composed" (*Publishers Weekly*), "taut and engrossing" (*Booklist*), and "evocative and beautiful" (*RT Book Reviews*), *Little Broken Things* is an absorbing and suspenseful story about two estranged sisters reunited by the unexpected arrival of an endangered young girl.

*I have something for you.*

Quinn Cruz and her older sister, Nora, have never been close, and in recent years their relationship has consisted mostly of infrequent, awkward phone calls and occasional emails. But when Quinn receives a cryptic text message from Nora one summer night, a chain reaction is put into motion that will change both of their lives forever.

Hours after sending the mysterious message, a haunted Nora shows up in provincial Key Lake, Minnesota, and her "something" is more shocking than Quinn could have ever imagined: a little girl.

Nora hands her over to Quinn with instructions to keep her safe and to not utter a word about the child to anyone—especially not to their buttoned-up mother, Liz. But before Quinn can ask even a single question, Nora leaves, and Quinn finds herself the unlikely caretaker of a girl introduced simply as "Lucy."

It's obvious that Nora has gotten involved in something way over her head—but what? As Quinn struggles to honor her sister's desperate request and protect a terrified child from the unknown, Nora must face matters head-on in a life-or-death struggle that demonstrates the lengths a woman will go to protect those she loves.

## Topics and Questions for Discussion

1. *Little Broken Things* explores motherhood in all its many forms. Tiffany and Liz are official parents, but Nora and Quinn also take on mothering roles in the book. What makes a good mother? Would you consider these women good mothers?

2. Liz is unlike the other characters in the novel. She's old-fashioned, patriarchal, and even a little racist. How does she change throughout the book? What do you think prompts this change?

3. In the novel, Nora sacrifices a great deal for Tiffany and Everlee. Why do you think she does that? Would you have done the same in her position?

4. Remembering her late husband, Liz muses: "Jack Sanford had not been a good man. True, he was steady and levelheaded and hardworking. He had made a way for himself in a world that favored the lucky, the people who were born with privilege and a place at the table. Jack Sr. had none of those things. But he took a small farmer's inheritance and made something of it, built a

legacy for his wife and kids and fought for it every day of his life. If he argued the validity of a bootstraps philosophy, it was only because he pulled himself up by them. A success story." Do you feel that Jack's challenges and determination in any way justify his actions?

5. Tiffany's story is one of heartbreak and loss. She leaves because she believes her daughter will be better off without her. Is this act sacrificial or selfish? Do you agree with her decision?

6. Nora thinks of her sister as "perfect little Quinn." In what ways does Quinn live up to that reputation? In what ways does she defy her sister's expectations?

7. Why do you think Tiffany named her daughter Everlee?

8. Although Liz is loath to admit that she and Walker have something in common, they are indeed both artists. Throughout the novel, what are some ways these two characters' art influences their worldviews?

9. Who is your favorite character in *Little Broken Things*? Why? Is there a character you don't like or don't understand? Explain.

10. Why do you think Liz's relationship with her daughters is so strained, and who—if anyone—is to blame? Do you have hope for them at the end of the book?

11. Throughout the novel, Everlee's paternity is in question. How does the revelation of her real father affect your reading of the novel? Does it change your perspective of certain characters?

12. Toward the end of the novel, Liz tells Macy: "I think I have a God complex." Do you agree that this affliction could apply to multiple characters in *Little Broken Things*? If so, which ones?

13. At the end of the novel, Tiffany makes a very deliberate decision that ends in Donovan's death. Is she a killer?

14. Walker names his sculpture *Elizabeth Undone*. Why do you think he does this? Is that an appropriate title for his piece?

## Enhance Your Book Club

1. Art plays an important role in *Little Broken Things*. Visit an art gallery with your book club, or if there is not one nearby, encourage book club members to share a picture of their favorite pieces of art.

2. Motherhood is a major theme in the novel, and many of us often forget how much sacrifice and love it requires. Take a moment today to thank your mother for the role she plays in your life. Send a card or flowers, or simply pick up the telephone. If your mother is no longer living, share a treasured memory of her with a friend or family member.

3. The Sanfords were known for their fabulous parties. Throw a party for your next book club meeting. Dress up, drink champagne, and enjoy some of the appetizers mentioned throughout *Little Broken Things* (e.g. endive stuffed with goat cheese and blood oranges; prosciutto-wrapped figs; or cherry tomatoes, mozzarella, and fresh basil skewers).

4. Like Everlee, many children from broken homes find themselves in difficult situations and could use a little kindness and help. Make a donation of clothing, toys, or money to your state foster care organization or bring grocery items to your local food pantry. You never know the impact your gift may have on a child and his or her family!